Princess Isabelle had always been consid___ the free spirit of the royal Bertrand family— _____ who professed to love her proposed _____ ___ ___ eartbroken by his betrayal- _____ __ ___ ___ e she's ever known—Isa_____ _____ _____ rt over. It is here, as she _____ _____ ___ independence, that sh_ _____ _____ istible Daniel Bronson, a se_ _____ ___ose drive and passion match her own_ _____ love challenges everything she's ever held true.

Daniel is a golden boy who has spent half his life on the road in search of the ultimate business deal. But from his first encounter with the sad-eyed princess, he finds it impossible to deny the powerful hunger she has awoken in him—a hunger that is deeper, stronger, and more powerful than he's ever known.

But can he convince the princess to trust in love—and persuade her that she is his one and only?

Please turn to the back of this book
for a special preview of Barbara Bretton's

Shore Lights

Available from Berkley Books in May 2003!

One and Only

Barbara Bretton

BERKLEY BOOKS, NEW YORK

ONE AND ONLY

A Berkley Book / published by arrangement with
the author

PRINTING HISTORY
Berkley edition / September 1994

For information address: The Berkley Publishing Group,
a division of Penguin Putnam Inc.,
375 Hudson Street, New York, New York 10014.

ISBN: 0-425-18882-5

BERKLEY®
Berkley Books are published by The Berkley Publishing Group,
a division of Penguin Putnam Inc.,
375 Hudson Street, New York, New York 10014.
BERKLEY and the "B" design
are trademarks belonging to Penguin Putnam Inc.

PRINTED IN THE UNITED STATES OF AMERICA

10 9 8 7 6 5 4 3 2

To J.S., who knows why

Acknowledgments

Special thanks to Dallas Schulze, who read the manuscript with a keen eye and a kind heart; and to Susan Feldhake, whose storytelling sense never fails to inspire me; and, as always, thanks to Robin Kaigh, my agent, for ten years of sound advice and valued friendship.

Chapter One

PERREAULT

Isabelle, second daughter of Prince Bertrand, stood beneath the porte cochere at the rear of the castle and watched as the taillights of Eric Malraux's Lamborghini were devoured by the Alpine darkness.

Tomorrow morning, society columns throughout the continent would be filled with vivid descriptions of how it felt to dance in the grand ballroom with the chandeliers of Austrian lead crystal blazing overhead, their dazzling light matched by the savage glitter of icy diamond earrings and bloodred ruby necklaces worn by women of consummate grace and beauty. Their gowns had shimmered with gold and silver lights reminiscent of the days when owning a king's ransom in jewels had been a right, not a privilege. The music of the past resonated everywhere that night, a glorious past that few guests could consider without experiencing a bittersweet sense of longing.

Isabelle hugged herself as a breeze, fragrant with pine, came down from the snow-capped mountains that surrounded the principality of Perreault. How could she think of the past when tonight she had taken her first step into the future, a future that sparkled more beautifully than any diamond possibly could?

Just one hour ago Eric had held her close in his strong arms as his honeyed kisses eased her passage from girlhood to womanhood. Her body tingled in each place that he had touched, as if shooting stars and comets were zinging through her from her head to her feet. Not that the act itself had been so wonderful. It had been messy and awkward and at times almost funny, but none of that mattered. She was in love!

At Christmas last, Eric had just been Honore Malraux's son, a quiet and handsome young man who'd been part of her life for as long as she could remember. A boy to dance with at royal soirees. Someone who knew her as Juliana's sister and nothing more, the girl who had been sent away to boarding school and forgotten. But then on New Year's Eve in the gazebo Eric had kissed her, and everything changed forever. Of course, she hadn't realized that fact at the time. She'd carried the memory of her first kiss back to boarding school, eager to share the experience with friends who had already leaped happily into the sexual fray.

Maybe there truly was a place for her in the scheme of things. Maybe her father would blink once, twice, then open his eyes to discover he had another daughter besides Juliana. Anything was possible, even being happy. If she could win the heart of someone like Eric, she could do anything at all.

A voice to her right broke through her thoughts.

"Will you be needing anything, mademoiselle?"

She turned to see Yves, master of all he surveyed, standing a few feet away from her. As always, his posture was rigid, his bearing more royal than hers, although he was only a servant.

"Is the party over?"

The man's bushy brows lifted. "*Oui*, mademoiselle. There is no one afoot, save the help."

Isabelle wrapped her arms about her slender torso, remembering Eric's touch. How could Yves look so dour on so special a night? "Is my sister still awake?"

His reaction was a classic Gallic shrug of his shoulders. "It is not my province to know such things, mademoiselle. That is Maxine's job, is it not?"

"Oh, you wonderful, stuffy old man!" Isabelle pressed a kiss to his leathery cheek. "Go into the kitchen and drink some champagne. I am certain there must be some Cristalle left. Enjoy it! I want everyone to be happy tonight!"

Yves muttered something about the dangers of the grape, but Isabelle merely laughed and gave his ear a playful tug.

"Oh, don't be so provincial, Yves," she said, laughing, as she led the way back inside the palace. "Don't you ever want to throw caution to the four winds and dance till dawn?"

For once Isabelle didn't notice the cold breezes racing through the castle as she hurried up the wide stone staircase, her slippers dangling from between her fingers. Her St. Laurent gown rustled with every movement. The skirt was suspiciously wrinkled with a huge emerald grass stain across the derriere. Isabelle considered it a mark of triumph, a medal of love, although she certainly didn't wish to encounter Maxine with the evidence of her liaison with Eric so clearly visible to all. Maxine's eagle eyes missed nothing. Isabelle's kiss-swollen lips would betray her in an instant to her governess. Thank heaven Yves was too bound by rules and time schedules to notice true love blossoming right before his weary eyes.

The castle overflowed with guests who had traveled to Perreault for the celebration, so she tiptoed down the long second floor hallway toward her suite of rooms. A woman's laughter, silvery and coy, spilled from one of the rooms, and Isabelle paused for an instant, head tilted, as she heard the distinctive voice of that American businessman she'd met earlier join the woman's. Bronson, wasn't it? Oh, he was handsome enough, but too aggressive by half. Isabelle wrinkled her nose. For some strange reason, American men had never mastered the fine art of subtlety. Why couldn't they understand the value of understatement, of flattery? These two contradictory terms were amazingly compatible in the hands of even the average European male.

Eric was so wonderful at both. He managed to make a woman feel beautiful and brilliant, charming and clever, all at the same time.

Mr. Bronson, however, was either unwilling or unable to make a woman feel anything but uncomfortable. She'd met him early in the evening. Of course, the brash American had been right on time, betraying his upbringing for what it was. No one arrived on time for parties. Certainly no one who mattered. She had been standing to Juliana's right on the receiving line, and Bronson had strode right up to her as if they were equals. She'd waited for the customary bow, but he'd just looked her straight in the eyes, practically challenging her to put him in his place. How could she refuse such an open invitation?

"Has no one ever told you about proper protocol?" she'd said as sweetly as she could manage. "You are expected to bow when introduced to royalty."

"Of course," he'd said, sweeping her body with his gaze. "Royalty." The wicked glint in his eyes told her that he didn't consider the last three members of the Perreault family to be terribly royal, but he'd bowed nonetheless. Isabelle had the feeling, however, that inside he was laughing.

When he'd approached her later for a dance, she had lifted the train of her peach-colored skirt and glided away with all the royal aplomb at her command. Besides, no man should be allowed to look at a woman the way he'd looked at her. His gaze was direct, sensual, almost threatening in its power. She'd turned away from him and stepped into Eric's arms, so happy to have a man as kind and sensitive as the young Mr. Malraux at her side.

But, then, what difference did it make? Obviously Mr. Bronson's method had been successful enough, if the muffled sounds of passion behind the door were any indication.

Smiling, she moved past his room. She wished him well tonight. She wished everyone well.

The spacious apartments she shared with her sister were at the end of the corridor. At the turn of the century this had been the nursery wing, furnished to accommodate the large families that had been part and parcel of the Victorian era. As the years passed, the royal family's size had decreased, until the whole of Perreault's monarchy consisted of Isabelle and her sister Juliana—and their father, of course.

The ornately carved oak door creaked as she pushed it open. "Juli?" She tossed her dancing slippers on a Chippendale chair in the corner, then dashed through her bedroom and the sitting room and into the room where her sister slept peacefully in her four-poster bed. Asleep! How could her very own sister sleep on the most important night of Isabelle's life? It was unthinkable. They'd been separated for so many years, but still they were sisters. Isabelle admired Juli's poise, her cool intelligence, the way she seemed to accept the world, flaws and all. Oh, there was still a certain awkwardness between them—after all, they had spent most of their lives apart. But Isabelle knew that there was no one else on earth who would understand the importance of her wondrous news the way her older sister would.

She leaped onto the feather bed and nudged Juliana's shoulder. "I have the most spectacular news, Juli! You must wake up."

Juliana was as fair as Isabelle was dark; as calm and cheerful outwardly as Isabelle was turbulent and prone toward black crises of the soul.

Isabelle knew if she was awakened in the dead of night,

she would snarl and grumble and not listen to one single word her sister had to say. Juliana simply yawned, her rosebud mouth forming a perfect *O*, then propped herself up against the eighteenth-century headboard and listened quietly as Isabelle recited chapter and verse about her miraculous, wonderful, altogether fabulous night.

"And that's not all." Isabelle lowered her voice to a sultry whisper, then held her hands a distance apart.

Juliana buried her face against her pillow. Even her delicate ears were bright red. You would almost think it had been Juliana, not Isabelle, who had spent the last fifteen years at convent school. "No!"

"Yes!"

"That's—that's impossible."

"I swear on the Sacred Heart and Mama's grave."

"But—how did he—how could you—"

"It's the most amazing thing," Isabelle said as she sprawled across the foot of the feather bed and stretched lazily. "I was scared to death when I first saw him, but it was as if we were made for each other, Juli. Truly, the whole experience takes much less time than I would have imagined."

"Was he gentle?"

"Gentle and sweet and so wonderful—"

"I cannot believe you have done it, Isabelle. Are you in love?"

"Oh, yes!"

"Does he love you, too?"

"I know that he does." Would a man ever do the things Eric had done to her—for her—if he didn't love her with all his heart and soul? Impossible, she thought. What they had shared was special. Surely no one on earth had ever known such happiness as she'd found in his arms.

"Robert?" asked Juliana.

"Niall?"

"Good God, no."

"Henry? Marco? That handsome American? I saw the way he was looking at you—"

Isabelle threw back her head and laughed. "You goose! It's Eric Malraux! How could you not know?"

There was a silence, deep as the darkness beyond the leaded glass windows. The type of silence that a wiser woman would have understood. Isabelle, however, was young and foolish and very much in love.

"I—I had no idea." Juliana looked down at her hands, as if embarrassed to know such intimate details about her sister.

"Oh, Juli, didn't you see the way he was looking at me at the New Year's party? The flowers he sent at Saint Valentine's Day when I was on holiday from school?" What on earth was wrong with her sister? Isabelle had expected squeals of excitement, at the very least, and a veritable barrage of questions.

"That was months ago," said Juliana in her soft, measured voice. "Certainly it was not something I remembered."

Isabelle was almost incandescent with pleasure. "To tell the truth, even I had almost forgotten that he'd kissed me in the gazebo on New Year's Eve. I was so caught up in flirting with Jean-Claude that night that I scarcely paid Eric any heed. I had never thought of him like that but—" She sighed and closed her eyes, remembering.

Juliana said nothing, but Isabelle was so swept up in her romantic reverie that she didn't notice.

"He swept me into his arms and kissed me right there in the gazebo with the snow swirling all about and the cold wind slicing through our clothing." She sighed deeply, theatrically, as she lifted her thick dark hair off the back of her neck. "It was the most exciting thing in the world." She laughed gaily. "That is, until tonight."

Juliana's eyes fluttered closed for a moment.

"Oh, Juli, did you ever in a million years think this would happen to me?"

"No," said Juliana, her eyes the color of the ice-crusted lake beyond their window. "I never did."

It isn't real—this can't be happening—doesn't he know how much I love him?

Juliana felt as if her heart was about to snap in two like a dried twig. A heaviness had settled in across her chest, pressing against her ribs and making it difficult to breathe. Dear God, how could it be that Eric didn't realize the depth of her emotions? She had loved him from her very first second on this earth. His was the face she saw when she awoke in the morning, the face she saw in her dreams at night. The face she wanted to see every day for the rest of her life.

". . . and then he brushed my hair from my face—oh, Juli, he was so wonderfully gentle—and said, 'Oh, Isabelle, you are . . .' "

Her sister's words came through a thick fog of pain.

This is only a story—another one of Isabelle's tall tales—I'll wake up in the morning, and it will all be just a ridiculous bad dream.

Hadn't it always been this way? From the moment she came into the world, Isabelle had captivated everyone. She hadn't cared a fig about rules or responsibilities; she had simply danced through life with an abandon few could equal. One day she would dream of being a siren of the silver screen, and the next day she planned to lead safaris in darkest Africa. Part gypsy, part Joan of Arc, Isabelle sparkled brighter than her dreams.

Focused and determined, Juliana allowed herself only the dreams that fit in with the reality of her life. A part of her envied her sister's freedom, but even as a small girl, Juliana had understood that the lure of freedom fell far short of the certainty of power.

She had been handed her dreams on the day she was born, and what separated her from her sister was the certainty that one day her dreams would come true. As heiress to the throne, it seemed inevitable that her future be linked to the future of a man of position and promise. How often she had prayed it would be Eric Malraux. Certainly it was a dream that would come true. A dream that she could will into fruition.

And now all hope was gone. With one swift and thoughtless blow, Isabelle had shattered Juliana's dreams.

Isabelle was still recounting her adventure, apparently oblivious to Juliana's pain. "He said I'm sexy, Juli! Can you believe it? My very first time with a man, and it all seemed so natural, so—"

"Please!" The word burst from Juliana's lips despite her efforts to control the anger building inside her. She took a deep breath, praying she could get through the next few minutes. "I mean, if you tell me everything, what will there be for me to discover when my turn comes?"

"But I thought we had a vow, Juli. I thought we'd promised that whoever was the first would share absolutely everything with the other. Didn't we?"

"Well, yes, but . . ." Her voice grew faint. *That was before you slept with the man I love. Before Eric took you to his bed.* That silly promise had been made years and years ago when they were prepubescent girls, giddy from holiday punch. "If you tell me everything, I shall not be able to look at Eric again without giggling."

"But it was so wonderful, Juli. I couldn't wait to tell you every last detail."

I would never tell anyone, thought Juliana. *I would hold it to my heart and keep it special, for the two of us alone.*

"You have had too much champagne," said Juliana after a moment. "Perhaps you should take a warm bath and go to bed."

Isabelle laughed, but her laugh no longer had the sound of girlhood about it. Her laughter told Juliana everything she didn't want to know. "No bath, Juli. I can smell his cologne on my arms. I can't bear the thought of washing it away."

Isabelle leaned over and kissed the top of her sister's

head, and for an instant Juliana imagined the scent of bayberry and spice. She could almost see Eric standing before her, knife in hand, ready to cut out her heart.

"Good night, Juli." Isabelle did a pirouette in the center of the room. "It really was a wonderful party, wasn't it?"

Juliana watched, spellbound, as her dark and fiery sister drifted from the room. Isabelle was everything Juliana had ever wanted to be, all passion and grace and daring.

You've lost, thought Juliana. *You waited too long and now you have lost.* Isabelle had walked through the door into womanhood while Juliana still sat on the sidelines, dreaming her life away. Her whole existence had been one of waiting for the moment when she would take her rightful place in the scheme of things. "This will all be yours one day," her father had said, gesturing toward the towering mountains and deep valleys flowered with alpine roses and deep blue lupine that were part of her homeland. "There is nothing more important in this world."

She lay back against her pillow, heart pounding with rage and pain.

How she wished she could close her eyes and will herself back into a dreamless sleep, anything to escape the vision of her younger sister in the arms of the man Juliana loved. Those long, splendid limbs of Isabelle's entwined with his. Eric's face, flushed with desire, coming closer and closer. . . .

She pressed her fists against her mouth, willing herself not to cry.

She'd been so careful, so fearful, so concerned with protecting her heart that she'd allowed the love of her life to slip through her clumsy hands.

"Fool," she whispered into the quiet of her bedroom. It hadn't been her heart she'd been trying to protect, it had been her position. The lust for power had taken hold of her, bending her to its will. The inevitability of power and the ways in which power could serve her well attracted her. She loved the way the servants bowed in deference when she passed. Sitting next to her father during a meeting with his ministers, seeing men of stature lower their graying heads to her, knowing full well she would one day hold their lives in the palm of her hand.

But since Isabelle's return to Perreault, Juliana had begun to perceive the other ways in which power set her apart from others. She'd been willing to wait for Eric, so certain had she been that the lure of power would prove as potent an aphrodisiac to him as a pair of open thighs. Maybe she'd been wrong, and the ancient lure of sex was more powerful than she had ever imagined. Isabelle had been willing to cast her fate to the winds of desire because she had nothing of value to lose.

As a little girl, Juliana had been aware of the way adults and children alike were drawn to the flame that was her younger sister. Governesses and nannies laughed at Isabelle's antics, even when those antics were in defiance of nursery rules. They despaired ever teaching the child to obey, but still they held her close and smoothed her ebony hair with loving hands. Juliana would sit quietly on her rocking horse, her pinafore scarcely wrinkled after a day at play, and watch Maxine double with mirth as Isabelle imitated their stern-faced tutor. Sweet Juliana with her soft voice and placid temperament rocked silently on her toy horse and wished her sister dead.

The day Isabelle left for boarding school, crying so hard Maxine feared the child would faint, Juliana had stood beneath the porte cochere and bitten the inside of her cheek to keep from laughing in triumph.

"Don't look so sad, lovey," Maxine had said, clutching Juliana to her ample bosom. "Our Isabelle will be home on holiday before we know it."

Juliana counted the days spent without her sister, savoring each and every one of them. With Isabelle away at school, the spotlight shone on her alone, white hot and intense. The way it should be. After all, the throne of Perreault would one day belong to her. It was her birthright and her privilege and not even her sister with her wild and beguiling ways could change that. But the love of the people, of their father? It seemed those were Isabelle's alone and always would be.

"It isn't fair," Juliana said, her voice rising in the lonely stillness of her room. "She cannot get everything she wants."

There was still a chance to change things if Juliana could only summon up the courage. Sexuality was a two-edged sword, and Isabelle wasn't the only one able to wield that particular weapon. Isabelle had drawn first blood, but Juliana would claim the prize. A bright future was there for the taking, and it was time Juliana claimed what was rightfully hers, beginning with Eric Malraux.

they'd been tailored on Savile Row. The prince had been expansive in his generosity. Women had been gifted with diamond stud earrings, while the men eagerly accepted elegant Swiss watches that would have fed a family of four for a year back home in Queens, New York.

Not that Daniel knew too much about what went on in Queens these days. It seemed he spent half his life on the road in search of the ultimate business deal. "You're just like your old man," his father Matty liked to say. "Can smell money two states away." *Hell,* thought Daniel with a rueful laugh, *make that two continents away.*

Getting an invitation to the Perreault Tricentennial Ball had been easy. All you needed was fame and a world-class fortune and you were in like Flynn. The famous and the infamous on both sides of the Atlantic had flocked to the tiny alpine principality in droves to be part of the festivities. Only an elite few, however, had been chosen to spend the night in the castle, surrounded by battlements and suits of armor and the ghosts of three hundred years of history, most of which had been spent in a dance of conquest and surrender.

Everywhere you looked, you could see evidence of a past that included a rich tapestry of splendor and savagery: the small towns, walled in stone to withstand ancient invaders; the freshly painted farmhouses whose walls still held the gunshot scars from more recent wars. History was in the road you walked on, the music you danced to, and the castle that dominated the entire landscape.

It was more opulent than Bronson had ever dreamed possible. You didn't grow up in an apartment overlooking a concrete playground and expect to spend the night with royalty. Hell, you were lucky if your dreams took you as far as the Hudson River. A tiny snowball of a country, Perreault was perched high in the Alps, hard to find and even harder to forget. Some said it was Perreault's inaccessibility that gave it its cachet; others said it was the aura of mystery and sadness that hung over the principality like a morning fog.

Either way, it wasn't much of a monarchy, but Bronson wasn't fussy. Castles still had the power to impress, and he wasn't afraid to admit it—at least, not to himself.

He looked over at the woman asleep on the pillow next to him. Greta was from one of those Eastern European countries whose borders were more flexible than the Pentagon's budget. Greta had long limbs and hair the pale gold of Dom Perignon. Her morals were dependent upon the occasion, and he was moderately glad he'd been able to rise to that occasion tonight.

There were rules for this sort of thing, and he'd mastered them the way he'd mastered the rules of business. Keep things light and breezy. Never mention anything as crass as a future together.

To his family's dismay, he'd reached his early thirties without forming the kind of alliance his parents believed necessary to survival. His one attempt at marriage had been more to placate his folks than to build a future, and it had come as a relief when his wife found a more welcoming pair of arms elsewhere.

He couldn't blame her. A part of himself was always standing aside, watching, wondering if happily-ever-after was possible or if the concept was just the collective fantasy of a culture raised on John Wayne movies and Disney World vacations. A fine Irish gloom had captured his soul at birth, and it seemed there had never been a time when he hadn't seen the dark cloud on the horizon, waiting to steal away the silver lining.

"The Golden Boy," they'd called him in the New York tabloids. The man with the Midas touch. Nobody suspected the layers of deeply rooted, old-fashioned Catholic guilt the good sisters of Saint Dominic had instilled in him over the years. *Prove it,* he heard them say. *Prove you have what it takes.*

And so he did. Over and over and over again, with each new deal taking him closer to the top.

Even Bronson's most vociferous detractors had to admit,

however, that he'd never once forgotten where he came from. How could he? The rhythm of the New York City streets was in his blood. But not the streets of Fifty-seventh and Fifth. The streets the Bronsons called their own weren't home to Tiffany's and Bijan; they were home to Sam's Deli and Nino's Pizzeria and Shamrock Realty where his old man had made his fortune, parlaying prewar apartment buildings into co-op urban dream machines for the average man.

His father had taken Daniel under his wing, exposing him to both the good and the bad the city had to offer. Matty had no illusions about the place of honor in business. He adhered to his own strict code of behavior, but he had stopped being surprised when others stumbled over their ethics.

"Take a good look around you, Danny," his father had said time and again. "You're no better than the rest of 'em. You only have more money."

Unlike Trump and his ilk, Bronson hadn't forgotten his roots. He built for those at the top of the ladder and those who had to reach up to touch the bottom. It wasn't unusual for him to have dinner with the governor and an ambassador or two at some posh Manhattan eatery, then show up a few hours later for a beer and a few laughs at a Queens neighborhood bar. You never knew when you might need a favor, and it was those no-bullshit blue-collar types from Ridgewood and Woodside who made his dreams possible. He wasn't about to forget that.

Sometimes he felt as if he was the only one who recognized the way the global economy was shifting. You'd have to be blind not to see the way the Japanese were nosing their way into the American mainstream. First it was cars, then VCRs. Before you knew it, they'd be buying up enough land to carve out a new country. And it wasn't just the Japanese who were expanding. Phrases like "global economy" and "world market" had taken on new meaning, and he wasn't about to let his patriotism get in the way of his pragmatism.

People had warned him that doing business with Prince Bertrand would be like dancing on quicksand. Like most Europeans he'd met, Bertrand was a natural pessimist. Both frugal and cautious, the prince had an appalling lack of interest in anything remotely resembling progress. So far, Daniel's best efforts had been met with nothing more than maddening courtesy.

Next to him Greta stretched lazily, a lean and gilded cream-fed cat. Those magnificent amber eyes fluttered open, and the look she gave him was pure heat.

"Good morning, darling," she said.

"It's not morning yet."

"How wonderful." She spread her perfect legs and opened her arms to him.

Sometimes being a red-blooded American male was a definite asset.

Yves was waiting at the foot of the winding staircase when Isabelle glided down from her bedroom suite early the next morning. Dressed in his formal daytime uniform, Yves held his bony frame erect, as befitted his position. His sparse, light-brown hair was neatly plastered to his head, and his narrow face held its perennially gloomy expression. Isabelle sighed. *Poor Yves. It must be terribly sad to be so old and to have no one to love.*

"Breakfast is in the garden room," he said, with obvious disdain. "Mademoiselle desires anything special?"

Isabelle tossed her dark hair and favored him with a smile. What on earth was the matter with Yves? God knew, he was always dour but the way he was looking at her was almost as if . . .

Ridiculous. He couldn't possibly know. If he hadn't known last night when the proof was right there in her eyes and on her lips, he would never know.

"Nothing special, Yves." She frowned when he didn't return her smile. "Coffee and melon will do."

"Je suis votre serviteur." The traditional statement of obeisance. He bowed, then left the room.

Let him have his dark and dreary thoughts. Isabelle had more wonderful things with which to concern herself. She dashed off toward the garden room where a bountiful repast was laid out on the sideboards, attended to by a bevy of fluttery young parlormaids with nary a thought in their heads. Yesterday she had been just like those girls, giggling and silly, wondering what life held in the palm of its hand for her.

Ah, but today she knew!

Today she knew that at the center of her future was Eric Malraux and their happiness stretched as far as the eye could see.

"Spreading lies, is it?" Maxine Neesom's broad Irish brogue grew stronger as she stared at her nemesis. "How dare you be saying such nonsense about one of my girls!"

Yves didn't flinch beneath her flinty gaze, and that unnerved Maxine more than his words had. Lord in heaven, could it be true?

"Honore Malraux's boy," Yves said with such authority that Maxine's indignation wilted before it. "I saw them near the garden with my own eyes."

"Ridiculous!" said Maxine with a snap of her broad fingers. "In this dreadful October cold? Never." Her beloved girl's first time would be on her wedding night in a beautiful room made perfect by Maxine. Maxine had been with the family from the moment when both of the royal sisters drew their first breaths. God willing, she would be with them when she drew her last.

Poor little things they had been, so tiny and defenseless. So forgotten. Their mother had been a flighty one, more concerned with dancing the night away than in seeing to it her own babies were cared for and happy. "No one could take better care of them than you, darling Maxi," the mother had said once as she kissed the babies good night before leaving for yet another cotillion.

Maxine, young herself and eager for adventures of her own, had known the cold fingers of dread along her spine that night, for with those careless words the lives of two helpless babes had been placed in Maxine's hands as surely as the rosary she prayed with each night. She squared her shoulders, feeling the sharp flare of arthritis in her neck and spine. The unmistakable sign that her youth was long gone and old age waited to enfold her in its cold embrace. Still, she had no regrets. She lived a good life and she had done her job well. She loved the girls with all her heart and soul and knew God would forgive her if the princess Isabelle occupied a bigger part of her heart than perhaps was fair. Juliana was self-contained and obedient; she would always fare well.

Isabelle, however, was ruled by emotions as fiery as her dark eyes and, as Maxine listened to Yves spin his tale, the truth of his words found its mark.

"I saw the mademoiselle with my own eyes last night," Yves continued, cool and calm as could be. "Grass stains across the backside of her fancy dress and a smile on her face that can mean only one thing."

Maxine drew herself up to her full height and looked the uppity butler right in the eye. "Coincidence," she said, almost as if she believed it. "And I'll be thanking you to keep your opinions to yourself." She lowered her voice and leaned closer to him. "One word of your suspicions to any of the servants, and I'll have your head on a silver platter or know the reason why."

"I do not gossip with the help, madame," said Yves with a regal snort. "I simply tell the truth."

With that he turned and disappeared toward the kitchen, leaving Maxine with the terrible feeling that disaster was right around the corner.

*   *   *

Isabelle stepped over to the sideboard and waved away one of the serving girls. She was about to help herself to a large plateful of eggs and kippers when she saw Bronson, that brash American, in the archway to the room. He looked different than he had last night in evening clothes. His dark hair fell artlessly across his forehead, shaggy and quite appealing in a rough-hewn way. Even from across the room she could discern the vivid green of his eyes. *Contact lenses,* she thought with a sniff. No one's eyes were that green.

But what on earth could possibly explain that almost laughable self-confidence? In her experience, the notion of failure was something that never occurred to Americans. Defeat simply wasn't in their national vocabulary. You had only to look at the way Bronson entered a room to know he wasn't the kind of man who took a backseat to anything or anybody.

She nodded toward him and dished up a more ladylike serving of eggs than she might have, had he not chosen that moment to present himself.

"Don't hold back on my account." Bronson executed a ridiculous caricature of a bow in her direction. "I like a woman with an appetite."

Isabelle ignored the slice of honey bread she'd coveted a second ago. "I'm afraid I am not concerned with what you do and do not like in a woman, Mr. Bronson."

"Suit yourself." He reached around her and grabbed himself a platter.

Isabelle watched in envy as he loaded his plate with everything that caught his fancy.

"You are allowed to return for more," she tossed over her shoulder. "No one will slap your hand."

"Thanks," he said, following her to the table near the French doors that led out to the garden. "I probably will."

She waited for him to hold out her chair. Cheerfully oblivious, he sat down and looked as though he was about to dive into his mountain of food when a cough from Isabelle caught his attention.

"Sit down," he said. "The food's getting cold."

"My chair."

He glanced over at it. "Louis Quatorze, is it?"

Muttering an oath in both French and Italian, Isabelle claimed her seat. A red-faced butler dashed out from the anteroom, but Isabelle waved him away.

"If you wanted me to hold your chair, you should have said so."

She glared at him across the table. "A true gentleman wouldn't have needed to be told."

He made short work of a croissant. "Like your boyfriend Eric?"

"Eric?" she said, eyes wide. "Do you mean Honore Malraux's son?" *Perfect,* she thought. Not too ingenuous. Not too arch. He'd never suspect a thing.

"Yeah," said Bronson. "The guy you're sleeping with."

She felt as if she'd been caught in flagrante delicto. "How dare you insinuate such a thing."

"I'm not insinuating anything," Bronson said, swallowing some black coffee. "I'm stating a fact."

"You know nothing about me," Isabelle said, cheeks reddening. "You couldn't possibly know with whom I spend my time."

"Wrong, princess. I know exactly what you were up to last night."

Her liaison with Eric flashed through her mind in glorious technicolor. "But you—I mean, we were—"

Bronson threw back his head and laughed. The sound was entirely too triumphant for Isabelle's taste. "You're going to have to work on that poker face. It'll get you in trouble one of these days."

"I shouldn't wonder that you spend time speculating on the lives of others, Mr. Bronson, for it is abundantly clear your own bedmate of last night has abandoned you."

That phantom grin of his teased the corners of his mouth.

"How do you know I had a bedmate last night?" he countered. "Maybe I spent it alone, thinking of you."

"A man like you? I cannot imagine you spend many nights alone." She treated him to a parody of her most flirtatious smile. "Thinking of me or otherwise."

"Don't waste your time batting your eyelashes at me, princess. I'm out of your league."

Isabelle laughed out loud. "What a high opinion you have of yourself. Are all Americans as self-satisfied as you?"

"Only the successful ones."

"Then I shudder to think of the future of your country. You are vulgar, egotistical, incredibly—"

"Good morning, all."

Both Isabelle and Daniel turned toward the doorway. Greta VanArsdalen, ex-wife of a notable Dutch banker, slithered into the room, a vision in cream-colored wool and silk. She exuded the ripe sexuality of a woman in her prime, a woman who knew the power of her allure and didn't hesitate to use it. Isabelle, newly attuned to the sensual byplay between men and women, knew instantly that Bronson and the sleek blonde had spent the night together.

Why was it that she'd never before realized how much she disliked Greta VanArsdalen?

"You're looking well, Isabelle," Greta offered as she glided over to the sideboard.

"As are you, Greta."

Greta's gaze landed on the collar of Isabelle's blouse. "How perfectly sweet," she purred. "Embroidered collars are so cunning."

Fine needlework was Isabelle's only claim to artistic talent. The woman's cutting remark found its target with ease. She was possessed of an almost irresistible urge to embroider the woman's mouth shut.

Greta cast a look in Bronson's direction. Isabelle could feel the heat from across the table. Suddenly she felt terribly young and extremely uncomfortable, and she welcomed the arrival of the other guests. In moments the room was filled to overflowing with Swedes and Japanese, Brits and Italians, until it seemed as if every nationality in the world was represented at the table.

But it was the only American at the table who commanded Isabelle's attention, and each time she looked at Daniel Bronson, he was looking right back at her and laughing.

She thought he was laughing at her. Maybe he had been, but he wasn't any longer. Damn it. She was a spoiled brat. Why couldn't she stay that way instead of turning into a real live human being in front of his eyes? He saw her uneasiness in the way she held her chin high and stabbed at her eggs with short, determined jabs of the sterling silver fork. He liked the way she used that fork. She might act like a pampered house pet but she also had a no-nonsense directness that would have made her feel right at home on the streets of Queens.

The idea of the glamorous Princess Isabelle strolling along Roosevelt Avenue, window-shopping at Woolworth's, and saying hi to the guys at the construction site on the corner brought a huge smile to his face, something he instantly regretted when he glanced across the table at her and caught the look in her eyes. *Damn it, princess,* he thought, ripping apart a piece of honey bread and smearing it with sweet butter. *I'm not laughing at you. Not really.* Who would've figured the girl with the sharp tongue would have such thin skin? He didn't want to think of her as a real live person with a breakable heart. He wanted to think of her only as another of Perreault's underutilized natural resources.

The word around town was that she was wild as an unbroken mare, as flighty and unpredictable as her mother, and twice as beautiful. While the old-timers on the staff despaired for her future, they still seemed to have a soft spot in their hearts for Isabelle, a soft spot that didn't exist for her sister Juliana.

Next to him Greta was going on about some idiotic horse show she was riding in next month in Philadelphia, and wouldn't he absolutely love to come to Philly to cheer her on? He grunted something noncommittal and shot another look at the dark-haired princess. Those high, almost Slavic cheekbones and her straight nose gave her face a chiseled quality, softened only by the huge dark eyes with the thick tangle of lashes that cast a shadow each time she glanced down at her plate. Her skin was pale, almost porcelain-smooth, with a patch of high color riding across each cheekbone.

It suddenly hit him that she wasn't half as smart or sophisticated as she wanted him to believe. She was a nineteen-going-on-twenty-year-old girl with a bad case of the hots for a guy who wasn't good enough to kiss her Maud Frizons. He'd overheard the servants talking about the little princess and Malraux's son, and it didn't take a rocket scientist to figure out what it was all about. She thought she was in love, even though Bronson could have told her that sooner or later the fog would lift and she would see Eric Malraux for the nobody he was. People often mistook loneliness for love and, unless he missed his guess, this was one of those times. Trouble was, if he told Isabelle right now, she wouldn't believe him.

Just because he was too old and too jaded to believe in happily-ever-after was no reason to deny the girl her dreams. He'd had a first time himself and dreamed those same dreams. She'd learn soon enough that life didn't always work out according to plan, not even for princesses with eyes dark as night.

But still there was something about her that called out to Bronson in a way that made him feel both powerful and vulnerable at the same time. Something that went beyond the allure of her cascade of dark curls or the sweet curves of her ripe young body and touched at the most primitive part of his soul. She shifted in her seat, brushing away a lock of hair with an elegant, artless gesture and for a moment,

Bronson knew exactly how she would feel in his arms. She was too young, too spoiled, too much trouble for a man as practical and pig-headed as he was, but still—

I'm not laughing at you, princess, he thought as he met her eyes. *I'm just wondering why I couldn't have been first.*

Chapter Three

Breakfast dragged on forever. There were so many people laughing about so many inconsequential things that Isabelle could scarcely manage to keep her mind on the foolish conversations flying about her head, much less respond in kind.

Only forty-five minutes until she was in Eric's arms once more. The thought was enough to make even this boring meal palatable. She sipped her coffee, listening for the deep roar of Eric's Lamborghini. Outside, a crisp autumn day beckoned, and she wished she could meet Eric down near the lake. Away from prying eyes, she could throw herself into his arms and—

Bronson's amused laughter brought her back to the breakfast table. "Come on, princess," he said in that infuriating American accent of his. "Dr. Wortham asked you a question."

Isabelle conquered her desire to kick him under the table. Instead she turned her attention to the physicist and managed to field some questions about Perreault's stand on global warming without making a total fool of herself.

"Very good," said Bronson a few minutes later as he joined her near the sideboard. "I almost believed you knew what you were talking about."

She cast him a look that would have destroyed a lesser man. "And what makes you think I didn't know what I was talking about?"

"Remember what I told you about your poker face? You lost it again back there."

Juliana would have graciously admitted her shortcomings and made it her business to introduce Dr. Wortham to an expert. "Does the doctor realize that?"

"Princess, if she doesn't, she'd better give back that Nobel prize."

"Oh, do be still," Isabelle hissed, putting her plate back down on the sideboard. "Who asked for your opinion?"

Bronson grabbed the honey bread from her plate and bit off a chunk of it. There was something almost primitive about the flash of white teeth, something disturbing and earthy, and Isabelle looked away. Thank God he wasn't her type at all.

"He's out there, you know."

"Who is?"

"Your boyfriend."

"Don't you ever tire of juvenile pranks, Mr. Bronson, or is it merely another facet of the remarkable American character?"

"You don't like Americans, do you?" he asked, narrowing his eyes as he looked at her.

"I like some Americans," she replied pointedly. "Those who understand that familiarity is something to be earned."

He grinned. "That doesn't change the fact that your boyfriend is outside."

"Impossible. He isn't due for another quarter hour." She

met his eyes. "Besides, he wouldn't wander through the garden. He would come inside. After all, Eric is like one of the family."

"Not if he wasn't alone."

To her horror, tears sprang to her eyes, and she blinked rapidly to stem the flow. "Eric wouldn't do that to me."

"Life is tough, princess," he said, his gaze intent upon her. "Things aren't always what they seem."

"You're despicable," she whispered. "I pity you that you find it necessary to hate those who are lucky enough to have someone to love."

He gestured toward the garden beyond the glass doors. "Go ahead. Find out for yourself. Just don't say I didn't warn you. I'll be waiting for your apology."

"You'll be waiting in hell for it, Mr. Bronson, because I would rather die than give you the time of day."

"You'll change your mind, Isabelle," he said, heading back toward the breakfast table. "Sooner or later, you'll come around."

Isabelle didn't linger long enough to try to untangle his words. With hasty apologies to the others, she dashed from the room. She could have let herself out the French doors and into the garden, but Bronson already had more than enough to amuse him, so she hurried through the hallway and into the kitchen.

"Princess Isabelle!" Olivia, one of the chef's assistants, leaped to her feet as Isabelle burst into the room. "Is there something I can do for you?"

Isabelle shook her head. "A back door," she said, glancing about the room. "We have one that leads into the garden, don't we?"

Olivia maintained her composure, even though Isabelle was certain the girl was filled with curiosity. "Through the butler's pantry and down the hallway to the right. It takes you to the rose garden."

Isabelle clapped her hands together. "Splendid! I'll be on the other side of the garden." Away from prying eyes watching from the French doors. She would die of embarrassment if Bronson and the other guests saw her scurrying down the path after Eric.

"Mademoiselle?"

"Nothing, nothing." She flashed the girl a quick smile. "Thank you, Olivia. If anyone should ask, you haven't seen me all morning."

"As you wish, mademoiselle."

The butler's pantry was an enormous, windowless room in which the bounty of harvests past rested on deep shelves that went from floor to ceiling, effectively hiding the door that led down to the cellar. Conserves, jams, jellies, and relishes vied for space with jars of Belgian carrots, raspberry vinegars, and cornichons. Glass bottles of pale gold olive oil rested next to enormous sacks of unbleached flour and winter onions.

She pushed open the back door and stepped out into the garden. Although it was late October, a few bloodred roses still clung to the thorny branches, their sweet fragrance softening the sharp, tangy air. The pathway divided at the edge of the rose garden, and she paused, her gaze drawn across the endless sweep of lawn. If she stood on tiptoe, she could make out a curve of driveway sheltered beneath the porte cochere. Sunlight glittered off the elegant angles of the familiar red Lamborghini, and her breath caught as if she'd received a blow to her chest.

She hesitated, then the sound of laughter, low and intimate, caught her attention. Turning, she peered through a thick rhododendron bush and looked toward the gazebo. Juliana and Eric were clearly visible, standing inside the gazebo. What on earth could they be talking about that would make Juliana duck her head and smile like that? And Eric certainly looked pleased with himself, albeit a trifle nervous. He wore a turtleneck sweater the color of jet, and she thought she'd never seen him look more romantically handsome. He had that elegant pallor she'd always associated with poets and artists, even though Eric had grown up surrounded by horses, not books and brushes.

He was leaning against the south side post, his golden head tilted to one side, while Juliana talked with what seemed to be great intensity, her pale hair whipping across her cheek in the breeze. Juliana looked so serious while Eric—darling Eric—looked serious and sincere and so absolutely adorable that Isabelle's heart melted.

"I know what you're doing," she called out as she approached the gazebo, "and I love you for it."

Juliana turned toward her sister, her cameo-perfect face composed and radiant. "Oh, I doubt that you do, Isabelle."

Isabelle climbed the three steps and went to Eric's side. "You cannot fool me, you two wonderful people. You're making plans for my birthday, aren't you?" In two and a half weeks she would be turning twenty years of age, and she knew that wonderful occasion would not pass without great fanfare. She linked her arm through Eric's. Especially not now. "Tell me, are we having a private party for family or a wonderful bash with no one over twenty-five allowed?" She gave Eric's arm an affectionate squeeze. "Why so silent? Has my big sister been telling you all of my dark and dreadful secrets?"

"Eric had some marvelous ideas," said Juliana, breaking in smoothly, "none of which you are to know about until the tenth of November."

"So you *were* plotting something wonderful for my birthday." She threw back her head and laughed with joy. "I knew it! Juli, you are so terrible at keeping secrets."

Eric cast a look back toward the garden room. "We seem to be attracting no small amount of interest."

Isabelle glanced over her shoulder. Bronson, arms folded across his broad chest, was watching the scene with blatant curiosity. "Oh, pay no attention," she said airily. "That obnoxious Mr. Bronson has nothing better to do than stick his nose into other people's affairs." Her choice of words brought a rosy glow to her sister's cheeks. "Oh, Juli!" She laughed and planted a kiss on Juliana's forehead. "Don't be so provincial. We're all adults now, aren't we?" Feeling amazingly smug and quite adult, she swung about and met Eric's eyes. "Juli knows all about us."

"I'd rather suspected as much."

"Are you angry with me?" She pressed kisses along his jawline. "Juli is my sister. I simply couldn't keep such wondrous news from her."

"Don't make our girl suffer, Eric." Juliana's voice was sweet and soft as springtime rain. "You know she finds it impossible to keep a secret."

Eric met Juliana's eyes, and Isabelle frowned at the look that passed between them. "Is something wrong?" she asked.

His serious expression dissolved into the pleasant smiling countenance she knew and loved. "Darling girl," he said, drawing her into his embrace. "There's nothing for you to worry about."

Juliana's laugh joined his. "She's much too curious for her own good. How on earth can we plan the world's most wonderful birthday party if she questions our every move?"

Isabelle relaxed against Eric, burying her face against the soft wool of his sweater. *Goose,* she thought. *Everything is absolutely fine.*

Maxine couldn't put her finger on what was wrong, but she knew deep in her bones that trouble was on the horizon. She hadn't slept well last night. Each time she closed her eyes, visions of some faceless, nameless terror forced her to sit upright with her heart pounding in her throat. She didn't know when the hounds of hell would come riding over the crest, but she could hear the thud of their footsteps as surely as she had heard the banshees howl the night the Princess Sonia had died.

How well she remembered that awful time. It had been the night of the hunter's moon sixteen years ago, a wild night of punishing winds and wicked rain. "You mustn't go out in this, madame," she had pleaded with Sonia as she helped the princess with her toilette. "There's evil afoot tonight."

Sonia had only laughed at her reflection in the beveled glass of her mirror and arranged a diamond comb in her upswept hair. "It is the Irish in you speaking, Maxine. A little rain shan't hurt me."

The cruel sparkle of diamonds in Sonia's midnight hair made Maxine shiver. "'Tisn't the rain what worries me," she said, smoothing a curl that tumbled from the princess's glamorous coiffure. "'Tis a feeling I have."

Sonia's laughter grew brittle. "Spare me your feelings. I know all about your feelings." She rose from the boudoir chair, all willowy grace and elegance. Sonia was everything Maxine could never be: beautiful, rich, and well loved. "I only wish someone would pay heed to my feelings for a change."

It had seemed to Maxine that people paid too much heed to the heartless Sonia's feelings, but she held her tongue. When you worked for royalty you quickly learned to keep your opinions to yourself, at least until you were safely belowstairs with the rest of the staff. Being Irish and naturally rebellious, Maxine had a basic distrust for royalty, even royalty as minor as the ruling family of Perreault. Royalty was nothing more than an accident of birth, the simple luck of being born on the right side of the sheets, in a palace rather than a cold-water flat. Maxine was paid to serve, and when it came to the little princesses, she loved as well. If only their mother were capable of the same emotion.

Rain beat fiercely against the window of the Paris apartment while vicious winds bent the graceful trees toward the pavement. Sonia, in her sleek black dress, stood at the window, her face raised toward the storm. "It's wonderful," she whispered, her voice vibrant with forces Maxine dared not contemplate. "Perfect."

"Madame," Maxine began, unable to stop herself, "I'm begging you to reconsider. . . ."

The deep roar of a powerful engine at the curb drowned out her words, and in a moment the princess was gone.

Even now, many years later, Maxine could conjure up the sight of Sonia, so ravishing in her black gown, as she dashed across the rainswept sidewalk and swung her elegant legs into the waiting sports car. So young. So foolish. So terribly, terribly selfish. Maxine saw that selfishness in the girls Sonia had left behind, and she had spent the last fifteen years battling against it. Isabelle was the spit of her mother, but Juliana, with her candy-box prettiness and spun-sugar blond hair, had inherited her mother's fatal flaw. There was something beneath the surface with Juliana, a note of steel, of hunger, that worried Maxine for it brought Sonia to mind more clearly than the wild beauty the younger girl had inherited.

Last night Maxine had thought about the curse for the first time in years. She had been standing in the doorway to the ballroom, watching as Isabelle danced with Honore Malraux. Something about the way her girl looked in the older man's arms triggered a fear inside Maxine that was beyond reason, conjuring up memories of a time when talk of the curse of Perreault had been on everyone's lips. Newspapers and slick, shiny magazines had devoted endless space to the chain of tragedies that dogged the royal family.

The loss of Bertrand's wife and the death of his sister's fiancé were grist for the gossipmonger's mill. To her endless regret, Maxine herself had devoured the details of the Princess Elysse's grief when her playboy fiancé had drowned in a boating accident. Years later, when she met Elysse at the castle for the first time, Maxine had been overcome with remorse that the good woman's loss had provided her with an hour's entertainment.

"You'd be too young to go walking down memory lane like that," she chided herself. Better to push these unsettling thoughts from her mind. There was much work to be done today, what with so many people in the palace for the celebration.

She hurried downstairs to fetch a packet of letters she'd promised to answer for Prince Bertrand and was passing by the wall of windows in the library when something caught her eye.

There, in the gazebo, were the two young princesses and Honore Malraux's boy. Juliana, a snow angel in her pale blond fur coat, was talking with great animation while Isabelle, a flash of ebony fire, had eyes only for Eric. Even from a distance Maxine could feel the intensity. She couldn't quite make out their expressions, the glare from the sun being what it was, but there was something . . . something.

Dread prickled its way down Maxine's arms.

"You would be lettin' your imagination run away with you, old woman," she said out loud. "How many times would you see the three of them together, as normal as you please?"

She reached into the capacious side pocket of her navy wool jumper and withdrew her spectacles. Not that she needed them, of course. She was only fifty-six and not prey to the ravages of time quite yet. It was just the glare and the way it streamed through the leaded-glass windows. Squinting, she looked back toward the gazebo. Ah, yes. There they were. She could see them quite clearly now. Eric had his arm about Isabelle's shoulders. Isabelle was looking up at him as if he were the sun and the moon and the stars, all rolled up in one quite average young man.

Maxine sighed. There was no denying that look on her beloved girl's face. She'd given herself to that pretty young boy, given away the most important possession a girl would ever have. People said virginity wasn't important any longer, that only fools worried about that tiny, trembling membrane, but Maxine knew otherwise. It mattered to men, being first. Oh, women could talk all they wanted about being equal and being free, but when the bedroom door closed on a bridal couple, a man liked to think he would be the one to teach his wife the ways of the world.

At first glance it seemed as if Juliana was looking upon her sister and her sister's young man with the fond benevolence of a woman much older and a great deal wiser. But then Maxine looked more closely. Juliana's smile was sharpened like a blade; her movements were quicker, more certain; and, dear God, she seemed to be focusing her attentions in on Eric.

Maxine took off her glasses, letting them dangle over her bosom from a long ribbon cord. It couldn't be. Surely she was misreading the expression on Juliana's face the way the gypsy lady used to misread the tea leaves after too much of the grape. Life was complicated enough without pitting sisters one against the other. Nothing good would come of a confrontation like that, nothing good at all.

Chapter
Four

If Isabelle had her way, she would have spent the afternoon in the gazebo with Eric. Instead she found herself perched on the high terrace at the rear of the palace, watching while men and women who should know better fired bullets at pieces of clay.

Cries of "Pull! Pull!" rang out in the Alpine stillness followed by the report of shotguns and peals of excited laughter. Her father's beloved Corgis, a gift from Queen Elizabeth II, barked accompaniment. Isabelle sighed and hugged her knees closer to her body. She was hopelessly awkward with pistols and shotguns. She hated the cold dead weight against her shoulder and cheek, hated the off-balance way she felt as she peered through the sight. The mere thought of pulling the trigger made her flinch. Juliana, of course, was expert at it. While Isabelle was stranded in that godforsaken boarding school, Juliana had been at their father's side, learning all the things that were truly important in Perreault.

"Good, isn't she?" said a deep male voice as the clay bird shattered overhead.

Isabelle groaned inwardly. Bronson, no less.

"Yes, she is," she managed. Why on earth did everyone find Juliana's proficiency with a shotgun so incredibly interesting? "Quite good."

"Why aren't you down there performing your royal duties?"

She ignored him.

"Can't shoot?" he persisted.

"Of course I can," she said with a short laugh. "There's nothing terribly special about that." She fixed him with a look. "Do you shoot?"

"Only to kill," he said. "Otherwise, it's a waste of good ammunition." If ever a man looked as if he'd have a taste for blood, it was Bronson. "Why aren't you down there with your pal?" he asked.

She gazed pointedly toward Greta VanArsdalen who idled near a Japanese businessman from Kyoto. "I could ask you the same thing."

His smile didn't waver, but she noted the steel behind it. "There's nothing between Greta and me."

"Oh, come now, Mr. Bronson. She made your alliance quite clear at breakfast."

"I didn't say we didn't have sex last night. I said there's nothing between us."

To her dismay, her cheeks reddened. "But you—I mean, you said you . . ."

His eyes raked her body, not in a sleazy fashion, but rather like someone reacquainting himself with the obvious. "I keep forgetting how young you are, princess. In case you don't know, sex and love are two different things." He paused, his vivid green eyes twinkling. "Or they should be if you're doing it right."

"That's despicable."

"That's the real world. I know you princesses don't have a lot to do with the real world, but the sooner you pick up on a few elementary points, the better off you'll be."

"I feel sorry for you, Mr. Bronson," she said, turning away from him. "You must lead a terribly lonely life."

They watched in silence as Juliana and Prince Bertrand engaged in some friendly competition. Her sister's pale hair was pulled back in a sleek French braid that bobbed merrily between her shoulder blades. The expression on her heart-shaped face was endearingly earnest as she listened to some advice from their father then blithely raised the rifle to her shoulder and took aim. The clay bird shattered and fell back to earth.

"You as good a shot as your sister?"

She shook her head, maintaining her silence, as Juliana's laughter floated up to the balcony. Her father's handsome face was creased with a broad smile, and jealousy, her old nemesis, clawed at her ribcage. Isabelle's breath caught as Eric moved out from the shadows and took his place next to Juliana. Bertrand stepped aside as if that were the most natural thing in the world. There was something so right about the scene, so deeply inevitable, that Isabelle struggled to maintain her composure.

"They make a great-looking couple," Bronson noted.

She refused to meet his eyes. Damn him. He was being tactful. Eric and Juliana made a stunning couple. You would have to be blind not to be struck by the sight of their two blond heads pressed close together as Eric helped Juliana reload. Isabelle suspected her sister could take the shotgun apart and put it back together again without anyone's help whatsoever.

"I know you don't believe it," Bronson continued in a voice more gentle than she'd heard from him before, "but one day you'll wonder what you saw in him."

"I love him," she said. "I'll love him until the day I die."

"Sure you will," said Bronson.

"You don't know anything at all," she snapped. "You wouldn't understand true love if you lived to be a thousand."

"You don't really believe that, do you?"

"I certainly do."

"And you think Malraux is your knight in shining armor?"

She hesitated. The biting edge to his words wasn't lost on her. "You make it sound so foolish. Why is it so hard for you to believe that two people can fall in love?"

"Go ahead, princess," Bronson urged. "Tell me you two will live happily ever after."

"We will," she snapped in exasperation. "Mark my words, Mr. Bronson. You'll dance with the bride before too long."

"Right," said Bronson, "and if I'm lucky, maybe I'll get to dance with you, too."

"You bastard!" Fury flooded her brain. All she could think of was wiping that malicious smirk from his face. She raised her hand, her palm itching to make contact with his cheek, and gasped in surprise as he deftly moved forward and pinned her hands behind her back while she prayed he wouldn't toss her over the railing.

"Don't even think it, princess. You're not going to get away with that crap with me."

She considered the wisdom of kicking him in the shins, but the set of his jaw forced her to reconsider. "You're hurting me."

"I'd turn you over my knee and paddle some sense into you if I thought it would do any good."

"How terribly macho," she said, praying she sounded braver than she felt. "I'm sure your female companions must enjoy walking three paces behind you."

"He's a schmuck," said Bronson. "You can find a thousand like him at the tables in Monte Carlo."

"And a million of you on any street corner in Manhattan."

Damn the quaver in her voice. "Why are you so hateful? What on earth have I done to make you treat me this way?"

"I hate to see people make mistakes."

"Loving Eric isn't a mistake."

"It's not love, princess, it just feels that way."

"You couldn't possibly understand anything about the way I feel. Why, I—"

With one swift movement he lowered his head, bringing his mouth against her mouth, kissing her hard and long. There was nothing tender about the kiss, nothing sweet or romantic. What there was, was heat. More raw fire than she would have imagined possible in a kiss. The fact that he had absolutely no business claiming her this way was almost secondary to the warmth radiating outward from the pit of her stomach.

His mouth was hard, demanding. He yielded nothing and demanded everything. And there was nothing—nothing she could do.

If he hadn't taken her by surprise, she never would have allowed such a thing to happen.

If he hadn't pinned her hands behind her so effectively, she would have pushed him away without a second thought.

If he—

"Is that you I hear, Mr. Bronson? We need to talk."

Heat was replaced by panic as her father's footsteps sounded on the stone steps, not thirty feet away from the balcony where they stood.

"See what I mean?" Bronson ended the kiss with the same suddenness with which it had begun. She struggled to regain her composure. "Lust." His grin was all too knowing. "Hard to tell the difference, isn't it?"

"Shut up," she hissed. "I have a good mind to tell my father what you did. He'd toss you off this balcony in a flash."

"Feeling guilty, princess? Doesn't Malraux—"

"So it was you I heard, Mr. Bronson." Bertrand's imposing figure appeared on the landing. Dressed in forest green cords and a coffee-brown suede jacket, he appeared more the country gentleman than the ruler of Perreault. A jaunty Irish cap, souvenir of his last visit to Dublin, perched atop his thick mane of silver hair. "And Isabelle." He bestowed his best smile on his younger daughter. "Juliana didn't tell me I'd find you here as well." He crossed the balcony to where she stood, radiating paternal warmth and concern. "Your cheeks are flushed, *cheri*. Perhaps you are cold?"

"N-no." She swallowed hard, studiously avoiding Bronson's eyes. "We—I mean, I was just . . ." Her voice drifted away. So did her father's attention. For once she was glad she'd failed to hold his interest.

"Isabelle was explaining some of the finer points of trap shooting," Bronson offered, his tone laconic. "She's an enthusiastic teacher."

Her father's smile was benign. "My daughter does everything with great enthusiasm."

"So I've noticed."

She couldn't help it. She looked up at Bronson, but his expression was as bland as his voice. No wonder he was so successful in business. He could lie with the best of them.

". . . much like my late wife," her father was saying. "All fire and emotion . . ."

Bronson's dark brows lifted, and Isabelle held her breath. *Don't say anything,* she pleaded silently. *If you ask one question about my mother, he'll turn away from me as if I were invisible.*

Prince Bertrand shook his head once, then twice, as if to bring himself back to the matter at hand. "We have some time before the afternoon hunt." He focused in on Bronson, using all of his formidable charm to coax a smile from the businessman. "You said you wished to speak with me about a particular matter?"

Isabelle watched as Bronson switched gears with the ease of a Maserati downshifting into a curve. "A very important matter," he said with none of the deference most men evidenced when speaking to her father. "Give me an hour, and I can lay out the whole project for you."

Her father blinked, then looked over at Isabelle. "The directness of Americans can be overwhelming, can it not?"

Isabelle bit hard on the inside of her cheek. "Quite," she said after a moment.

"In the library, then," said her father.

"I'll get my portfolio," said Bronson, "and meet you there in five minutes."

"My daughter will be joining us, if you don't mind."

Bronson's emerald eyes twinkled as he looked over at Isabelle. "I don't mind at all."

You have a lot to learn about Perreault, Mr. Bronson, she thought. Second daughters didn't attend meetings with businessmen from America, no matter how important those businessmen thought they were.

Bertrand turned to Isabelle. "Tell Juliana to make her apologies, then come to the library. Our guests can amuse themselves for an hour, I have no doubt."

She noted the disappointment on Bronson's face and enjoyed it. "It's been . . . interesting," he said, sweeping past him with all the aplomb at her command.

"We'll do it again," he said.

"I doubt that," she murmured as she reached the staircase, then paused. Looking back over her shoulder, her gaze was caught and held by the telltale pink lipstick smudge near the left corner of his mouth. Smiling, she turned and hurried down the stone steps. She hoped he had the devil of a time explaining that smudge to Greta VanArsdalen.

Daylight was cruel to the castle, Daniel noted as he followed a middle-aged parlormaid up a back staircase to his room on the second floor. Much as the uncompromising sunlight pointed out each wrinkle on the pleasant woman's face, it also highlighted the castle's considerable problems. Chunks of stone were missing from the walls, the lighting was quixotic at best, and puddles of rainwater had him hopscotching his way down the hallway. The air was damp and downright cold, and he wondered if the slightly lopsided windows at the landing kept out any but the gentlest of alpine breezes. Daniel wasn't given to romantic flights of fancy, but he could almost swear he heard the clanking of armor in the distance.

"Your room, m'sieur." The parlormaid swung open the heavy oak door and stepped aside.

Bronson found himself reaching for his pockets but stopped before he made a total ass of himself. The place looked so much like a broken-down old hotel that he'd almost tipped the woman. "Thanks," he said, smiling.

The woman nodded. "I wait to take you back to the library."

"Not necessary. That I can find."

She hesitated. "The castle is large, m'sieur. It is so easy to get lost."

It took some effort, but he convinced her he'd be able to find the library without a guide. Truth was, he could have found his room on his own as well, but the help here seemed to think outsiders couldn't find the bathroom without a map. He could be as dense as the next guy, but at least he had a good sense of direction. His problem had to do with the opposite sex. If someone could hand him a map to help him understand women, that would be something he could use.

Admit it, he said to himself. *The little princess really had you going for a while down there.* He was a sap, a fool. Hell, he was an asshole for letting himself get taken in like that by a kid. And that's all she was, a kid. A girl. Yeah, she had the body of a woman, but he could see she was still wet behind the ears when it came to the battle of the sexes. She still believed in fairy tales, happily-ever-after, and that love triumphed in the end. Maybe it had something to do with growing up in a castle, surrounded by every romantic cliché Walt Disney had ever dreamed up.

Still, there was something about Isabelle's words that had reached down into Bronson's gut to a place he'd long forgotten. *I'll love him until the day I die.* . . . He blinked, startled by the clarity of the voice inside his head. Sweet, throaty, part English boarding school, part Parisian boîte. The starry-eyed little princess with the midnight eyes thought she was in love with a guy who wasn't half good enough for her.

Had anyone ever said that about him? He couldn't remember. He'd been so busy making money that he hadn't paid a hell of a lot of attention to things like falling in love. But listening to Isabelle, seeing the look in her eyes as she watched that Malraux kid with her sister, he'd felt a stirring of something that wasn't lust. Lust, at least, he could understand. It was something he was familiar with.

What Isabelle had triggered in him was more complicated. He felt sorry for her. He understood her. He could see what was happening even if she couldn't, and if there was any way at all that he could spare her the inevitable, he would. He had the strangest feeling that they were somehow kindred spirits and that notion disturbed him even more than the fact that he might not cut a deal with her father.

"You're losing it, Danny," he said aloud, grabbing his portfolio and heading for the door. Let the little princess chase after lover boy. There wasn't anybody alive who hadn't had his or her heart broken at least once. It came with the territory.

Maybe it would even do her good.

Chapter Five

"Good to have you home," said the customs inspector at JFK as he handed the passport back to Daniel. "The Jets always lose when you're out of town. You sure you didn't take their whole offensive line with you?"

Daniel laughed and slipped the leather passport case into the breast pocket of his trench coat. "Defense," he said, reaching for his bag. "That's the real name of the game."

"Amen to that," said the inspector with a sage nod of his head. "You got some clout in this town, Mr. B. Why don't you see what you can do to get us some new talent?"

"We've got the talent," said Daniel as he headed for the door. "The thing is, we don't know how to use it."

A slicing wind blew off Jamaica Bay, swirling the gum wrappers and cigarette butts into whirlpools in the rainswept gutter. A toddler squalled at his mother's feet while she argued with a skycap. The sound of her voice was all but drowned out by the roar of a 747 climbing into the sky beyond the airline terminal. The damp air smelled of salt water and jet fuel with a measure of plain old air pollution thrown into the mix just to remind him that this was New York.

Home.

Dirty, noisy, hard to love but even harder to forget. He was glad to be back where he belonged.

A black Lincoln Town Car with the license BRON-CO idled at the curb outside the International Arrivals Building. A gray-haired man stood next to it, its door flung open, while he engaged in animated conversation with a Russian emigré cab driver who'd apparently just missed clipping the left front fender.

Daniel nodded toward the cabbie, then turned toward the Lincoln's driver. "Problems?"

"Guy needs to get his eyes examined," the gray-haired man shot back. "God damn menace on the road."

Daniel eyeballed the Lincoln. "I don't see any damage."

"No thanks to him. If I didn't have the reflexes of an eighteen-year-old, he'd have creamed me."

Daniel approached the cabdriver, who was watching them with the fierce intensity of a cossack warrior. "You okay?" he asked.

The driver nodded, casting a suspicious glance over Daniel's shoulder. "He shot out in front of me like a—" He fumbled for the English words, then launched into a burst of Russian that didn't require a translator to be understood.

Daniel knew all about his father's kamikaze driving skills. Reaching into his pocket, he pulled out a pile of francs, British pound notes, and a serious array of dollars. Peeling off a twenty, he handed it to the guy who grunted his thanks and climbed back into his cab.

"You've gotta stop picking fights, Pop," Daniel said, walking back to the Lincoln and flinging his bags into the backseat. "Especially when you're driving this damn hearse."

His father tossed him the car keys and climbed into the passenger's side. "Everybody's a critic. I don't hear any thanks for picking up your sorry butt."

"Thanks," said Daniel, starting the engine and adjusting the mirrors. Sometimes he wondered why his old man bothered to keep Ted on retainer. More often than not, Matty drove himself wherever he needed to go.

Matty pressed a button and brought his seat to a reclining position. "So how'd it go?"

"It didn't," Daniel said, pushing into the flow of traffic. "Bertrand doesn't believe in progress of any kind. I probably blew it when I handed him the specs on the project. He'd rather drink brandy and talk about the good old days."

"I told you he wasn't going to budge." Matty's sphere of interest extended far beyond the city limits. "Bertrand's the kind of guy who'd be happiest living a hundred years ago."

"He practically is."

"Beautiful country."

"That's not a country, Pop, that's an E-ticket ride at Disney World." He started to laugh. "Can you believe their goats wear little bells around their necks? I thought I was listening to the 'Hallelujah Chorus'!"

"Atmosphere," said his father. "If they could bottle the stuff, they wouldn't be in the mess they're in."

"Yeah, well, I couldn't even convince him to put in a ski lift."

"What about Malraux?"

"If Honore has his way, the place'll be the Las Vegas of the Alps. He barged in on our meeting, and Bertrand just smiled and invited him to sit down."

Matty's face darkened. "Sorry to hear that SOB is still on the scene. After that problem in Singapore, I had him pegged for some jail time."

"You've got to be kidding. His type never gets caught. It's a law of nature."

"How about his son? Last I heard the kid was in Cannes, squiring some Italian widow with unlimited funds."

Daniel's jaw tightened. "I don't know about the widow, but he's sleeping with one of the prince's daughters."

Matty glanced at him. "Best way to get power is to marry it. When Bertrand dies, Malraux's kid'll be sitting pretty."

"Not that pretty," said Daniel, trying to keep his tone even. "He's seeing the younger daughter—" He hesitated, now knowing exactly why.

"Never last," said Matty sagely. "Malraux isn't going to waste a son on the second daughter."

"My thoughts exactly."

His father cast another glance in his direction, this one more curious than the last. "I hope she knows there's no future in it."

Daniel shrugged. She was young and more naive than he'd have thought possible. "She's a princess," he said. "She'll land on her feet." He merged left around a tow truck.

"Might as well toss the specs into the circular file," Matty said. "You don't want to tangle with Malraux."

"The hell I don't. That's the kind of bastard I live to beat."

"You don't beat men like that, Danny. You just slow them down for a while."

Traffic slowed to a crawl, and he looked at his father. "What's with you, Pop? I've never heard you talk like that before." He'd inherited his fighting genes from his old man.

"A feeling," Matty said after a moment. "Can't put my finger on it, but something's telling me a ski lift in Perreault isn't worth bumping up against Malraux."

The first snows came to Perreault in early November— heavy, drifting snow with frigid Siberian winds that sent the old men scurrying into the cafés in search of warm brandy and memories of their younger days.

Prince Bertrand opened the doors to his chalet high up in the mountains, thus officially declaring the start of ski season. The fact that they had to cross the border to actually ski seemed odd to everyone but him.

Family business kept Eric traveling through most of the month. He sent Isabelle an enormous bouquet of roses for her birthday, but it was still no substitute for the comfort of his presence. Her father hosted a small party in her honor, but it appeared to Isabelle that most of the guests were more interested in the menu than the occasion.

Honore Malraux, however, showered her with attention. He was flirtatious, albeit in his courtly fashion, and extremely apologetic for sending Eric away on so many business trips. Honore saw to it that she never lacked for a dance partner, and if it seemed that he held her a trifle closely, she chalked that up to her lack of sophistication.

"That dark sweep of hair," he mused, his tone light and uncomplicated, "those devastating eyes. You are your mother come back to life . . . even more beautiful, if that is possible."

She had heard those words before, of course, but always couched in disapproving tones. "I know so little about my mother, Honore. Not even Maxine will say more to me than I can discover for myself in old newspaper clippings."

"Come," he said, sweeping her toward the library. "We will talk."

"I want to know everything," she said minutes later as she sat down opposite him. "How she spoke, how she walked, the music she liked to listen to . . ." She waved her hands in the air. "I want to know it all."

"She loved Bach better than Beethoven," Honore began, "but she loved American jazz most of all. . . ."

Two hours later Isabelle dried her eyes and impulsively hugged Honore as they left the library. "That was the most wonderful birthday gift anyone has ever given me."

Honore's handsome face beamed with pleasure. *"Je suis votre serviteur."* The traditional phrase of obeisance. He kissed her left cheek and then her right. "Isabelle." His voice had a different note, strange yet oddly familiar.

She took a step backward. For one terrible instant she had the insane notion that he was about to kiss her. The expression on his face shifted, then his features settled back into their normal pattern. She felt almost giddy with relief. What a goose she was to even think such a thing.

"Life will be good to you, I promise," Honore said as they walked together to the ballroom. "No matter what happens, you must remember that."

An attractive Swedish industrialist claimed her as soon as they reached the entryway, spiriting her onto the dance floor before she could ask Honore exactly what he meant.

Eric came home a few days before Christmas. He seemed charmingly uncertain in her company, the way she imagined a man would seem when he was about to propose marriage to the woman he loved.

When her father summoned her to the library on the morning after Christmas, Isabelle knew there could be but one reason: Eric had asked for her hand.

As soon as she entered the room she became aware that her father had been drinking. Not a great deal, for Bertrand never did anything to excess, but enough so that the room held the slight bouquet of warm brandy. His pipe rested on the small mahogany table to the right of his leather chair, next to a copy of a Maigret mystery novel and a stack of unanswered correspondence.

"I know I'm late, Papa," she said, kissing him on the forehead, "but I was embroidering a cape for Maxine to wear to church on New Year's Day and—well, one thing led to another and before I knew it, it was eight o'clock." She offered up her very best smile and perched on the arm of his chair, ignoring the chair next to him. "You do forgive me, don't you?"

The corners of his mouth lifted in a quick smile, but that smile came and went long before it reached his eyes. "There is nothing to forgive, Isabelle. This is a talk between a father and his daughter, not a military engagement."

She rolled her eyes comically. "I do not think Yves would

agree with your assessment. He chided me in the hallway for keeping you waiting."

Bertrand chuckled, but Isabelle was quick to note that the furrows between his thick brows grew deeper. A chill ran up her spine once again, and she slid from her perch on the arm of the chair and claimed the seat next to him.

He pointed toward the decanter of brandy on the side table. "Please help yourself."

Isabelle shook her head, then took a deep breath. "I'd be happy to pour for you."

"Later, perhaps." His eyes met hers, then he looked away toward the window. "There is a matter of great importance—"

"Oh, Papa!" She leaped to her feet, her apprehension vanishing. "I know what you're going to say!"

"Isabelle, please sit down. This is—"

"About Eric, isn't it?"

"Yes, but—"

"Then I do know what this is about! How could I not when—"

"Isabelle! Sit down."

With exaggerated movements, she sank back into her chair. How like Papa to rely on tradition and ceremony. She could barely suppress a smile. "You were saying, Papa?"

He glanced toward the bar. "Perhaps a touch, if you would."

Moments later, she handed him his snifter, then sat down again. This was not going as she'd imagined it would. She waited as he took a long drink of cognac.

"You have been seeing Honore's son, have you not?"

She nodded. "I have."

His eyes closed for a moment. "And you're fond of him?"

She nodded again. "Oh yes." *Say it, Papa! Just say it so I can shout my happiness to the entire world!*

"I only wish it could be different."

"What?" She must have missed something.

He leaned forward and reached for her hand, but she had

the arms of the chair in a death grip. "This is very difficult, Isabelle. I only wish there were another way—an easier way to tell you."

The air in the room grew thin, and she struggled to draw a breath. A twisting mountain road—the black sheen of ice—she'd lost her mother that way years ago. Dear God, she couldn't lose Eric . . .

She lowered her head, unable to meet her father's eyes. "Say it. If something's happened—if he's dead—please say it."

"Dead?" She looked up to see incredulity in her father's eyes. "The boy is fine."

Relief was as painful as anxiety had been. "Then what is it?" she asked, exasperated. "If he's come to ask for my hand in marriage, why don't you just say so?"

"Because he hasn't asked for your hand, Isabelle. He has asked for your sister's."

Three weeks later, on a cold January afternoon, the wedding of Juliana and Eric took place at the Cathedral of San Michel.

This is real, Isabelle thought. Not a dream. Not the product of a fevered mind. The scent of flowers, the angelic voices of the choir, the expectant hush from the guests crowded into the cathedral—it was all happening now, in this place, at this moment in time.

It should be me, she thought as a shaft of longing, hot and violent, pierced through her. *This should be my wedding day. He should be my husband. . . .* She turned away, unable to bear the sight, and her eye was caught by the unrelenting gaze of Daniel Bronson, the American business-man who had predicted that her fairy tale with Eric would never work out. *You're wrong,* she thought, daring him to laugh in the face of her heartbreak. *People make mistakes. Eric and I are meant to be together.*

But he didn't laugh. He didn't even crack a smile. He simply watched her with a look in his eyes that came perilously close to pity, and that look hurt more than his laughter ever could.

She let her own gaze drift. How many of those good people knew that her heart was breaking? She'd been so indiscreet, so eager to share her happiness with the world. Had she told each and every one of them that she loved Eric, that the future was theirs for the taking? Dear God, how could she face them? Their pity was almost palpable, reaching out to clutch at her soul.

She clutched her skirts and left the altar, heading for the door that led to the sacristy. The image of Juliana's face, a pleat of concern marring her porcelain forehead, followed her. Let them wonder why she had bolted. Let them think she'd had too much to drink last night and was about to lose her breakfast. Anything was preferable to this public humiliation.

A buzz of conversation followed her, but she didn't care. She needed to be alone, to gather her wits about her and rest a cloak of Dutch courage on her shoulders for what lay ahead.

She felt Maxine's hand on her shoulder, but she refused to turn around. "Let him go, lovey. It's over."

"It's not over," she said, biting back her tears. "He doesn't love her. He loves me."

"'Tisn't you he married, lovey. 'Tis your sister."

She pulled away, then whirled about to face the older woman. "Leave me alone! You don't understand. You don't know how it feels."

"I know a broken heart is nothing to be ashamed of."

"They all know," she said, tilting her head in the direction of the church. "I couldn't stand it any longer. They were all watching me, feeling sorry for me. . . ."

Maxine snapped her fingers. "As if it matters what they'd be thinking. Hold your head high, my girl, and take your place at your father's side in the receiving line. The rest will fall into place."

She caught a glimpse of herself in the shiny marble

surface of a pillar, amazed that her heartache didn't show. Only the glitter in her eyes gave her away.

"This won't last, Maxi," she said, straightening her shoulders. "Eric loves me. He'll come back to me."

"They're married, lovey." Maxine's voice caught, but Isabelle refused to acknowledge the emotion behind the words. "In the eyes of God, he belongs to her."

"No," said Isabelle. "He belongs to me."

The little princess was out of control.

Even across the crowded cathedral Daniel had noted the wild fire in her dark eyes, recognized her pain. From the very beginning, he'd known that this was where she'd end up, standing there in her pretty yellow dress, watching while the man she loved claimed his future at her sister's side.

Men like Eric Malraux didn't waste their time on the second princess in line. Perreault might not amount to much in the economic scheme of things, but the Malraux family hadn't gotten what they wanted by settling for second place.

You bastard, he thought as Honore said something to his plain little wife. He'd sold his zero of a son to the highest bidder, and now Perreault was his personal playground. He'd build his glitzy palaces where rich people with nothing to do met other rich people and compared notes and, in the process, he'd become wealthier than in his wildest dreams.

Daniel told himself he'd come to the wedding to make a last-ditch attempt to sway Bertrand over to his side. Through the years Monaco had become a joke, the very name a synonym for emptiness, and it would be a damned waste of potential if this picture-perfect country followed suit. The wedding was only a good excuse to fly across the pond and put his proposal to Bertrand one last time.

The music of the recessional flooded the cathedral. The bride and groom linked arms and began the long walk back up the aisle as man and wife. He had to admit Juliana was radiant. He'd never thought much about that word before but apparently even he knew it when he saw it. The happy groom, however, had the look of a deer caught in the headlights of an eighteen-wheeler.

A match made in heaven, like it said in the tabloids? Not very likely.

The pews cleared one by one as the guests streamed from the church. Daniel was about to take his place with the rest of them when he saw a lone figure appear to the side of the altar. A shaft of sunlight found her, gilding her thick tumble of dark hair and illuminating her skin. He felt an uncharacteristic tug of emotion.

She stood with her spine straight, chin held high, as gutsy as she was beautiful. He knew her heart was breaking and he found himself admiring the strength that enabled her to be there at all.

Then he remembered who she was, the spoiled little princess with the sharp tongue and fiery temper who'd told him in no uncertain terms what he could do with his opinion of her love life. She didn't need his sympathy. Hell, she'd probably toss it back in his face without a backward glance.

"M'sieur?" The woman next to him touched his elbow then gestured toward the aisle. *"S'il vous plait?"*

He stepped out of the pew to let her pass. The church was just about empty. He looked back at the little princess who'd been joined by her nursemaid. The red-haired woman said something to the girl, but the princess said nothing. She gathered her skirts, lifted her chin, then glided up the aisle in her pretty yellow dress as if the celebration belonged to her.

If he'd been expecting to see heartbreak on her beautiful face, he was mistaken.

He saw defiance.

"Mr. Bronson," she said as she swept past him on her way toward the vestibule. "Do save me a dance, won't you?"

Her smile was dazzling, but not quite dazzling enough.

"Not bad, princess," he said, falling into step with her, "but it still needs some work."

He detected a flash of fire in her dark eyes, but the smile never faltered. "Whatever do you mean, Mr. Bronson?"

"The poker face. It gives you away every time."

"What a wonderful imagination you Americans have," she said, a bite hidden in her sugar-coated words. "No wonder you've given the world so many cultural treasures."

"I wouldn't know about treasures," said Daniel, grinning. "I've always been a pop culture kind of guy."

"How surprising," she drawled. "And here I imagined you were haunting the latest exhibition at the Louvre."

"Forget the Louvre, but if you want someone to tell you how Gilligan managed to get off his island, I'm your guy."

She looked away, but not quickly enough. "I don't know what you're talking about."

"Sure you do," he said, positive he'd seen her smile actually reach her eyes. "Europeans talk a good show when it comes to culture, but you gobble up our TV shows like they're 'Masterpiece Theatre.'"

"You certainly do think well of yourself, don't you, Mr. Bronson?" She paused a few yards from the doors to the cathedral.

"Give me an hour, princess, and I'll show you why."

She shuddered theatrically. "You're much worse than I'd feared."

"But a hell of a lot better than you think."

Her cheeks reddened. "I doubt that, Mr. Bronson." She turned to leave the church.

"He's not worth the heartache, Isabelle," he said to her retreating back. "None of us are."

He wasn't at all surprised when she didn't stop to answer him.

Chapter
Six

"Champagne!" Isabelle spun away from the arms of an Italian auto baron and placed her hands on her hips. "My kingdom for more champagne!"

Gianni Vitelli, twice married and looking for wife number three, threw back his head and laughed. "*Cara,* you surprise me. Surely your kingdom is worth more than a glass of wine."

"Such insolence!" Isabelle pretended to strike him an invisible blow. "Champagne or it's off with your head."

Vitelli was rich, but Isabelle was royal. Fortunately, those things still mattered to some people. He scurried away to do her bidding while Isabelle, laughing, swayed to the music.

The other dancers on the floor laughed along with her, as Isabelle had known they would. There were unwritten rules attached to mingling with royalty. Enjoying their jokes, however feeble they might be, was one of them. Isabelle could have placed her hands under her arms and clucked like a chicken, and within a heartbeat the titled and untitled alike would be clucking right along with her.

Everyone, that is, except for that annoying American, Bronson. It wasn't that he did anything untoward. He was far too clever for that. No, he danced with the ladies and chatted up the men, but the whole time Isabelle knew he was laughing up his sleeve at the lot of them.

The orchestra segued from a fox trot into a sedate waltz. She watched as Margot Hofmaier, of the Liechtenstein Hofmaiers, batted her false eyelashes in Bronson's direction and was rewarded with an invitation to dance. Margot had the subtlety of a cow in heat, and wasn't it just like a man to respond to such a blatant overture.

It occurred to her that they needed to be brought down a peg and, with a toss of her head, she set out to do exactly that.

Dancing up to the couple, she tapped Margot on her plump white shoulder. "Be a darling, won't you, Margot— I'm simply longing to dance with Mr. Bronson."

"Next dance," Bronson said, meeting her eyes over Margot's hennaed head.

Margot cast a quick, satisfied look in Isabelle's direction.

"I adore waltzes," Isabelle said, shadowing their movements with sure and graceful steps.

Margot's shoulders and cheeks reddened to match her hair, and she stumbled but quickly regained her composure. "I prefer fox trots," she began. "Perhaps—"

"I'm sure the princess won't mind waiting her turn." The look the American gave her was enough to make Isabelle's blue blood boil. She wanted to slap his face. She chose, however, to ignore him and press her advantage with Margot.

"Thank you ever so much, darling Margot." Isabelle neatly replaced the middle-aged woman in the American's arms. "I'll return him to you just the moment the dance is over."

"Nice trick," Bronson said as she looked up at him. "Too bad it didn't work."

"Of course it worked," she said, unable to mask her delight. "We're dancing, aren't we?"

"Not anymore." With a mock bow, he released her, then turned to head toward the French doors leading out to the terrace.

Murderous rage filled Isabelle's breast, and she started after him.

"Cara." Gianni Vitelli appeared at her side, bearing a flute of Dom Perignon. "I live to serve."

She took the glass, blew him a kiss, then continued toward the French doors. She'd make it up to the handsome Italian later. Right now all she could think about was giving the obnoxious American businessman a piece of her mind.

The raw beauty of the night stopped her in her tracks. The stars overhead were shattered crystal against a moonless sky, and the only sound was the low rumble of the heaters, positioned at discreet intervals along the perimeter of the terrace. She drew in a long breath, cold air mingled with the scent of pine and the sharp smell of an approaching snowstorm.

It took her eyes a few moments to adjust to the absence of light as she searched for Bronson. There! Over in the far corner she saw the red glimmer of a glowing cigarette. A cheap American brand, no doubt.

She gulped some champagne then stalked over to where he stood, looking out into the blackness. She stopped mere inches away from him, demanding his full and utter attention with the force of her will.

"I should throw this champagne in your arrogant face."

He didn't even have the decency to meet her eyes. "I wouldn't try it."

"Oh, that's right," she said. "Didn't you once tell me you would hit a woman?"

"If she pulled a stunt like that, damn straight I would."

"How perfectly Neanderthal of you."

"I'm funny like that, princess. Hit me, and I'm damn likely to hit you back."

"A real man wouldn't behave like that."

"Yeah? Well, a real woman wouldn't embarrass another woman the way you did back there."

Isabelle dismissed his criticism with a wave of her hand. "Margot knows there was nothing personal about the exchange."

"You're probably right," he said. "Most of the people around here seem to accept lousy behavior as the norm."

"I'm so sorry if we've offended you. How could I have forgotten America is the last bastion of polite society on earth."

"Hell of a lot more polite than anything I've seen here tonight."

"Then why don't you go home, Mr. Bronson, where the atmosphere suits your sensibilities?"

He looked at his watch. "My plane leaves in ten hours and eleven minutes."

"And I suggest you be on it."

"Don't worry about it, princess." The look he gave her was anything but flattering. "There isn't anything here to keep me."

There was something about his words—or maybe it was the way he said them, or maybe it was the feeling that there was no one on earth who understood one blessed thing about her. Whatever it was, the tears she'd been holding back all day burst forth with a vengeance, and she sank down onto a bench and began to sob.

"Jesus Christ," Daniel muttered under his breath. "Don't cry."

He came from a long line of men who were lousy at dealing with crying women, and from an equally long line of women who knew exactly how to use that to advantage. He was the worst of the lot. The sight of a woman dissolved in tears usually reduced him to a useless blob of testosterone.

He stood there staring down at her while she sobbed into the hem of her fancy ballgown, and felt an alarming rush of something too close to affection for his own comfort. This wasn't some poor kid with a broken heart. This was a rich brat, born on the right side of the royal sheets and determined to make sure everyone on the planet knew about it. She was the kind of woman he disliked on sight. She was arrogant, self-centered, and—damn it—crying as if her heart would break.

"For Christ's sake," he said, grabbing her hands in his for a moment. "You can't keep crying into your dress."

She didn't even look at him, just grabbed hold of his jacket and buried her face in its dark folds. Her tears were hot, quickly saturating his shirt and warming his skin. So many tears. . . .

He looked down at her, mesmerized by the way her dark hair fell across her face, the way it shimmered in the starlight. If this was an act designed to tug on his heartstrings, she deserved an Oscar. He wanted to gather her up into his arms, kiss away the tears, then make love to her right there on the terrace.

The fact that she'd probably have him sent to the guillotine if he tried it wasn't enough to dissuade him, but the fact that she'd already been hurt enough was.

He groped through his pockets for a handkerchief.

"Here." He pulled one from his inside breast pocket with a flourish. "This beats using a St. Laurent for a tissue."

She reached for the square of linen gratefully. "It's—it's n-not St. Laurent," she said between sobs. "It's a Ch—Christian Lacroix."

He couldn't hold back a grin. "I never was very good at playing Name-the-Designer."

She waved her hand in the air with the gesture he'd come to know. "You can g-go now."

"You're finished with me?" He should have known better than to feel sorry for her.

She nodded. She didn't know him well enough to recognize the menace in his words. "I want to be alone now."

"A minute ago you wanted to throw your champagne in my face." And a minute ago he'd wanted to kiss away her tears. Thank God he'd stopped short of making a total ass of himself.

"That was before. Now I wish to be left to myself."

"We don't always get what we want." His glance strayed toward the glittering ballroom where the happy bride and groom commanded the dance floor. His meaning was unmistakable.

Her teary dark eyes suddenly flashed with fire. "Don't you dare say anything!"

"I could have said, 'I told you so.'"

"An admirable display of restraint on your part."

"Wish I could say the same about you. Dancing on the tabletop was hardly your shining moment, princess. Your old man should've locked you in your room and thrown away the key."

"I'm high-spirited," she said with a toss of her head. "It's expected of me."

"No," he said slowly, "what's expected of you is that you take a backseat to your sister."

"You don't understand how it is."

"Maybe not, but lover boy out there sure as hell does."

She rose to her feet, her slender frame visibly shaking with anger. "Don't you dare say anything bad about Eric!"

"I wasn't about to, princess. On the contrary, I was going to pay him a compliment."

Even in the darkness of the terrace he saw the look of suspicion on her face. "I find that hard to believe, Mr. Bronson."

"He's a lot smarter than I'd figured. If you're going to dally with the prince's daughter, why not dally with the one who'll inherit the throne?"

She turned away from him, and for a moment he almost regretted the harshness of his words. But just for a moment. Someone had to tell her the way the game was being played.

"I could spell it all out for you," he said, his tone a bit softer, "but somehow I don't think you'd believe me." Unpaid debts, broken promises, and cold-blooded family mergers were hardly the stuff of dreams.

She wheeled around to face him again, and for a second he saw the woman behind the beautiful mask. "I'm not a fool," she said, her husky voice etched with pain. "I know what my father and Honore are about with this match. Eric had no choice. He's not to blame for what's happened."

"And what about your sister?"

He heard her intake of breath. Now he was getting somewhere. "She has always done what was expected of her."

"Even sleep with the man you love?"

Isabelle reacted purely from instinct. He understood that. He even welcomed it. All of her rage, all of her heartache came together as the crack of her palm against his cheek-bone rang out in the still night air.

He winced and moved his jaw back and forth with comic deliberation. "Not bad," he said, touching the curve of his jaw.

"Not half good enough," she retorted. "I only wish I'd helped you part company with your teeth."

"I'm not the one you hate," he said quietly. "I'm just the one who's around."

She wanted to hate him. With every fiber in her being she wanted to despise the air he breathed, the ground he trod upon. Only Maxine had ever talked to her the way Bronson had, with so little concern for who she was and her station in life.

Or with so much honesty, a voice inside her added.

Her eyes filled with another appalling flood of tears, and she held them back with the sheer force of her will.

She turned her empty crystal flute upside down on the marble bench. "I need more champagne."

"What's wrong? Reality rearing its ugly head?"

"That's exactly what's wrong," she said with an attempt at gaiety. "This is a wedding. Everyone knows that weddings and champagne go hand in hand."

"You've had enough."

"My dear Mr. Bronson, I have yet to begin." She narrowed her eyes and looked at him. "Gianni Vitelli was only too happy to fetch more champagne for me."

"I just saw him dance by with Margot Hofmaier. Want me to whistle for him?"

"The only thing I want is for you to disappear from the face of the earth."

"Will you settle for me disappearing from Perreault?"

"With pleasure."

He had started to say something when Maxine, in her best dress, appeared in the doorway.

"You've lost your mind, is it, lovey? Your father has been looking for you, and I've exhausted my excuses." Maxine glanced over at Bronson, who'd stepped further back into the shadows. "You needn't try to hide, Mr. Bronson," said Maxine. "Everyone knows you're out here with my girl."

Isabelle's spirits lifted. "Everyone?"

Maxine looked from Isabelle to Bronson, then back again. "'Tis a romance in the making to those who wouldn't be knowing the truth."

A chance to make Eric jealous! It was all too perfect. She met Bronson's eyes. "You owe me a dance."

He didn't say anything at all. The moment stretched like an overused elastic band. Maxine coughed politely, but still he said nothing. Isabelle knew he was capable of just about anything. He could refuse her as easily as not, but she knew somehow deep in her soul that this time he would come to her rescue.

Daniel told himself he was doing it strictly for the shock value, but he couldn't make himself believe it. There was something about walking into a glittering ballroom in an ancient castle with a beautiful, dark-eyed princess on your arm that could turn the most hard-headed Yankee into a believer.

Every eye in the place was focused on the two of them as they made their way to the center of the dance floor. Prince Bertrand, his brow furrowed, watched from the corner of the room where he'd been engaged in conversation with Honore Malraux and the minister of finance, a laughable title, considering the economic situation.

With a courtly bow, Bronson swept the dark-haired princess into his arms. She favored him with an enticing smile. The exuberant strains of a Strauss Waltz swelled all around them as they began to move together to the music. Her color was unnaturally high, her laughter brittle. The sparkle in her eyes could only be described as dangerous.

"He'll never make you happy," Daniel said as they spun past the hapless Eric and Juliana.

"And to think I had believed you to be a clever man," she said in her sweetly accented English.

"You've got a lot going for you, princess. A hell of a lot more than you think."

"There's no reason to be nasty."

He laughed. "You're so damn used to being second that you don't have any idea what you could do if you put your mind to it."

"I know what I want," she said, her gaze straying toward the bridegroom.

You're too strong for him, princess. You'll chew him up and spit out the bones.

But Daniel said nothing. Somehow it seemed like the least he could do.

* * *

Although it galled Isabelle to admit it, Bronson was a marvelous dancer. He held her close, but not too close, leading her through some tricky footwork with agility and a positively wicked sense of rhythm. His body was big and uncommonly broad. The fact that his wide shoulders were a gift of nature and not a clever tailor was not lost on her. She felt almost guilty noticing such things about another man, but the facts were impossible to ignore. It was enough to make her reconsider her opinion of stodgy, puritanical American businessmen.

They didn't talk, which was probably a blessing, since talk between them always gave way to arguments. She found it quite enough to be seen in his arms, looking for all the world as if that was the only place on earth she wanted to be.

She glanced up at Bronson through her dark lashes. If only he were more flirtatious, more openly predatory the way he'd been the first time they'd met. She was slightly disgruntled that he'd chosen this moment to abandon his pursuit. How wonderful it would have been to see Eric defending her honor as the American kissed her soundly.

"If you think I'm going to kiss you, you're wrong."

Was the man a mindreader? "The last thing on earth I want is to be kissed by you." She sounded quite convincing.

"I suppose that's why you were staring at my mouth."

"You flatter yourself."

"Sometimes, but this isn't one of them."

"I know you find me attractive."

"Not half as attractive as you find yourself."

"If I'm so terrible, why did you kiss me the last time we met?"

That predatory gleam in his eyes reappeared. "Good memory, princess."

This wasn't going at all the way it was supposed to. "Another man would be flattered by my attentions."

"I've just never much liked being used—not even by a beautiful woman."

She tried to look away, but he wouldn't let her.

"If you want something, princess, just ask for it."

What a horrible man he was. "You remind me why I prefer European men to Americans."

"You can push European men around. No secret there."

She almost snorted with laughter. "A European man understands the subtext of a conversation."

"I understand the subtext better than you think, princess."

"Meaning?"

"If you want me to kiss you, just ask me. I'd be happy to oblige."

She tossed her head. "I'd rather kiss a garden snake."

He looked toward Eric and laughed. His meaning was all too clear.

"Say it, Mr. Bronson, and I shall see to it that you spend the night in jail."

"You're trying to make him jealous, and I'm the lucky guy you've found to help you out. I can handle that."

She stopped. "I no longer wish to dance with you."

"What if I told you lover boy was on his way over here?" Bronson spun her into a wide arc, cleverly masking her misstep. "Don't worry about it, princess. I'll stake my claim and turn him away."

"Turn him away? If you so much as—"

"Relax," Bronson said with a shake of his head. "I'll take a hike as soon as he taps me on the shoulder."

He was as good as his word.

"You look beautiful, Isabelle." Eric swept her into his arms, and it was all she could do to keep from bursting into tears and embarrassing them both.

"Oh, Eric—" Her voice caught on his beloved name. "I wish—"

He stopped her with a look of such tender concern that her heart seemed to turn over in her chest. "Trust me, darling girl. Nothing can come between us. I promise you that."

She pressed her forehead against his shoulder, her tears turning the fabric of his jacket even darker. "It hurts so much," she whispered. "Every time I think of you and Juli, I—"

"Don't think about it," he said, his lips grazing her hair. "I promise you we'll be together. You have my word."

But there was still tonight. Eric and Juliana alone in a room with a four-poster bed and candles and the good wishes of everyone who wanted a happily-ever-after ending to their love story. The thought of them together, limbs tangled, made Isabelle feel wild with despair.

If he truly loved her, he'd never do something like that, no matter what promises they'd made before God and man.

"Eric." Her voice was low. Urgent. "Swear to me that you won't—"

"Don't speak of it," he said. "You must trust me, darling girl. This is what our fathers want, not what I want. You must believe that."

She looked at Honore Malraux who was watching them from the archway. "We should talk to your father," she said as desperation mounted. "I know he holds great affection for me. We'll tell him that we're in love—that we want to spend our lives together. I know he'll understand, Eric. I'm sure he will."

She wanted him to pledge his eternal devotion, swear that he would never touch another woman, not even Juliana. Her eyes sought his.

But he wasn't looking at her. He was looking at her sister. *His wife.*

The new bride wore a going-away suit of winter white silk with matching hose and pumps. The groom wore a dark suit, striped tie, and a smudge of crimson lipstick just beneath his left ear. No one thought anything of it. It was a wedding, after all, and weddings meant kissing and being kissed by damsel and dowager alike.

"Please, everybody! One more time!" The photographer gathered the family into a tight knot beneath the porte cochere.

Click. Bertrand with the happy couple.

Click. Honore and the happy couple.

Click. The happy couple kissing sweetly for the camera to the delight of the crowd of well-wishers.

"Now the two princesses, if you please." The photographer hunkered down to get the best shot. *"Mesdames, s'il vous plait."*

Isabelle had not spoken a word to her older sister since that horrific night when her world fell apart. Standing arm in arm, her pain captured for all eternity on film, was more than she could fathom. "I cannot possibly—" She stopped. The silence around her was deafening. Maxine looked as if she were poised at the edge of a cliff. Eric refused to meet her gaze. Juliana was looking down at her tiny, perfectly manicured hands. She deliberately avoided looking over at Bronson. She could only imagine the look of smug satisfaction on his face.

She wanted to turn away from them all and run back into the castle. She'd done nothing wrong, committed no crime, and yet she felt as if she was being punished. *Don't make me do this,* she pleaded silently. *I hurt so much I can scarcely breathe.* She met her father's eyes and saw the sharp edge of indifference just beneath the paternal glow.

She moved into position next to Juliana.

"Closer," the photographer urged. "Ahh, yes. So lovely. The dark and the light. . . ." He snapped the shutter three times in quick succession. He motioned toward Eric who stood quietly next to Prince Bertrand. "And now the new husband joins them."

Isabelle stiffened with apprehension. She couldn't catch her breath. She felt as if all of her emotions were trapped inside her throat, choking off the air. To his credit, Eric looked as if he were being sent to the guillotine. He stepped between the two sisters. Isabelle wondered if anyone in the entire country missed the irony.

I can't do this, she thought wildly. Pathetic, that's what she was. Second best in everything, even when it came to the man she'd loved. Standing there with the happy couple, she looked exactly like what she was: the sister who'd been left behind. If only—

"Wait a minute!" All eyes turned toward Daniel Bronson as he stepped forward. "I should be in this picture, too." He strode toward Isabelle and took his place beside her. Juliana and Eric stared at the two of them in disbelief, and Isabelle realized it was now or never. She tossed back her hair, lifted her chin, and flashed Bronson her most dazzling smile.

"Of course, darling," she said, motioning for him to stand next to her. "How could we have taken a picture without you?"

The photographer went wild with excitement. He murmured things about symmetry and beauty as Isabelle and Daniel posed with the bridal couple. Bronson's bold gesture had changed everything. She could just imagine the whispers, the speculation, the absolute envy of the women who'd thrown themselves at the handsome and brash American. She glanced toward Eric. He met her eyes, his expression openly curious and obviously pained. She simply widened her smile and linked her arm with Bronson's.

"Thank you," she whispered to Bronson as the photographer began to snap his pictures.

"You owe me, princess," he said.

"Whatever you want, Bronson. A donation to your favorite charity."

"No," he said, grinning. "I can think of something better." He lowered his head.

She lifted her chin. "You wouldn't."

"Damn right I would."

"With everyone looking on?"

"That's the point, isn't it?"

"Mr. Bronson, I—"

His kiss was fierce and swift. All around them people laughed delightedly and called for more.

"Smile for the camera, princess," he said as he broke the kiss. "Let's give 'em what they want."

If only she could remember what that was.

Chapter
Seven

He wasn't going to think about her again.

That's what Daniel told himself when he left Perreault a few hours after the wedding. He'd helped the little princess out of an embarrassing situation, and she'd introduced him to the millionaire from Kyoto who was looking to back a Japanese-American development deal outside the city.

Isabelle had made it through the wedding with her pride intact, and Daniel boarded his plane with entrée to a business opportunity that would make his plans for Perreault look like small potatoes. It was almost enough to make him forget how much he hated flying.

Back in New York, he threw himself into his work with renewed enthusiasm. The Kyoto millionaire faxed him the specs for a planned community that combined the best of both cultures, and Daniel was off and running. He barely noticed when winter melted into spring. Meetings. Midnight brainstorming sessions. Endless talks with government officials over the advisability of the deal.

Spring slid into summer, one of those hot, muggy New York summers that made the concept of hell a little easier to understand. Daniel returned from a preliminary trip to Japan where he met with Toshiro Umeki and Umeki's partners in the speculative venture. He'd taken a crash course on Japanese sensibilities and had managed to get through seven days of excruciatingly polite business meetings without embarrassing himself. One of the businessmen had suggested taking a mountain hike, and Daniel had blanched at the thought. There wasn't much in life that scared him at ground level. Raise the altitude, and it was a different story entirely.

He found himself thinking about Isabelle at odd moments and wondering if she'd finally come to terms with her sister's marriage. He'd heard through the international grapevine that Juliana was pregnant. A fact like that would make reality hard to ignore, even for the stubborn little princess.

"Looks like the marriage is working," his father had said to him over a game of pool at the Golden Cue. "Nothing like a baby to cement family ties."

"Kids don't solve every problem," Daniel had pointed out as he ran the table.

"Your sister Cathy is pregnant again."

"Terrific."

"Her baby is due next month."

"Great."

"And your cousin Steve—"

"Don't tell me," said Daniel as he reracked the balls. "He's pregnant, too."

"You're a wiseass, Danny," Matty had commented with a shake of his head. "Life's passing you by, and you're too busy making with the one-liners to give a damn."

"Not everyone's itching to join the diaper brigade, Pop. There are enough rug rats in this family to go around."

"One day you'll find out what it's all about, Danny. Family's everything in life. Everything else is a distant second."

A couple of times he'd seen Isabelle's picture in one of the gossip rags his assistant Phyllis was so crazy about. "Princess Isabelle Leads Royal Brat Pack," one headline had screamed when Isabelle and Stephanie of Monaco cohosted a gala in Monte Carlo. She'd been seen at one time or another on the arm of an Italian industrialist, a Russian expatriate poet, and a low-ranking member of the British royal family. He wondered if she'd slept with any of them and then he cursed himself for giving a damn.

There was a loneliness in him these days that nothing could reach, a bone-deep need for something he couldn't define. He felt as if he'd lost some essential part of himself and didn't know where to look in order to recover it.

The truth was, anyone with eyes could see that something was bothering Daniel. His sisters continued to speculate over the problem, but by tacit agreement they refrained from asking any questions. His brothers chalked up Daniel's mood to too much time playing desk jockey, while his parents assumed he'd had his heart broken by the Ford model he'd been seen squiring around Manhattan last year.

He knew he was asking for trouble, showing up at the family house in Montauk for the annual mid-summer barbecue, but when Connie Bronson threw a party, she expected her children to show up, no matter how old they were.

As usual, traffic on the Long Island Expressway was bumper to bumper, and he didn't make it to the compound until nearly six o'clock. The entire brood was down on the beach where Matty was barbecuing ribs, hot dogs, chicken, and sirloin steaks while Connie worried about whether or not they'd have enough potato salad and cole slaw.

It wasn't that Daniel didn't enjoy bonding with his

siblings. Normally he would've been down there on the beach with the rest of them, bringing the same intensity to a game of volleyball that he brought to the boardroom. Today, their good-natured concern was getting on his nerves.

It took his niece Katie to zero in on the matter with the laserlike precision of a six-year-old.

"What are you doing?" She stood in the doorway to the library. She wore a hot-pink ruffled bathing suit, hot-pink thongs, and an oversize pair of polka-dot sunglasses. Her strawberry-blond hair was piled on top of her head and secured with one of those scrunchy rubber bands. She was about as cute as they came and she knew it.

"Reading," he said, smiling as she sashayed into the room.

"Grandpa said to tell you it's time to eat." She placed her hands on her waist and jutted out her jaw in a great imitation of Matty. " 'Two minutes or I'm eating his steak!' "

He tugged at one of her curls. "You tell Grandpa I'll be there."

"Grandpa said not to come back without you."

A copy of *People* magazine lay open on the table in front of him. It was the last thing he wanted Katie to notice and the first thing she went to.

"Ohhh." Her big blue eyes took on a dreamy expression as she examined the two-page spread. "A princess!"

He grabbed the magazine and flipped it shut. "Let's go outside, Katie. You don't want Grandpa to eat all the hot dogs, do you?"

"I want to see the princess." Her eyes filled with tears.

He knew they were probably crocodile tears, but it didn't matter. He knew when he was licked. He flipped open the magazine and handed it to his little niece. "One look, then we'd better get outside."

"She's so pretty," Katie cooed, looking at a picture of Isabelle that was part of an article on lesser European royalty. "Look, Uncle Danny! Isn't that you?"

He mumbled something about Juliana's wedding.

"You met two princesses!" It was obvious he'd just risen several notches in Katie's estimation. "Did you dance with them?"

He couldn't help grinning. "Both of them."

"Ohh." Her voice went soft with wonder. "Did they wear crowns?"

"Not that day, Katie."

"Princesses are special," she told him in a tone of utter seriousness. "They always marry princes."

"Not always. Sometimes a princess can marry a frog."

"No!" she said, giggling. "A princess kisses a frog, and then he turns into a handsome prince and they live happily ever after."

"You sure about that?"

"Everybody knows it," she said solemnly. "Would you like to marry a princess?"

"I don't want to marry anyone, Katie. At least not for a while."

She studied him curiously. "Mommy says you've let all the good ones get away."

"Your mommy might be right."

Katie pointed at a picture of Isabelle. "Maybe you could marry her."

He believed in telling kids the truth, but this time he was willing to make an exception. Life had a way of screwing up most fairy tales soon enough. Katie deserved to hang on to a few of her illusions, at least until her next birthday. He didn't want to be the one to tell the little girl that there were two princesses and that the odds of a happy ending to this particular fairy tale were a million to one.

Gianni Vitelli was six feet two inches of rippling inanity. His conversation was limited to soccer, wine, and the weather, and most of it was in Italian, but Isabelle didn't mind. The last thing on earth she wanted was conversation.

She wanted bright lights, loud music, beautiful people—and lots of champagne.

"We drink champagne?" Gianni asked as the sommelier approached.

"Of course we do, darling!" Isabelle reached across the table and patted him on the hand. "Champagne is mother's milk to me."

Gianni chatted on about soccer—or maybe it was the unutterably beautiful summer weather. It didn't matter. Isabelle smiled at the right moment or murmured something appropriate. Gianni would never know the difference. They were both using each other for the same purpose: to brighten the spotlight they each craved. Isabelle found herself wondering if that was as much as a woman could ask of a relationship.

As far as she could tell, love had precious little to do with marriage. Certainly it hadn't in the case of Juliana and Eric. In the six months since their wedding, Eric had been away on business at least half the time, and when he was in residence at the castle, Juliana expected him to wait upon her hand and foot.

"Cara."

She blinked, bringing Gianni's handsome face back into focus.

"I apologize," she said with her most winning smile. "You were saying?"

He gestured toward a table near the huge picture window. "The husband of your sister, no?"

Isabelle turned around in her chair, and her gaze locked on the table near the terrace doors. Her heart seemed to stop beating inside her chest. Eric was engaged in a tête-à-tête with Mireille Dubois, a tarty little cabaret singer better known for her boudoir gymnastics than her vocal abilities. Mireille, her dyed red hair tumbling about her face and shoulders, seemed mesmerized by Eric's every word.

The music shifted into a dreamy tune, and Isabelle extended her hand toward Gianni. "We must dance," she said, looking at him through lowered lashes. "I have heard wonderful things about your talents."

"Many talents, *Principessa*. Many talents for you to explore."

Gianni danced well, but not as well as Daniel Bronson. Oddly enough, Isabelle had retained a strong sensory memory of the way she'd felt in his arms. It came to her at the strangest moments, that sensation of being in a safe harbor. Ridiculous, really, considering the fact that she barely knew the man.

Unlike the American, however, Gianni could easily be maneuvered, and within moments Isabelle found herself standing in front of Eric and Mireille.

"Mireille!" Isabelle cooed in the way of her set. "How splendid to see you." She kissed the air in the vicinity of the singer's cheeks then turned to Eric whose face was flushed an unnatural shade of red. Playfully she gave his tie a tug. "And my darling new brother-in-law." She marked his cheeks with the touch of her lipsticked mouth. "How naughty of you not to offer me a ride in the Lamborghini!"

Eric had the decency to look embarrassed. He nodded toward Gianni who was busy chatting up Mireille and taking stock of her many unnatural assets.

"My father and Mireille are doing business together," he said, forcing a note of casual indifference. "We were just now discussing a contract for Mireille to appear at Father's—"

"Oh, Eric! Don't bore me with such foolishness," said Isabelle with a wave of her hand. "Business is so dull. Surely you can find better things to do with your time." She cast a knowing look toward Mireille who was dimpling artfully for Gianni.

"Isabelle—" He lowered his voice. "Darling girl, surely you don't—"

"Think you're having an affair with Mireille?" She shrugged her shoulders, allowing the straps of her beaded dress to slip just a fraction. "Certainly it's no business of mine."

He rose to his feet. "Darling girl, can I convince you to dance with me?"

"One dance," she said, giving him her hand. "I should hate to keep you from your little songbird."

"She means nothing to me."

"Really?" Isabelle arched a brow. "And Juliana?"

"I have the utmost respect for your sister."

"I didn't know respect resulted in pregnancy, Eric. I must remember that."

"Why do you torture me, Isabelle, when you are the one who is keeping us apart?"

She tossed her head. "I'm not the one who wears a wedding ring."   •

He stopped dancing and drew her into an anteroom near the door to the restaurant kitchen. With a flamboyant gesture he removed the etched gold band and pressed it into her hand.

"Take it," he said, his golden hair glittering in the overhead light. "Do with it as you will."

"What if I took it to Juliana and told her we were lovers?"

"Then that is your choice."

"I want my own ring," she said, meeting his eyes, praying he could see the longing that was tearing her soul apart. "I want a home of my own."

"And those things will happen, darling girl, I swear it." He drew her into his arms. His words were tender. His promises were sweet.

And, dear God, how she needed to believe him.

It was wrong and she knew it, but by the time Eric turned the Lamborghini onto the road that led to the chalet, Isabelle had convinced herself that she no longer cared. She'd spent her entire life waiting for someone to love her, and now that she'd been given this second chance she wasn't going to let anything or anyone stop her. Juliana had married him, but Isabelle owned his heart and that gave her the right.

Eric unlocked the door to the chalet and ushered her

inside. It smelled of damp earth and pine, and she walked across the front room and flung open the windows to the sweet night air. He switched on the lamp in the corner. The faded divan near the fireplace beckoned to her.

She perched on the window seat and drew her knees up under her chin. A faint crescent moon rode high in the sky. She watched as it vanished behind a drift of clouds, only to reappear a few moments later.

"Do you want some music?"

She nodded. "That would be nice."

Seconds later the painfully glorious sound of Mozart reached out to embrace them.

"We could dance," Eric said, standing before her.

"To Mozart?"

He smiled and held open his arms.

She rose from the window seat and stepped into his embrace. They stood motionless in the center of the room, their arms around each other.

"So long," he murmured, kissing her on the side of her neck. "How could you believe I would ever let you go?"

She started to say that the fact of his marriage was a fairly good clue, but she bit back the words. What on earth was the matter with her? She'd dreamed of this moment for six long months, and now that it was here, she'd almost ruined it with a slash of her sharp tongue.

"Soon we'll be able to be together for all time," he said, kissing her jaw, her throat. "Three short weeks . . ."

His kisses were intoxicating but apparently so were hers. "But Juliana isn't due until October."

He shook his head. "Three weeks," he repeated.

"That's not possible."

"Darling girl," said Eric with a chuckle, "surely I must know. I have been counting the days until—" He stopped. He met her eyes, and in that instant the final puzzle piece dropped into place.

"My God!" She pulled away from him, stumbling in her haste to put distance between them. "How could you?"

"Darling girl, I can explain. I—"

"Be quiet!" Her voice resonated with her pain, her humiliation. "Don't say anything! You cannot say anything I wish to hear." What a fool she'd been to believe he loved her, that his marriage to Juliana had been nothing but an arrangement between two families. The proof of that was in the date of conception.

"It happened," he continued. "I don't know how. I didn't want it to, but Juliana—"

"Spare me," Isabelle snapped. "None of this matters— you don't matter."

He grabbed her by the forearms. She struggled to pull away, but he held her fast. "She came to me, Isabelle. She said things—" He glanced away for an instant. "I'd never seen her that way. There was nothing I could do—" His yelp of pain mingled with the crashing brilliance of Mozart.

"I can only hope I broke your leg!" Isabelle roared. "Consider yourself fortunate that I did not reach my goal, or there might never be another child!"

Pain was a living force tearing its way through her body. She couldn't think over the rush of blood pounding wildly in her ears. Her sister . . . her sister . . . she had to get out of there . . . she had to get as far away from this insanity as she possibly could.

She grabbed for the key ring resting atop the mantelpiece.

"Isabelle!" Eric lurched toward her, favoring his right leg. "It's dark—you've had too much champagne. Let me—"

"Don't touch me!"

"I'll drive," he persisted. "You can't—"

"Good-bye, Eric," she said as she opened the front door. "I'll tell your wife you'll be home late tonight."

The Lamborghini skidded on the first in a series of hairpin curves that marked the beginning of castle property. Isabelle gripped the wheel more tightly and eased up on the gas pedal. Another mistake like that, and she'd find herself at the bottom of a three-hundred-foot cliff. She'd already wrecked her own car. Adding another to her list would hardly endear her to anyone.

Maybe it really didn't matter. Maybe the thing to do was drive as fast as the Lamborghini would allow in an attempt to keep one step ahead of the pain that had her in its grip and refused to let go.

I'll love him until the day I die. . . . I feel sorry for you, Mr. Bronson. . . .

She laughed out loud, the sound carrying a note of hysteria. He'd tried to tell her the affair was doomed, but she'd been too blinded by love to listen. That brash American with the Midas touch had seen it as clearly as he saw the numbers in one of his financial reports.

"I should have listened to you," she said into the stillness. No one else had had the guts to tell her that the whole thing was impossible. Only Daniel Bronson had taken her measure and told her the truth.

Had he known that Juliana and Eric were having an affair, or had the affair started after the Tricentennial Ball? Not that it mattered any longer, but Isabelle was seized with the need to know everything.

She gunned the engine, leaping forward into the blackness. She wanted to revel in her pain, bathe in scalding tears, beat her breast, and curse the gods for letting her be such a fool.

Her face burned with shame as she thought of her sister and the man she loved together in bed. How they must have laughed at poor little Isabelle, so young and so naive.

Foolish enough to believe that someone might actually love her.

Juliana watched her sister with detachment. There was something unseemly about such an unbridled display of emotion.

"It's late," she said as another vase went winging its way toward destruction. "You are obviously in no condition to talk rationally. Perhaps we can continue this discussion tomorrow."

Isabelle's eyes were wild with emotion. Her cheeks were flushed and streaked with tears. Juliana could not remember a time when her sister looked less attractive.

"It doesn't matter to you, does it?" Isabelle shrieked. "My feelings, my happiness, my future."

"Perhaps if you thought less of yourself and more of Perreault, your future would be of greater consequence."

A porcelain statue crashed against a bookshelf. "I don't give a damn about Perreault, and neither do you."

"You're wrong, Isabelle. I care a great deal."

"I don't believe you."

Juliana smiled. "As you wish."

"You're so cool about this," Isabelle said, moving closer. "I may not matter to you, but I know who does. Your precious husband."

"Spare me your lies," Juliana said in her most imperious tone of voice. She had heard her share of rumors about Eric and chose to deal with them by pretending they didn't exist. Eric appreciated his position too much to endanger it.

"He still wants me."

"He never wanted you. He took what you offered."

"Ask him," Isabelle challenged, recovering too quickly for Juliana's taste. "He'll be home soon."

Juliana fingered the pearls at her neck. "I'm afraid you're mistaken. Eric is away on business."

The glint in Isabelle's eyes grew wilder. "Eric was at the Savoie with Mireille Dubois."

"You're a liar."

"It would appear your loving husband is the liar."

"I know what you're doing, and it won't work. You're pathetic, Isabelle, truly pathetic, and I am bored with you." She turned toward the door. "Good night."

In an instant Isabelle was in front of her, barring the way. "I can prove it." Isabelle reached into the pocket of those ridiculous satin shorts and pulled out a set of keys. She twirled them in front of Juliana's eyes. "Look familiar?"

"Car keys prove nothing," Juliana said. She linked her hands over her stomach. "Move, please. I am fatigued."

Isabelle hesitated, her gaze lowering to rest briefly on Juliana's belly. She took a deep breath. "A Porsche, Papa's Daimler, your Rolls." She fingered the keys one by one. "Still think it's a coincidence?"

"You took them from our bedroom." Juliana snatched the keys from her sister. "Eric is in Italy. What need would he have for his keys?"

"Eric is at the chalet."

"You lying bi—" Juliana raised her hand, but Isabelle grabbed her wrist.

"You have already hurt me more deeply than any blow possibly could," she said, "but I will not let you hurt me again."

Juliana did not look away. This would make the next month or two rather messy, but she was glad her sister finally knew. She'd waited a long time to savor her triumph to its fullest. "I'd wondered when you would realize."

"Your stupid little sister finally knows the truth."

"It was never a secret," Juliana said. "Certainly everyone else realized it long ago."

Isabelle looked down, struggling with tears. Juliana noted the action, recognized the meaning, but Isabelle's pain meant nothing to her.

"It's better this way," she said as Isabelle's shoulders heaved with her sobs. "Eric was quite embarrassed by the way you have been throwing yourself at him. Perhaps now you can get on with your life. Aunt Elysse would so love to have you visit her in New York. You might—" Isabelle withdrew something else from her pocket, something round and golden, and held it up to the light. "Wh-what is that?"

"Your husband's wedding ring." She tossed it to Juliana, but it hit the edge of the bar and rolled across the floor. "You might ask yourself how it came to be in my possession."

"You'll pay for that," Juliana said, her voice low with menace. "I promise you, you'll pay for that."

"I already have," Isabelle said as she turned toward the door. "I loved him first, didn't I?"

"No fish!" Juliana's voice pierced the silence of the breakfast room the next morning. She tossed the menu plan at Yves. "How many times have I told you I absolutely abhor fish and will not tolerate it at my table?"

"Many times, madam," said Yves. Both his tone and his expression were carefully neutral. He had seen to it that the detritus of last night's disruption had been cleaned up, but had not alluded to the incident in any way. "I shall convey your displeasure to the cook."

"And convey the message that the cook's services are no longer required. He is terminated as of now."

"But, madam, we—"

"Now!"

Yves bowed stiffly. "As you wish, madam." He backed out of the room then disappeared down the corridor.

Pompous fool. As if anyone cared what he thought about the subject. There were times when Yves acted as if he ruled the house and the rest of them were his loyal servants.

She pushed back her chair and waited a full ten seconds before a red-faced footman raced into the dining room to help her. Certainly her father had never endured such an indignity.

"Has my father returned yet from his walk?"

The footman shook his head. "N-no, your highness. The prince took the dogs from their kennels and left before seven."

"That will be all."

The footman bowed, then backed out of the room with the same obsequious agility that was Yves's hallmark. There were people who found that type of behavior a horrifying throwback to the Middle Ages. Juliana unabashedly enjoyed it and, she suspected, so would most people if they were the object of such slavish servility. Honore understood. She smiled as she thought of her father-in-law. Somehow she never had to explain herself to him. Honore knew that she was everything Isabelle was not, and he seemed glad of it.

If only it were that easy with his son.

She walked slowly from the dining room, aware of the dark pain in the small of her back. She hadn't slept a wink last night: That nasty bit of excitement in the library had sent her adrenaline flowing, and she'd found it impossible to close her eyes. The adrenaline, she suspected, was also to blame for the twinges of pain she'd felt intermittently deep in her belly. Unfortunately there were still three long weeks to go until she delivered her son.

And it had to be a son. Power in Perreault, such as it was, passed directly to the first male child, regardless of the royal rank of the child's parent. Indeed, if her aunt Elysse had borne a son, Juliana would not be in a position of power today. She shivered at the thought of how close she might have come to losing all that she held dear.

A parlormaid dropped a quick curtsy as Juliana passed her in the hallway. Juliana nodded in acknowledgment and continued walking. Like her father, she thought best when she walked, even if the process was more difficult now than it should be. Last night she had come close to allowing emotion to override her common sense. Men were weak creatures. She understood full well why Eric would seek out the company of a mindless piece of fluff like Mireille Dubois. Isabelle, however, was another story. She'd rather see her husband dead than in the arms of that duplicitous bitch.

She paused for breath in the enormous center hallway, leaning against a pillar for support. If only she were in charge now, she would send Isabelle away post haste and Maxine with her. She would see to it that Eric had a title, the first step toward bolstering his fragile male ego. And she would welcome her father-in-law's new ideas with open arms.

"Madam?" Yves made his way across the hall. "The cook has asked me to beg your forgiveness."

Her expression remained impassive, and she watched, fascinated, as Yves seemed to grow smaller before her eyes.

Yves cleared his throat. "He askes you to look upon him with generosity and accept his apologies for his grievous mistake." All said with a French accent that would have done Charles de Gaulle proud.

Juliana, cool and collected, met his eyes. "Am I to assume the cook also wishes that I restore him to his position on the staff?"

Yves nodded. "That is indeed his wish, madam."

"His wish is denied." A surge of adrenaline flooded through her veins at the look of disbelief on the man's narrow face. This was power, and she found she loved it. "One month's salary and the usual references."

"But, madam—"

"That is all, Yves." *Unless you wish to join the cook on his search for a new position.* "And you are not to trouble my father with this matter. He gave me full authority over household matters, and I will not be challenged. Do you understand?"

"I understand, madam."

She turned and headed for the main door. "I am going for a walk in the garden. If my husband telephones, please ask him to leave a number where he can be reached."

"As you wish, madam."

So quick. So easy. With a word she could cast a person into oblivion or make his fondest dream come true. How was it she'd never realized all that was within her grasp?

That taste of power had been intoxicating. The only thing in her life that came close to the sensation was making love with her husband. Perhaps the two sensations were more intertwined than one might think at first observation. Once again it occurred to her that the acquisition of more power could ensure Eric's place by her side.

In the distance she heard the strident yipping of her

father's infernal Corgis. She despised those horrid little dogs, all haunches and teeth and bad dispositions. Oh, yes, there would be many changes when she acceded to the throne, and it would start with those canine ferrets.

She wrinkled her nose at the slightly blowsy look of the roses. They were past their peak, petals wide open to the sun with the faded look of a once-beautiful woman lifting her face toward the light. She preferred the controlled beauty of the privet hedges, predictable angles and lines with a purpose beyond the ornamental.

The garden was neatly bordered with a stone fence punctuated by a gate at the far end. She pushed open the gate and continued walking. The dogs were making an unconscionable amount of noise. A faint hint of alarm mingled with her curiosity as she followed the well-worn footpath into the woods.

"Ridiculous," she said out loud as the cathedral of leaves overhead rustled in the summer wind. This odd sense of approaching destiny was more than likely the result of her advanced state of pregnancy, nothing more. The barking of the dogs grew louder as she plunged more deeply into the forest. "Papa!" she called out. "It's Juliana."

No response save for the barking of the dogs.

Her heart beat more rapidly in earnest. "Papa!" she called, more loudly this time. "Where are you?"

She jumped as she felt something brush against her ankle. Looking down, she saw one of her father's dogs, leaping about as if possessed.

"What on earth—?"

The small dog growled ominously, and she took a step back, but then the animal ran forward a few yards, as if trying to tell her something. She supposed the little horror wanted her to follow it into the woods where it would turn her into a human sacrifice.

"Papa!" Her voice rang out. "Please come and fetch your dog before it bites me!"

Still no response.

"All right," she said to the dog. "I'll do as you say." She followed the animal through some brush ripe with berries then into a clearing.

She glanced about, her hands linked across her belly, then saw a knot of Corgis clustered around her father's prone form. She was at his side as quickly as her bulk would allow.

". . . pain . . . my jaw . . . shoulder . . ." His words were slow and indistinct. "I need . . ." His eyes closed, and she watched, fascinated and horrified, as beads of sweat broke out along his brow.

She felt useless standing there while he writhed in pain, but her belly was so large she couldn't bend over to wipe his forehead.

"Help," he said, clutching at his left shoulder. "The doctor . . . quickly. . . ."

"Of course, Papa," she said. "Immediately."

She looked down at him for a long moment, memorizing the furrows and planes of his face, then turned and slowly walked back toward the castle.

The *New York Times* broke the story about Bertrand's death on one of the inside pages—three column inches of text accompanied by a small picture of Juliana and Eric standing, griefstricken, at the gravesite. Matty saw it first. He called Daniel to pass on the news.

"Damn glad you didn't get involved with them," Matty said. "Malraux will have that place tied up in red ribbons before the grass grows over the grave."

"You have a way with words, Pop," Daniel said, thinking about the charming silver-haired prince he'd met just a few months ago. "I wonder—" He stopped.

"You're wondering about the other princess."

"She's going to have it rough," Daniel said, wishing his father wasn't so good at finishing his sentences for him. "She was the odd one out when Bertrand was alive. It's only 'going to get worse." A lot worse, if his gut feeling about Juliana was on target.

"They'll work it out fine without you," said Matty. His words were punctuated by puffs on a cigar. "That's one thing about royalty, Danny: It's a job for life. They take care of their own."

You're wrong, Pop, thought Daniel. The memory of the way they'd all closed ranks at Juliana's wedding, as if Isabelle didn't exist, lingered with him. So did the depth of her loneliness.

They spent a few minutes talking about a real estate deal on the Upper West Side, then broke the connection. Daniel buzzed for Phyllis, who popped up seconds later in the doorway.

"You rang, boss?"

"Send some flowers or whatever to Prince Bertrand's family in Perreault."

Phyllis jotted something in her ever-present notepad. "Birth? Anniversary? Wedding?"

"Death. The prince, a few days ago."

"His poor daughter," Phyllis said, looking genuinely concerned. "Just married, about to have a baby, and now she's inherited the throne. I wouldn't want to be her for a million dollars. Her freedom is gone before she even had a chance to enjoy it."

"This from the raging royalist of Queens?"

"I'm not stupid, Daniel. I want the perks, not the pressures."

"So what do you think'll happen to the other sister?" He managed to sound only mildly curious.

"Judging from what I've been reading, she'll probably marry one of those rich Euro-types she's been partying with."

He scowled. "What do you mean, partying?"

"Honey, if half the stuff they're printing about her is true, this girl has a track record Carl Lewis would envy." She paused. "For heaven's sake, Daniel, don't look at me like that. You asked, and I told. It's just an opinion."

"Too goddamn much gossip," Daniel muttered, crumpling up a piece of paper and aiming it for the wastebasket across the room. "What the hell ever happened to privacy?"

Phyllis stalked out of his office, mumbling something about tyrants under her breath. Knowing Phyllis, Daniel guessed she was probably wondering why all the interest in Isabelle.

He really didn't give a damn what happened to the little princess. She wasn't his responsibility. Hell, they barely knew each other.

Still, the thought of her in the arms of one of those professional boyfriend-types he'd seen roaming through Europe made his gut knot up. Despite her interlude with Eric Malraux, the dark-haired princess still had the fires of righteous innocence burning in her heart. Even Daniel, who wasn't particularly good at navigating emotional landscapes, could see that she still believed in a love that would last a lifetime. All it would take was two or three more mistakes on the scale of Malraux and she'd turn into one of those hollow-eyed women who relied on cabana boys for their self-esteem.

But hell. It wasn't his problem. Any last, lingering hope for a deal with the principality had died with Bertrand, and now that Daniel was negotiating hot and heavy with the Japanese, the odds were he'd never cross paths with any of them again.

Chapter
Eight

Elysse, sister of the late Prince Bertrand and ex-wife of too many men—both noble and otherwise—to count, checked the last of the wardrobe trunks lined up in her foyer, then nodded toward the doorman and his assistant. "If you would, gentlemen, I'll be forever in your debt. The nice man in the big black limousine will help you load them in the boot."

Isabelle watched the proceedings with alarm. "Aunt Elysse! How can you do this to me?"

"Quite easily, my dear." Elysse checked her makeup in the mirror of her gold compact. "I am more than willing to put a roof over your head and food in your stomach, but I simply cannot live with you. And certainly not during August in New York. You are demanding, foolish—although not unintelligent—and altogether too loud and too young for my aging tastes. I shall simply remand myself to my home in Bermuda as is my custom and wait for the storm to pass. I will see you again in the spring, by which time I hope you will have found your own residence."

"I can't live here by myself."

"You won't be living here by yourself," Elysse pointed out. "You have Maxine."

"But Maxine doesn't know anything more about New York than I do!"

"And think of the fun you two will have learning all about it."

"You simply cannot do this to me."

"I can and I must," Elysse said, sliding on her gloves. "I am old, I am tired, and I need time and space for myself. My banker will take care of the apartment's carrying charges and the utilities. There is food in the pantry and a well-stocked freezer. After that, my dear, I'm sure you'll find a way to fend for yourself."

"But who will clean up after me?"

Elysse rolled her blue eyes in despair. "How I thank God that I left Perreault when I did and learned to be an independent woman. I shudder to think that there was a time when I believed the world owed me a living."

Isabelle brushed away her words with a wave of her hand. "Yes, but who will do the cleaning?"

"A service will come in every Friday, my dear, but you are on your own the rest of the time." Elysse pointed to her cheek. "Now if you will kiss your aunt good-bye, I must be on my way."

Isabelle did as she was asked. Her aunt smelled of Chanel No. 5 and impatience. "Why on earth did you invite me to live with you if you weren't going to be here?"

"My dear, you had an abysmal interlude in Paris, and we both agree you were faring equally badly in London. What choice was there? I couldn't bear to see you thrown to the wolves. You're quite a delectable little morsel, and they would have devoured you in one bite." She shrugged her narrow, elegant shoulders. "We are family, but that does not mean we must live together under the same roof. Need I say more?"

"No," said Isabelle, "I would rather you didn't. You make me sound like an undisciplined ogre, unfit for human company."

Elysse's laugh rang out. "*Au contraire,* my darling. You're a most amusing and beautiful child, and it is my fondest hope that one day you will become a quite satisfactory woman. But I see no need to share that journey with you. *Au revoir,* Isabelle. I will see you again in April."

Isabelle stormed back into the kitchen where Maxine sat nursing a pot of tea and reading the newspaper.

"Well, the traitor has run out on me," she announced, slumping into a chair opposite Maxine. "Once again my own flesh and blood has seen fit to desert me."

Maxine looked up at her. "'Twould seem you have been left with more than you deserve, lovey, considering the way you've been acting."

"Please do not start with your criticisms again, Maxi. I am simply not in the mood."

"This is the life you've been given, and it is high time you made your peace with it."

Isabelle shot Maxine a perfectly foul look. "If you're so dreadfully unhappy with me, Maxine Neesom, why don't you go back to Perreault and play nursemaid to Juliana's child?"

"You know the answer to that as well as I do, lovey. When I chose you, I broke my ties forever." Maxine resumed reading her newspapers.

Isabelle swiped a chocolate donut from the platter in the center of the table and stalked back into the living room. In the two months since her father's death, Isabelle had bounced from place to place, trying to find somewhere she could put down roots, even temporarily.

One week after Bertrand's funeral, Isabelle had found herself expelled from her homeland with nothing more than her wardrobe trunks and Maxine by her side. Juliana had maintained her icy silence where Isabelle was concerned, empowering Yves to deliver the nasty bit of news. There was little doubt that the man enjoyed it. Somehow Juliana had managed to turn public opinion against Isabelle, and that extended to the castle staff. "Her wild ways took their toll on her father," went the whispers. "She broke his heart in two."

She knew that wasn't true, that she had existed in the shadows of her father's life. To break someone's heart meant that you had held a place within it, and Isabelle knew she never had.

"Pack everything," she'd instructed Maxine, "because I will never return."

"Rash statements are the most often regretted," Maxine had said. "This is the place of your birth. One day you'll return."

But Isabelle was beyond reason. Perreault had been a dream to her, a distant vision of something that could never be. In a way there was a certain relief in knowing that it was over.

Paris, however, proved a disaster. The Hotel George V was very pricey, something she had never thought about before. Two weeks into their stay, the manager had appeared at their suite with the embarrassing news that the castle had refused payment and would mademoiselle please make other arrangements.

Unfortunately, mademoiselle hadn't given much thought to things like hotel bills. Those mundane details had always been taken care of by the anonymous accountants laboring away in the castle offices.

She and Maxine had moved on to London where Isabelle and her friend Gemma quickly discovered that they were too old to be roommates again. Isabelle embroidered some flashy designs on a plain silk dress and left it behind as a thank-you gift, although she suspected just seeing her departure might have been gift enough.

"I have a brother in Dublin," Maxine had offered. "He might be willing to let us stay with him for a spell."

But Isabelle had had other ideas. How many times had Aunt Elysse said Isabelle would love New York City? Maybe the time had come to find out for herself.

"Well, you certainly found out, didn't you?" Isabelle said as she looked out the window at the street below. New York was louder, dirtier, and faster than she'd ever imagined. It was also more expensive, more dangerous, and more exciting than in her wildest dreams. Just walking three blocks to Trump Tower was an adventure. But she had counted on having her aunt there to guide her through the maze that was the Big Apple. And, she must admit, to be there to pay the bills.

Maxine had checked the pantry and freezer and clucked that the supplies wouldn't last forever, and they'd best be thinking about the future. The last time Isabelle had given serious thought to her future, she'd believed marriage would be at the heart of it. Now, whenever she turned her thoughts toward that particular road, all she saw was darkness.

Phyllis burst into Daniel's office, waving a copy of the *New York Post*. "She's in town! Page six says she's living right near Trump Tower."

Daniel leaned forward and switched off the tape recorder. "Don't you ever knock, Phyl? I'm trying to practice my Japanese."

"Forget your Japanese," his assistant said, shoving the newspaper under his nose. "The princess is in town."

Somehow he knew she didn't mean Diana. "I don't have time for this today. I'm leaving for Tokyo next week and I still haven't got past *domo arrigato.*"

Damn it. He didn't want to look. He'd done a pretty good job of keeping the princess tucked away in some far corner of his brain and intended to keep her there.

"I'm not going to leave until you look at it."

He knew Phyllis well enough to realize she meant

business. "Okay," he said, reaching for the newspaper. "If that's what it takes to shut you up." He glanced down at the photo. "What the hell—?" Her hair was piled atop her head, diamonds dangled from her ears—and she was carrying a bag from Gristede's? He looked up at Phyllis. "Is this your idea of a joke?"

"No joke, boss. That's hot off the presses. I couldn't believe it, myself." Phyllis leaned across the desk. "You should call her, Daniel. Invite her to lunch." She grinned. "Invite me to lunch with the two of you."

"Forget it."

"She's all alone in the city," Phyllis urged. "She could use a friend."

"We're not friends."

"So make friends with her. You danced with her at her sister's wedding, didn't you?" Her expression grew sly. "You need a social life, Dan-o."

He skimmed the story that accompanied the picture. "Sounds like she's doing okay without me. Lunch at Le Cirque and dinner at 21. She could give lessons."

Phyllis yanked the paper away from him. Rolling it into a tube, she tapped it against her hand. "God, how I'd love to hit you in the head with this."

He couldn't help laughing. "What is it about me that makes women want to hit?" The little princess had threatened him repeatedly, and once he'd even let her connect.

"Figure it out," Phyllis snarled, then stomped back out to her desk.

"If you're so damn interested, why don't you call her?" he said as the door slammed shut behind her. "Like we'd have a chance," he muttered, staring out the window at the traffic on Park Avenue. She was royal and she was beautiful, which made her as useless as two left shoes. She also had a bad temper, no visible talents, and lousy taste in men—and she didn't like him any more than he liked her. He and his ex-wife had had more than that going for them, and they'd ended up in divorce court, bickering over the china service.

No doubt about it: He and the princess were a match made in romantic hell, and the sooner he got that through to his libido, the better off he'd be.

He didn't need her. He didn't want her. And he sure as hell wasn't going to call her.

New York was a big city. There had to be room enough for both of them.

By the first week of October, Isabelle had decided that New York City was nothing more than a collection of small towns loosely linked by a common language—or at least what approximated a common language. She'd never imagined English could be spoken in so many different ways, but one month in Manhattan had shown her how wrong she was.

The tiny blurb that had appeared in the newspaper a few weeks ago had been the start of her introduction into the social whirl of the city. All it had taken was one sharp-eyed photographer, and her phone began to ring off the hook with invitations to gallery openings and galas and lunches. Royalty was a valuable commodity in New York City, and she found herself doted upon in a most agreeable manner.

Even her needlework engendered comment. Juliana had not only held up her trust fund, but also she had seen to it that Isabelle's wardrobe had yet to arrive. Isabelle, hungry for pretty clothes, had dressed up some plain garments with beadwork and fancy stitchery, and overnight the well-dressed ladies who lunched were oohing and ahing as if they were vintage Diors.

"Americans certainly do eat a lot of lunches," she said one morning as she poured herself a cup of tea and joined Maxine at the breakfast table. "I have a noon luncheon engagement tomorrow and a one-thirty on Wednesday."

Maxine scowled in her direction. "And wouldn't I be wishing I could spend my days eating fancy food off china plates."

"Oh, for heaven's sake, Maxi!" Isabelle buttered a piece of toast and reached for the marmalade. "Nobody told you to get that idiotic job. We're doing just fine." Maxine had taken a clerical job at a Seventh Avenue dress factory called Tres Chic.

" 'Just fine' isn't good enough," Maxine said. "One rainy day, and we're in trouble."

"You sound like one of those worrying women in the ladies' magazines." She bit into the toast, then added another layer of marmalade.

" 'Twould be nice if I wasn't the only one doing the worrying."

"We have nothing to worry about, Maxi, can't you understand? Any day Aunt Elysse's lawyer will get my trust fund released and have it deposited at a local bank. It's just a matter of time."

"Too much time, if you ask me," Maxine sniffed.

"Well, no one is asking you."

"You'd be asking me to do everything else around here."

"Is it my fault no one thought to teach me how to cook?" Or iron a blouse. Or balance a checkbook. The list was endless. "I'm getting quite tired of hearing about my shortcomings." She added yet another layer of marmalade to her toast. "I'm certain there is something I'd be good at, and sooner or later I shall discover what it is."

Maxine watched as she took a bite of toast. "We can't be buyin' new clothes on our budget, missy."

Isabelle's eyebrows lifted dangerously. "Are you implying something, Maxine?"

Maxine's face remained impassive. " 'Twould be a shame for those lovely clothes to go to waste."

"You think I'm getting fat."

"I wouldn't be saying that."

"Then what would you be saying?" She mimicked Maxine's particular rhythm with wicked precision.

"That there might be something better to be doing with your time than eating fancy meals with useless people."

Isabelle leaped to her feet and ran to the refrigerator. She flung open the door then pointed at the contents inside.

"Leftovers, the Americans call them," she announced to Maxine and anyone else who might be in earshot. "My fancy luncheons and dinners are providing sustenance for us both."

Maxine made a dreadful face. "Food that isn't fit for a rabbit."

"We don't all require potatoes, Maxine."

"Don't you be turning your sharp tongue against me, missy. I'm gainfully employed and I have half a mind to find myself my own little place closer to the shop. There are times when a body needs some peace and quiet."

"That's what *Tante* Elysse said."

"And what would that be tellin' you, lovey?"

"That you've become bloody impossible since you started working at that factory," Isabelle snapped. "That Igor must be a dreadful employer."

"His name is Ivan, and he is fair-minded and generous." Maxine paused a beat. "Which is more than can be said for some."

Isabelle tossed her hair back with a quick, sharp gesture. "If Igor's so wonderful, why don't you go and live with him?"

"And don't be thinking I haven't considered such a thing."

"Maxi!" Isabelle was stricken with horror at the thought that Maxine would actually leave her. "You wouldn't— would you?"

Maxine's smile was too sly for Isabelle's taste. "You'll be makin' your own dinner tonight, lovey. I have a date."

Isabelle's jaw dropped open. "With Igor?"

"Ivan. And I won't be tellin' you that a third time." Maxine placed her napkin on the table and rose from her chair. "Now, if you'll be excusin' me, lovey, I am off to work."

"Good," said Isabelle as the door slammed shut behind Maxine. "I am quite tired of your company as it is."

A fitting retort, but somehow it didn't satisfy the way it

would have a few short months ago. Since her father died, there had been too many changes for Isabelle's comfort. Leaving Perreault forever hadn't hurt half as much as leaving behind her dreams of a happy future shared with the people she loved and who loved her. If it weren't for Maxine's steady presence, there were times when Isabelle feared she would cease to exist with no one in the world to notice or care.

A pang of conscience gnawed at Isabelle as she thought of Maxine slaving away at that dress factory. The woman had left behind a life of relative ease in order to follow Isabelle into exile, and how had Isabelle shown her gratitude? She hadn't, that was how. She had accepted Maxine's loyalty as her due, then watched as the woman ventured out into the hostile world in search of employment. Lately all Maxine did was talk about this Ivan person. He seemed nice enough. After all, he had sent over a stack of samples, plain silk shirts and dresses in classic styles that would soon bear more famous labels. Still, Isabelle was of a mind to march over to Seventh Avenue and take a look at this man who suddenly figured so prominently in their lives.

But it was dreadfully hot out, and the air conditioning inside the apartment was so comfortable that Isabelle sat in front of the television for the next two hours letting herself float on a sea of surreal entertainment. American television was the most amazing thing. Twenty-four hours a day she could flip on a channel and find someone waiting to entertain her in a wonderfully mindless fashion.

After lunch she thumbed through the stack of mail that had been accumulating in her basket, stacking invitations in one pile and bills in another. There was an odd request from a man named Silverstein who claimed to be a producer of something called "The Morning Show." She couldn't imagine what he could possibly want with her. Gemma had sent an amusing note about her latest conquest, and Isabelle smiled as she read it. Gemma certainly hadn't done much smiling while Isabelle and Maxine were in residence.

Isabelle considered jotting off a quick response, but a fascinating chat show had just begun on a cable station, and she found herself staring, mesmerized, at the flickering screen.

"Our topic today is fractured families," said the serious young star of the show. "Why they break apart . . . how to put them back together." Three real-life families sat right there on the stage, willing and eager to spill their deepest secrets before the television camera.

Another chat show followed with a different serious young star. "Famous people, infamous lives. Join us as some of your favorite movie stars tell about the sorrow behind the glamour."

Andy Warhol had said everyone in America would be famous for fifteen minutes, and Isabelle sat up straight in her chair as she finally understood what he'd meant by that.

She glanced toward the stack of magazines piled on the table next to her. Whole issues were devoted to the cult of celebrity, and it seemed those celebrities were getting rich simply for being famous. She couldn't cook or clean or type or do any of the other things average people did to earn a living, but there was one asset that she'd possessed since the day she was born: She was a princess with a story to tell, and American television was the place to tell it.

She plucked Silverstein's note from the stack and kissed it. Unless she missed her guess, "The Morning Show" would be the start of something wonderful.

Chapter Nine

Dressing room one at the ABC studios was a ten-by-twelve-foot rat hole of a place, crowded with garment racks, rickety stools, and more pots, jars, and bottles of makeup than Daniel had seen in one place in his entire life.

"C'mon, Mr. Bronson." The makeup artist motioned him toward a stool. "It's almost showtime."

Daniel took a seat, keeping one foot on the ground for balance.

"Number two," the woman mumbled. "Maybe a three base. We'll talk about the eye cover later."

Daniel stood up. "We'd better talk about it now. I thought you were going to comb my hair."

The woman gave him the once-over. "I'm not a magician, honey. You need yourself a haircut."

He looked at his reflection in the mirror. "You might be

right." He looked back at her. "What's all that stuff about number two?"

"Makeup, honey. Gotta even up that skin tone for the camera."

"I like my skin tone the way it is."

"Well, sure you do, but you're gonna look like day-old toast to the viewers."

"Sorry," Daniel said. "I'll take my chances."

"Your choice," said the makeup artist with a shrug. "Your father never gives me any trouble." Matty Bronson was a frequent guest on many of the local television and radio shows.

"Believe me when I say I wish my father was here right now." Matty had been scheduled to appear on "The Morning Show" for a segment on people who were born rich versus people who worked their way up from the bottom. An unexpected bout of flu had caused Matty to back out and Daniel to be pushed into the spotlight in his father's place, despite the fact that he had just stepped off a plane from Japan two hours ago and was facing terminal jet lag.

He reluctantly submitted to a brief encounter with a puff of powder.

"Such great raw material," the red-haired woman said with a sigh. "I could have done wonders with you." She tossed the cotton puff into a wastebasket. "Tell Matty that Sheila was asking for him."

"Will do." He turned to leave, then paused in the doorway. "Any idea who else is on this show?"

She rolled her eyes. "A former child star, a man who made millions in salad dressing, and—"

"Two minutes!" A fresh-faced intern raced down the hall. He skidded to a stop in front of Daniel. "You Bronson?"

"That's me."

"Your spot's up next. Come on."

Daniel followed the kid down a long, drab corridor, picking his way across a maze of thick cable, skinny wires, and discarded paper cups. He recognized some of the famous names on the doors, noting with amusement that the glamorous world of show business looked anything but glamorous from this side of the footlights.

"So what can I expect?" Daniel asked as the intern pushed open the heavy red door that led into the studio itself.

The kid cast a look over his shoulder. "Didja do a preinterview?"

He shook his head.

"Great," mumbled the kid. "Okay, it's like this: This guy named Bob Harris is subbing for the host. He does all that celebrity shit in syndication. Anyway, he'll set up the whole segment, they bring you out, you do two minutes of shtick, the rest do their thing, and they take a few phone calls. Piece of cake."

"Shtick? What the hell do you mean, shtick? I'm not a comedian, I'm a businessman."

The kid shot him a look. "Same thing, isn't it?"

"Sweetheart, you look like a million bucks!" The hairdresser turned Isabelle's chair toward the mirror. "Whaddya think?"

Isabelle nodded at her reflection. "Wonderful eye makeup, but isn't my hair a little—big?"

"You're a gorgeous girl, honey. You wanna stand out in a crowd, don't you?"

Isabelle touched the top of her hair and stared as her hand bounced off the surface. "I always thought I did stand out in a crowd."

"Well, sure you do, but this is TV. You need a little extra oomph."

"Oomph?"

"You know. Pizzazz."

Pizzazz was almost as bad as oomph, but Isabelle got the general picture.

"Does this outfit have enough—oomph?"

The hairdresser inspected her slinky royal blue chemise.

"Must've cost a mint. Get a load of that beading along the neckline."

"I did the beadwork."

"You?" The hairdresser inspected the work more closely. "Great job. You woulda thought a machine did it."

Isabelle, uncertain if she had been complimented or insulted, merely smiled.

The television studio was a confusing maze of corridors, doors, trailing wires, and harried people. Isabelle followed a frantic young man through that maze.

"Damn," the young man muttered as they stopped in front of a closed door. "The red light is on." He glanced at his watch, and Isabelle noted the beads of sweat at his temples.

"What is going on?"

"The show, that's what. God, my ass'll be grass."

The notion of green grass sprouting on the man's derriere made Isabelle laugh out loud. "The American idiom is surely filled with surprises."

The man shot her a look. "Idiom, shmidiom. You're up next, and we can't get inside until the damn light goes out."

"They'll wait for us," Isabelle said.

"Honey, you're not back in the palace. This is the US of A. People don't wait for anybody."

"But if I'm the star of the show, they'll have to, won't they?"

The man rolled his eyes. "You've got a lot to learn about living here, sweetheart."

Moments later, the red light went out, the door swung open, and the man pushed Isabelle toward the light.

"Be funny," he advised, "be sassy, and sparkle!"

Sparkle, thought Isabelle. *I can't do that.*

"Ten seconds," yelled a skinny black woman with red hair. "Five . . . four . . . three . . . two . . . we're on."

"Welcome back, everybody." A man's voice rang out. Isabelle rose on tiptoe in an attempt to see over the cameras but failed. "My name is Bob Harris, and we're talking about fame and fortune. You've already met Carl Lindemann and little Sallie Gleason who had to work hard for every penny they earned. Now let's introduce the other side: two lucky people who were born with platinum spoons in their mouths. Let's welcome—"

"Go!" The young assistant placed his hands at the small of Isabelle's back and pushed. She stumbled forward into the blinding lights. She couldn't make out the audience or the crew; all she could hear was the applause drawing her in. Straightening her shoulders, she lifted her chin and walked toward the set.

Bob Harris was a jovial sort. He extended his hand, then kissed her on the cheek. It took all of her self-control to keep from dressing him down. You would think an Englishman would have more respect for royalty, but he was in America now, where such things didn't matter. How quickly they all forgot the things that were truly important in life.

She nodded toward the two guests already standing there, then turned toward the fourth guest as he stepped into the spotlight.

"Bronson!"

He stopped a few feet away from her. "What are you doing here?"

"I was about to ask you the same thing."

The audience erupted with laughter. Both Isabelle and Daniel started and glanced about, as if they'd forgotten where they were.

"What have we here?" asked Bob Harris as they took their seats on either side of him. He winked into the camera. "Is there something going on that we should know about?"

Isabelle tossed her big hair off her face and smiled. "Mr. Bronson and I are old friends," she said with false cheer. "We met last year at the Perreault Tricentennial. He and Greta Van—"

"In fact, the princess and I danced at her sister's wedding," Bronson broke in smoothly, meeting her eyes. No one had eyes that green, she thought. They had to be contact lenses. "Her waltzing needs a little work."

"Americans!" she said breezily. "So in love with truth as they perceive it. Whatever happened to the graceful social lie?" She hoped everyone recognized him for the skunk he was.

"Fighting words," bellowed Bob Harris, current purveyor of glitz and glamour. "Now let's get to the heart of it. You two lucky people were born rich. Why work if you don't have to?"

Bronson obviously found the question beneath contempt. "Once you get out of school, it's up to you to build your own life. Trust funds only go so far. You have to rely on brains and ambition to take you the rest of the way."

"Easy for you to say," said Lindemann, the salad dressing king. "I didn't go to Harvard Business School. I had to start from scratch. Worked three jobs just to get my seed money."

"Right," said little Sallie. "Bet you didn't have to audition for jobs when you were still in training pants. Try being three years old and on unemployment. Does something to a person's self-esteem, I can tell you that."

"Absolutely," Isabelle chimed in, feeling one with them all. "Can you imagine how it feels to be cast to the four winds by your own sister with nothing but the clothes on your back?"

Bob Harris seized the moment. "Do you mean your sister, Princess Juliana, the ruler of the little principality of Perreault, threw you out of the castle?"

There was a gasp from the audience.

"I certainly do," said Isabelle, warming to the subject. She cast a quick glance toward Bronson and was rewarded by the look of surprise on his face. "She threw both Maxine and me—"

"Maxine?" Harris broke in. "Is Maxine another princess?"

"Maxine is my governess." Bronson's groan was audible over the laughter of the audience, and she leaned across Bob Harris to glare at him. "I'll thank you to keep your opinions to yourself, Mr. Bronson."

"No, no," said Bob Harris. "We'd love to hear what Daniel has to say, wouldn't we, audience?" Wild applause confirmed his opinion. Harris really was the most annoying man.

Bronson met her eyes. "I think a family's problems should remain that family's business."

"Spoilsport," said Harris, turning away from Bronson. "I know we're all interested in the princess's story."

"Thank you so much, Mr. Harris," said Isabelle with a sweet smile. So much for Bronson's opinion. "It's terribly difficult to be alone in a strange city with no one to help you find your way. I have done my solitary best to—"

"What about your governess?" Daniel interrupted.

"You make governess sound like a dirty word," Isabelle snapped. "It's not an unusual occupation."

"Aren't you a little old for a nanny?"

"And aren't you a little old to be working for your father?"

"I work with my father, not for him. There's a big difference."

"I'm afraid that difference escapes me."

"The difference is, I don't travel around with my own personal slave."

"How dare you! Maxine is not my slave. In fact, she's working for a man named Ivan on your Seventh Avenue in order to make ends meet."

"To make ends meet? You have your nanny out there in some sweatshop while you sit around on your royal—"

"Finish that sentence, Mr. Bronson, and I shall see to it that your attorneys are kept busy for the next six months."

He remained unchastened. "Where are you living, princess? The penthouse of the Plaza? Big comedown from the castle, isn't it?"

"Not that it's any of your business, I am living with my aunt."

"Rent free?"

"Yes, but—"

"And you still need to have your nanny out there bringing in some bucks?"

"For your information, my sister cut me off without a *sou*. All I have is what I brought out of Perreault with me, and as my aunt does not have unlimited funds, we are doing the best we can."

"You mean your nanny is doing the best she can. What are you doing, princess?"

Isabelle opened her mouth to speak, but no words came out.

Bronson, the wretch, grinned at her. "Come on. You must be doing something constructive."

"I'm here, aren't I?" she said in exasperation.

Bob Harris laughed louder than anybody. "I've never heard a talk show called constructive before."

"I'm quite serious," Isabelle persisted. "One afternoon last week I took stock of my skills and I realized the one thing I was quite adept at is being famous."

"I didn't know being famous was a skill," Harris said.

"Of course it is. Isn't that what you Americans do best?" She launched into a spirited description of the television shows, books, magazines, and radio programs she'd come in contact with since her arrival in America. "It seems to me that being famous is a full-time occupation in this country. How else can you explain the existence of Charo?" She offered a dazzling smile to the camera. "This is the land of opportunity, and since I am in need of gainful employment . . ."

The audience burst into uproarious applause, and Isabelle found herself positively basking in their approval. The director signaled Bob Harris to cut to a commercial.

"Two minutes thirty, folks, then we're back on," called an assistant.

Little Sallie ran off for the ladies' room. The salad dressing king waved frantically for the makeup artist to powder down the shine on his bulbous nose. Bob Harris unclipped his mike and strolled over to chat with the audience, which left Daniel and Isabelle alone beneath the lights.

"You're looking good, princess," he said. "I like your hair big like that."

"Don't talk to me. And don't insult my hair."

He ignored her warnings the way he always did. "Were you telling the truth before?"

"Of course I was."

"Juliana tossed you out?"

"As soon as the funeral was over."

"What happened?"

"That, Mr. Bronson, is none of your business."

"You'll spill your guts on television, but you won't tell me?"

"I don't like you, Mr. Bronson, and you have made it abundantly clear on many occasions that you don't like me, either."

"I like you."

"You can't even say that with a straight face."

"I want to know what happened with your sister."

"Then you can fly to Perreault and ask Juliana. That is something I will not talk about with anyone."

"I bet it has something to do with that sleazeball you were in love with."

"Shut up."

"She get tired of sharing him with you?"

"Why do you find it necessary to attack me at every opportunity?"

"I'm not attacking you, princess, I'm—"

"Ten seconds, everybody!" barked the director as the other guests rushed back into the spotlights. "Four . . . three . . . two . . . we're back!"

Her confrontation with Bronson during the commercial break had Isabelle's temper flaring. Fortunately, she was able to turn her fire into something approximating sparkle. The audience seemed to love it. And they especially loved it whenever she and Bronson got into one of their heated discussions. The phone calls were witty and complimentary, especially the ones that inquired about her dress. Isabelle was happy to oblige with information about Ivan's factory and her own talent with a needle. How it must infuriate Bronson to play second-fiddle to an article of clothing! There were an appalling number of questions about their relationship, but both Isabelle and Bronson stated in no uncertain terms that they were not involved with each other.

The hour was up too quickly.

"You were wonderful, Princess Isabelle." Robert Silverstein, the producer, hesitated a moment as if unsure of protocol, then extended his hand. "The phone banks are lit up like Christmas trees. We've already had two hundred questions about your dress alone."

"I had a simply marvelous time," she said. Except for Daniel Bronson, she had. "I cannot remember when I last enjoyed myself so much. And you can tell anyone who asks that the dress is an original from Tres Chic."

"You're going to have your fifteen minutes and then some," Bob Harris chimed in. "I have a number of projects in the works. You'd be a natural in a fashion segment. Give me your card, darling, and my people will call you."

"I don't have a card," Isabelle said with a toss of her head, "but I'd be happy to write my number down for you if you'd like."

"Oh, I'd like," said Harris with a roguish wink. "You don't know how much I like . . ."

Daniel watched the proceedings with disgust. They were slobbering all over her like a pack of dogs in heat. She'd hit upon exactly the right blend of brashness and naïveté that Americans loved, and by the time the show was over she'd had the audience ready to fly over to Perreault and take Juliana to task for casting such an adorable little princess into exile.

"Nice job, Mr. Bronson." The director popped up at his

elbow. "I liked that story about your father and the sail-boat."

"Too bad he wasn't here to tell it."

"Oh, you did just fine," she continued, oblivious to his mood. "We only received a few phone calls of complaint."

"Complaints?" He looked down at her. "Complaining about what?"

She stepped back. "Oh, nothing terribly important. A few people thought you were treating the princess with a lack of respect. But don't worry: Everyone else thinks you two are having an affair!" With that she turned and hurried off to catch up with the salad dressing king.

An affair? Not too likely. They couldn't say two words to each other without erupting into fireworks of a different kind. He watched as Isabelle dimpled for Bob Harris, little Sallie, and assorted members of the crew. Somewhere under all that bravado was a real live woman. Too bad he'd never get to meet her.

He wheeled and headed for the exit. He still had time to go to the office and knock off some work before jet lag kicked in big time.

"Mr. Bronson!"

No way was he going to turn around.

"Mr. Bronson!"

He pushed open the door and strode down the corridor.

"For God's sake, stop this instant and talk to me!" Petulant. Imperious. Pure Isabelle.

To his surprise, he stopped. "Okay, princess, spit it out. I'm not in the mood for more crap."

She looked like she wanted to introduce his face to her fist. "You owe me an apology."

"The hell I do."

"The way you talked to me back there was unconscionable."

"It's a free country. I thought that's part of what you liked about America."

"You were making fun of me, and I do not appreciate it."

"I did exactly what you wanted me to do. I fed you the straight lines and you ran with them. You wanted to be famous, and now you've got your wish."

"I want you to know that everything I said today was true."

"Who said it wasn't?" Why did she have to look so damn vulnerable when she was angry? If she cried, he'd be a goner.

"I can tell by your expression that you don't believe me." Her dark eyes looked suspiciously wet.

"What difference does it make if I believe you or not?"

"Damn it, Bronson! Why do all New Yorkers answer a question with another question?"

"I don't know," he said, grinning. "Do you?"

Their eyes met.

The moment lengthened.

She didn't blink or get teary or dimple at him. Her gaze was direct and uncompromising. Lethal. He'd been a pretty good sprinter in college. If he bolted for the door now, he could probably make it to Eighth Avenue before she got to the corner.

"Have time for a cup of coffee?" he asked against his better judgment. Everything that had happened so far today had been against his better judgment.

"I don't drink coffee, but I should love a cup of tea."

Then she smiled. A real smile that made the sad light in her dark eyes vanish and sent thirty-four years of defenses crumbling into a pile at his feet.

The coffee shop was located a block south of Columbus Avenue on the ground floor of a modest office building. A menu was pasted to the front window with a few items crossed out in black Magic Marker. A hand-lettered sign, "Baklava fresh daily," was taped above it. Daniel held open the door for Isabelle, and she stepped inside. A faint haze of cigarette and kitchen smoke filmed the air. The blare of a radio competed with the cook's muttered oaths as he cracked an egg onto the grill.

"Don't sit at the counter," a waitress tossed out as she hurried by balancing a trio of plates. "Nobody's working the counter."

Isabelle stopped and looked toward Daniel for instruction.

"Over there," he said, pointing toward a booth near the rear.

"This is wonderful," she said as she slid across the bench. "I've only seen places like this in films. I didn't believe they really existed—" She stopped. "Why are you looking at me that way?"

"Every time you say something like that I think, 'She's got to be kidding.' Then I remember who you are."

"I doubt if you ever forget that, Mr. Bronson. You certainly remind me of the fact of my birth at every opportunity."

The waitress stopped at their table and looked at them. "What're you having?"

"Tea," said Isabelle. "No cream. Lemon on the side. Served in a large mug not a cup. And honey if you have it."

"We don't have honey."

"Raw sugar, then."

The waitress looked toward Daniel as if he were an interpreter. "What's raw sugar?"

"Brown sugar if you can't provide raw," Isabelle said, annoyed. "Thank you very much."

"About the mug, I can't make any promises."

Isabelle waved her hand in the air. "I am certain you will do your best."

Bronson placed his order. The waitress understood him perfectly.

"Is my accent that incomprehensible?" she asked as the waitress hurried away. "People are always giving me the strangest looks when I place an order."

"It's not what you order, princess, it's the way you do it."

He got up and shrugged out of his coat, then reached for her shawl. She watched him as he looked around for a coat rack. His chestnut hair was longer than the last time, streaked blond in places by the sun. It gave him an agreeably rakish quality that provided a counterpoint to his urbane choice of clothing. His eyes were the same vivid green that she'd remembered, a color so intense and vital that again she thought it couldn't possibly be real.

He was bigger, though, than she'd remembered, his shoulders broader, his legs longer and more powerful. It was as if he was most himself in the city of his birth, drawing upon the power of the streets and avenues and making it his own. Although it didn't make a jot of sense, she noticed her heart was pounding so hard inside her chest that she found it difficult to breathe.

He found a hook near the back wall and hung the coat and shawl. His walk was both elegant and athletic. How he managed the combination was beyond her. Why it should matter was even more of a mystery. The man meant nothing to her. Fate might see fit to throw them together time and again, but in the grand scheme of things, their lives could never mesh.

He sat down opposite her.

"So tell me, princess, did she kick you out for sleeping with her husband?"

She bristled. "He wasn't her husband when I was sleeping with him."

"Small distinction when you're the wounded wife."

"I don't care to talk about this, Mr. Bronson."

"I think you do."

"How could you possibly know what I want to talk about?"

"Call it a lucky guess."

She refused to acknowledge the fact that he was right. Or the terrifying suspicion that they were inching toward uncharted territory. He had no business knowing her so well when he really didn't know her at all.

"She stole Eric away from me." Her words tumbled together in her haste to be rid of them. "She slept with Eric while he and I were involved. She was pregnant when they got married."

"When did you find this out?"

"The night before Papa died." Quickly, sparing no one, not even herself, she laid the whole ugly story out on the table before them. "If he hadn't forgotten to keep the phony due date straight, I would have slept with him that night at the chalet. I had believed—I had convinced myself that he loved me and that after the baby was born, he would leave Juliana and marry me."

"He'll never leave her, princess, and it has nothing to do with you."

"I know," she said, looking down at the paper place mat on the tabletop. "Eric is a coward."

"He's also his father's pawn. When he married your sister, he married her for life. His old man's not about to let go of the keys to the kingdom. Not for something as unimportant as happiness."

"I fear it isn't much of a kingdom." She loved her homeland, but she wasn't blind to its shortcomings.

"Wait'll Malraux puts up his casinos. You won't recognize the place when he's finished."

She shuddered. "I don't want to talk about that."

"Can't say I blame you."

A flash of memory returned. "Didn't you have some plans for Perreault, as well?"

"Could've made a big difference to your economy."

"And to yours as well."

"It's a dead issue now, princess. I just came back from Japan a few hours ago."

"Were you on holiday?"

"Business. I'm going back at the beginning of the year to oversee the project."

"You certainly don't waste time on regrets, do you, Mr. Bronson?"

"Not if I can help it." That piratical grin slashed across his face.

The waitress appeared next to them. "Okay, coffee regular and tea, lemon on the side, with some kind of fancy sugar. Anything else?" They both shook their heads. She slapped their check facedown on the table. "Have a nice day, folks."

Isabelle watched as he lifted his cup of coffee and brought it to his mouth. A powerful image of herself in his arms, his lips hot against hers, seared her brain, and she shook her head to be rid of it.

He put down the cup. His hands were large, the fingers tapering. They were beautiful hands, capable hands. Hands that would know how to gentle a woman, how to give her pleasure.

An odd sensation of destiny was building inside her chest, and she knew the only way she could deal with it was to run for her life. She stood up. "This has been delightful, Mr. Bronson, but I must dash." She would put distance and time between them, anything that would make this strange feeling disappear.

He grabbed her wrist. His fingers encircled it with room to spare. "Not yet."

She made to pull away, but he held her fast. "There's really nothing else to say."

"Have dinner with me."

"No."

"We need to talk."

"We don't talk, Bronson," she said, a wild laugh escaping her lips. "We argue, and I'm sick unto death of arguing."

"My name is Daniel."

Oh God. "Dinner would be a dreadful mistake. We can't spend five minutes with each other without getting into a row."

"The problem isn't that we don't like each other, princess. The problem is that we want each other."

Her body flamed with sudden heat. "Speak for yourself."

Dear Lord, she sounded soft, yielding—eager. "I'm not looking for a man. I don't want anything except to be left alone to live my life."

"When I thought you were still sleeping with that bastard, I wanted to kill him." His voice was low, filled with dark promise.

"You're scaring me, Bronson."

"I'm scaring myself. Everything about this is wrong, but I don't give a damn."

He released his grip on her wrist. She didn't move away.

"Tell me I'm crazy, and I'll leave you alone."

"You're crazy." Her voice was a whisper.

"I'm not going to leave you alone."

"And you're a liar." Her eyes fluttered closed for a moment. "I'm glad."

He told her what he wanted to do to her right there backed up against the wall of the coffee shop. A line of fire blazed from her brain down to the juncture of her thighs. He brought her right hand to his mouth, then kissed the inside of her palm. Her nipples grew hard in response.

"The waitress," Isabelle said. "She's watching us."

He tossed a twenty-dollar bill down on the table, then held out his hand to her. "Come on, princess. Let's see what this is all about."

Chapter Ten

Daniel's apartment was an eight-room duplex on the top two floors of a building that overlooked Central Park. The elevator operator smiled at them as the doors slid open. "Good to see you home, Mr. Bronson," he said as they exited the car on the forty-ninth floor.

Bronson met his eyes, equal to equal. "Thanks, George. Regards to Emma and the kids. Tell Jason I hope he wins the quarterback spot on his team."

"Will do, Mr. B. That'll make his day." The man nodded politely toward Isabelle.

She looked at Bronson curiously as he unlocked the door to his apartment. She wouldn't have figured him to take note of elevator operators or the other people who served him. In the world she came from, they were an invisible part of the landscape of privilege. To Bronson, however, they were real people with names and families.

He swung open the door and motioned her inside.

"It's a little stark," he said as he closed the door behind them. "I'm not much on decor."

She glanced around, quickly noting the white walls, the uncurtained windows, the black leather couch in the middle of the room. Her eye was drawn to an oil painting resting against the far wall. The slashes of crimson paint seemed to throb with life.

"That's magnificent," she said, moving toward the canvas.

He followed her gaze. "My sister Pat's husband is an artist." He moved toward her.

"You should hang it properly. If you leave it like that, the canvas will warp."

"I'll get around to it."

She couldn't tear her eyes away from the bloodred splashes of paint. "You should do it now. It would be a shame if—"

"Quiet, princess."

"—the canvas shifted or—"

"Shut up."

He reached for her, and she was in his arms in the space of a heartbeat. "You're going to kiss me now, aren't you?"

He crushed her closer to his body, so close his heat became her own. "That was the general idea."

"This seems a wonderful time to do it."

"My thoughts exactly."

She lifted her chin. He lowered his head. His breath smelled faintly of coffee. She wrapped her arms about his neck, threading her fingers through the cool, silky strands of his hair. Hunger rose within her, dark and magnificent, a hunger like she had never known before. There was nothing safe about this man, nothing deferential or yielding.

"Open for me, princess," he whispered against her mouth. "Let me taste you."

Her lips parted on a moan. He claimed her swiftly, his tongue sweeping across her teeth, tasting, savoring, drawing her into a sweetly fatal battle of parry and thrust, domination and surrender. She wanted more. She slid her hands inside his jacket and frantically worked to strip him of it. He shrugged out of the garment, then threw it across the room, followed quickly by his tie. He pulled her shawl off her shoulders, and it fell to the floor, a pool of black silk.

Still it wasn't enough. She fumbled with the buttons of his shirt. He reached behind her and tugged at the zipper of her dress. She felt a rush of cool air on her heated flesh, then gasped as he pressed his hand flat against her skin, matching her heat with his own. She bared his chest to her eyes and mouth. The mat of thick hair was soft against her cheek. The smell of his skin made her feel faint with longing. He was more beautifully made than a man had a right to be.

"This isn't enough," he said, his voice a low rumble against the curve of her breast.

"I know," she whispered in a voice that seemed to come from far away.

Claiming her mouth again, he swept her up into his arms and strode down the hallway, not breaking the kiss. There was a door at the far end of the corridor. He kicked it open with his foot. They fell to the bed together in a wildly erotic tangle of limbs. He pulled away long enough to strip off his clothes.

"Stop." Her voice was husky with desire. "Let me see you."

He towered over her as she looked up at him. His body was tanned a light gold all over, except for the faint outline of a small bathing suit. His chest and arms were powerfully muscled. He stood wtih his legs apart, and a deep throbbing pulse came to life between her own legs as she stared at his erection. He was the most beautiful man she had ever seen, and she wanted him in a way that defied reason.

She lay there trembling as he knelt on the bed beside her. The bodice of her dress had fallen off her shoulders. The skirt was bunched around her hips. The intensity of his gaze both thrilled and terrified her. Instinctively she made to cover herself, but he stopped her.

"You're beautiful," he said, stroking the line of her calf with his index finger. "So small, so perfect."

She gasped as he encircled her ankle with his hand then bent to place his mouth against her instep.

"Don't," she whispered. She felt vulnerable and uncertain, more innocent and untried than when her dreams had been the dreams of a virgin.

"I'm going to love you, princess, every inch of you. And I'm going to make it last."

Shoes, panty hose—her clothing vanished. He took her to a place she'd never been, a place she'd never imagined. She came to life wherever he touched, as if she'd been waiting all her life for the heat of his mouth to awaken her. Her foot, her ankle, the muscle of her calf, the tender flesh of her inner thighs, the—

"No!" This was insane. He couldn't. She shouldn't let him. "You can't possibly want to—"

"I want you to open for me, princess," he said for the second time, his mouth against the most sensitive part of her body, the most secret. Her hips began to move to a deeper rhythm, and she felt herself tumbling over the edge. "You're so sweet, princess, hot and wet—"

Her cry of pleasure filled the room as he flicked his tongue against her swollen flesh, then covered her with his mouth. Wave after wave of sensation swept her farther out into the dark sea of sexuality.

Still it wasn't enough. The aching void inside could be eased only one way, the oldest way on earth, the most wondrous. His mouth left a hot, wet trail along the flesh of her belly and ribcage. He drew each nipple into his mouth in turn, suckling hard, causing her womb to contract violently in response. She trailed her fingernails across his nipples, then moved down across his belly until she found him. She took him in her hand, the hard length of him smooth and hot beneath her fingers. She wanted to run her tongue up his shaft, taste him, know that she had demanded this fierce response from him.

But Bronson had other ideas. He pushed her back on the mattress, then spread her thighs with his powerful hands. "Tell me what you want, princess."

She reached for him. He leaned away.

"You know what I want."

"Say it, princess. Let me hear you say it."

The words tore from her throat. "You, Bronson. Damn it, I want you."

He'd waited a long time to hear those words. Longer even than he realized. The sound of her husky voice saying his name was almost enough to bring him to climax. But he wasn't going to cheat either one of them out of one second of pleasure, not if he could help it.

He positioned himself between her slender thighs. She had a tiny birthmark to the right of her navel, fashioned in the shape of a heart. He leaned forward to kiss it, catching the scent of her, feeling her warmth. She whimpered in the back of her throat, arching her back off the mattress. Those dark, unfathomable eyes never left him. She watched, eyes widening slightly, as he entered her, and he couldn't remember a moment more powerfully sexual. Or more dangerously real.

It was the last thing he remembered before insanity took hold. They came together with heat and urgency, a mating so primitive that no words could contain the powerful emotions he felt as he buried himself inside her body.

She rose to meet his thrusts, wrapping her legs about his hips and working her muscles in a way that made him groan out loud. She urged him on with hands and mouth and thighs until he came violently, his body wracked with waves of pleasure so intense they bordered on pain.

Afterward, after the storm had passed, they lay together, still joined, her breasts pressed against his chest, her long, dark hair obscuring her face. He touched her cheek with his finger, then brushed her hair back. She nuzzled against him like a kitten.

"You okay?" he asked.

She nodded. "Mmm."

He listened to the sound of their breathing, the faraway rumble of traffic on the street below, the ringing of his telephone. He waited for the inevitable moment when he'd grow aware of his cramping muscles, of the hour, of the need to reclaim himself from the situation, but it didn't come.

Sex was an old and familiar pleasure, but there was nothing familiar about the way he was feeling right now. He felt complete, as if it had taken this moment with Isabelle in his arms to put all the puzzle pieces of his soul into place.

An illusion. It had to be. Some kind of sleight of hand that occurred when the sex was volcanic and the stars were in the right position. It would diminish with repetition, fade away until the whole thing became a question of bodies, not souls. Nothing this good could possibly last. No man in his right mind would want it to.

The second time they made love slowly. There was a sweet grace to their movements, a tenderness that bordered on sacramental. They climaxed together, one ripple of sensation after another, so deep and intense that it seemed as if they were one person.

Neither spoke of it afterward, but it was there in the room with them, this sense that physical pleasure was only part of what had happened between them.

"Do you remember the first time we met?" she asked as he drew a quilt up over their naked bodies. "The first moment?"

He lay down again and pulled her close until she was lying across his chest. "This time last year. The Tricentennial." He kissed her mouth. "You were wearing a shimmery peach-colored gown, and your hair was stacked up on top of your head. I kept wondering what you would do if I pulled out the pins and let it tumble around your shoulders. When I asked you to dance, you told me to go to hell."

"I would never have said something so common."

He laughed. "You're going all royal on me, princess."

"If I recall, you didn't ask me to dance with you, you asked me to go out onto the terrace for some nefarious reason of your own."

"I'd forgotten that part."

"If I'd known how wonderful it would be, I might have said yes."

"What would you say if I told you I'd only wanted to ask about my chances with your old man and the ski resort?"

"I'd say chivalry was dead and buried, and there was no hope left for civilization as we know it."

"What else do you remember, princess?"

She looked at him curiously. "Can it be the great and mighty Daniel Bronson is fishing for a compliment?"

"The hell I am."

"The first time I saw you I thought you were too handsome for your own good, too arrogant for my taste, and too opinionated to ever do business in Perreault."

"Three strikes," he said. "I'm surprised you didn't have me tossed in the dungeon."

"I also thought you were incredibly sexy."

"Keep going."

"So did that cow Greta VanArsdalen, if I remember correctly."

He flipped her onto her back and pinned her to the mattress. "You were going to say that on TV this morning, weren't you?"

"If you hadn't stopped me, I would have."

"It was a weekend fling, princess. I never saw her again."

"Do you make a habit of that sort of thing?"

"Weekend flings? I'm not looking for a commitment, if that's what you mean."

"Good," she said, "because I feel the same way."

"So what is this, princess? What are we getting into?"

"An affair. Sex without complications. When it's over, we say good-bye and go our separate ways." She paused. "Why are you looking at me like that? Isn't that exactly what you desire in a relationship?"

"Yeah," he said, "but it doesn't sound the same when you say it."

"My father played me for a fool, Daniel. So did my sister and her husband. I think that is quite enough for one lifetime."

"I won't hurt you, princess," he said quietly. "That's the one thing I can promise you."

"Don't make promises," she said, placing her finger against his lips. "Just kiss me."

When Isabelle awoke, the room was bathed in the muted blues of dusk. For a moment she didn't know where she was and she sat up in bed trying to place her surroundings. Daniel mumbled something in his sleep, and she nearly jumped out of her skin in surprise. The whole incredible afternoon came rushing back in on her in extraordinary detail. So that was what all the fuss was about. She'd never imagined the infinite variety possible between a man and a woman. Certainly she had never suspected it during her months with Eric. She didn't know whether to be thoroughly ashamed of herself or wake Bronson up and do it all over again.

She touched his shoulder. "Daniel." No response. She said his name again, but he was deeply asleep. Jet lag, the result of his trip home from Japan, had finally set in, and she knew he would be out for hours. In truth she was glad, for it made things much easier.

The warmth of the bed, the solid strength of his body, the feeling that she'd been moving toward this moment since the day she was born—none of it was real. She couldn't allow herself to believe it was possible.

Gently she pulled the covers up over his chest, then slipped from the bed. If she didn't leave now, while she still could, she might never leave, and the thought of needing him that much terrified her.

Gathering up her clothes, she padded into the enormous marble bathroom adjacent to the master bedroom to reassemble herself as best she could.

Twenty minutes later, reasonably well put together, she sat down at his desk and wrote her telephone number on the back of one of his business cards. Returning to the bedroom, she pinned it to her pillow with one of her brooches, kissed his forehead, then let herself out of the apartment.

The next move was his.

"And where in the world have you been, lovey?" asked Maxine when Isabelle returned. "The telephone has been ringing off the hook and myself without a clue what to say. I was thinking of calling the authorities."

Isabelle tossed her shawl across the Queen Anne desk in the foyer. She had been hoping to have the apartment to herself for a few hours in order to collect her thoughts. She simply wasn't ready to share what had happened, not even with Maxine.

"What are you doing home early, Maxi?" She kissed the older woman on the cheek. "Shouldn't you be at work?"

"And who could work with the whole world beatin' a path to my door? 'Tis a wonder I didn't lose my job."

"For heaven's sake, will you calm down and explain to me what is happening?"

Maxine pointed toward the answering machine and a two-inch stack of messages next to it. "This is a country of craziness, that's what it is. You would think these people have nothing better to do than waste their time listening to other people's troubles."

Isabelle pounced on the messages and riffled through them. Given the extraordinary turn of events with Daniel, she had forgotten their television appearance. "My God, Maxi! *People* magazine wants to do a three-page story on me!" She glanced at the next few slips of paper. *Harper's Bazaar* and *Vogue* wanted to feature her on their covers. "I cannot believe it. People want to order a dress like the one I'm wearing! They don't even care about the price."

Maxine looked as bewildered as Isabelle felt. She informed Isabelle that the telephones at Tres Chic had been ringing all afternoon with pleas for information on how to order the Princess Isabelle dress seen on "The Morning Show."

Isabelle's story of royalty on the rocks had sparked the public's imagination. Americans loved what they called the "underdog" and the notion of a poor little rich girl cast out into the big cold world with only her governess for company and a trunkful of beautiful clothes. This was even better than glamorous Princess Diana or Fergie because it was happening right there in the US of A.

Isabelle dialed the buyer at Bonwit Teller. "I'm not a dressmaker," she said apologetically. "I only did the needlework."

"Who cares?" the woman responded. "Just put that beadwork on a burlap sack with your name on it, and we're talking six-figure profits."

It was the same with Bloomingdale's and Lord & Taylor.

Maxine called Ivan and asked him to come over immediately, and by midnight Isabelle realized that they were on the verge of major success. She popped the cork on a bottle of Aunt Elysse's best champagne and poured them each a glass. "America!" she said, raising her glass high. "The land of opportunity!"

"From your mouth to God's ear," said Ivan, clinking his

glass against Isabelle's and then Maxine's. "Seventy years I wait to make a name for myself, and it takes you one hour on television to do it for me!" He muttered something in Russian, and they all laughed, even though only Ivan knew what he was saying.

Ivan was a most delightful man, and Isabelle wasn't blind to the affection present between him and Maxine. It seemed that years ago Ivan had been a tailor for the Bolshoi Ballet, slaving away with nothing but a dream to keep him going. When Rudolf Nureyev defected to freedom in the 1960s, Ivan defected with him. Unfortunately Rudi went one way, Ivan went another, and poor Ivan had been slogging for a living ever since.

Maxine, the worrier, refused a second glass of champagne, declaring the celebration both premature and excessive. "The girl puts a few fancy stitches on a dress, and she thinks she'd be inventin' the wheel. Nothing lasts forever, I say, and you would do well to be rememberin' that."

Isabelle winked at Ivan. "We know nothing lasts forever, Maxi. That's why we intend to make the best of it while it does last."

Maxine shot them both a withering look. "Opportunists. This country is filled with nothing but opportunists." Her withering look embraced Isabelle's dress as well. "My sweet girl dressed like a common—"

"Stop while you can, Maxine," Isabelle warned sweetly. "You told me to help with the household expenses, and I have finally found a way that will help not only us, but Ivan as well."

"Would you be listenin' to Miss High-and-Mighty. Nobody would pay a brass farthing for those dresses if you weren't a princess."

"You're right, Maxi, and we intend to exploit that fact for everything it's worth, don't we, Ivan?"

Ivan, oblivious to the implied insults, poured some more champagne. He and Isabelle toasted princesses and embroi-

dery and were about to offer a toast to syndicated daytime
television when Maxine grabbed the bottle.

"Enough with this nonsense! 'Tis unseemly, that's what it
is. You don't see Princess Diana peddling her wares on
television like a common shop girl."

"If I had Princess Diana's jewelry, I wouldn't have to,
either. This is the real world, Maxi. Aren't you the one who
told me to get out there and do something?"

Maxine knew when she'd been bested, but to save
face, she muttered something about Isabelle finding herself a husband instead of wasting her time on television
shows.

"I don't want a husband," Isabelle said, the memory of
her hours in Bronson's bed heating her blood. "Every man
I've met since we've been here has bored me to tears."
Which neatly excluded Daniel since she'd met him in
Perreault.

"I have a nephew," said Ivan. "Drives a limousine, got a
house on Long Island, and four weeks' paid vacation every
year. You could do worse, Izzy."

Izzy? Somehow it made her feel very American, and she
smiled.

"I know of one who wouldn't be letting you best him,"
said Maxine, her expression sly. "Daniel Bronson."

She couldn't possibly know anything, Isabelle told herself. The trick was to stay calm and act natural. "What a
ridiculous thing to say. You know perfectly well that Mr.
Bronson and I are not fond of each other."

"I know what I saw today on the telly, and a picture is
worth a thousand words."

"She's right, Izzy. I saw it, too."

"Ivan, please! Mr. Bronson and I don't even like each
other."

Ivan shrugged his shoulders. "So when does like have
anything to do with love? I know sparks when I see them,
and you two had sparks."

"You could do worse, lovey," said Maxine. "I'd feel

better if I knew that when I die I could leave you in his hands."

Isabelle was still laughing an hour later when she said good night. Maxine would die right on the spot if she knew that was exactly where Isabelle had spent the day: in Daniel Bronson's hands.

Chapter
Eleven

Apparently Maxine and Ivan weren't the only ones who thought Bronson and Isabelle had chemistry.

The *New York Daily News,* the *Post,* and *Newsday* all said that they were a real-life Sam and Diane, whoever they were, and gave their battle-of-the-sexes exchange on "The Morning Show" a collective thumbs-up. The general consensus was that if Isabelle and Daniel weren't having an affair, it was simply a matter of time.

Even Isabelle had to admit that the still photos from "The Morning Show" were provocative. There was no mistaking the body language or the intensity. They were tuned in to each other, to the exclusion of everyone else in the studio. Her face flamed with the realization that what had been so obvious to everyone watching the show had taken both of them by surprise a few hours later.

Maxine left for work a little before eight o'clock just as the telephones began to ring with more requests and invitations and offers for Isabelle. When the intercom buzzed a half-hour later, Isabelle was juggling two phones and the beginning of a headache.

"Delivery for you, ma'am," said the doorman. "I'm sending Barney up with it."

"Roses!" she exclaimed when she opened the door. She quickly put her phone call on hold. "How lovely!"

"Better clear off a table, ma'am," said Barney as he handed her a bouquet of bloodred American Beauties. "Somebody musta bought out the entire florist's shop."

Barney didn't exaggerate. White roses, pink roses, yellow roses by the dozens, followed by an enormous live bush of pink tea roses for the terrace. A tiny rhinestone tiara peeked out from among the blooms. The card was signed simply, "Daniel." She smiled as she held the card in her hand before slipping it into the pocket of her trousers.

He called a little before nine-thirty. "Your phone's been busy, princess."

She leaned against the edge of the desk and pressed the phone closer to her ear. Her headache immediately disappeared. "Everything has gone crazy here since yesterday, Daniel." She told him about the dress orders, her needlework, and Ivan. "And now the apartment is filled with the most beautiful roses in the world."

"Not half as beautiful as you."

She laughed. "I'm not accustomed to being complimented by you. I don't know what to say."

"Say you won't leave like that next time. I would've liked waking up to see your face."

"Two compliments in a row." How could she tell him she'd left because she needed to know that she could. "Does this mean we're actually beginning to like each other?"

"Anything's possible."

She thought about the things they'd done the day before,

the things they'd said. "This is certainly not a normal love affair, is it?"

"Not by a long shot. Maybe that's why we were so damn good together."

She hugged the phone more tightly. "We were, weren't we?" she asked. "Very good together."

"I want to see you tonight."

"I want to see you, too, Bronson."

"I thought you were calling me Daniel."

"I'm a creature of habit. Besides, you don't call me by my Christian name."

"Does that bother you, princess?"

"Not a whit. Does it bother you, Bronson?"

"Not if you . . ." His request was simply put and quite thrilling.

She found herself smiling broadly. "I'll consider it."

"Eight o'clock," he said. "I'll pick you up at your aunt's place."

"No! I mean, you don't have to do that. I can find my way around the city."

He wouldn't hear of it. "Besides, I wouldn't mind meeting that nanny of yours."

"I don't think that would be such a good idea."

"What's the matter? You don't think she'll like me?"

"It's not that." Frantically she cast about for an excuse. "Maxine goes to bed early."

"Eight o'clock?"

"I mean, she's been working late."

"Princess, are you sure there is a Maxine?"

"Of course there is a Maxine, and you'll meet her very soon, Bronson. I promise."

Either television talk shows were more popular than he'd thought, or everyone Daniel knew had a hell of a lot of time on their hands. Whatever the reason, it seemed as if everyone in New York City had caught "The Morning Show" yesterday.

Cabdrivers, the guy who sold newspapers at the corner kiosk, his mother who swore she never watched anything except "Guiding Light," everyone had seen his appearance on the talk show and everyone had an opinion. "Say hi to the princess!" the guy buffing the lobby floor had called out as Daniel entered the Bron-Co building. "I'd give up democracy any day for someone like that."

Poor guy didn't know how close he came to losing his teeth.

Get a grip on yourself, he chided as he stepped onto the elevator. *Stay cool.*

The elevator operator was a new guy. He glanced at Daniel when he entered the car, then glanced at him again. "Don't I know you from someplace?"

"You might," said Daniel. "I own the company."

"No, that's not it," said the guy. "Someplace else."

Gimme a break. Not that goddamn TV show.

The guy smacked his forehead. "You were on TV yesterday! 'The Morning Show'—all about big shots, right?"

"Yeah," said Daniel, thinking fondly of automation. "Big shots."

"You and that duchess—"

"Princess."

"Yeah, the way you and that princess were going at it, I figured you had to be an item."

"We're not an item."

"Yeah?" The guy didn't look convinced.

"You heard it here."

The car shimmied to a stop, the doors opened, and Daniel exploded into his office.

"Say one more word about the television show, Phyl, and you're dead meat," he announced as he tossed his coat on the rack in the anteroom.

Phyllis had always been fearless. "'Hollywood casting directors, take note,'" she read from the *Wall Street Journal.* "'Handsome millionaire and beautiful exiled princess are—'"

Daniel grabbed the paper and crumpled it into the wastebasket on his way into his office. "You're hanging by a thread, DeRosa. Don't push me."

"You can't fool me with that grouchy act," she called after him. "You love this! You and a princess on national television!"

He loomed in the doorway. "National? What are you talking about, national?"

"They're syndicated, boss. Didn't anybody tell you?"

"Son of a bitch!" He slammed the door shut behind him. He and Isabelle had a snowball's chance in hell of maintaining their privacy. His intercom buzzed.

"I don't want to talk to anyone, Phyllis."

"It's your sister, the doctor."

"Especially my sister the doctor."

"She says it's an emergency."

"She always says it's an emergency. Tell her I'll call back."

A second later the intercom buzzed again. "She said she won't hang up until you talk to her."

"Great. I hope her phone bill goes through the roof."

"I'm going to put her through," said Phyllis. "I don't need this aggravation."

"This'd better be good," he warned before Cathy had a chance to say a word. "I'm not in the mood."

"Hello to you, too," said Cathy, her tone huffy. "And here I am, just calling to tell you I understand."

"Understand what?" He sounded suspicious and with good reason.

"Why you've been keeping such a low profile the last few months. A princess, Danny! I'm impressed."

"It's not what you think." At least, it hadn't been until yesterday.

"Feeling protective, are we? That's one of the first signs. Mom is already talking about silver patterns."

"Tell Mom to cancel her order," Daniel snapped. "There's no wedding on the horizon."

"You know Mom. She sees everything in terms of happy endings. Seriously, though, she's thrilled that you're seeing someone."

"Who in hell said I was seeing anyone? I was on a TV show, for God's sake."

"I saw the way you were looking at her, Danny. We all saw the way you were looking at her. You'd have to be blind to miss the signs. You can't tell me you don't feel something for her, because I won't buy it."

"What the hell is wrong with the bunch of you?" he exploded. "Doesn't anybody in this damn family think of anything except my marital status?"

"Touchy, aren't we?"

"Can you blame me?" he shot back. "I'm thirty-four years old, Cathy. I made my first million before I turned twenty-one. Believe it or not, I can take care of my own goddamn love life without any help from you."

He slammed the phone down in its cradle and looked around for something to punch. That's what was wrong with his office. Nothing to punch. He made a mental note to have maintenance install a speed bag in the corner especially for times like this. With a family like his, times like this came with regularity.

He pushed back his chair and stood up. Tension was coiled inside his chest and winding tighter. He paced the length of his office, trying to work off his anger. He and the princess had enough things working against them. If they added public opinion to the mix, they might as well call it quits now.

Damn it, he didn't like waking up to find a note pinned to his pillow. He'd wanted to see her beautiful face, hear the sound of her gentle breathing, feel the softness of her breasts against his chest. What the hell was wrong with her, disappearing like that without even saying good-bye?

As if that wasn't bad enough, she wouldn't let him pick her up at her aunt's apartment. She was busy setting boundaries, building fences between them that he found himself wanting to blast his way through. He'd never met a softer woman with a harder edge in his life. Hell, for all he knew she was still in love with her sister's husband. If he had half a brain left in his head, he'd keep that in mind.

She was too complex a bundle of woman for his taste. She was young, strangely naive about some things, and yet she possessed that European sophistication that made him feel backward and gauche. They didn't speak the same language or want the same things from life; and no matter how long she lived in the United States, she'd always be royalty, and he'd be a guy whose relatives crossed the ocean in steerage. The gulf between them was wider than the Atlantic, and nothing he could say or do would ever change that.

Still there was something else going on between them, something deeper and stronger, more powerful than anything he'd ever known before, and that something had been there from the very first time they met. They understood each other on a level that went beyond words. Too bad the words they managed to find kept getting in the way. Yesterday, with her naked in his arms, he'd found himself thinking about next week and next month, projecting the two of them into a future his family had always told him he would want.

"Well, the joke's on me, folks." He stood by the window and looked down at the traffic moving slowly down Park Avenue. The little princess said she didn't want a commitment. She wasn't looking for anything more than a pleasurable interlude. Most women wanted the night before to slide into the morning after. He woke up to find the bed empty and the scent of her perfume in the air. She didn't want what he couldn't give, and he wished he could be happier about that fact than he was.

* * *

Honore had said the groundbreaking for the casino would happen before the first snows. A site had been chosen that fronted the lake, and Juliana had been quite impressed by the architect's rendering. Her lingering doubts about the advisability of courting the gambling trade had been replaced by a modest optimism.

It was now late October, however, and still the ground remained unbroken. Juliana had questioned her father-in-law about it the day before yesterday, only to have him kiss her cheek and tell her not to worry.

As if that were possible, given the state of Perreault's financial affairs. Despite the delay over the groundbreaking, Honore had been a godsend. Why he chose to stand beside her and offer his support was a question she dared not ask. She only knew that she blessed him every time she sat down with the Minister of Finance and considered the disaster her father had left behind upon his death. "What on earth is this?" she had asked Honore, her eyes brimming with tears. "Where did these debts come from? My God, Honore, we owe you millions of francs!"

In a tender voice Honore had explained that her father had been a wonderful ruler but a dreadful businessman. He had offered to forgive the debts, but Juliana would not hear of it. Putting aside her reservations, she had granted him the right to build his casino complex with her full cooperation. It was the least she could do. If Honore called in the debts, the entire principality would be in ruin.

Under the circumstances, how could she possibly complain when Malraux family business kept her husband traveling much of the time?

"Madam, the periodicals you requested have arrived."

Juliana looked up from her correspondence to see Yves standing in the doorway. "Thank you, Yves. You may bring them in."

Moments later he reappeared with a box filled with newspapers and magazine clippings arranged in date order.

"Will there be anything else, madam?"

She shook her head. "No, Yves. You may go now."

"Je suis votre serviteur." He bowed, then left the room.

It had not taken long for news of Isabelle's escapades in America to reach the castle. *Tante* Elysse had fired off a blistering letter to Juliana, taking her to task for casting the poor child into the night without anything to call her own. Juliana had wanted to point out to the woman that she was writing her letter from her beach house in Bermuda and not from the poor child's side, but she controlled the impulse. Her aunt's opinion was of little interest to her. Elysse had turned away from Perreault long before Juliana was born. There was no reason to pay any attention to her ramblings at this late date.

She reached into the box and withdrew a sheaf of newspaper clippings. Isabelle on television. Isabelle coming out of a boutique, packages in hand. Isabelle at the Russian Tea Room, Lutece, and 21.

Juliana leaned forward, intrigued. Isabelle on the arm of Daniel Bronson? She should have known the slut would not remain without a man for long. Isabelle's choice surprised her, however. Certainly she could have done better than be bedded by an American.

How gratifying to know that perhaps he was the best she could do. She wanted nothing but the worst for her beloved sister.

Last month Honore had suggested that Juliana free her sister's trust fund. "It serves no purpose, dear child. Let the girl have her money. What she does with it cannot compromise your happiness in any way."

Juliana had considered his suggestion then rejected it. It appeared that Isabelle had overcome her financial difficulties through an appalling bourgeois clothing venture. Juliana saw no need to help fund the undertaking.

"I will not reward treachery," she said to her father-in-law. "Not for any reason."

Neither she nor Honore mentioned Eric's part in it. Honore understood his son's shortcomings. Juliana was willing to overlook them. He was her husband. And, if the gods were with her, one day soon he would be the father of her son, the next ruler of Perreault.

The intercom on her desk buzzed. The nanny, a plain-faced Swede, informed her that Victoria had been bathed and awaited her mother's good night.

"I am unavoidably detained," Juliana said smoothly. "I shall see her in the morning for breakfast."

The nanny began to protest, but Juliana cut her dead. It was growing harder and harder to find help who understood their place. Certainly she need not spend her time explaining herself to an employee. Victoria was four months old. It was highly unlikely she would know the difference between her mother and her nanny. If she did, she would learn to adjust the same as her mother had before her.

For the first few weeks, Daniel's apartment on the forty-ninth floor was their refuge from the world. He gave Isabelle her own set of keys on their second night together. Both were equally surprised, but neither said anything about it. Isabelle was determined to maintain her own sense of herself despite the overwhelming urge to seek safety in Daniel's arms. As for Daniel, he veered between admiration of her burgeoning independence and the strong male desire to own her.

Isabelle discovered that being profitably famous was a time-consuming venture, something Daniel could have told her if she had asked. Based on the incredible volume of orders for the "Princess dress," Ivan had hired an advertising agency to put together a promo campaign featuring Isabelle, and she spent a goodly number of hours posing for a camera in a series of beautifully embroidered dresses. Ivan was a clever businessman, and he'd divided the line into ready-to-wear and custom made. In a moment of rash enthusiasm, Isabelle had agreed to personally embroider two dresses a month for women willing to pay the price. To her amazement, the price was enough to feed a family for a year.

Daniel had a few anxious moments in late October when it seemed as if the Japanese investors would back out of the deal with Bron-Co, but thanks to Matty's shrewd business sense, the deal held firm. Unlike New York's other real estate baron, Donald Trump, the Bronson family's fortune was built on a solid and wholly owned foundation of already developed real estate properties that were bringing in steady profits.

Maxine, of course, knew all about Daniel, but Isabelle stubbornly refused to bring the two of them together. Introducing him to Maxine would make the whole affair seem much too important, much too permanent, and she kept coming up with lame excuses to keep them apart.

In mid-November, Daniel finally had enough of Isabelle's reluctance and, over dinner at his apartment, he issued an ultimatum.

"Either you introduce me to Maxine in the next ten days, or it's over between us." He handed her a sizzling platter of shrimp scampi, then dished one up for himself.

"Whatever you say." Isabelle breathed deeply of the wonderful aroma. "You, Mr. Bronson, are the world's most wonderful chef. These shrimp smell divine!"

"To hell with the shrimp," he said, sitting down opposite her. "Did you hear what I said?"

She popped a shrimp into her mouth and sighed with rapture. "Food of the gods! Handsome, rich, and a wonder in the kitchen. I—"

He grabbed her plate and yanked it away from her. "No answers, no food."

"How dare you!"

"Can the royal outrage, princess. It won't work this time. I want to meet Maxine."

"Good heavens," she said with an amused laugh. "Why all the fuss? Of course you can meet Maxine." Even if the thought did send flutters up her spine. "Perhaps around Christmas."

"Perhaps next week."

"Next week she'll be in Florida with Ivan at a trade show."

"Thanksgiving at the latest."

"When is Thanksgiving?" she asked.

"Fourth Thursday in November."

"It's an important American holiday, isn't it?"

He nodded. "You're avoiding the question, princess."

"My shrimps are getting cold."

"Screw your shrimps."

"Bronson! Your language is appalling."

"And it'll get a hell of a lot worse if you don't answer me."

"This is quite unfair," she said, bristling with indignation. "All of this fuss about meeting Maxine while you have kept your family hidden from me as if they were figments of your imagination."

"My family's an open book," he said. "Pick up any newspaper or magazine, and you'll find something about one of us."

"I know. I spent an afternoon in the library last week." Her grin was sheepish. "There are certainly a lot of Bronsons."

"And you want to meet them?"

She nodded. "It only seems fair." Perfect, she thought. He'd made it quite plain that he wanted to keep his family and his affair with Isabelle separate. Now perhaps he would forget this obsession with meeting Maxine.

"I'll pick you up four o'clock the day before Thanksgiving."

She stared at him. "What?"

"You want to meet my family. They want to meet you.

They throw a big bash out at the house in Montauk on Thanksgiving and they asked me to invite you. I didn't think you'd be interested." His look sharpened. "Ask Maxine, too, if she's not doing anything."

She was so surprised that she dropped her fork. It clattered against her plate, then slid to the floor at her feet. "I don't know—I mean, that's such—" She stopped. "I don't know what I mean."

"Yes or no, princess? Meeting my family isn't that big a deal."

But it was, and they both knew it.

Maxine Neesom was a handsome woman in her midfifties. Her hair was a deep red, graying slightly at the temples, and she carried herself with an air that could only be described as regal. Daniel Bronson wondered if she came by it naturally or through osmosis.

The moment she opened her mouth, however, he knew. Maxine was as real, as solid, as his parents. And every bit as blunt.

"So, Mr. Bronson," she said, opening the door and ushering him inside. "I'm thinking it's time we met."

He extended his hand, and they shook. Her grip was every bit as firm as he'd expected. "I've been thinking the same thing, Ms. Neesom."

He followed her into the living room, a comfortably elegant mix of antiques and starkly modern pieces that he found agreeable.

"My girl isn't here yet," Maxine said as she motioned for him to sit on the sofa, "but she said for you not to be worryin'. She'll be here any time."

Daniel nodded. At the moment he was more interested in getting to know Maxine.

She crossed to the bar. "I'd be offering you something fancy, but Elysse only keeps the basics."

"The basics are fine with me, Ms. Neesom."

"Whiskey?"

"Straight up."

Her broad face was transformed by her smile. "A fine choice, Mr. Bronson. A fine choice."

"My name's Daniel."

She considered him for a long moment. "Maxine to all who know me."

She poured them each a tumbler of whiskey.

Daniel lifted his glass. "To Bertrand."

Her eyes filled with tears. "God rest his dear soul."

They each took a long swallow.

Maxine lifted her glass. "To my darling girl."

"To the princess."

They sat together for a few minutes in companionable silence. Finally, he couldn't take it any longer. "Are you really her governess?"

"I suppose you'd be askin' because I look too young, but I've cared for the child since the day she drew her first breath."

"You love her, don't you?"

"Like she was my very own flesh and blood."

"And you want to know if I'm a decent, upstanding citizen."

"'Tis easy enough to find out about you, Daniel Bronson. That big fine Irish family of yours is known to everyone in this city. What you are to Isabelle is what would be turnin' my hair gray."

"You don't have to worry, Maxine. We have an open and honest relationship. No game-playing."

Maxine sniffed. "When a man and a woman come together, game-playing is unavoidable." She frowned at him. "You're old enough to know that."

"The princess isn't much of a game-player, Maxine." He took a gulp of whiskey. "She's set the rules between us."

"And you'd be going along with them?"

"With a few exceptions." He leaned forward, balancing

the whiskey glass on his knee. "Are you going to ask me my intentions?"

Maxine shook her head. "I wouldn't be needin' to, Daniel Bronson. One look at your face tells the tale."

Chapter
Twelve

"A truck?" Isabelle asked. "You drive a truck?"

Daniel inserted his key into the lock of the shiny black vehicle. "What did you think I drove?"

"I don't know," she said, amazed. "A Porsche. Maserati. Something—smaller."

"Welcome to New York, princess. If you're going to travel our roads, a truck's the best way to do it."

Four-wheel drive. Extra-heavy-duty shocks and suspension. Antilock brakes. She had no idea what he was talking about, but it all sounded quite exotic and terribly impressive.

She gauged the distance between the ground and the body of the truck. "I don't think I can do this without a stepladder."

"I had the running board removed a few weeks ago. Come on, I'll give you a boost."

He gripped her around the waist and lifted her into the air, swinging her up and into the passenger seat.

"Buckle up," he said, climbing into the driver's seat.

She did as she was told.

"This is marvelous, Bronson," she said as he pulled away from the curb and moved into the heavy city traffic. "The view is splendid from up here."

"It was this or a tank," he said as they neared the Queensboro Bridge. "Anything smaller is fair game in this city."

"Listen to you. There are times it sounds as if you hate this city."

"Sometimes I do. There's so damn much wrong with it and so much that isn't being done to make it right."

"Perhaps you should consider running for office." She grinned at him. "Mayor Daniel Bronson has a nice ring to it, has it not?"

"Forget it. Bureaucratic red tape brings out the worst in me."

She thought about the homeless people she'd seen sleeping on benches and in the doorways of expensive boutiques. "The first thing I would do is make certain everyone had a place to live."

He shot her a quick, curious glance. "That's what we're working on, princess. It takes time." Bron-Co was involved in a number of inner-city renovations designed to help house the homeless and disadvantaged in safety and comfort.

"So tell me, Bronson: What did you and Maxine talk about while you waited?" She'd begged the photographer to let her go early, but he had flatly refused. The thought of Maxine and Bronson alone together had sent her imagination down some frightening paths.

He looked over at her. "Nothing much."

"Surely you talked about something."

"Nothing you'd be interested in, princess."

"She must have told you stories about me."

"Why do you think we talked about you?"

"Isn't it obvious? I'm the only thing you two have in common."

He laughed out loud. "She loves you like a daughter."

Isabelle relaxed—at least a little. "She orders me about as if I were her daughter. She can be a most infuriating woman."

"I liked her." He grinned. "And I think she liked me."

Isabelle wasn't entirely certain what she thought of that turn of events, so she kept silent. Maxine certainly knew enough embarrassing stories about Isabelle to fill a book.

He pointed out the sights as they bounced across the rutted road called Queens Boulevard. His family owned an amazing number of office and apartment buildings. They even owned a pool hall and a night spot that boasted flashing lights and a crowd of oddly dressed young people waiting on line to get inside.

"We're stopping here?" Isabelle asked as Daniel angled the truck into a parking spot.

"For a minute," Daniel said, setting the brake. "Sal and Rose aren't coming out until tomorrow afternoon, and my mother needs the turkey in the morning."

"I'm utterly confused."

"Great," said Daniel with a grin. "That's the best way to approach Thanksgiving with my family."

He helped her from the truck and headed toward the Golden Cue.

"A billiard parlor, Bronson?" Isabelle stopped dead in her tracks. "I don't think—"

"Not good enough for you, princess?"

She hesitated. "I've seen American billiard parlors in movies. I hardly think they're the kind of place where . . ." She allowed her voice to trail off delicately.

Bronson laughed and swung open the door. "After you, princess."

Isabelle lifted her chin and stepped inside. The room was loud, smoky, and dim lit. A pair of elderly men sat near the plateglass window arguing heatedly about something called the Mets. A middle-aged woman in a pair of gold Spandex stretch pants leaned over a jukebox, a cigarette dangling from her lips. A young guy clad in black leather winked at her over his pool cue.

Isabelle didn't know whether to laugh or cry.

"Bronson," she said, looking up at him, "this is making me terribly apprehensive." This was the type of place that bred gunfights the way ponds bred mosquitoes.

"Hold on, princess," he said. "It's about to get interersting." He cupped his hands around his mouth. "Yo, Sal! Get your butt down here with that turkey before I raise the rent!"

Isabelle watched in utter shock as the room came to life.

The woman at the jukebox spun around at the sound of Daniel's voice. Her heavily made-up eyes widened in surprise, then she launched herself across the room with her arms spread wide. "Danny! Where you been keepin' yourself anyway?"

Daniel staggered under her onslaught then planted a kiss on her cheek. "Good to see you, Helen. How's the grandkids?"

"Four of 'em now," Helen said, casting a curious glance at Isabelle. "And my youngest daughter is expecting her first in May."

"Better watch out," called one of the old men near the window. "Pretty soon she's gonna catch up with you Bronsons."

The young guy in leather approached them. Isabelle had to swallow down the urge to hide behind Bronson.

"Hey, Dan." The two men slapped hands together in a very odd fashion. "How's it goin'?"

"Not bad, Frankie. You coming tomorrow?"

Frankie nodded. "The old man says it might be his last Thanksgiving, and the whole family's gotta be together."

To Isabelle's horror, the two men burst into laughter.

"That's disgraceful!" Isabelle snapped. "How dare you make light of another's impending doom?"

Daniel placed his arm around Isabelle's shoulder. "Sal's been saying the same thing since I was five years old, princess. He's healthy as a horse."

"My old man'll live to be a hundred," said Frankie, "and he'll be buggin' me on the day he dies."

"Damn straight," said a voice from the doorway. A gray-haired man stepped into the room. "Now will one of you bozos help me with this goddamn turkey before I bust an artery?"

By the time she and Daniel left the Golden Cue, Isabelle's head was spinning. Daniel loaded the enormous fowl into the rear of the truck, then helped her into the passenger seat.

"Bet you never thought you'd be sharing a ride with a twenty-six-pound bird," he said as they eased back into traffic.

"I should say that's a fair statement."

"You're looking a little shell-shocked."

"I'm feeling shell-shocked."

He laughed. "Sal isn't always that hyper. He was excited to meet a real live princess."

"He thought I was from Peru," Isabelle said with a shake of her head.

"Sal's short on pronunciation but long on heart."

"Where on earth do you know him from?"

"He's my dad's best friend." He shot her a sidelong glance at a traffic light. "They went to school together."

"And your father still keeps up with him?"

"My old man's not about to let a few million dollars get in the way of a good friendship."

"Sal said your family owns half of New York City," she said as they drove past the sports restaurant Daniel's father had built years ago near the site of the World's Fair.

"We're working on it."

"How does it feel to be so wealthy?"

"How does it feel to be a princess? If it's all you've ever known you have nothing to compare it to."

She thought of the stories she'd heard about Matty's rise to wealth. "I thought your father was a self-made man."

"He is, but by the time I came along, he was on his way. Trust me, princess. My childhood was anything but deprived."

"Will all of your brothers and sisters be at your parents' house?"

"Getting cold feet?"

"You must admit you do have an uncommonly large family, Bronson."

"What can I say? We're Catholic."

He had her laughing out loud as he described each of his siblings in trenchant detail. By the time he launched into capsule portraits of their spouses, Isabelle was holding her sides.

"And there must be nieces and nephews," she prodded, eager to know more.

"Eleven of them." He chuckled. "Katie's going to go crazy when she meets you. She wants to be a princess when she grows up."

Sudden tears burned behind her lids. "I think she can do better than that." In truth, little Katie already had. Katie had a family who loved her.

The princess didn't think he noticed, but Daniel had a sixth sense when it came to a woman's tears. All that talk about family coming so close on the heels of her father's death had obviously triggered a rush of emotion. Her face was turned toward the window as she pretended to be fascinated by the lights of Nassau County as the truck zoomed past. Once again he was acutely aware of the differences between them, not just in experience but in expectations.

He accepted the idea of happiness as a matter of course. The princess didn't quite believe it existed, and he wondered if she ever would.

* * *

Isabelle dozed for a while, her face pressed against the window of the truck. She woke up at the Patchogue-Shirley exit where Daniel found a McDonald's and introduced her to her first Big Mac with fries. Daniel laughed at the way she gawked at the cardboard carrying case for the sodas and the hamburgers wrapped in paper. It was all quite overwhelming.

"American cuisine not up to your standards?"

She nibbled at a French fry. "American cuisine is wonderful," she said with forced brightness. "It seems I'm simply not as hungry as I thought."

The truth was that Isabelle was fighting a dreadful attack of nerves that had her stomach too tied up in knots to eat. The closer they got to Montauk, the more apprehensive she became. His family was so big, and it sounded as if they all actually liked each other. She had no idea how they would feel about her coming into their close-knit world—not that she was likely to be a permanent part of that world. Both she and Daniel knew the likelihood of that occurrence was too tiny to merit thought.

"The princess is here! The princess is here!"

Isabelle stopped dead in her tracks in the driveway. "What on earth—?"

Bronson put his arm around her shoulder and squeezed. "That sounds like Katie. She's six years old. She's the one who wants to be a princess when she grows up."

She glanced down at her corduroy trousers and woolen cape. "I hope she won't be disappointed. This is hardly Cinderella's ball gown."

"Don't sweat it, princess. You couldn't disappoint her if you tried."

Isabelle plunged her hands into the pockets of her trousers so no one would see them tremble. The last time she'd been this nervous was the day her father asked her to present his thirty-minute speech to the Perreault Agricultural Collective on the benefits of compost to a group of disgruntled farmers.

The driveway was crowded with automobiles. Daniel's truck was parked between two other similar-looking vehicles. The Bronsons obviously enjoyed their trucks. A Mercedes nudged a Volvo while a Porsche was half in, half out of the garage. There were other cars, as well, but she wasn't close enough to see their make. Not a limousine or Rolls-Royce in the assortment.

She could hear the ocean beyond the house. The crisp air carried with it the wonderful smell of salt water, and she wondered if she'd get the opportunity to see the light of the full moon dance across the waves.

The house itself was huge and rambling with four wide steps that led up to a spacious porch. She and Daniel had no sooner reached the top step when the front door swung open, and she found herself swept into the foyer on a sea of Bronsons.

"Forgive us if we don't know the right protocol," said a comfortably round, dark-haired woman who introduced herself as Daniel's mother, Connie. "But we want you to know that any friend of Danny's is a welcome guest in our house." Connie then proceeded to execute an off-balance curtsy, hanging onto her husband's arm for balance.

Matty Bronson pumped Isabelle's hand. "A pleasure, Princess Isabelle. I knew your father and respected him. It's a great loss."

She looked into his green eyes—now she knew where Daniel got them—and saw nothing but sincerity. "Thank you, Mr. Bronson. I shall always miss him."

"Enough with the Mister business," said Matty gruffly. "The name is Matty."

"Please call me Isabelle," she said. She felt a tugging at her sleeve and looked down into the blue eyes of the most adorable little blond girl she'd ever seen.

"Are you really a princess?" asked the child. She wore a

bright-blue nightshirt and huge slippers in the shape of bunny rabbits.

Isabelle crouched down. "I'm really a princess."

"My name is Katie. I wore a princess costume for Halloween. My mommy made it for me."

"I'm sure you were a beautiful princess, Katie. Did you have a tiara?"

Katie popped a thumb in her mouth. "Wha's that?"

Isabelle ruffled her hair with her fingers. "A crown," she said. "A beautiful sparkling crown to show everyone you're a princess."

"Are you married to a king?" asked Katie.

"Katie!" Her mother's warning voice rose above the crowd.

Isabelle smiled. "I'm not married to anyone," she said easily.

"Do you want to be married?" Katie asked. "I do. I want to marry a handsome prince."

"Don't you remember what I told you, Katie?" Connie Bronson spoke up. "Uncle Danny and the princess are good friends."

Katie digested that bit of information, then asked the inevitable question. "Are you and Uncle Danny going to get married?"

"I'm not going to get married for a very long time, Katie." She stood up again. God only knew what the next question might be.

"Nice save," muttered Daniel. "By this time tomorrow you'll have it down to an art form."

Isabelle quickly decided she would settle for remembering everyone's names. The sheer number of relatives was daunting. Four sisters, two brothers, six spouses, and a slew of children, most of whom Isabelle wouldn't meet until the morning. Blue jeans and T-shirts seemed to be the accepted uniform on both men and women alike. They were loud and friendly, and she had to keep reminding herself that each and every person in that room was a millionaire, for none of the obvious trappings of wealth were visible. For one thing, there wasn't a servant in sight.

"Certainly your mother doesn't care for this house herself," she said as Daniel led her upstairs to the room they would be sharing. "A house this size should have a staff of at least five."

"Mom has help," Daniel said, ushering her into a large, L-shaped room at the far end of the hall, "but she and Dad don't believe in asking anyone to work on holidays."

It was more than Isabelle could comprehend. "At home it is considered an honor to serve. Especially at times of celebration."

"Here it's considered a job."

The difference defined all that separated her experience from Daniel's. "There is much I don't understand." She sank onto the edge of the bed. "There are times I feel as if I had been dropped into your country from another planet entirely."

He sat down next to her. "My family can be overwhelming. Want me to ask them to back off?"

She shook her head. "It isn't them, Daniel. I suppose I am tired, that's all." She had spent most of the day posing for a magazine cover and granting radio interviews. "The same questions over and over, as if there is nothing more fascinating in this world than to live in a castle and have people bow to you."

"You have to admit it looks pretty glamorous from the outside."

"You have no idea, Bronson. Simply no idea."

He watched as she rose from the bed to unpack her clothing. It was the closest she'd come to talking about her life in Perreault since the day she'd told him about her sister's treachery. He found himself wanting to know more, wanting to discover what had caused that look of sadness in her dark eyes. She gave her body to him but she withheld her soul, and he knew that the time was near when that would no longer be enough to satisfy him.

*   *   *

Breakfast on Thanksgiving morning was Isabelle's first crisis.

"Everyone shifts for themselves around here," said Matty when she and Daniel entered the bustling kitchen. "Eggs, pancakes, bagels—make whatever you like."

Connie and one of her daughters were busy stuffing the turkey Isabelle and Daniel had picked up from the pool hall. Two of her other daughters were standing at the island counter, preparing vegetables and laughing together. One lovely red-haired woman sat in a rocking chair near the window, nursing an infant. Through the window Isabelle could see Daniel's brothers and brothers-in-law cutting and stacking wood near the end of the patio.

The room was a whirlpool of activity, and Isabelle froze in place.

"C'mon, princess. How does an omelette sound to you?"

"It sounds wonderful," she said, "but who is going to prepare it?"

"No servants on holidays," he reminded her, the slightest edge to his voice. "You're going to have to pitch in."

"There's one slight problem," she said as her cheeks grew hot with embarrassment. "I've never cooked a breakfast before."

"You're joking." He looked at her more closely. "You're not joking? You don't know how to cook?"

"Don't seem so surprised," she snapped, lifting her chin. "It is not on the list of necessary skills for a princess."

"Didn't they teach you anything in that fancy boarding school you went to?"

"They taught me to be a snob."

He grinned. "I have a feeling you didn't need many lessons, princess. It seems to come naturally."

She couldn't help it. She started to laugh, and that started Daniel laughing and before she knew it, the entire kitchen echoed with the sound. Her embarrassment and discomfort evaporated as if it had never existed.

"She doesn't know how to cook," Daniel announced to the throng. "Any suggestions where to start?"

"Scrambled eggs," Matty called out from behind his newspaper. "Easiest way to learn."

Connie, elbow deep in turkey, made a face. "Nothing is easier than a fried egg, sunny side up."

Katie tugged at the sleeve of Isabelle's cashmere sweater. "I can make scrambled eggs."

Isabelle looked at Daniel. "Tell me that isn't true."

Pat, Katie's mother, looked up from the carrots she was slicing. "Progressive day care," she said with a friendly smile. "Katie can cook scrambled eggs, toast, and squeeze fresh orange juice."

Isabelle rolled her eyes comically. "Is there some way I can enroll in this progressive day care school?"

If there had been any lingering doubts about their royal visitor, that remark dispelled them. As friendly as they had all been before, the atmosphere changed as she threw herself wholeheartedly into the challenging business of scrambling an egg.

"Now I know why Daniel is such a wonderful chef," she said to Connie as she moved the eggs around in the pan. "He comes from a family of wonderful chefs."

"I'm not so sure wonderful is the right word," Connie said, "but I always say if you like to eat, learn to cook."

"I wonder why I never thought of that."

"Because you're a princess," Daniel said, buttering some toasted slices of rye bread.

"But your family is rich," she persisted, lowering her voice. "Nobody has to do any of this. Why do they bother when it could all be done for them?"

He didn't say anything for a long time, long enough for her to worry that she had said the wrong thing.

"Daniel," she whispered as they carried their plates to the table. "If I've said anything untoward, I apologize. I just want to understand." Normal everyday life was so far beyond her experience that she found it difficult to grasp.

"I don't know what to tell you, princess," he said, holding her chair for her. "Maybe it has to do with being a family."

She looked around the huge, sunny kitchen. Connie and her daughters. Cathy nursing her baby. Little Katie sitting on her grandfather's lap while he read to her from the newspaper's comic strips. Three generations under one roof, gathered together to thank God for the blessings of the past year.

Daniel touched her arm. "The eggs are great. Give them a try."

She nodded. In truth she wasn't sure she could swallow around the huge lump knotted in her throat. *You're a rich man, Bronson,* she thought. *Richer than you'll ever know.*

After breakfast Daniel loaded the dishwasher, then went outside to lend a hand stacking the woodpile. Isabelle offered her help with the vegetables, and Connie handed her a knife and a pile of potatoes. Isabelle stared at them for a long moment, then began to scrape away at the skins the way she'd seen the kitchen maids at the castle do. She scraped away as much potato as she did skin, but nobody uttered so much as a peep of criticism. From potatoes she moved on to cauliflower, breaking apart the snowy white heads into florettes. She rinsed the florettes beneath cold water as Connie instructed, then piled them high in the basket of an enormous steamer.

"This is quite enjoyable," she said, drying her hands on a linen dishtowel. "It's really a very satisfying endeavor."

The women laughed, but there was nothing mean-spirited about their laughter. "Sometimes it is, sometimes it isn't," said Cathy, a psychologist and new mother. "It's the one household chore, however, that I won't turn over to someone else."

"Cooking is love," said Connie. "Plain and simple."

"I had never thought of it as anything more than nourishment," said Isabelle. She stopped for a second and smiled. "Except when Maxine would smuggle Sacher tortes and warm milk upstairs when I was home from boarding school."

"Oreos and cold milk," said Pat with a sigh. "Best snack in the world."

"Oreos?" asked Isabelle. "Is that a sweet?"

"She doesn't know Oreos!" Cathy leaped to her feet. "Ma, you do have some, don't you?"

"With this crowd?" Connie rolled her eyes skyward. "Pantry. Second shelf from the top, right-hand side."

Oreos were a success as were Fig Newtons and graham crackers. Isabelle was less than impressed with packaged chocolate chip cookies and cheese-filled pretzel nuggets. Twinkies, however, were the hands-down favorite.

"Junk food," said Isabelle, savoring the words as much as the taste. "I fear I will not have room for dinner."

Matty, who had just popped back into the kitchen to look for his glasses, heard her. "You need a long brisk walk along the beach," he stated in a tone that brooked no argument. He glanced at her attire. "Those little shoes aren't going to cut it."

"I have some Reeboks upstairs," Cathy said. "I think we're about the same size."

"And a heavy jacket," Matty advised. "The winds can be pretty brutal."

Five minutes later Isabelle, bundled in borrowed clothing, set off across the back lawn with Daniel's father. Daniel, who was playing football with his brothers and brothers-in-law, started to join her, but Matty waved him off. Daniel met Isabelle's eyes, but she smiled and gestured for him to continue playing. There was something familiar about Matty Bronson, even though she had met him less than twenty-four hours earlier. He emanated a sense of solidity, of strength, that she found herself drawn to, much as she was drawn to those same qualities in his son.

She followed Matty down a steep wooden staircase.

"We lost a lot of beachfront a few years ago during the

nor'easter," Matty said as they crossed the sand. "A lot of the newer houses got washed out to sea."

He pointed out one of the rebuilt houses, precariously perched on stilts that tempted Mother Nature to lash out and prove her power over mankind's follies. How typically American to believe in a future so bright that not even the untamed forces of nature could dampen your optimism. It was a far cry from the stone castles and brick estates of her own upbringing, where homes were built to withstand not only the forces of nature but the onslaught of man as well.

They talked idly as they walked along. Matty told her about the lighthouse at the tip of the island. "I suppose two hundred years of history doesn't sound like much to you," he said with a shake of his head. "Around her it borders on antiquity."

"One of the boarding schools I attended was built during the reign of Queen Elizabeth." She paused, then laughed. "The first one, that is."

"A lot of history within the walls of your own castle, Isabelle. I only wish I'd made it back to Perreault for the Tricentennial. It would've been great to see Bertrand one more time."

Isabelle looked out toward the water, focusing on a fishing boat cutting across the choppy waves.

Matty put his arm around her shoulder and gave a quick, awkward squeeze. "Didn't mean to bring up a sad subject, Isabelle. I apologize."

"You need not apologize for a thing," she said, meeting his eyes. "I know my father thought highly of you. Now I understand why."

"One thing I never did understand was what your old man saw in Honore Malraux."

Isabelle stiffened slightly. "Honore is a lovely man, Matty. He's been very good to my family."

"The only family Malraux is good to is his own," Matty said. "That conniving son of a bitch has left a trail across Europe you wouldn't believe."

"I have heard the talk," Isabelle conceded, "but the man I know is different indeed."

"Glad you're out of there," Matty said. "You're better off over here, making a fresh start."

Isabelle smiled. "Fresh starts, as you put it, can be frightening."

"Not for you," Matty said with a grin much like Daniel's. "I've got a feeling you're going to do just fine on this side of the Atlantic."

They sat down on an overturned rowboat near the water's edge. Isabelle drew her knees up under her chin and wrapped her arms about her legs.

"Do you miss Perreault?" Matty asked, zipping up the front of his jacket as high as it would go.

She considered his question. "Not very. In truth I never spent all that much time there."

"You and your sister were in boarding schools."

She shook her head. "Only I was," she said quietly. "Juliana was tutored at home."

"Nothing wrong with being homesick. Danny had a beaut of a case when he went off to college. He called so much I threatened to get a WATS line installed in his dorm."

"But you still took his calls."

His expression was puzzled. "He's my son. My flesh and blood. You don't turn away from family."

"But there are times when family turns away from you."

"I know what happened," he said, his gruff voice sounding oddly gentle. "It won't last, Isabelle. You and your sister will get back together. Blood tells."

"I'll never go back there." The vehemence in her tone shocked even Isabelle. "I no longer care what happens to any of them."

"You feel that way now, but it'll change. Home is the one place you can't escape."

"That's not my home, Matty. I don't think it ever was."

He patted her hand, and they sat together in silence, watching the play of sunlight on the gray-blue ocean and the way the seagulls darted beneath the whitecaps in search of food. What would it be like, she wondered, to be part of a family like Matty's? To know you were loved no matter what, that home was there waiting for you, however far away you wandered.

As the day wore on, the house continued to fill with family and friends until Isabelle wondered if the crowd would spill out onto the deck and down to the beach. She helped set the enormous table in the dining room and the three additional tables in the foyer and kitchen. Apparently it was an American custom to seat the children at their own table, separate from the adults. Graduation to one of the adult tables was viewed as a welcome rite of passage. One of Daniel's nephews, a handsome young man named Tony, was having his first holiday meal with the adults, and he didn't hesitate to lord it over his siblings and cousins.

Sal and his wife Rose arrived *en famille* a little after three o'clock. Isabelle greeted the retired butcher with a warm hug.

"I told ya so," Sal said, turning to grin at his wife. "I did meet the princess at the pool hall last night."

"Oh, great," said Rose, rolling her eyes in mock dismay. "As if he doesn't already think who the hell he is."

The Brooklyn contingent of Matty's friends arrived in Bernie Pearlstein's rented minivan while the rest of the Queens brigade came out on the Long Island Railroad.

Dinner was loud, raucous, filled with arguments about everything from sex to politics to religion. Sal argued energetically with his best friend Matty, a multimillionaire, about the stock market. Cathy, the psychologist, tried to mediate, but both her father and godfather told her to mind her own business because they were thoroughly enjoying themselves.

Everyone, it seemed, also had an opinion about Daniel's business dealings in Japan. She listened as Daniel detailed the hotel-convention center he was building outside Tokyo.

"You've got a lot of work ahead of you, Danny," said his father. "Better brush up on your Japanese. After New Year's, you're gonna be needing it because you can't postpone the trip any longer."

"I don't see why you can't send one of those fancy executives," Connie grumbled. "You pay them enough. Can't they make sure things get off to a good start?"

"This company was built with hands-on supervision," Matty said with conviction, "and that's the way we're gonna continue." The Bronson name stood for quality, and nobody cared more about keeping it that way than another Bronson. "Bad enough you've put this trip off as long as you have."

January, thought Isabelle, feeling a wave of sadness wash over her. *January is when it will end.*

Daniel made them all laugh with his attempts to speak Japanese. Isabelle did her best to join in, but her heart simply was not in it. It was one thing to realize nothing lasted forever. Knowing when it would end—and how— was something else.

Cathy, the psychologist, tossed a piece of dinner roll in her brother's direction. "Wouldn't you love to be the poor sap stuck next to Danny on a fourteen-hour flight?"

"Claustrophobia?" Isabelle asked when the laughter died down.

"It's not the space," Daniel said, glaring at the rest of his family. "It's the altitude."

"You're afraid of flying?"

He nodded. "Despite the best efforts of my psychologist sister."

"I cannot imagine you being afraid of anything."

"Yeah, well, we all have our Achilles' heels. Mine kicks in about ten feet above sea level."

"You must have hated Perreault," she said with a shake of her head. "Especially the castle."

"Let's say I didn't spend a lot of time looking out the window. When I get around to building my dream house, it won't be five thousand feet up."

After dinner, Isabelle volunteered to help with the cleanup, but Connie wouldn't hear of it. "You're our guest, honey. We put you to work this morning. That's enough for one visit. Go! Have fun!" With that she placed her hands at the small of Isabelle's back and gave her a gentle shove in Daniel's general direction.

"I feel so useless," she said to Daniel as they went for an after-dinner stroll on the beach. "Everyone is so accomplished, so productive. All of your sisters are doing something marvelous with their lives, raising families, helping people, running companies. I cannot think of one productive thing I have done in my entire life."

"You put Ivan's factory on the map." Daniel stopped walking and drew her into his arms. "He's made more money in the past two months than he has in his entire life. I'd say that's being productive."

A brisk wind was blowing off the water. She reached up to brush a lock of hair off his forehead, then looped her arms around his neck. "I haven't seen much of you today, Bronson."

"I didn't think you'd noticed. You and my old man were thick as thieves."

"Jealous?"

He chuckled. "Should I be?"

"He's a wonderful man," she said in a teasing voice. "Warm and funny and quite attractive." She paused for dramatic effect. "Almost as handsome as his son."

"My whole family is taken with you, princess. Even Uncle Quinn who doesn't like any of us."

"I'm taken with them—even Uncle Quinn."

"They want you to come back for Christmas."

"How do you feel about that?"

"I want you to be with me for Christmas," he said bluntly. "The rest of it is negotiable."

Her heart seemed to turn over in her chest from the sheer force of the emotions his words evoked. *Nothing lasts,* a small voice warned. *Especially not anything as wonderful as this.* The specter of Daniel's trip to Japan threw a long shadow.

They made love that night in the big bed near the window, bathed by the light from the full moon. Once again he took her to a level of passion that bordered on the mystical, and she found herself crying softly against his shoulder after she climaxed.

She couldn't explain it when he asked, couldn't find the words to describe the bittersweet mélange of joy and sadness that filled her heart as she lay there in his arms. She knew that in this world nothing lasted forever, but would it be tempting the fates if she asked that the wonder they'd found together last a little bit longer?

Chapter Thirteen

The offices of Patrick Marchand were situated a few blocks from Harrod's in an office building that had never quite recovered from the blitz.

Juliana, wearing dark glasses and with her pale hair hidden by a Hermes scarf, waited for the driver to open the door of her limousine.

"You will wait for me here," she instructed the driver as she stepped from the car. "I do not know how long I shall be, but I expect you to be here for me."

The driver tipped his hat. "Right you are, miss. You look out the window and you'll see Clarence waiting here just like you asked."

She wrinkled her nose at the clumsy attempt at familiarity. How odd it felt to venture forth without the protective trappings of her position. It made her feel vulnerable, a feeling for which she had little patience.

But it simply couldn't be helped. She needed secrecy, someone who understood the necessity for discretion. Certainly she could never have turned to anyone at home. Indeed, not even in Paris could she have been guaranteed the confidentiality necessary for the task. The Malraux name was even more famous than her own, at least within certain cosmopolitan circles.

Quickly she made her way through the crowd of pedestrians that clogged the sidewalk, hurrying about on their sad little chores. It was hard to imagine what they did with their time. She rarely gave much thought to how other people lived their lives. She found the problems of others to be of paramount disinterest, and never more so than now when her own life teetered on the verge of ruin.

Marchand's office was on the second floor. Juliana stepped carefully over some cigarette butts and disgusting wads of chewing gum scattered like confetti on the stairs. She hated disorder; dirt was incomprehensible. If the man hadn't come so highly recommended, she would turn on her heel and flee.

She breathed a sigh of relief when she stepped into the anteroom. The walls were lacquered a restful shade of icy gray with the slightest blue undertone. The fitted carpet was the same hue but in a darker tone.

His receptionist, a slim young woman with a sleek cap of honey-blond hair, smiled up at her. It was obvious the receptionist recognized Juliana, but she gave no indication of undue curiosity. "I'll let Mr. Marchand know you have arrived."

Moments later, Marchand stepped into the anteroom. He was a tall, good-looking man of about fifty who understood the proper way to treat a woman of Juliana's position. Instantly she felt as if there might be hope.

He ushered her into his office, then offered her a chair. She removed her sunglasses and unwrapped the scarf, folding it into a neat square and placing it in her lap.

"May I offer you some tea, Princess Juliana?"

She shook her head. "I should like to proceed."

"As you wish." He looked down at a foolscap pad positioned in the center of his desk blotter. "You say your husband has been straying. . . ."

After a weekend in Montauk coping with his family's brand of controlled chaos, Daniel usually was glad to return to Manhattan. The city's insanity seemed tame compared to a few days spent in close proximity to the rest of the Bronson clan. More often than not, he was glad to say good-bye to the woman who had accompanied him. He was a loner by nature. Sharing space didn't come easily. Solitude was as important to him as companionship was for someone else.

Adding Isabelle to the mix changed everything. Watching her laugh with his family, making love to her by the light of the full moon, and catching another glimpse of the real woman behind the smile awakened in him a longing that went far beyond sex. He found himself wishing the weekend didn't have to end and that they didn't have to say good-bye now that it had.

He parked the truck two blocks away from her apartment, then walked her to her door.

"I'm going to miss you," she said, kissing the underside of his jaw as they clung together in the foyer.

"You don't have to," he said, holding her close. "The truck's parked in a legal spot for a change. I'll spend the night."

He sensed a slight pulling away. "I don't think that's a good idea."

"Had enough of me?" *Cool it, Danny. You sound like a kid.*

She kissed him again. "That isn't possible. It wouldn't be fair to Maxine. She's a very old-fashioned, traditional woman. Besides, she thinks of me as her daughter."

Normally he would have accepted her explanation. Tonight he pushed a little harder. "I have a big, empty apartment, princess. Come home with me."

"I don't think so."

"You don't think so or you don't want to?"

"You're sounding angry, Bronson."

"I'm not angry. Just looking for an answer."

"Fine." She pulled away, turning into the little princess right before his eyes. "I'm tired and I have a long day tomorrow, and it might be better if I spend the night alone."

He raised his hands, palms outward. "Okay. Great. Whatever you say, princess. I live to serve."

"Oh, do be quiet!" she snapped. "That's a perfectly dreadful thing to say."

It was a cheap shot, and he knew it, fueled by the unsettling feeling that she was about to slip through his fingers like quicksilver. "You're right," he said. "I'm sorry."

She touched his forearm. "I had a grand weekend."

"So did I."

"I could be persuaded to try my hand again at scrambled eggs tomorrow night."

"Around seven?"

"You might want to eat a nutritious lunch, Bronson, as a precautionary measure."

He forced a smile. "I'll do that."

"Your family are wonderful," she said, using that odd Euro-grammar that he was finally getting used to. "Thank you for inviting me."

He pulled her to him and claimed her mouth with a kiss that carried with it all the fear and anger that had been building inside him these past few hours. She would go so far and then retreat, as if she couldn't quite believe that what they had together was real. He had the feeling that one day he would open his eyes and she would be gone, vanished like a dream.

She was soft and yielding in his arms, as warm and womanly as he could ever desire, but the sense that the ground was shifting beneath his feet remained long after they said good night, reminding him of all the reasons why it didn't make sense to get more involved.

"Great job, Princess Isabelle." The star of the radio program stood up and extended his hand. "You handled those phone calls like a pro."

"Thank you, Mr. Beaumont. You made the experience very enjoyable."

She glanced at her watch. Not yet noon, and she'd already put in a full day. A breakfast interview with *Women's Wear Daily* and visits to three different talk radio shows. At two o'clock she was slated to meet Maxine and Ivan at Tres Chic to be fitted for the only evening gown planned for the Princess collection. The wonderful weekend with the Bronsons seemed a lifetime ago. If only it hadn't ended with pointed words. Those pointed words echoed in her mind all night, making it almost impossible to sleep.

Liar, she thought as she rode the elevator down to the main lobby. The truth was much more complicated than that. She missed the feel of his body next to hers, the distinctive smell of his skin, the sound of his breathing in the heart of the night. She'd never imagined that what happened in bed between a man and a woman could be so powerful or that it could affect her in such a fiercely primitive way.

The elevator doors opened. She strode across the lobby, her thoughts tangled.

"Darling girl!"

She slowed her step for a moment and glanced around. Shaking her head, she continued.

"Isabelle! You must stop, darling girl, I've come a long way to see you again."

A hand on her shoulder. A familiar laugh. The floor tilted beneath her feet, and she found herself in the one place where she never thought to find herself again. In the arms of Eric Malraux.

*   *   *

"Maxine, Maxine, Maxine. Where is your brain, woman? Five minutes I'm talking to you, and you haven't heard one word."

Maxine shook her head as if trying to clear the cobwebs. "I'm sorry, Ivan. Now what is it you were saying?"

Ivan launched into a list of facts and figures about the Princess line while Maxine struggled to keep her mind on his words. All morning long she'd had the terrible feeling that disaster was lurking right around the next corner. It was the same dreadful feeling she'd experienced those last months in the castle.

She and Ivan had spent a wonderful weekend with his married daughter and her family in the countryside of northern New Jersey. It felt like home there, a gentler version of the mountainsides of Perreault. Ivan promised to take her to the house he owned in the Poconos in Pennsylvania, and Maxine looked forward to it.

The only disturbing event had been that first night when Maxine had sat bolt upright in bed, certain she had heard the unearthly wailing of a banshee, but the next morning Ivan's daughter Natalie had laughed and said it was only the sound of the neighbor's beagle howling at the full moon.

"Maxine!"

"Something's wrong, Ivan," she said, tears welling in her eyes. "I don't know what it is, but something dreadful is coming, and we can't do a thing to stop it."

"You're a superstitious Irishwoman, Maxine Neesom. The girl is fine. She'll be here in an hour for our meeting, and you'll see for yourself. Now put your mind to business."

Isabelle was bored. Deeply, profoundly, irrefutably bored. She stole a glance at her watch. A scant ten minutes past one o'clock. She and Eric had been together less than an hour, and she found herself praying for an earthquake or some other act of God to help her break free. He claimed he'd been in a taxicab on his way to *Tante* Elysse's apartment when he'd heard her on the radio and instructed the driver to take him immediately to the station. The story was meant to impress, but it left Isabelle even more bored, as if that were possible.

"More wine, darling girl?"

She shook her head. "Thank you, no. I have a long afternoon ahead of me."

"You've barely touched your food. Your appetite always charmed me."

"I must be coming down with a cold," she said. "I am feeling a trifle under the weather."

He considered her closely. "You are different, Isabelle. I cannot place exactly in what way, but you are not the same woman who left Perreault."

Her laugh was brittle. "I should hope not. Experience changes a woman, Eric. Even a woman as foolish as I was."

"You were never foolish, darling girl. It is I who—"

She raised her hand. "I'm afraid I do not wish to continue this conversation, Eric. I agreed to join you for lunch because you claimed there was a matter of some importance that needed to be discussed. Thus far I have heard nothing of any consequence."

"So wonderfully hot-tempered." He leaned back in his chair and favored her with a tender smile. "I have always envied you for living to the full extent of your emotions."

She pushed back her chair, causing a bevy of waiters to race to her assistance. "I'm sorry, Eric, but there is no point to this conversation. I appreciate the opportunity to see the photos of Victoria and the fact that you seek rapprochement for Juliana and me, but I am simply not interested." She tucked her purse under her arm. "And I venture to say my sister is not interested, either."

"Juliana is with child once again."

Isabelle's brows lifted. "So soon? Victoria is—what? Four months old?"

"Juliana is eager to have a son."

"Terribly eager, I should say. I cannot imagine that it is good to space children so closely together."

"Your sister is a determined woman. She usually gets whatever she desires."

"I know," said Isabelle. "I have had firsthand experience."

"We need time to talk, Isabelle. There are many things that need to be said, and we cannot say them all over such a short lunch."

"I have said everything I wish to say, Eric, and I have heard a great deal more than I wished. Have a pleasant trip back to Perreault."

"When will I see you again?" he persisted as she gathered up her belongings. "I will be in town for another two days."

"No, Eric." His meaning was unmistakable. "Not in this lifetime."

"Surely you must know how I feel—how I have always felt. . . ."

She left the restaurant, knowing he would be delayed paying the bill. The fates were with her, for a taxi was discharging a passenger right there at the curb. She claimed it like a native New Yorker, slamming shut the door behind her.

"Where ya goin', lady?" barked the cabbie.

"Anywhere," she said, sinking down into her seat. "As long as it's far away from here."

"This was the single smartest thing I ever did." Daniel reared back and landed another punch. "Should be standard office equipment."

Phyllis, notebook in hand, stood in the doorway and watched as he hammered the speedbag with a flurry of punches. "You didn't learn this in Harvard Business School."

"Even Harvard Business School doesn't know everything, Phyl." Another barrage of punches, each one harder than the last. "Some of the best moves you pick up on the street."

"You don't expect me to talk business while you're bobbing and weaving, do you?"

"I'm listening." A quick right then a left. "It helps my concentration."

"Well, it's blowing the hell out of mine." Phyllis rose to her feet. "Let me know when you're finished, Rocky. Then we'll talk." She paused in the doorway. "By the way, Isabelle called while you were on long distance with Umeki. She's canceling dinner."

He peppered the speedbag with jabs. "She want me to call her?"

"I'm just your assistant, boss, not your social secretary. You figure it out." She closed the door behind her.

Daniel hauled off and battered the speedbag with everything he had. When he finished, he debated the wisdom of doing it all over again, but his hands ached and his muscles felt more tense and knotted than they had before he started.

She was pulling away from him. It hadn't taken long. He'd felt it last night, heard it in her voice. All of that damn talk about Japan hadn't helped. What woman would want to sit there and listen to the man she was sleeping with talk about flying off to Japan to live for a few months? Absence didn't make the heart grow fonder. Absence made you forget. She knew it, and so did he.

"For the thousandth time, Maxine, nothing is wrong. I do wish you would stop asking me that. You're becoming quite annoying."

"The feeling is on me, lovey, and it won't be going away just because you say it should. Something is wrong, and I won't be resting until you tell me what it is."

"There's nothing to tell." Isabelle yawned and poured herself a glass of tea from Ivan's samovar. "Gigi's finished with the fitting. I believe I'll go home. I am exhausted."

"You should take a nap before himself comes over."

Isabelle glanced away. "I left a message for Daniel. I'm not much in the mood for dinner tonight."

"Aha!" Maxine stood in the doorway. "You are not leaving, lovey, before you tell me what it is you're hiding."

Isabelle opened her mouth to lie but was shocked to find the truth springing to her lips. "Eric is in town."

Maxine made the sign of the cross. "Mary Mother of God, what would he be wanting with us?"

Isabelle gave her a sidelong glance. "Not us, Maxine. Me."

"And I hope you'd be sending him packing."

"No," said Isabelle, "I sent myself packing right after lunch."

"Don't be tellin' me you ate lunch with him."

"Yes," said Isabelle, lifting her chin. "I was curious as to what he wanted."

"Curiosity can lead a person to ruin."

"Oh, for heaven's sake, Maxi. We shared wine and poached fish, not an assignation. I wanted to hear about Juliana—about the baby. Is that a crime?"

Maxine muttered something dark, but Isabelle paid her no heed. The woman was always hearing banshees in the night and feeling the cold hands of fate against the back of her neck. She blessed herself again.

"Will you stop that," Isabelle snapped. "He's a fool, not a monster."

"Fools can be more dangerous."

"Agreed," said Isabelle. "And that is why I walked away from him."

"And how did you feel, lovey, when you did that?"

"Free," said Isabelle. She sighed. "He showed me pictures of little Victoria. It hurts to know I have a niece whom I'll probably never meet. Juliana is pregnant again, Maxi. Can you believe that?"

"Poor little tykes to be brought into a world of confusion."

"Victoria is beautiful," Isabelle mused. "So fair—with huge blue eyes like Daniel's niece—"

"Daniel will agree with me," interrupted Maxine. "Time and distance are what should be between you and Eric."

"You're not to tell Daniel about this."

"You wouldn't be keeping secrets from him, would you, lovey?"

"We're not married, Maxi. It isn't necessary that he know everyone I see and everything I do."

"I doubt if Daniel would be seeing it that way."

"Don't you dare say one word to him, Maxi."

"'Tisn't my business to be sticking my nose in where it doesn't belong."

"Good," said Isabelle.

"Terrible," said Maxine. "Why hide something if you have nothing to hide?"

Daniel threw himself back into work with the same intensity he'd brought to hammering the speedbag. Phyllis left a little after six. "Don't work too hard," she said. "You've got a seven-thirty breakfast meeting with Dershowitz at the Plaza."

"Yeah, Phyl," he mumbled, engrossed in the specs on the Japan project. "You, too."

The telephone rang a few times around eight o'clock, but he ignored it. He didn't give a good goddamn who called. If it was important, they'd call back. If it wasn't, the hell with them.

A few minutes later he heard a knock on his door. "What is this?" he mumbled, tossing down his pen. "Goddamn Penn Station?" He crossed the room and opened the door.

"Sorry to bother you, Mr. B.," said Fred, the head of security, "but you weren't answering your phones."

"Is there a problem, Fred?" He wasn't in the mood for conversation. Not tonight.

"Seems you got a visitor downstairs. She says you're expecting her."

"I'm not expecting anybody."

Fred lowered his voice. "It's that princess, Mr. B. She doesn't much like being told no."

"Send her up." He turned away from the puzzled man as he tried to regain control of his emotions. He didn't like being taken by surprise.

What the hell did she want? he wondered, as he pushed papers around on his desk. Was she coming to tell him it was over?

A soft tap on the door. "Bronson." An even softer voice. "May I come in?"

He didn't look up. "Do what you want."

"Not a very warm welcome." A hint of arrogance laced her honeyed tones. He heard the click of the lock.

"You're the one who canceled, princess, not me."

He heard her footsteps approaching his desk. "I brought dinner with me."

"I'm not hungry."

"Pastrami on rye, pickles, cream soda." No response. "Phyllis said that was your favorite meal."

"Phyllis should mind her own goddamn business."

"Look at me, Bronson."

"I'm not in the mood for game-playing."

"I don't want to play games," she said, sweeping his papers off the desk.

"Son of a bitch! You—" He looked up. Her dark eyes were lit from inside with flame. Her hair was wild about her face. She shrugged off her wine-colored coat, then tossed it to the floor.

"Make love to me, Bronson," she said, lifting herself onto his desk. "Right here. Right now."

"What's going on?"

"I need you." The expression on her face brought him immediately to a fever pitch.

With a moan he crushed her to him, plundering her mouth, stealing her breath and making it his own. She moved against him with abandon, as if she couldn't get close enough to him, couldn't make it happen fast enough.

He pushed her skirt up around her waist, then tore her panties from her body with one fierce movement. She was ready for him, more than ready, throbbing and wet and eager. She fumbled with his fly, her hands trembling with need. He freed himself from his trousers and briefs.

"Slide to the edge," he told her, cupping her heat with his hand. She did as told, shivering at the feel of the cool wood against her legs. He spread her thighs. She was all pink and moist, beautiful everywhere.

"Now," she said, her voice a whisper. "Please—now!"

The sound of her voice was almost enough to bring him to climax. Clasping her buttocks, he lifted her hips and plunged himself into the warm softness of her body. They both came almost immediately in strong, fierce spasms that erased everything but the primal need to own each other, body and soul.

Afterward they didn't talk about what had happened between them. They had said all that needed to be said without words, which suited them both. Words always got them into trouble, pushing them apart when they longed to be together.

They picnicked on the floor of his office. Isabelle spread her coat facedown on the thick carpeting, then set out the sandwiches and pickles on paper plates she found in the supply cabinet adjacent to Daniel's office.

"It isn't cooking," said Isabelle as she settled herself down next to Bronson, "but you must admit I assemble quite a nice meal."

He grinned at her over his pastrami. "You're a regular Julia Child, princess. I'm impressed."

She narrowed her eyes. "Are you making a joke at my expense?"

"I never joke about pastrami on rye."

He opened her bottle of cream soda for her, then laughed as she got up to search the supply closet for a glass.

"You could drink it straight from the bottle," he suggested.

She shuddered melodramatically. "Heaven forbid!"

"Once a princess—"

She tossed a paper cup at his head. "I'm well on my way to becoming an independent working woman, Daniel Bronson, and I should thank you to remember that."

"That reminds me," he said, gesturing toward his cluttered desk. "I have the prelim advertising forecast Ivan wanted."

She leaned forward. "And—?"

"Things look great." He reeled off a few specifics. "Right product, right market, right spokesperson. It doesn't get much better than that, princess, not first time around."

"Oh, thank God!" she whispered. It was really going to happen. They were on their way to even greater success.

"The only thing you have to worry about is overexposure."

Her eyes widened. "The dresses are too short?"

He started to laugh. "Don't touch those hemlines. Overexposure means you're getting too famous too fast, princess. It's time to scale back until the line debuts, then you hit 'em with both barrels."

The metaphor was a bit fuzzy, but Isabelle understood the meaning. "What should I do?" she asked, pouring some cream soda into a cup. "Find myself some mountain hideaway and stay there until next spring?"

He met her eyes. "You could come to Japan with me."

She stopped pouring cream soda. "Would you repeat that?"

"You heard me, princess. I'm asking you to come to Japan with me."

She stared at him, her thoughts leaping in a hundred different directions. "Japan! I never—I mean, I'm so—" She started to laugh. "Are you sure?"

"Now who's answering a question with a question?"

"I know, but I never expected this."

"Neither did I. When push came to shove, I couldn't imagine being without you."

"I'm flattered."

"Yeah, but you're still not answering me."

"Six months is a long time, Bronson. I have responsibilities now. Maxine and Ivan rely on me."

"If you don't want to—"

She scooted closer to him. "I do want to," she said, reaching for his hand. "More than anything in the world. It's just—"

"Five and a half months."

She grinned. "Two months."

"Four and a half."

"Two and a half."

"Four."

She made a show of figuring out the dates. "Three and a half."

He scowled, but she could see the twinkle in his eyes. "How about you just bring your cute little ass over there as soon as possible, then go home whenever you want to?"

"I'd never want to leave you, Bronson," she said quietly, "but I cannot abandon Maxi and Ivan."

"You're changing, princess."

"Disappointed?"

"No," he said. "I think I like it."

Tell him, lovey. She heard Maxine's voice as clearly as if she were in the room with them. *'Tisn't good to keep secrets, no matter how innocent.*

She took a deep, steadying breath. "Bronson," she said, meeting his eyes, "I bumped into someone today. . . ."

Ten days after Juliana met with Marchand in his London office, a courier arrived at the castle with a sealed envelope. Juliana retreated to her private suite, locked the door behind her, then opened the envelope with the pointed blade of a sterling silver Georgian meat skewer that she used as a letter opener.

Her hands shook as she removed the packet of photographs. She could scarcely read the note attached, even though it was typed and in clear, concise English. She sank onto the edge of her bed and, drawing a deep breath, looked at the first photograph. Blood thundered in her ears, making it hard to think. Eric, clearly enjoying himself, was dancing hip-to-hip with a beautiful young woman whose dress was more imagination than fabric. The fact that his hand rested on the woman's derriere was not lost on his wife.

It was nothing more than she'd expected, and for that she was grateful. Honore had done his best to help Juliana to understand the way it was with a man, but in her heart she rejected his explanation. Reflexively her hand caressed her burgeoning belly. This pregnancy was as distasteful as the last, but there was no escaping the necessity of bearing a male child.

Her father-in-law had also been painfully blunt in his explanation of the arcane laws governing accession in Perreault. The possibility that Isabelle might bear a male child before she did made Juliana feel physically ill.

That a child of that bitch in heat would ever rank above the issue of Juliana and Eric's marriage—it was simply unthinkable.

She looked at the second and third photographs, but they were variations on the same theme. She began to relax as she flipped through a dozen more, then found another note, this one handwritten, attached to the last batch. "New York City," it read. The date was a few days earlier.

New York? Eric had said he was going to Buenos Aires. She supposed it was possible that there had been a layover in New York, but the thought did not console her. She tossed the note down on the bed then turned to the photos.

Her sister, dark hair flowing loosely about her shoulders, faced the camera. She looked aloof, a trifle bored, very beautiful. Eric leaned across the table, deep in conversation. She couldn't see the expression on his face and for that she was grateful.

"It doesn't matter," she told herself, repeating it like a mantra. Eric belonged to her in every way in which a man could belong to a woman. As long as she held the reins of power in her hands, he would continue to belong to her. His father had made that promise to her on her wedding day, and Honore would never let her down.

This was Isabelle's doing. She could feel it in her bones. Eric would never seek Isabelle out like this. There was nothing Isabelle could possibly offer him that was worth risking all that he already possessed. Yes, she was sure it was Isabelle who sought him out, trying to use her feminine wiles on him for some obscure purpose. Money, more than likely. The thought of her sister reduced to begging caused Juliana's lips to curve in a smile.

But there was the future to think of. Honore had urged her to release Isabelle's trust fund. Perhaps the time had come to heed his suggestion.

Telling Daniel about seeing Eric was a small moment in the fabric of their relationship, but it represented a turning point. Daniel wasn't thrilled that Eric had shown up in New York and he was even less thrilled that Isabelle had gone to lunch with him.

"He's a son of a bitch," he said bluntly, "and his father's a son of a bitch. You're better off without either one of them."

"Agreed," Isabelle had said. "And I love it that you're jealous."

"Jealous? The hell I am."

"You are, Bronson," she'd said. "Nobody has ever been jealous over me before. I think it's delightful."

"I think it sucks, but I'm glad you told me." He glared at her, and she loved it. "Just don't think that changes the fact that I don't want you to see him again."

"I won't see him again," she retorted, "but that's because I don't wish to see him again. You're the only man in my life, Bronson, like it or not."

"I like it," he snapped.

"Good," she snapped back. She couldn't remember the last time she felt so happy.

The next few weeks passed in a blur of activity. Christmas in New York was a season unto itself. Isabelle embarked on a round of parties, interviews, and photo shoots. She was becoming quite well known in the city. Cabdrivers beeped their horns when they saw her. "Yo, Princess!" one shouted to her just the other day. "Give 'em hell on Letterman tonight!"

Ivan had read the advertising forecast and agreed that it made sound business sense for Isabelle to step into the shadows after the holidays, which made her trip to Japan with Daniel possible. A major ad campaign would begin with a vengeance in April, with Isabelle as spokesperson and model.

The only thing wrong with her life was the idiotic cold she'd caught during a photo shoot on the Staten Island ferry and the fatigue that wouldn't quite go away. But those were small blotches on an otherwise wonderful landscape.

Two weeks before Christmas she was sipping her morning tea and thinking about her luncheon appointment with Daniel's sister when the telephone rang.

"We need you to come in and sign some papers, Princess Isabelle," said her banker. "Your trust fund was wired to the bank this morning."

"My trust fund—I do not understand."

"Apparently your sister had a change of heart and released the funds."

Isabelle doubted if Juliana would have had a change of heart unless considerable pressure had been brought to bear. What pressure she couldn't imagine, since the attorneys she'd hired had thus far seemed inept. "You are quite sure the funds have been received?"

"All that is required is your signature on some papers and the transaction will be official."

"I'm shocked."

The banker laughed out loud. "That is the exact response I expected."

She glanced at the clock. "I can be there within the hour."

"And that is the other response I expected."

Isabelle made a face at the telephone as she hung up the receiver. She hated to be deemed predictable in any way, especially by someone as dull and boring as a banker.

But she was too excited to stay annoyed at anyone today. Her trust fund! She'd never expected to see it again. It wasn't a fortune, but it would go a long way toward establishing her independence. When *Tante* Elysse returned in the spring, Isabelle would be able to find her own apartment, one large enough for a suite for Maxine and enough privacy that Daniel could spend the night.

All that wonderful money, and all she had to do was sign her name to a few papers.

Was it only only a year ago when she'd been eagerly awaiting Christmas Day, pathetically certain that Eric would ask for her hand in marriage and lead her off into a life of bliss?

"Never again," she vowed as she hurried toward the bedroom to get dressed. She would make her own decisions, chart her own course through life, and she would never, ever depend on a man for her happiness. Not even on Bronson.

Chapter Fourteen

"There's one stipulation," said the banker as Isabelle made to put pen to paper. "One that might make you reconsider."

Isabelle, who had been happily spending her money in her mind, looked up at the serious young woman. "Does it include a pact with the devil?"

The woman stared at her blankly. "Excuse me?"

"Sorry," said Isabelle. Was there a law against bankers with a sense of humor in this country? "And what is the stipulation?"

The banker looked at the ceiling, at the floor, everywhere but at Isabelle.

"For heaven's sake, will you just tell me?" Isabelle asked in exasperation. "Short of giving up my firstborn, how terrible can it be?" Probably some ridiculous, outdated marriage clause or something equally antiquated.

"You are not to return to Perreault if you wish to keep the money."

"Is that all?" Isabelle signed her name with a flourish. "I have no intentions of returning there as long as I live. This simply makes it official." She smiled broadly at the banker. "Now do I get my money?"

"Miss—er, Princess Isabelle, certainly you don't want me to hand you that sum of money in cash."

"Well, I suppose not. Where will you put it?"

The banker launched into a long and detailed explanation of all the ways in which Isabelle's money could grow even larger.

"Fine, fine," said Isabelle in exasperation. "But do I get a checkbook?"

She sailed out of the bank on a cloud of excitement, thinking about all the wonderful things she could do with that money—all the wonderful things she could buy. That beautiful cashmere set Maxine had been coveting, head-to-toe formalwear for Ivan, and for Daniel—

She stopped in her tracks. What for Daniel? She couldn't think of a single thing that he might like. She'd found a Saint Christopher medal the other day in an antique store and, cleaned and polished, it made an attractive gift but certainly nothing spectacular. She knew Saint Christopher had fallen from vogue, but as the patron saint of travelers he seemed a perfect choice for her reluctant globetrotter. Still, that wasn't enough. She wanted to find something smashing, so absolutely perfect for him that he would be left speechless. She might not know what the perfect gift was, but she knew who would.

An hour later, Isabelle rose to her feet as Cathy approached her table at La Cucina off Fifth Avenue.

Isabelle kissed the woman on both cheeks. "I am desperate for help."

Cathy sat down opposite Isabelle and placed her purse on the empty chair next to her. "So much for small talk. What's wrong?"

"I'm desperate," Isabelle repeated as the waiter gave them each a menu. "Christmas is days away, and I have no idea what to buy for Daniel."

Cathy laughed and reached for her glass of water. "What to buy for the man who wants nothing—the question that's been plaguing the entire family for years. He's impossible, isn't he?"

"Dreadfully so. I was hoping you might have some suggestions."

"Last year we settled on a fly-without-fear class at JFK. As soon as he heard the classes were held on a flight to Washington D.C., he backed out of it."

It was Isabelle's turn to laugh. "He's not a collector, he doesn't have hobbies, and he's not a clothes horse."

"Narrows the field, doesn't it?"

Isabelle leaned back in her chair and sighed. "I am at my wits' end."

"You could buy him something for his truck."

Isabelle made a face. "New tires are not terribly romantic."

"God knows he could use something to dress up that monastic apartment of his."

"I though of having that beautiful oil painting framed, but he'd notice if it disappeared."

Cathy shook her head in dismay. "He still hasn't gotten around to it?"

"It's leaning up against the wall. I was horrified."

"My brother marches to his own drummer. I guess after thirty-four years he's not about to change."

"I don't want him to change," Isabelle said, "but I do wish he was easier to buy presents for." She brightened. "A ski weekend in Vermont might be wonderful."

"Danny on a mountaintop willingly? I've seen him turn green on the top rung of a stepladder. I don't think he'd go up a mountain if it was a question of life or death."

"That does tend to rule out skiing," Isabelle said ruefully.

"How does he feel about scuba diving? At least then he would be below sea level."

The two women laughed out loud.

"So tell me," Cathy said after they placed their orders, "are you ready for Japan?"

Isabelle arched a brow. "Daniel told you?"

"Let's just say I figured it out. I didn't think he'd be able to tear himself away from you for six months. Not after the way he kept postponing the date."

"I thought he kept postponing the date because of other commitments."

"You're the other commitment, Isabelle. I thought you realized that."

She hadn't, but it was a wonderful thing to know. "Well, I'll only be there a month or so," she said. "I couldn't possibly leave Maxine and Ivan in the lurch, not with the line about to launch."

"How do you feel about long-distance romances?"

"A personal question, isn't it, Cathy?"

"Sorry. Occupational hazard." She grinned. "So how do you feel about long-distance romances?"

"That they're a poor substitute for the real thing." She toyed with her water glass. "And that if the man is as wonderful as Daniel, they are well worth the undertaking."

"Have you ever considered going into my line of work?" Cathy asked. "Sounds like you have a pretty good grip on what's important." Isabelle sneezed. "Now if you could just do something about that cold . . ."

After lunch they strolled up Fifth Avenue admiring the shop windows and chatting about Christmas traditions in both the United States and Europe. Cathy determined that Isabelle should see one of New York's favorite traditions, the huge Christmas tree at Rockefeller Plaza. Towering over the skating rink, the one-hundred-foot lighted tree was a breathtaking sight. The two women ordered hot chocolate and watched the figure skaters in their colorful costumes as they glided about the rink.

"Isn't this foolish?" Isabelle blotted her eyes with a lace-trimmed handkerchief. "I've never been so sappily sentimental as I've been the past few weeks."

"Love and Christmas," said Cathy with a sigh. "You don't need a Ph.D. to know it's a lethal combination."

Love? thought Isabelle with a start. That couldn't possibly be true. They were infatuated with each other. Certainly they lusted after each other. Sometimes they even liked each other. But love? That was something else entirely.

She considered saying all of that to Cathy in just so many words, but that seemed more effort than the subject warranted, and so she sneezed again instead.

"It wasn't supposed to be this way," Isabelle sniffled into her handkerchief on Christmas Day. "How could this possibly happen to me? I haven't had a cold in years."

Bronson handed her a huge glass of orange juice and two aspirins. "You've got one now," he said, watching while she swallowed the tablets. "Let's hope it's not the flu."

"It wouldn't dare be the flu," she said. "We leave for Japan in seven days, and I have seven weeks' worth of running around to do."

"I don't think you're going to be doing much running around, princess. Not in that condition."

"I refuse to stay in this condition," she said, her voice a miserable shadow of itself. "I can't stay in this condition. Damn it, Bronson, it's Christmas Day!"

"And we're spending it together just like we planned."

"You needn't be sarcastic."

"I'm not being sarcastic. It's a statement: Today is Christmas, and we're together."

"I look dreadful," she said, touching her red nose. "And I sound even worse."

He grinned. "We're together, but I didn't say we were having fun."

"I'd throw my pillow at you, but I don't want you to catch my germs."

"I appreciate that," he said dryly. "If I postpone that trip one more time, there'll be an international incident."

She sank down into her germ-riddled pillows, feeling dreadfully sorry for herself. How could he even talk about that stupid trip when she was feeling so miserable? Nothing seemed normal. Not her fingers or toes, not the thoughts inside her head. She felt as if she'd been taken over by an invading army and her defending troops had fled. "You should be with your family, Bronson, not cooped up with me in this awful apartment."

He shot a look at the clock across the room. "You're right. If I leave now I could be there by dinner."

"Fine," she snapped. He'd obviously been making an attempt at humor, but she refused to respond. "Leave me alone. Why should you be any different? Maxine deserted me, and now you're planning your escape."

"Maxine didn't desert you. You told her to go."

"Yes, but I never thought she would take me up on it." Maxine and Ivan went to his daughter's for dinner. Maxine had cooked an authentic Chanukah meal for Ivan and his family the previous week, and now Natalie was returning the favor with a Christmas feast.

"Don't offer what you can't deliver, princess. That's the first rule of doing business."

"I'm not in business," she retorted, reaching for a fresh handkerchief.

"Jeez, you're tough to take when you're sick."

Her eyes welled with tears. "See! You are angry. I knew it. Your entire family is probably angry with me."

He sat on the edge of the bed. "That's one of the good things about having a big family: Nobody notices if someone's missing."

She waved her lace-trimmed handkerchief in the general direction of the living room. "I've done all the shopping. The packages are wrapped. And now there's no one to give them to." She burst into tears.

"Damn it, princess, quit crying." Daniel hated the way he

felt when she cried, all clumsy and uselessly male. "You'll be better in a day or two, and we'll drive the presents out to Montauk."

"Y-you would do that for me?"

"Sure," he said. He'd walk the presents out to Montauk if she would stop her crying. "If you want to deliver your presents in person, you'll deliver your presents in person."

"Oh, Bronson . . ." She dissolved into another bout of weeping that had him pulling his hair out in frustration. The past few days she'd been like a human roller coaster, all towering highs and staggering lows. Talking to her was the equivalent of riding the Cyclone at Coney Island without a seat belt.

"What?" he asked, pacing the room. "What's wrong? I know getting sick for Christmas is a bummer, but it's not the end of the world."

She cried even louder.

"I'm calling a doctor," he said, heading for the phone. "You must have one hell of a fever." That was the only explanation he could come up with. Either that or insanity ran in her family.

"Damn it, Bronson, don't call the doctor." She punctuated her words with a sneeze. "I'm crying because I took ill before I could find a suitable present. I'd searched and searched for something big and wonderful. I even asked Cathy for ideas. I thought I'd have a few more days to look for the perfect gift, but then I took ill and . . ." She trailed her hand in the air as her words faded away.

He looked down at the medal hanging around his neck from a silver chain. "I always thought they gave Saint Christopher a raw deal. I had one of these when I was in high school. It's good to have him back on the job."

"He's the patron saint of travelers."

"I know." Actually, he loved the medal. It meant more to him than any fancy sweater or leather briefcase she might have found in some pricey, impersonal shop. Too bad she didn't realize it.

"I thought it might help you with your problem."

"According to my travel agent, you'd need Saint Jude for that."

Isabelle frowned. "Saint Jude?"

"Patron saint of hopeless cases."

"I'm fearless," she said between sneezes. "I'd fly in anything. The Concorde—a Piper Cub—a helicopter—" The sneezes outnumbered her words, and she fell back against the pillows, grabbing for tissues.

"Thanks, princess," he said. "You're great for the ego."

She looked up at him. "You must have done a good deal of shopping for Christmas, what with the size of your family and all."

"Yeah," he said. "I'm a shopping fool."

She waited, her foot tapping impatiently beneath the covers. He looked at her, his expression bland.

"If you're trying to torture me, Bronson, it's working quite well."

He slapped the heel of his hand against his forehead. "Damn! You're looking for a present."

She glared at him. "That might be nice, considering you forgot my birthday last month."

"I didn't forget it, princess. I didn't even know it was your birthday until you told me."

She hated logic. Especially male logic. "If you don't have a present for me, why don't you just say it? I won't be angry."

They could have heard his hoot of laughter back home in Perreault. "You don't fool me, princess," he said, still laughing. "You're thinking dungeons right now, aren't you?"

"No," she snapped. "I'm thinking guillotines."

He reached into the inside pocket of his jacket and withdrew a square box wrapped in shiny silver paper and tied with a big red satin bow. "I think this has your name on it."

Delightedly she reached for the box. Jewelry, she thought,

as she untied the ribbon. A ring. Definitely a ring—diamonds—mabye sapphires and diamonds. Dear God, could it possibly be an engagement ring? Wouldn't that be an odd twist of fate, to receive an engagement ring when she was no longer certain she wanted to marry? But how romantic—how wonderful—how—

"Oh," she said, as she lifted the top of the box. "A bracelet." It was a beautiful bracelet, a coil of thick, heavy gold with a spray of tiny diamonds on the clasp and a gold tiara charm dangling from it.

"Look inside."

"You had it engraved." She peered at the cursive letters. The date. His initials. Her initials. "How wonderfully sentimental. I'm surprised you didn't add your social security number."

"What's that supposed to mean?"

She blinked at him. "What do you mean, what's that supposed to mean? It was a declarative sentence, quite self-explanatory, even with my accent."

"If you don't like the bracelet, just say it."

"I love the bracelet, Bronson," she said through clenched teeth. "I'm not sure about the tiara."

"It's a crown," Bronson said.

"It's a tiara," she corrected him.

"The jeweler said it was a crown."

"Is the jeweler a princess?" she asked sweetly.

"If you love it, why haven't you put it on?"

"I wasn't certain it looked quite right with my nightgown." She snapped the bracelet around her left wrist. "See? Chanel couldn't have done better." She realized she was acting like a spoiled brat, but she couldn't stop. The flu must be altering her brain waves or something. *You idiot! You didn't want a ring from him. He didn't give you a ring. You don't want a commitment any more than he does. You should be happy!*

"Remind me to give you a gift certificate for Valentine's Day, princess."

With that he turned and stormed out the door.

From somewhere on the next floor she heard the strains of "Jingle Bells" being played. "Oh, do shut up!" she muttered and then burst into tears.

An hour later he returned wih Chinese food, vanilla ice cream, and a huge red poinsettia.

"Oh, Bronson," she said, beaming. "You didn't have to do that."

"Yeah," he said. "I think I did."

"Are you implying that I need to have my feelings soothed with presents?"

"Looks that way, doesn't it?"

They were off and running again, arguing over his hot and sour soup and her dish of Ben and Jerry's.

All things considered, it was the best Christmas either one had enjoyed in years.

Juliana slipped down the worn staircase and headed for the library, clutching her robe tightly about her body for warmth. Outside the winds beat ceaselessly against the walls of the castle, searching for any chink in the stones, any opening. On nights like these it seemed the castle was losing the battle. Frigid drafts of wind swirled about her ankles, curling beneath the hem of her ivory cashmere robe and making her shiver.

The dying embers of a fire still burned in the library fireplace. She drew her father's chair closer to the hearth and curled up in it, as much as her belly would allow. She had thought she would go utterly mad from the noise of music and laughter and endless conversation. By the time their guests had all retired to their respective rooms, Juliana's nerves were so raw she felt like weeping. Weeping would be a relief. She would welcome anything that would help dissipate the awful tension building inside her chest.

Honore had insisted that a Christmas gala was not only proper but necessary. "It's time to open the doors again, Juliana. We must think of the future."

She watched the dwindling fire as bitterness gnawed at her breast. She'd wanted to ask Honore what future he was talking about, for surely there was no future on the horizon for Perreault. They were deep in winter's grasp, and still the projects Honore espoused existed only on paper. For two days she'd watched while a veritable army of revelers availed themselves of her hospitality, and for what? Honore claimed this was a necessary part of the process of building good will with the same people who would soon frequent the casinos. All of which would matter only if the casinos one day came to pass, something that Juliana was beginning to doubt.

Honore had been quite pleased when she'd informed him that she'd released Isabelle's trust fund into her sister's hands. "You are a wise woman," he had said approvingly. "Better to annihilate an enemy with benevolence than anger her with justice." There was something wrong with that aphorism, but she chose not to pursue it.

So many parts of her life seemed to be spinning out of control: the nonexistent casino project, Eric with his constant traveling and lackluster lovemaking, Victoria who cried each time Juliana took her in her arms, and the most painful disappointment of them all—she laid her hands across her belly—the sonogram run last week had shown the child she carried was healthy, was developing on schedule, and was a girl. Honore had suggested she abort the child, but Juliana had been horrified. "You could try again almost immediately, my dear, and thus have the son you desire."

She had been so offended that he quickly apologized for his faux pas. "It's a new world, dear child. Choices are in our best interest." Juliana, however, strongly disagreed. Taking an innocent life was wrong.

It was the not-so-innocent lives that didn't bear closer examination.

Be careful what you wish for. The truth of that statement

made her laugh out loud. Locked away in the bottom drawer of her father's old desk was more information than she had expected or wanted. The pictures of her husband and Isabelle had torn at her heart, but she had found a way to deal with the threat. The information she now possessed was beyond her comprehension. The scope of it, the sheer ugliness of what was revealed in those papers had stunned her into silence. Money laundering was the least of it. The thought of drugs being moved through the principality made her blood run cold.

She knew Eric couldn't possibly be involved, if for no other reason than he lacked the cunning to carry out his part in the scheme. Honore, however, was another story. She had not been deaf to the whispers. Still she could not allow herself to confront him. The truth was, she needed her father-in-law. Bertrand had left behind an ocean of debts, both to Honore and to others. Honore had forgiven Bertrand's debt to him; the other debts remained outstanding, a constant source of deep embarrassment for Juliana and the principality.

"You are not to worry, dear child," Honore had said. "I will see to it that everyone is taken care of."

She would not question how. That was up to her father-in-law. He had made her marriage possible, and for that she would forgive him almost anything.

By the twenty-seventh of December, Isabelle was forced to admit her cold was getting worse instead of better. She and Daniel were due to leave for Japan in five days, and she hadn't even begun to pack or do any of the thousand things she needed to take care of before they left.

"Thank you for seeing me on such short notice, Dr. McCaffree," she said as the young woman entered the examining room.

"Problems don't come on a time schedule," the doctor said, flipping through Isabelle's chart while she talked. "It hasn't been that long since your last visit, has it?"

"September," said Isabelle. "You changed my birth control prescription."

Dr. McCaffree nodded. "Now what seems to be the problem?"

Isabelle sneezed.

"I see. Have you anything to add to that description?"

"Only that I require the services of a miracle worker. I'm short-tempered, tired all the time, and my throat is raw. I feel absolutely dreadful and I am due to leave for Japan on the first of January."

"We'll have to see about that." She withdrew a tongue depressor from a jar. "Open, please—that's it—I don't like the look of that throat. Stay open, Isabelle, while I take a culture."

Fifteen minutes later, the doctor came back into the room. "There's good news and bad news."

Isabelle sniffled then blew her nose. "Yes?"

"You don't have strep throat, but you do have a rotten case of flu, and it's going to get worse before it gets better."

"I can still go to Japan, can't I?"

"Of course you can," said the doctor, "only not on the first of January."

"But—"

"No buts. You could damage your hearing permanently if you fly before we clear up the ear infection you have brewing. I'll fill out a prescription and—" She stopped. "Are you sexually active, Isabelle?"

Her cheeks burned. "What on earth does that have to do with an ear infection?"

"If you're pregnant, I'll need to choose a different medication. We'd hate to expose the fetus to any side effects."

"I am—active, but I don't see how I can possibly be pregnant. I've taken my pills regularly."

"Only abstinence is foolproof, Isabelle. The bathroom is the second door on the right. You'll find a specimen cup on the ledge above the sink."

*   *   *

It's not possible, Isabelle thought as she waited by the telephone for the results a few hours later. She'd taken every one of her pills exactly when she was supposed to take them. The odds of becoming pregnant were so slim that she was being ridiculous to even entertain such a notion.

Dr. McCaffree was just being cautious. Americans loved to sue their doctors. McCaffree was merely exercising the prudence necessary in such a litigious society.

She tapped her fingers against the edge of her night stand. If only she didn't feel so dreadful, she'd go for a walk, anything to break the tension.

"Lovey, I made some—"

Isabelle fairly jumped out of her skin. "Maxine!" Her voice was down to a low rasp. "Must you sneak up on me like this? Consider knocking next time."

Maxine stood in the doorway balancing a tray of food. "I'll be overlookin' your bad mood while you're sick."

"How kind of you," she drawled in a particularly obnoxious tone of voice. "What do you want?"

Maxine looked pointedly at the tray. "I thought you'd be wantin' to play a game of canasta. What would you be thinkin' I want, lovey, me with a tray of food in my hands?"

"I'm not hungry."

To Isabelle's dismay, Maxine bustled into the room. "Hot chicken soup is what you'd be needin'."

"Chicken soup?" Isabelle had to laugh. "Is this Ivan's idea?"

"Better than these modern medicines that drain a person's wallet. I don't see that doctor making you well."

"I haven't started taking the pills yet."

"All this fuss and feathers for nothing." Maxine put down the tray on top of the dressing table then handed her a steaming bowl of soup. "Eat. Feed a cold, starve a fever."

"Will you take that out of here?" Her voice was strained with agitation. "I cannot bear the smell."

"I'm not leaving until you eat something."

"Maxine, I warn you—"

The telelphone on the nightstand rang, and Maxine reached for it.

"No, Maxi!" Isabelle caught the panic in her tone and took a deep breath. "I'll answer it." She waited a moment. "It's personal, Maxi."

"No need to spell it out, lovey. I know when I'm not wanted."

It was Dr. McCaffree. Isabelle clutched the receiver as if it were a lifeline.

"My nurse is calling the pharmacy right now, Isabelle. We're going with the secondary antibiotic." The doctor paused.

Isabelle swallowed hard. "I'm pregnant?"

"The test was positive," said Dr. McCaffree, "and I'm as amazed as you are."

"No," said Isabelle with a nervous laugh. "There is no one more amazed than I."

"Remember that nothing is infallible," said the doctor. "Not the birth control pill and not even the pregnancy test. I cannot confirm your condition without a physical examination."

"If I'm pregnant, how far along would I be?"

The doctor sighed. "I realize how frustrating this must be for you, but again I cannot hazard a guess without performing an examination. I'm sorry, Isabelle. I wish I could be more informative, but I cannot."

"I don't see how this can be happening. I've never given thought to having a child." She'd always believed motherhood to be somewhere down the road, years and years away.

"There are options available to a woman," McCaffree went on.

"No! I meant it's not that I—" She sighed. "I don't know what I mean."

"The first thing is to take care of that flu. Then we can discuss what's next."

Isabelle listened, her mind numb, as the doctor fired off instructions.

"Isabelle!" McCaffree's voice penetrated her fog. "Have you been listening to me?"

"No," said Isabelle, "I'm afraid I haven't."

"That's what I thought. Now write this down: Next Thursday, ten A.M. We'll know more after that."

Isabelle hung up the telephone, and a thousand crazy questions leaped into her mind. Dear God, was it possible that she was indeed pregnant? Next Thursday seemed such a long time from now, endless hours of waiting and wondering.

Even if her flu magically vanished between now and then, she couldn't leave for Tokyo before she saw Dr. McCaffree again. Daniel had postponed his trip many times before. She was certain he would do so again.

"Poor little thing," Maxine said to Daniel when she opened the door to him on New Year's Day. "She hasn't been out of bed in days. Too sick to do much more than lie there and cry her eyes out."

Daniel strode down the hallway toward Isabelle's bedroom. Damn it. The last thing he wanted to do was leave her, especially when she was so sick.

He tapped on the door. Nothing. He tapped again, then opened the door.

She was sitting upright in bed, surrounded by more junk than he'd ever seen in his entire life. Huge bed pillows, a half dozen afghans, books, magazines, needlework, and a remote control for the TV in the corner. The nightstand boasted a crystal pitcher of orange juice, a jug of water, two crystal tumblers, an ice bucket, and a Wedgwood candy dish piled high with cough drops. She wore a lace-trimmed yellow nightgown. Her hair was knotted on top of her head. Dark shadows ringed her eyes, and her cheekbones stood out in sharp relief in her drawn face.

"You look like hell," he said, staring at her pale face. "I can't believe those circles under your eyes."

"Thank you so much," she managed, her voice a hoarse whisper. "You look like hell, too."

He went to sit down on the bed next to her, but she frantically waved him away, muttering something about germs.

"I told you not to come over," she said. "Believe me, you don't need to catch this flu."

"I came to say good-bye."

Her eyes widened comically and, to his amazement, her mouth actually sagged open.

"It's January first, princess," he said. "My plane leaves in four hours."

"You're joking."

He stared at her. "Do I look like I'm joking?"

"You can't possibly be leaving for Japan."

This wasn't going well at all. "This can't be coming as a surprise to you."

"Of course it's a surprise," she said in what was left of her voice. "I never thought you'd go without me."

"I can't postpone it again."

"You postponed it before."

"That's why I can't postpone it now."

"I can't believe you'd leave me."

"You'll get over the flu and you'll come to Japan. It's not like you're on the list for a heart transplant."

She glared up at him through watery eyes. "You could certainly use one."

"Hey, I'm sorry you're having a bad time with the flu and you can't leave with me, but there's nothing I can do about that."

"You could if you wanted to."

"I should've known," he said, his temper finally exploding. "You can take the princess out of the castle, but you sure as hell can't take the princess out of the girl."

He'd never seen anyone look imperious in a nightgown

before, but Isabelle managed to do it. "That, Mr. Bronson, is the most ridiculous statement you have ever uttered."

"You could fly over in a couple of weeks," he said, with less enthusiasm this time. "That would give me a chance to get settled."

"I'd rather spend a week in hell."

"A week alone should qualify."

"I hate you," she said, bursting into tears. "I wish I'd never met you."

"Right now, princess, I'm thinking the same thing."

Maxine tapped on the door. "Your driver buzzed, Daniel. He said for you to mind the time."

"Do hurry," Isabelle said. "I should so hate for you to miss your plane."

"I'll call you when I get to Tokyo."

"Don't bother," she snapped, wiping her eyes with the back of her hand. "I have nothing to say to you."

"Great," said Daniel, turning toward the door.

"Great," mimicked Isabelle, glaring at his back.

He paused in the doorway and looked back at her. "If you decide you want a man and not a servant, give me a call."

Isabelle grabbed the first thing she could find on the nightstand. He disappeared down the hallway just as the pitcher of orange juice crashed against the wall. If only it had been his stubborn, insensitive head. . . .

Chapter
Fifteen

"You're pregnant," said Dr. McCaffree on Thursday morning.

Isabelle lifted her head and tried to peer over her sheet-draped knees. "Are you sure?"

Dr. McCaffree placed one hand on Isabelle's belly and palpated. "I'm sure."

Isabelle felt as if her brains had suddenly disappeared and only cold, dead air space remained. "How far along am I?"

"I would estimate that you're at the end of your first trimester or the very beginning of the second."

"But I thought pregnant women had morning sickness and strange cravings and . . ." Her voice, still scratchy from the flu, trailed off miserably.

"You're one of the lucky ones." The doctor stripped off her surgical gloves. "Why don't you get dressed and we'll talk in my office?"

Isabelle shook her head, clutching the dressing gown close to her chest. "Now, please. This is crazy. I just don't see how—"

"You've been having sex, haven't you?"

"Yes, but—"

"Then that's how, Isabelle. Sometimes nature is stronger than anything modern medicine can come up with to master her."

"That's all terribly poetic, Dr. McCaffree, but I think it's disgraceful that a woman can't count on something as important as birth control pills."

McCaffree reached for Isabelle's chart. "You came to see me the middle of September. That's when we did a physical and changed your prescription." She met Isabelle's eyes. "Were you with anyone then?"

Isabelle shook her head. "The first time was at the beginning of October."

McCaffree sighed. "And when did you begin the new prescription?"

"The beginning of October."

"That would explain it." The doctor said something about fluctuating hormonal levels and other technical niceties, none of which made any impression on Isabelle. McCaffree was quiet for a moment. "Now this is only a guesstimate— we'll know more after we run a sonogram—but how does June thirtieth sound to you?"

"Dreadful." She felt the hot flush of embarrassment color her face and throat. "I'm sorry. I can't believe I said that."

"No apologies necessary. I've seen every reaction there is to see when it comes to pregnancy, Isabelle. Mixed feelings are quite common when you're dealing with a life-altering experience like parenthood."

"Parenthood?" She buried her face in her hands, feeling dizzy. "I can't even imagine wearing maternity clothes."

"If you're beginning your fourth month, as I suspect you are, you'll be wearing them very soon." Dr. McCaffree smiled. "Think of it as a new market, Isabelle: hand-embroidered designer gowns for the mother-to-be."

Isabelle left the office with a pamphlet of information, an appointment card for a sonogram, and prenatal vitamins. She had also been issued a stern warning to finish her prescription antibiotics because it was important that she regain her strength as quickly as possible.

"Hey, Princess Izzy!" She glanced up to see a cabdriver cruising slowly along the curb. "Need a lift?"

She smiled and waved him on. It wasn't terribly cold out, and she was bundled up well. She needed fresh air, anything to help her think her way through this mess. The notion of going back to the apartment and facing Maxine's well-meaning concern was more than she could bear. Dear God, what would Maxi say when she found out Isabelle was pregnant?

And there was Ivan. The poor man had sunk every penny he owned into making a success of the Princess line. Without a real live princess, it was doomed before it debuted.

She refused to think about Daniel. He'd called her twice since arriving in Japan, but both times she'd refused his calls, forcing Maxine to say she was sleeping. Sooner or later she'd have to speak to him, but she wasn't looking forward to it. How dare he be halfway around the world when she needed him most?

You should be used to that, Isabelle. Has anyone ever been there when you needed help? Only Maxine, and it was long past time that Maxine had the chance to build a life of her own. Maxine and Ivan were an unlikely combination, but there was no denying the very real affection between the two of them.

A DON'T WALK sign flashed, and she stopped at the corner a block away from the apartment. Two businessmen to her left argued loudly about the Dow-Jones average while a young woman in tights and a bright red leather jacket jogged in place ahead of her. She glanced to her right and found herself looking at the most pregnant woman in the Western Hemisphere. The woman was about Isabelle's height and age, but there all resemblance ended. Her coat was stretched across a belly that looked as if it had been inflated with a bicycle pump into a cartoon version of pregnancy. Isabelle winced just looking at her.

"If you ask me, I'll scream," the woman said, to Isabelle's shock. "I know what you're thinking."

"Everyone seems to know what I'm thinking," Isabelle said. "I've been told I have a terrible poker face."

The woman nodded. "Stay away from Vegas, Princess."

Did everyone know who she was? Isabelle wished she could help herself, but she continued to stare at the woman's belly.

"Six months, since you didn't ask," said the woman as they started across the street. "Can you imagine what I'll look like at nine months?"

Frankly Isabelle couldn't. Her own pregnancy was beginning to seem frighteningly real.

A few minutes later she let herself into the apartment. Maxine was still at work. Dropping her coat over the back of a chair, she walked down the hall to her bedroom, walked across the room to her bed, climbed beneath the covers, and pulled them over her head—as good a way as any to cope with the next six months.

It was Tuesday night in New York, wasn't it? Daniel hesitated, his hand on the phone. Maybe it was Tuesday morning. Wait a minute. It was Tuesday morning in Tokyo which meant it was Wednesday—

Forget it.

He slammed the phone back down in its cradle. What the hell difference did it make anyway? She wasn't going to take his call as she hadn't taken the two that came before it. Any way you cut it, three strikes and you were out. Or should be, if you had a functioning brain.

On Christmas Day he should have realized that they were

on the fast track to the finish line. The way she'd acted about the bracelet would have tipped off a smarter man. But then, a smarter man never would've gone back to the apartment lugging Chinese food, ice cream, and flowers like some psychotic, sex-obsessed wise man bearing tribute.

Good word, tribute. Exactly what that spoiled, foul-tempered ersatz princess wanted. He'd known cleaning women who had more compassion for people in their little fingers than Isabelle had in her whole perfect, luscious, incredible body.

"Son of a bitch!" He glanced around the austere hotel room. It was too quiet. Too uncluttered. Too much like his apartment back in New York. Lately he'd found himself craving chaos and noise the way he once craved solitude and silence. The least the hotel should've done was install a speedbag for him. Instead, the concierge had looked at him as if he'd asked for an AK-47 and a target.

It always came down to sex. He and Isabelle had their problems, but when it came to what went on between the sheets, they were a match made by the gods. The more he had, the more he wanted. A simple equation, but one that had kept the most unlikely couples together through the ages. Too bad it wasn't going to be enough for them. No, he thought, pacing the room. He and the little princess had to talk to each other, try to have a relationship, when what they should've done was screwed each other's brains out until the thrill was gone and they could say good-bye and mean it.

If she wanted to talk to him, she could damn well pick up the phone and call him.

He was through.

"Lost your mind, lovey, that's what you've done. Living in the middle of nowhere in the dead of winter and with you in a family way. 'Tisn't right, I tell you. Nothing good can come of it."

"Oh, be quiet, Maxine. If I have to listen to you complain for the next two hours I'll go mad."

"I second that," said Ivan, behind the wheel of his 1976 baby blue Cadillac. "You want to hear complaints, Izzy, come to the office. Complaints she's got plenty of. Good ideas?" He shrugged his shoulders. "Not so many."

"Fine," said Maxine, going all huffy. "I'm no fool. I'll not be saying another word about the subject. Any subject."

Isabelle met Ivan's eyes, and they both burst into laughter. It was the first good laugh Isabelle had had in the two weeks since she'd discovered she was pregnant. Maxine wouldn't be able to hold her tongue long enough for them to cross the Delaware River into Pennsylvania.

She patted Ivan's hand affectionately. What a dear man he was. When Isabelle announced her decision to leave the city for a while in order to think through the tangle her life had become, Ivan had immediately stepped forward and offered the use of his cabin in the Poconos.

"Fancy it isn't," he'd said in his inimitable way. "Hot water, cold water, appliances, and a bed. You want the Plaza, don't come to the Poconos."

Isabelle didn't want the Plaza. She didn't know what she wanted except the chance to be alone. The enormity of her situation had finally hit her, and she'd experienced a blinding flash of revelation. She was pregnant. It didn't just mean a fat belly and huge dresses and puffing and panting on a delivery table. Inside her body another person was growing bigger every day, a person who was totally dependent upon her for all of his or her needs. Oxygen. Nourishment. Security. Not just for nine months, but for the next eighteen or twenty years.

And she'd have to teach the child so many things— things she had yet to learn for herself.

Was it any wonder she'd stayed in bed for two days with the covers pulled over her head after Dr. McCaffree had given her the news?

Finally it occurred to her that even if she stayed under the covers for the next six months, she couldn't avoid the inevitable; and so she got up, got dressed, and set about the task of building a life, which wasn't easy, considering she had no idea where to start.

God must have been watching over her when He'd seen fit to convince Juliana to release the trust fund. Knowing that she had a nest egg to fall back upon did make facing the future a tad less terrifying.

More and more it looked like she would be facing that future alone. Bronson had called twice, and she'd refused to speak to him. She'd been positive he would call again, the way men did in the romantic films she loved, but he didn't. She'd been tempted to phone his assistant Phyllis for his number in Tokyo, but pride prevented her from doing so. She'd also considered calling Cathy or Matty just to say hello, but they would have seen through that ruse in the blink of an eye.

You have a lousy poker face, princess, Bronson had said a long time ago, and she finally understood what he meant by that.

Ivan's "cabin" was really a small A-frame chalet-style house set at the foot of a mountain. It boasted a view of Lake Wallenpaupack, two working fireplaces, and the most comfortable—if unattractive—furniture Isabelle had ever seen.

"The kitchen's all electric," Ivan said, pointing out the stove and refrigerator and dishwasher as if Isabelle wouldn't recognize the appliances without a guide. "You get into any trouble, you call me."

Isabelle had purchased a microwave at Macy's before leaving the city and was sure it would be her passport to culinary delights from the frozen food counter of the local market. "I'll be fine, Ivan." She gave him a hug. "I appreciate this more than I can say." Preserving her anonymity had been important to her, given the circumstances. She would decide when or if to tell Bronson about the baby.

She didn't want his family reading about it in some sleazy tabloid publication.

"Are you sure you don't want me stayin' with you, lovey?" Maxine asked as she and Ivan made their good-byes. "'Twould be no hardship on me to live in the mountains."

"I need time to think, Maxi." She hugged the woman tightly. "And I need to be alone." Eric had found her in New York, and Honore had called on New Year's Day to wish her well. Isabelle had stood near the answering machine, listening to his familiar voice as he left his message. She didn't want to talk to him. She didn't want to talk to anyone associated with her old life. The only person she wanted to talk to was Bronson, and he was no longer calling.

"We'll be here every Sunday," Maxine said as Ivan nodded his head. "If you need it, Ivan's old Volkswagen is in the garage, and the keys are on the pegboard."

"And I have the phone numbers of the doctor, the police, the fire department, the nearest neighbor, and the taxi company on the pegboard, too. Don't worry," she said, laughing. "I'll be fine."

"And what about himself?" Maxine asked, referring to Daniel. "What do I say if he calls?"

Isabelle blinked back sudden tears. "He won't be calling, Maxi."

"But if he does?"

She sighed. "Just take his number, and I'll call him back." The odds of that happening were a million to one.

Isabelle had a difficult moment when Maxine and Ivan backed out of the driveway, then disappeared down the long dirt road that led to the highway. She wanted to race after them and beg them to stay, throw herself upon Maxine's ample bosom and cry until she couldn't cry anymore. But she didn't. Instead, she stood by the mailbox and waved until she couldn't see them any longer and then she went inside and cried until she couldn't cry any longer.

When she finished crying, she felt better. She inspected

each room, looked inside the closets, peeked under the beds, checked the view from every window, and tried the toilet and the sink. She was alone. For the first time in her life she had no one to rely upon for her day-to-day existence but herself—a scary enough proposition under normal circumstances, but with a baby growing inside her womb, it acquired monumental importance.

She'd kept her sonogram appointment before leaving for Ivan's cabin. Lying there with the gel and the sensors and wires attached to her abdomen, she'd experienced a visceral connection to the baby within, a rush of emotion so strong that it dwarfed anything she'd felt before. *Be healthy,* she prayed as the technicians bustled around, twisting dials and making jokes. *Be healthy and strong.* . . .

"You're beginning your fourth month," Dr. McCaffree had said afterward. The due date was June twenty-eighth. The doctor volunteered to tell Isabelle the sex of her baby, but Isabelle refused the offer. It was enough to know the baby was healthy. Now it was up to Isabelle to make certain things stayed that way.

She squared her shoulders and marched into the kitchen, secure in the knowledge that if all else failed, she knew how to make great scrambled eggs.

"It's the most amazing thing, Maxi," Isabelle said a few weeks later. "I went to bed my normal self and when I woke up this morning I found I could no longer wear my own clothes!"

They were at a small shopping mall near East Strouds-burg where Isabelle was searching for stylish maternity clothes. Isabelle had convinced them that biweekly visits were frequent enough, but she'd been unable to convince either one of them that she could manage her own food shopping. Her refrigerator and freezer bulged with supplies. Isabelle found herself wondering if she'd have to invite everyone in a ten-mile radius to help her eat it all.

Maxine was being unusually quiet, at least for Maxine.

Ivan had gone off to Sears to buy new tires for his Cadillac while they shopped for clothes.

"Look at this, Maxi." She stopped in front of a very modern-looking store. "Red Hot Mammas."

Maxine looked utterly horrified. "There is nothing for you in a store like that."

"Oh, of course there is, Maxi. I want something with a little pizzazz."

"Pizzazz?"

"You know," said Isabelle. "Flair. Style. Fun."

Maxine's lips were pursed tight with disapproval. "You were raised to have a sense of dignity," she said as Isabelle led the way into the boutique.

"I was raised to be a princess," Isabelle said, admiring a plaid woolen jumper and tights. "Times change, Maxi. It's time we changed with them."

"He called."

Isabelle kept her focus on the plaid jumper. "When?"

"This morning. Just before we left."

"What did you tell him?"

"That you were out, lovey, just as you told me to."

"Good," said Isabelle fiercely. "Let him wonder what I'm doing." She paused a beat. "Did he say anything?"

"He inquired after my health."

Isabelle bristled. "And did he inquire after my health? I was the one who was sick."

Maxine reached into her capacious leather satchel and withdrew a piece of paper. "This is his number, lovey. Call him. Tell him about the child."

"I wish you'd mind your own business, Maxine Neesom. If I want advice from you, I shall ask for it."

"Stop putting me in the center of your business, missy, and maybe I'll stop giving advice."

Isabelle snatched the piece of paper from Maxine, then tucked it into the pocket of her trousers. Whether or not she called Bronson was nobody's business but hers.

"If you dare tell Daniel about the baby, I'll have you drawn and quartered."

Maxine sniffed. "Somebody should be telling him about the baby before the child can do it himself."

"I need this time alone, Maxi. I need time to think this through."

"'Tis nothing to think about, if you ask me."

"I want to do this on my own."

"I wouldn't be thinking you got this way on your own."

"Damn it, Maxi! This is my baby, and she deserves a mother who knows how to take care of herself." Not some pathetic little princess incapable of balancing a checkbook or boiling water.

From the look on Maxine's face, the woman didn't believe it was possible for her to learn.

A big snowstorm was expected, and so Maxine and Ivan left before dinner. Isabelle had planned to make omelettes and French fries and was disappointed when she lost her opportunity to display her culinary talents. The fact that both Maxi and Ivan looked relieved was not lost on her.

After they left, she made a cheese omelette and toast for herself, then ate the meal in front of television in the living room. It made her feel terribly American and, she hated to admit, terribly homesick for Daniel. She wasn't sure if you could be homesick for a person and not a place, but that was the best word to describe the deep longing she felt for his company.

She found herself growing weepy during a comedy show about a boisterous American family who seemed to enjoy each other's company as much as the Bronsons enjoyed each other.

Why on earth did every thought bring her back to Daniel?

"Goose," she chided herself as she loaded the dishwasher and pressed the button to start the cycle. If he appeared right now in the kitchen, they would no doubt be arguing with each other before the dishes were clean. They were a dreadful match. They had been from the first moment they laid eyes on each other at the Tricentennial Ball. The sexual chemistry was there, but everyone knew that wasn't enough. A man and a woman had to be able to talk to each other and, up until now, they hadn't been able to manage it.

The piece of paper with the telephone number rested on the end table near the sofa. She circled it as if it were a coiled snake ready to strike. Sooner or later she was going to have to talk to him, even if she didn't tell him about the baby right this minute. Why not break the ice now?

She had no idea what time it was in Tokyo, but she decided it didn't matter. If he was groggy with sleep, she'd have him at a disadvantage—a notion that gave her great pleasure.

She dialed the country code then the number. An English-speaking clerk answered the telephone, and Isabelle asked for Daniel's room. A pause. A series of clicks. The sound of a phone ringing.

"Bronson here."

He sounded not only wide awake, but as argumentative as ever. To her dismay, her nerve was rapidly disappearing. *Hang up!* urged the coward inside her. *You don't have to talk to him at all if you don't want to.*

"If you have something to say, say it," Bronson commanded, "or I'm saying *sayonara.*"

"You're certainly in a terrible mood."

A pause. She wondered if he was surprised to hear her voice. "It's five in the morning, princess. I'm always in a terrible mood before the sun comes up." He didn't sound very surprised. Or very happy, for that matter.

Silence. A long, drawn-out silence. She had the feeling that silence could last a lifetime if they allowed it to.

"Well," she said with false cheer, "Maxine said you called."

"Did I leave my onyx cufflinks at your apartment Christmas Day?"

"You called to find out about your cufflinks?"

"Sentimental value. Did I leave them there?"

"I certainly haven't seen them." Onyx cufflinks? Who on earth would call from Tokyo about onyx cufflinks? Onyx wasn't even a precious stone.

"I put them down on your nightstand before you lobbed that juice pitcher at my head. Would you take a look?"

"They're not there."

"Maybe they rolled under the bed."

"They're not under the bed."

"Take a look, damn it, princess. I want those cufflinks."

"Take a look yourself," she snapped back. "I'm not in the apartment."

"What do you mean, you're not in the apartment?"

"You certainly do have trouble with declarative sentences, Bronson. I am living elsewhere."

"Where?"

"That's not your concern."

He muttered something profane that made her smile and cradle the telephone closer. "Is Maxine with you?"

"Not that it is any of your business, but no. Maxine is at *Tante* Elysse's."

"What the hell's going on? Why aren't you at the apartment?"

"I needed a change."

"Are you in the hospital? Did that flu turn into pneumonia?"

"No, it didn't." She paused for effect. "And how kind of you to enquire after my health."

"Who's with you, princess?"

She placed her hand against her belly. "I'm alone." In a manner of speaking. "Things have been quite hectic the past few weeks, and I needed time to gather myself together."

"A hotel," he said, sounding insufferably smug. "The old Helmsley Palace. I hear the room service is great."

"A cottage," she said, sounding equally smug. "No room service."

"A princess living like the common folk? You've got to be kidding."

"Never more serious, Bronson. I owe you a debt of gratitude for teaching me the art of the scrambled egg."

"Where is this cottage?" he asked. "The corner of Fifth and Fifty-seventh?"

"I'm not going to tell you."

"I'll ask Maxine."

"I told her not to give you that information."

"I can be very persuasive, princess."

"And I can be very, very royal." She paused. "Or have you forgotten that?"

"I haven't forgotten anything." His voice was different, lower, the tone more mellow. "Not one single thing."

"I should be ringing off now," she said. "It's time for bed."

"Give me your phone number."

"I think not."

"How can I call you if I don't have your number?"

"You can't." She smiled. "If you need to speak to me, leave a message with Maxine."

"That's ridiculous."

"That's the way it's going to be, Bronson."

"You're a pain in the ass."

"American men," she said with an exaggerated sigh. "Such a romantic race. Now say good night, Daniel, because I'm going to ring off and go to bed now."

"Hey, princess, I have one question: What are you wearing?"

"Right now?"

"Right now."

She looked down at her oversized pink-checked flannel nightgown and thick white socks. "Nothing," she said with a saucy grin. "Absolutely nothing."

She hung up on him.

Just like that.

She'd dropped that enticing bombshell in his ear, then clicked off as if she'd said good-bye and good luck.

Daniel reeled off a series of pungent oaths as he replaced

the receiver in the cradle. *Nothing—absolutely nothing.* He didn't have to try very hard to conjure up a picture of how she looked.

And she knew it. That was the hell of it. There'd never been any doubt the power she had over him. One look, one touch, and he was seventeen again, all hormones and enthusiasm.

He reeled off another series of oaths, punctuated by a scowl in the general direction of New York City.

But she wasn't in Manhattan, was she? She'd picked up and moved to some godforsaken cottage, and he didn't even know what state she was in.

His onyx and gold cufflinks winked at him from the top of his dresser. Pretty lame excuse for a telephone call. What he should have done was told her to put her royal butt on a plane bound for Tokyo where they could talk this whole goddamn mess out face to face. He should have told her that he'd rather exchange barbs with her than drink champagne from the slipper of the most beautiful—and sweet-tempered—woman in the world.

He should have said a lot of things but now he couldn't say any of them. All he could do was sit there and stare at the telephone and wait for her to call again.

If she called again.

Chapter
Sixteen

She called again five days later.

"You're getting better, princess," he said, cradling the receiver between his shoulder and ear. "At least the sun's already up this time."

Her throaty chuckle did amazing things to his blood flow. "You know me, Bronson," she said airily. "Always thinking of others."

"So how's life in your little cottage in the middle of nowhere?"

"Absolutely splendid. I made my first spaghetti dinner yesterday, and it was an unqualified success."

He laughed. "Somehow I can't picture you slaving over the sauce."

"I'm evolving, Bronson. Why, I venture to say you wouldn't recognize the new me."

"So what are you wearing today, princess?" It was early in the morning for this kind of torture, but beggars couldn't be choosers.

"Nothing terribly interesting."

"A dress?"

"Not exactly."

"One of your embroidered tops?"

"No." A long pause. "An ivory lace teddy with spaghetti straps."

Amazing how fast a man could get ready for action. "Any—anything else?"

"Do ivory stockings count?"

He swallowed hard. "Stockings or pantyhose?" He hated pantyhose.

"Stockings," she said. "And a garter belt."

The kind a man could rip off with his teeth. "This is how you dress in a rose-covered cottage?"

"I dress for myself, Bronson, not for the building I'm living in."

"I'm having a hard time reconciling the Happy House-keeper with the Playboy bunny wardrobe."

"I'm terribly sorry to hear that," she said, not sounding sorry at all. "I, however, am having no trouble with the concept."

"You're trying to drive me crazy, aren't you, princess?"

"Whatever gave you that idea?"

"The garter belt was a pretty good clue."

He felt her laugh deep in his gut, in his chest where his heart pounded double time.

"It was wonderful talking to you, Bronson, but I must go now."

"Expecting company?"

"No," she said. " 'Moonlighting' reruns are about to come on."

It was his turn to laugh. "You're becoming a real little American, princess. I'm proud of you."

"Thank you," she said in her most regal tone of voice. "I

now also have a working knowledge of 'Laverne & Shirley,' 'Happy Days,' and 'Cheers.' It occurred to me that we had little in common, so I decided to catch up on my popular culture." She paused. "An historic record of American life."

"I'm flattered." It was hard to imagine the glamorous Isabelle as a couch potato.

"You should be. Some of these shows are quite odd, Bronson."

"You should try watching them in Japanese."

"That must be interesting."

"You could find out for yourself."

"You'll videotape them for me?" she asked, all innocence. "How kind of you."

"You know what I'm talking about."

"Tell me."

"That plane ticket is still valid. Tokyo's a fascinating city. I'd like to show it to you."

"I would advise you to get your money back, Bronson. Right now I believe we're better off with half a world between us."

"Because we can't stop fighting with each other?"

"No," she said with a soft laugh. "Because when we're together we can't stop making love long enough to find out if we can ever make friends."

The moment she hung up the telephone she wanted to dial him back and tell him that she was wrong, that she wanted to be with him in Tokyo, that she missed the sound of his voice, the feel of his skin, the look in his eyes when they made love. Talking to him had awakened a storm of emotions inside her heart, a wild rush of longing that stole her breath away.

But she'd done the right thing. Sex was wonderful, but there had to be more, especially with a child on the way.

She rose from her chair, her movements a bit more awkward than they'd been the week before. She was on her way into the kitchen to make a pot of tea when she caught a glimpse of herself reflected in the television screen. Her hair was scraped back into a scruffy ponytail. Her face was devoid of makeup. Instead of a sexy confection of lace and ribbons, she wore a man's shirt with the sleeves rolled up, navy blue maternity slacks, and a pair of slippers. Her belly was definitely rounded. In profile it was finally becoming obvious that she was pregnant and not fat, a fact for which she was profoundly grateful.

"Would you like me this way, Bronson?" she asked her reflection. No glamour. No garter belts or slinky stockings. Not a princess, but a woman. And a pregnant one at that.

Placing her hands on her belly, she admired her reflection. She was well into her fourth month and she—wait a minute. She held her breath and pressed her palms more closely against her belly. A slight rippling motion deep inside—more a quickening than anything else. Her imagination perhaps, or could it be something more wonderful, more amazing, more thrilling even than the act that had made it possible?

"Oh, Bronson," she whispered, tears welling. "We're having a baby."

A miserable February rain sliced across the crowded London street as Juliana cautiously made her way to the door of Patrick Marchand's offices. She was at that stage in her pregnancy when walking was a triumph of will over gravity.

Wouldn't you think the man could afford an office with a lift, she thought as she slowly climbed the steps. With what she'd been paying him these past months, surely he could do better than this dilapidated building. She consoled herself with the fact that it no longer mattered. After today Marchand would no longer be in her employ, and he could situate his offices in the middle of Piccadilly for all it mattered to her.

"Princess Juliana, I am pleased to see you." Marchand nodded his thanks to the receptionist who had ushered Juliana inside. "You are looking quite well."

He drew up a chair for her and, with great solicitude, helped her to sit down. She removed her soft cashmere scarf, folded it into an oblong, then rested it on her lap next to her purse and leather gloves.

"I am here to settle accounts, Mr. Marchand," she said without preamble. She wanted no paper trail to link her with the investigation, a simple and clean transaction in cash.

His thick brows drew together in a look of concern. "You are displeased with our work?"

"On the contrary. I am no longer in need of further information." She opened the clasp of her Chanel bag and removed an envelope. "I believe this settles all debts." She slid the ivory vellum across the desk toward Marchand, who proved to be quite a gentleman. Arching a brow, she said, "I am surprised to find you a trusting man, Mr. Marchand, considering the business you are in."

He smiled and placed the envelope in his desk drawer. "My profession has made me an expert judge of character, Princess Juliana. You would not cheat me out of my fee. It is in other areas that I should keep careful watch on you."

Juliana nodded and gathered up her belongings. "A wise man, Mr. Marchand, and another reason why it is time to terminate our association."

He swiveled around in his chair and plucked a folder from a hanging file. "I have some additional information you might be interested in. It is in rough form, but it may be of interest."

She hesitated. She already knew as much as she cared to about her husband's wandering eye. "I think not."

He slid the folder across the desk toward her. "There are no other copies on file, Princess Juliana. I would prefer if you disposed of this material as you see fit."

She had no intention of reading the material, but she tucked it under her arm and left. She would simply file it all away and forget it.

Curiosity, however, was a potent emotion, and by the time she arrived back at the castle, she found it impossible to ignore the folder. Eric was off somewhere with his parents, Honore and Celine, to some family function that Juliana had begged off on, claiming the discomfort of pregnancy as her excuse.

"I'll take a light supper in the library," she said to Yves as he took her coat and scarf in the front hall.

"As you wish, madam." He bowed and hurried off to do her bidding.

A fire danced merrily in the hearth, welcoming her. The library had always been her favorite room in the castle. Sometimes she thought she caught the aroma of Papa's pipe, the rich bouquet of his cognac.

She shook her head, trying to banish the unwanted memories. It hurt too much to think of him. He came to her sometimes in her dreams. That haunted look in his eyes, the deep furrows and lines of his face, the Corgis yapping about him as he lay on the cold, cold ground—

"Madam."

She spun around to see Yves standing in the doorway. Was she imagining the look of disappointment on his face?

"Perhaps a cup of tea would be advisable while cook prepares supper." Correct—always so correct.

She nodded, moving toward the window while he set up the service on the sideboard, then quietly left the room.

She sat down on a straight-backed chair near the hearth and opened the file. How boring. Much of it was a rehash of the same business Marchand had reported earlier. She trailed her finger down a column of addresses; all purportedly represented foreign offices of Malraux International but were of questionable intent.

"Foolishness," she said, flipping quickly through a stack of photographs of Eric. It didn't matter where he'd been or with whom. He belonged to her and always would, if only because his father willed it.

A son, she thought as the daughter in her womb kicked violently against her rib. *A son would tie the Malraux family to the throne into the next century and beyond.*

She slid the photograph into the locked file she kept in the bottom drawer of her father's desk. She flipped quickly through the rest of the papers: scraps of foolscap, index cards, note paper. A fax transmission from a New York City phone number. The handwriting was large and scrawling, very American and difficult to read, the ink fading on the thermal paper.

It was dated mid-January, just a few weeks ago.

"I don't want to see this," she said, her hands beginning to tremble. "I don't want to know any more."

But she couldn't look away. She saw her sister's name. The address of a Dr. Joan McCaffree. And one simple sentence that changed her world: "Sonogram verified princess's pregnancy—it's a boy."

"It was the strangest thing, Maxi," said Isabelle as she carried the platter of toasted cheese sandwiches to the table. "I have dreamed of Mama every night for the past two weeks."

Maxine's blue eyes filled with tears. "'Tisn't surprising, considering your condition. Most young women turn to their mothers in times like this."

Isabelle walked over to the window and tapped against the glass with her knuckles to summon Ivan and his son-in-law for lunch.

"Now, that's exactly what's so strange about the dream," she said as she opened the refrigerator and withdrew a carton of skim milk and a big bottle of cream soda. "I am but a child in the dream, no more than five years old. Mama is sitting at her dressing table, and I'm watching as she pulls the stopper from a bottle of Bal a Versailles and touches the crystal to the base of her throat."

"How often I saw Sonia do exactly that," said Maxine, her voice rich with sadness. "I would stand in the doorway and watch as she coiled that thick dark hair into a chignon . . . that foolish, beautiful girl."

"Honore once told me she loved to dance, that she would whirl from partner to partner and never grow tired."

"Your mother was a woman of great charm. All who met Sonia fell under her spell."

"But she wasn't a good mother, was she?"

Maxine met her eyes. "Is that what Honore told you?"

Isabelle shook her head. "No, but when I combined his memories with my own, it was not difficult to arrive at that conclusion." She sat down across the table from Maxine and reached for the woman's hand. "Tell me, please, Maxi. I find myself thinking about Mama all the time, wondering if I will find a way to keep from making her mistakes."

"The fact that you would be askin' me that question tells me you will be a good mother to that babe you're carrying."

"And Mama?" Her voice was a whisper.

"Sonia was not meant for the life of wife and mother, lovey. She lived for sensation." A bright comet arcing across the sky, then vanishing in a burst of light and heat. "You mustn't condemn her."

"Did she have an affair with Honore?"

"Where on earth would you be getting an idea like that one?"

"I don't know," Isabelle said slowly. "A hunch . . . a feeling. There was something about the way Honore talked about Mama. It was in his voice."

"Honore Malraux is a good businessman, but he is not a friend, lovey. Not to any of us."

"Maxine! I've never heard you say something against Honore before."

"Like father, like son," Maxine continued. "It's Honore who'd be pulling Eric's strings, make no mistake about that. He was as much responsible for Juliana's marriage as your own dear father was."

"He called again, didn't he?"

Maxine nodded. "Mark my words, the man is up to mischief. You are seeing a very important man, lovey. That fact would not be lost on Honore."

Isabelle made an impatient gesture with her hands. "I do not care about Honore and his business dealings, Maxi. I only care where it concerns my mama."

Maxine sighed. "Your mother was an impetuous woman, lovey. You mustn't condemn her for that."

"I don't condemn her, Maxi. I only find myself lying awake at night wondering how I will know what to do with a child, how I will keep from making some terrible mistake that will perpetuate itself through the generations."

"Ah, lovey," said Maxine, drying her eyes. "I'm thinkin' you've become a woman at last. Now, if you would just tell Daniel about the child . . ."

"You're a day early, princess," said Daniel when he answered the telephone that night. "I wasn't expecting you until tomorrow."

"Am I that predictable?"

"Only to me."

"Maxine and Ivan were here today," she said, launching headlong into meaningless conversation. "Ivan and his son-in-law cut some more wood for the fireplace."

"Are you having a bad winter?"

"Not very bad." She laughed. "At least not by Perreault standards. It's hard to believe spring is only a month away."

"I miss you, princess."

She started. "What did you say?"

"I miss you."

The baby moved within her womb, almost as if he or she had heard Daniel's words. She took a deep breath. "I miss you, too."

"I'm not just talking about sex."

"Neither am I."

"Maybe I could fly home for a day or two. I find myself lying awake at night trying to picture your face, your smile."

"No!" She forced her voice down to more normal

volume. "I mean, I'd never ask you to do that, what with the way you feel about flying and all."

"I have an in with Saint Christopher."

"You're wearing the medal."

"All the time."

"And what else?"

"Use your imagination."

She was almost afraid to. "You haven't asked me what I'm wearing today, Bronson. I'm disappointed in you."

"Okay," he said, a low rumbling laugh floating through the wires and curling around her eardrum. "Let's hear it."

"Sweatpants, a baggy T-shirt, and floppy slippers."

"You're kidding." He paused. "Aren't you?"

"Afraid not."

"Any diamonds?"

"Not a one."

"I thought no princess worth her tiara goes out without diamonds."

"I wear one piece of jewelry, Bronson, and that's a gold bracelet a very wonderful man gave to me for Christmas."

It was his turn to sound surprised. "I thought you hated it."

"I never said that."

"You looked like you wanted to throw it at my head."

"I was dreadful that day," she said, "and I apologize. It never occurred to me that I might have hurt your feelings."

"It never occurred to you that I even had feelings."

She couldn't deny the truth. "I'm learning, Bronson, that's all I can say. When you grow up the way I did, it's difficult to know the boundaries." She thought of the endless stream of servants, the fancy schools, the buffers between herself and the real world. "I wish I could explain what it was like."

"I'm here," he said, "if you feel like talking."

"There is so much to say . . . so many things I have not thought about in so long." She laughed. "I do not know where to begin."

"Anywhere, princess." His voice was warm, caressing. "I've got all the time you need."

She leaned back in her rocking chair and closed her eyes. "I remember my mother sitting at her dressing table . . ."

They talked five days in a row. Long, intimate conversations about family, about dreams, about everything except the future. He was that rare specimen: an adult who liked his family, who understood its importance in the framework of life. And he was smart enough to know how rare a thing that was. Isabelle envied him his childhood with her entire being. But never once did he say he wanted a family of his own.

On the sixth day she took a car into Manhattan for her monthly appointment with the obstetrician Dr. McCaffree had suggested. "Right on schedule," said the doctor. "Keep doing what you're doing."

She rode back home in a quandary. Tell him, Maxine had said. A man should know he's about to be a father, Ivan had scolded. *What are you waiting for?* her own conscience demanded. *Tell him!*

She dialed his number as soon as she reached the cottage. If she had her time zones straight, it was four A.M. in Tokyo. "Sorry if I wake you up, Bronson," she murmured as the operator rang his room, "but at least I know you'll be there."

The telephone rang ten times, twenty, twenty-five. She slammed down the receiver. It must be—what? Four in the morning? She dialed again. This time she let it ring thirty times with the same result. "Message, please?" asked the telephone operator. "None," she growled. The Japanese were much too polite for the message she wanted to leave.

"I was in Hokkaido," he said when they connected a few days later. "The back of beyond."

She brushed away stupid, ridiculous tears. "I was so worried."

"You, princess? I would've figured you'd throw the telephone out the window."

"That was what I wanted to do the first four times I called. Then I started to worry."

"I like the sound of that."

"That I worried about you?"

"Yeah," he said. "That you cared enough."

This is it. This is the time. "Bronson, there's something—"

"Could it wait until next time, princess? Hastings is at the door. We have a plane waiting to take us to Kyoto for a meeting."

Isabelle sighed. Maybe it was a sign from the gods. "It can wait, Bronson." It had waited almost six months already.

He was due home the middle of May. That gave her two more months to figure out how to tell Daniel he was going to be a father.

". . . Hastings is doing a damn good job," Daniel said, finishing up his second progress report for the month of April. "We're running ahead of schedule. By the time I sign off, we'll be well under way."

"I've gotta hand it to you," said Matty, his voice loud and clear despite the miles, "this time last year I wouldn't've given you a plugged nickel for your chances over there. When you're right, you're right, Danny. If Malraux hadn't established a beachhead, I'd say give Perreault another shot."

Daniel flipped closed his portfolio and stashed it back in his briefcase. "So how's everything back home?"

"Patty's expecting."

"Again?"

His old man laughed. "She said she's going to have a son this time no matter what."

An odd twinge of pain settled itself beneath Daniel's rib cage. It felt a hell of a lot like envy.

"Did you hear me?" Matty boomed.

"Sorry, Pop, bad connection. What did you say?"

"I thought I saw Isabelle the other day at Madison and Sixty-third."

The twinge of pain intensified. "I don't think so, Pop. She's off somewhere communing with nature."

"It sure looked like her. She was in the backseat of a Lincoln Town Car. I thought it was my car at first, then I saw this real pretty girl with a big head of hair."

"A lot of pretty brunettes in this world." It couldn't be Isabelle. She was in the country somewhere. She wouldn't lie to him about something like that.

"Yeah, there are," said Matty, "but you know the way she tosses her head back and all that hair goes flying?"

"Hadn't noticed," Daniel mumbled. *Like hell.*

"Just a thought," said Matty. "Forget I said anything. I probably need new glasses."

The doorbell rang as Maxine and Ivan were sitting down on the terrace to a fine boiled dinner of corned beef, cabbage, and potatoes.

"Can't a body enjoy a meal without being bothered?" Maxine grouched as she rose from her chair and tossed her napkin down on the table. "I'll send whoever it is packing before he can open his mouth."

"Faster even," said Ivan.

It rang a second time, and she swung open the door, ready to do battle. A man stood on the welcome mat. He was of moderate height, moderate build, with a thick head of silver hair and a big smile. He reminded her of someone, but she couldn't quite place who it was.

"How're you doing?" he asked, extending his right hand. "You've gotta be Maxine. I've heard a lot about you."

Maxine had lived in New York long enough to look at his extended hand with suspicion. "And who might you be?"

"Matty," he said, shaking her hand firmly. "Matty Bronson."

"Would you be Daniel's father?"

He nodded. "I am and proud of it."

"He's a fine boy."

"That he is."

Gazes steady, they took each other's measure.

"Would Isabelle be in?"

Maxine shook her head.

"Would she be back soon?"

Maxine again shook her head.

"Has she gone away?"

Maxine hesitated. "You might be sayin' that."

"And what else might you be sayin', Miss Neesom?"

"She has a foul temper, Mr. Bronson. I can't vouch for what she might do if I told you."

"My son has a foul temper as well, Miss Neesom. He'd sell all of my stocks in Bron-Co if he knew I was here."

Maxine had the heart of a romantic and the soul of a born matchmaker, and she knew an opportunity when she saw one.

"Come in, Mr. Bronson, and I'll tell you a story if you promise to keep it a secret."

"Call me Matty."

She dimpled. "And you can call me Maxine."

She proceeded to tell him everything, right down to the placemats Isabelle was using on the kitchen table.

"They are making a terrible mistake," said Matty with a shake of his head.

"Of course they are," said Maxine, "but they're too stubborn to admit it."

"My son is pigheaded."

"And my girl is stubborn as an ox."

"It's about time he had himself a kid."

"And that baby will be here before Isabelle gets 'round to tellin' him she's expecting."

"We have a problem."

Maxine nodded. "What are you going to do? This is a secret, after all."

He looked at her and smiled like the cat that ate the

canary. "I'm going to call him," he said. "What did you think I was going to do?"

"Saint's be praised!" She leaped up and planted a kiss on Matty Bronson's cheek. "A man after my own heart!"

"Buckle up, Mr. Bronson." The flight attendant flashed a bright, professional smile. "We'll be landing at JFK shortly."

Like he'd have unbuckled the belt while he was suspended in a flying tin can thirty-nine thousand feet above the ground. "Thanks," he said.

"And return the tray—"

"—to the original, upright position."

Her smile widened. "You know the drill."

"By heart."

She hovered a few moments. He wasn't rude, but he didn't encourage her, either, so she moved back through the first-class cabin to chat with the other passengers.

He was beyond small talk. A part of him still couldn't believe that less than twenty-four hours ago he'd been asleep in his Tokyo hotel room, thinking about the plumbing facilities at the work site. Matty's call had come out of the blue. "We've got us a situation brewing here, Danny," his father had said. "I want you to catch the next plane out."

"What the hell's going on, Pop? Why can't you handle it?"

"Because your mother'll have my head on a platter if I don't take her to Florida this weekend to see her sister Flo."

Daniel had named three other executives, all of whom were equally qualified to handle any emergency. Matty would have none of it.

"Just get your butt on a plane," Matty had said. "A car'll be waiting for you."

"This damn well better be good," Daniel muttered as he strode from the International Arrivals building.

"Hey, Mr. Bronson!" A skycap with a familiar face hailed him near the taxi stand. "Been a long time."

"Sure has." Daniel scanned the street for the Bron-Co car. "How've you been?"

"I was workin' over at Teterboro Airport—right near home—for a while but I got laid off."

The guy's name came back to him. "Glad you got your old job back, Joe. Watch out you don't hurt your knee again."

"Thanks for rememberin', Mr. B." He paused. "You still seein' the princess?"

Daniel laughed. "Unless you know something I don't know."

The skycap disappeared back into the terminal.

"Hey, Danny!" Another familiar voice. "Over here!"

His father waved to him from the other side of the street.

They exchanged greetings as Daniel climbed into the Lincoln.

"I thought you and Mom were in Florida."

"Tonight," said Matty around his cigar. "Frank has the day off."

"Don't tell me he had another kid?"

"Tonsils," said Matty.

"His kids?"

"Frank's."

Daniel shrugged out of his jacket and tossed it in the backseat as his father gunned the engine. "So where's the fire?"

"Patience, Danny," said Matty. "Patience."

"Hey, Pop," Daniel said ten minutes later. "Manhattan's that way."

"I know," said Matty.

"And you missed the turnoff for the expressway."

"I'm not heading out to the Island."

"So where the hell are we going, Pop?"

"You'll see." He glanced over at Daniel. "Why don't you grab some shut-eye? I have a feeling you won't get a hell of a lot of sleep tonight."

Daniel was a couple of decades past obeying his old man,

but he hadn't slept in a day and a half, and if Matty's broad hints were any indication, he had a hell of a lot of work ahead of him.

When he opened his eyes two hours later, he was in the middle of a forest—at least it seemed like a forest. Mountains jutted up toward the sky. Big trees grew thick along a country road that hadn't seen a repair crew in a generation or two.

"Where the hell are we?"

"Sit tight. We're almost there."

"Where the hell is 'there'?"

"Isabelle."

Maybe it was jet lag because nothing registered on him. "Isabelle?"

"You know," said Matty around another cigar. "The princess."

"There's a town named after the princess?"

"Snap out of it, Danny. I'm taking you to see your girlfriend."

They pulled into a rutted driveway and rolled to a stop next to a beat-up VW bug.

"Last stop," said Matty.

"Okay, Pop. The joke's over. What in hell's going on?"

"Get out." Matty leaned across and opened the door. "I have a plane to catch."

"You're gonna pay for this, Pop." Daniel climbed out of the Lincoln. He grabbed his jacket and bag from the backseat. "How do I get back from here?"

"Don't worry about it, Danny. I don't think you're gonna want to."

With a beep of the horn, Matty backed out of the driveway and disappeared down the road.

Daniel took a look at the simple A-frame house. He thought about the princess. No way could he bring the two images together. Whatever his father had up his sleeve, there was no way it included Isabelle. Not here.

He strode up the path and knocked on the door. No answer. Terrific. He knocked again and listened. He heard the sound of a radio or television inside, then the sound of slow, deliberate footsteps heading toward the door.

"I'm on my way. Just be patient!" That throaty voice, the half-aristocrat, half-siren accent. That mane of dark hair— the sleek little body—

The door swung open. She was more beautiful than he'd remembered. That perfect little face with the high cheekbones and those big dark eyes that had haunted his dreams the last few months.

"Oh my God!" Her beautiful eyes widened in surprise, then brimmed with tears. "Bronson!"

She threw herself into his arms. "Whoa, princess! You're—" He stopped. She met his gaze. His entire life passed before him.

She took his hands and placed them on her belly. "Welcome home, Daddy."

Chapter Seventeen

Sometimes a man doesn't know what he wants until it's staring him right in the face.

For Daniel, thirty-four years of living finally made sense the moment Isabelle placed his hand against her belly and he felt their baby move. Everything she was, everything he wanted to be—all of it was right there beneath his palm, growing stronger and larger every day within the nurturing darkness of her body.

At another time in his life and with another woman, his surprise would have been shock, colored by anger and reluctance. Now he was surprised rather than shocked. He would have felt trapped before; now he experienced a sense of rightness that gave depth and meaning to every breath he took, every beat of his heart from this moment forward.

He drew her into the circle of his arms and kissed her

deeply, hungrily, wishing he could find the words to tell her what was in his heart.

She broke his kiss. "Say something, Bronson. You have to be surprised."

"That doesn't begin to cover it." He cupped her belly again, trying to comprehend a miracle. "When were you going to tell me, princess?"

"I tried," she said, brushing a lock of hair off his forehead with her hand. "It isn't the type of announcement that lends itself to long-distance phone conversations." A furrow appeared between her brows. "How on earth did you find me here? Why aren't you in Japan?" She peered out the living room window. "And how did you get here?"

"Matty."

She started to laugh. "And I'll wager I know who told him."

"Maxine?"

"She has threatened on more than one occasion to tell you about the baby herself."

"I wish she had."

Isabelle shook her head. "No. It was better this way."

"I should've been here with you."

"If you were with me, nothing would have changed between us, Bronson. We wouldn't be having this conversation. I'd still be looking for you to do my bidding."

"I've never been much for taking orders."

She waved her hand in the air. "Yes, but I had many years of practice in getting what I want from people. It was not one of my more endearing traits, as you've pointed out on many an occasion."

He stepped back and took a long look at her. "You've changed."

Her face lit up with a smile. "You've never seen my hair in a ponytail before."

"And I've never seen you in maternity pants, either. It's something else."

"Eighteen extra pounds can change a woman."

But it was more than that. She was more womanly, more centered, as if she'd lived a lifetime in the few months they'd been apart. She told him where the bathroom was, and he went to wash up while she made some coffee. It was a tiny room with a stall shower and a simple sink and vanity. Her red plastic toothbrush hung from the holder. A bright pink plastic drinking cup rested next to the biggest crystal bottle of perfume he'd ever seen. The room smelled of Comet and Chanel No. 5, and he laughed out loud as he thought of the little princess cleaning the toilet.

"I made tuna fish salad this morning," she said as he entered the kitchen. "I haven't mastered anything too terribly complicated yet, but I handle the basics quite well."

"Come here," he said, sitting down at the table.

She dried her hands on a paper towel and walked toward him. Her gait was measured, as if her center of gravity changed with each step. She was dressed simply: black tights, a white sweater with the sleeves pushed up to the elbow, and the bracelet he'd given her for Christmas. Her breasts were rounder than before, their fullness swaying beneath the soft fabric of her sweater. Her belly was an act of God. She wore no makeup. He knew he would never see a more beautiful woman.

He motioned for her to sit on his lap.

"I might hurt you," she said, cheeks reddening.

"I'll take my chances."

She eased herself down and looped her arms around his neck. "You couldn't possibly know how much I've missed you, Bronson."

"I think I can.

"I hope you enjoyed your freedom, princess, because it's over for both of us. From here on, we're in this thing together."

She bristled. Just enough so he was reassured the real princess wasn't hidden away in a pod in the basement. "I have my trust fund now and before long I'll have a real income from my venture with Ivan. I don't need anyone's help in caring for the child."

"I need to be part of this, princess. My kid's not going to grow up wondering who his father is or why he's not around."

"If we could be half as successful as your parents have been, I would consider myself blessed." She held his face in her hands, her dark gaze intent, as if she were hungry for the sight of him. "Every night I have the same dream, that we're together in a beautiful house on top of a mountain with three beautiful children and family all around us."

"I can go for all of it except the mountain."

She laughed and nuzzled against the side of his neck. "All right, we'll substitute the ocean."

"Perfect." He paused. "Three kids?"

She nodded. "And not a one will go to boarding schools or have to make an appointment to talk to us." Her voice broke. "I never want them to feel they can't count on their family the way I did. I want them to know so much love that it will warm them for the rest of their lives and give them strength."

"I'm not going to leave you, princess," he said as the loving yoke of commitment settled itself across his shoulders. "You'll always be safe with me."

They sat together in the kitchen, arms around each other, as the long shadows of afternoon fell across the tiled floor. She listened to the beating of his heart against her ear. He felt the movement of their child beneath his hand and he knew that there was nothing he wouldn't do to keep them safe from harm.

Juliana was delivered of a girl on the fifth of May. Her labor was long and arduous, and she begged her doctor for something that would dull the agony. "Better for the child if you do not," the doctor had said while crushing pain wracked her body.

"I don't give a bloody damn about the child," she cried. "The child is nothing."

Neither the doctor nor his nurse mentioned her outburst, but each recognized that it was not the usual ragings of a woman in transition.

They said Allegra was a beautiful infant with her fair curls and cornflower-blue eyes, but her mother saw nothing but failure each time she looked at her. Eric was attentive and loving, but Juliana saw the disappointment on his face, and she felt that disappointment through to her marrow.

Her mother-in-law, Celine, sent flowers from her villa on the Mediterranean and a note saying she would return to Perreault in July when she intended to shower the child with grandmotherly affection.

Honore, however, was on hand for the birth and the christening. He held the child while Father Guilbeaux baptized Allegra as he had baptized three generations of Perreault royalty. No one could know by looking at Honore that he had suggested that Juliana abort the child just six short months before. After the service, he took Juliana aside and pressed into her hands the deed to one hundred acres of French farmland.

"There is a clinic in Geneva," he said, linking her arm through his, "that performs miracles in gender selection. There is no reason to allow fate to make these decisions for you."

He looked so disappointed in her. She couldn't allow him to feel that way when he alone controlled her happiness, her future with his son. "I want the name of the clinic and the address," she said. "I intend to waste no time."

The look in his eyes was worth the prospect of enduring another nine months of torture.

There was no way to avoid the necessity of another timely pregnancy. Not with Isabelle big with child, a son only eight weeks from being born.

Lately, Isabelle was never far from her thoughts. The fool probably had no idea that the son she was carrying would be the rightful heir to the throne. Not that it was of any consequence. Isabelle was an acquisitive little creature. She would never endanger her precious trust fund by taking a jaunt across the Atlantic to visit her family. All Juliana needed was the time to produce a male heir of her own. Certainly her own child, the issue of her marriage to Eric, would be more desirable than the bastard offspring of her sluttish sister, no matter the dates of their birth.

Isabelle and Daniel spent an amazing two weeks in Ivan's Pocono hidaway, discovering that even without the balm of sex, they enjoyed each other's company immensely. The chalet was smaller quarters than either one of them was accustomed to, but somehow neither found the closeness anything but delightful. Isabelle wondered if the day would ever come when she would take for granted the miracle of companionship, of feeling cherished and protected.

What she enjoyed most was the ordinariness of it all. The minutiae of daily living filled her heart with joy: seeing Daniel's face the last thing at night, awakening in his arms as the first light of day streamed through the bedroom windows; long walks down country roads, planning their child's future right down to what college she would attend. All these were small joys to be savored.

They had their spats—silly, heated arguments about toothpaste caps and breakfast choices—but in all of the important matters they were in perfect accord. The happiness they'd found together mattered, and they were both willing to work hard to hold onto it.

At the end of the second week, Daniel decided it was time for them to move back to the city, and reluctantly Isabelle agreed. Their baby was due in six weeks, and a two-hour drive to the hospital didn't seem prudent to either one of them.

Maxine welcomed them back with open arms and an impromptu party. Ivan was thrilled to see the embroideries Isabelle had worked on since his last visit. Her unexpected pregnancy had thrown advertising for the Princess line into a state of confusion; the dresses she had worked on while in the Poconos helped soothe his frazzled nerves.

Of course, Matty had spread the word about the baby, and Isabelle fielded a score of happy telephone calls from various Bronsons. "Beware," Cathy Bronson-Bernier warned her over a giggly lunch at Serendipity. "My family believes in the guerrilla-ambush style of baby shower. You won't be safe between now and your delivery date."

Isabelle laughed so hard that tears ran down her cheeks as Cathy detailed the bizarre yet touching rituals that surrounded the American baby shower. "I can't escape this tradition?"

"It's inevitable," said Cathy, "and it'll happen when you least expect it. I was waltzed right out of my office by two women in fake nurses' uniforms. They put me in a stretch limousine and whisked me off to a beautiful little inn near Cold Spring Harbor on Long Island where everyone I've ever known and everyone I'm related to jumped out from behind the potted palms and yelled, 'Surprise!'"

There was little Isabelle could say in response. The whole thing was so far beyond her experience that it sounded like fantasy. When she went home that evening, she related the story to an amazed Maxine and a very amused Daniel.

The idea of living separately was no longer an option for Isabelle and Bronson. His apartment was spacious but needed considerable work to make it suitable for a family. *Tante* Elysse had delayed her return to Manhattan until September, and Isabelle hoped that the redecorating would be finished by then. When she told Maxine there would be a suite of rooms for her, Maxine shocked Isabelle by announcing that she was moving in with Ivan as soon as Isabelle was settled back home after delivery.

Love was in the air. Isabelle teased Maxine that the wonderful romance novels she adored had transferred their magic to their lives. Maxine just smiled. The sparkle in her eyes, however, told the tale.

*   *   *

Despite her best intentions, Juliana found herself growing more obsessed with Isabelle as the days wore on. A small story in French *Vogue* had awakened the sleeping monster of jealousy, and Juliana felt the nip of its fangs in the soft flesh of her heart. Who but her sister, her blessed-by-the-gods sister, could turn a schoolgirl's recreation into a successful endeavor? Every young woman in Perreault could wield a needle with equal skill. It was a commonplace art, almost vulgar in its accessibility. Well suited to Isabelle, all things considered.

She ripped the page, complete with a photo of a radiantly pregnant Isabelle, from the magazine and tossed it into the wastebasket beside the desk. Even her dreams of late had been filled with images of the dark-haired princess. She glanced toward the locked desk drawer where she kept Marchand's reports. She didn't have to see the photos of Isabelle and Eric again to call to mind each and every nuance of expression and gesture. If only she could remember how many trips abroad Eric had made last year after Bertrand's death. It seemed as if he'd been away much more than he was at home, traveling to all of the major cities where Malraux International kept an office.

How many other times had her husband and sister been together when a camera had not been present? In Paris after Isabelle left Perreault? In London when she stayed with that Gemma creature? Or New York—over and over and over? All along Juliana had assumed that the child her sister was carrying had been fathered by that American businessman. But in truth that child could belong to anyone. Surely Isabelle had not confined her amorous athletics to two men. The child could be Gianni Vitelli's or any number of men who had squired Isabelle during the months after Juliana and Eric announced their engagement.

But you know the truth, a voice whispered deep inside her head. *The child is Eric's—Eric's son—the rightful heir to the throne.*

She rose to her feet, her heart thudding painfully. Honore had made an appointment for her to see a specialist at the clinic in Geneva, but that wasn't for another two weeks. Fourteen days suddenly seemed too long to wait. She fumbled through the leather-bound address book resting next to the desk blotter. Why on earth didn't she have the phone number of the clinic? It was her business, after all, her future at stake.

Angrily she made her way down the hall to Honore's office. He never locked the door. He was too much the gentleman to make such a statement about the honor of the inhabitants of the castle.

He wasn't in his office. A sleek chrome Rolodex sat at right angles to the multiline telephone system he'd had installed a few months earlier. She flipped through the cards, names both familiar and famous leaping out at her as if illuminated by a spotlight. No clinic. She pushed aside the chair and opened the top drawer. A pair of gold pens, a sterling silver letter opener, a magnifying glass in a velvet pouch, an almost-empty pack of Player's cigarettes and a book of matches with the Malraux International logo embossed at the upper left-hand corner. She tried the three drawers on the right—nothing. Top drawer on the left. The file drawer on the bottom. Hands shaking, she pushed past hanging folders filled with spreadsheet printouts, press clippings on different MI undertakings—

She stopped, bile rising to her throat. She lifted one thick folder from the drawer and opened it. Her legs buckled, and she sank to the chair, its casters skidding against the carpet. There, in a silver frame, was a picture of her sister. Across the bottom of the photo were the words "Love, Love, Love," penned in a familiar, exuberant hand. Isabelle wore a white evening gown with a wide neckline that bared her shoulders. She was posed in the garden, near the privet hedges Juliana loved so well. The castle's western turrets were plainly visible behind them. The look in her eyes was challenging, blatantly sexual, oddly cynical. Her dark hair was swept off her face into a tight chignon, and it struck Juliana that she had never seen her sister wear such a severe hairdo.

She peered more closely at the photo. The hedge barely reached Isabelle's hips. *Impossible,* she thought. It had been years since the hedges had been that low. Not since their mother—

"My God," she whispered. "Mama?"

"Good evening, Juliana."

She jumped at the sound of Honore's voice in the doorway.

"Juliana," he repeated. "I am surprised to see you in my office." He still wore his topcoat and a copy of *Paris-Match* was tucked beneath his arm.

She said nothing, simply clung to the photograph, her heart pounding madly inside her chest.

"Your mother was a beautiful woman," he said as he stepped into the room, tossing *Paris-Match* onto a chair. "That is my favorite photograph of her."

She struggled to regain her composure. "Wh-why do you have it here? Did Papa give it to you?" *Don't tell me,* an inner voice begged. *Please don't tell me the truth.* It was only a photograph, after all. A photograph of a woman long dead and buried. Whatever it had once meant to Honore and her mother could be of little importance now.

"My darling child," he said, closing the door behind him. "How much you have to learn. . . ."

Maxine settled down in the kitchen with a pot of tea and a stack of romance novels for company. Ivan had flown down to Florida for a trade show. "Come with me, Max," he'd said. "Some sun. Some sand. Who knows what could happen?" Maxine had been tempted, but with Isabelle's due date a month away, she had found it impossible to leave. Ivan was understanding, but Maxine knew he looked forward to the day when the baby was born and she would be free to move in with him.

The apartment was quiet except for the city sounds that

floated through the open window. Isabelle and Daniel had retired for the night. It made Maxine's heart ache with joy that her girl had finally found a man capable of loving her the way she'd always needed to be loved. Daniel was a good man. Strong, powerful, but blessed with a kind heart that made him able to stand up for himself when Isabelle grew too full of herself. Which, even Maxine had to admit, was often.

It felt right, all of it. Maxine's only regret was that she'd been forced to choose between Juliana and Isabelle. She loved both girls, there had never been any doubt about that, but Isabelle—headstrong, impulsive, loving Isabelle—had always held a special claim upon her heart.

She sighed as she poured herself a cup of bracing tea. Why was it that the simplest things in life proved to be the most difficult? Love should be as direct and powerful a force in life as it was between the pages of the books she enjoyed. What a shame it was that a happy ending could not be guaranteed for all.

She'd dreamed of Juliana two nights ago. Juliana stood in the castle garden, near the privet hedges. She wore a long white gown that had once belonged to her mother, Sonia. There was a child at her ankles and one in her arms. Maxine had an impression of danger, of destiny, and then in a flash Juliana was gone. Maxine had awakened, startled to find herself in her own bed.

Are you happy, child? she wondered now as she listened to the traffic sounds from the street below. *Did you make the right choice?*

"I cannot bear this another second," Isabelle declared over breakfast one morning.

"'Tis almost your time," said Maxine, buttering a toasted English muffin.

"Just a few more weeks." Daniel poured them all some orange juice. "You'll be able to see your feet again soon, princess."

She looked at them blankly for a moment. "I'm not talking about my pregnancy," she said, laughing. "I'm talking about my baby shower." She turned to Daniel. "I implore you, if you have any idea when it will be, please tell me! The suspense is impossible to bear."

"I'm the last one my family would tell."

"Look at me," Isabelle said, moving her hands across her belly. "If they don't hurry up and surprise me, they will have to hold their party in the hospital." She looked at Maxine. "Do you know anything, Maxi?"

Maxine shook her head. "And you would be thinkin' I'd have my invitation by now."

Isabelle continued to worry the subject to death during breakfast. By the time the plates were loaded into the dishwasher, both Maxine and Daniel were happy to escape to their respective offices.

"Fine," said Isabelle as the door closed behind them. "Desert me in my hour of need."

She wandered through the apartment, feeling restless and vaguely annoyed. She was tired of waiting for the baby, tired of being fat, and most especially she was tired of waiting for that bloody baby shower to occur. Each time she went out she half-expected to be whisked away to one of those wonderful parties Daniel's sister had described. Wishing wells, layettes, silly guess-the-baby's-sex contests—the more she heard about this American custom, the more she looked forward to it.

She wanted to gather experiences into her arms like a bouquet of flowers. This was her life, the place where she would finally put down roots. She and Daniel didn't have to be married to provide a solid foundation for their child's future. Dreams of gold wedding bands and sacred vows had vanished with Eric and Juliana and their travesty of a marriage. What she had with Daniel was all that she wanted. To ask for more would be to tempt fate.

Now and again, when she was very tired and her guard was down, she found her thoughts drifting back toward

Perreault and her old fantasies about the way life should be. She imagined returning with Daniel and their beautiful baby, and asking Father Guilbeaux to baptize the infant the way he had baptized Isabelle and her father and her father's father before him. And she would finally meet Victoria, her beautiful niece who—

Fortunately, this foolish line of thought was broken by the ring of the telephone. Isabelle was delighted when her obstetrician's service asked if she would mind changing her appointment to this afternoon instead of later this week. Maybe if she got out of the apartment she could take her mind off this baby shower that wasn't.

She showered, then dressed carefully in a pair of crisp white pants, a black silk T-shirt, and a linen jacket in a beautiful shade of teal blue. High heels were temporarily eliminated from her wardrobe, at least until she regained her old center of gravity. She slipped her feet into a pair of white leather sandals, then grabbed her purse. If her baby shower turned out to be held in her obstetrician's office, she was not going to be taken entirely by surprise.

The doorman wasn't on duty, so she stood on the curb, debating whether to walk the six blocks to the doctor's office or hail a cab. It was a beautiful day, with clear blue skies and lots of sunshine. She knew the walk would do her good, but pregnant princesses attracted more than their fair share of attention, and the ten-minute walk might take closer to an hour. She was about to raise her arm and flag down a taxi when a sleek black limousine rolled to a stop in front of her. An attractive older woman in a pale blue Chanel stepped out, followed by a tall gentleman dressed in a perfectly tailored dark suit.

Smiling, the woman stepped forward. "Princess Isabelle?"

Isabelle nodded, hopes rising. *It's inevitable,* Cathy Bronson-Bernier had said about baby showers. *It'll happen when you least expect it.*

"We'd like you to come with us, if you please."

"How wonderful!"

The two well-dressed strangers met each other's eyes.

The woman's smile widened. "I am pleased to find you so agreeable."

"Of course I'm agreeable," said Isabelle as they led her to the car. She looked from the woman to the man, then back again. "I had been told to expect a guerrilla-style ambush, but this is actually quite civilized."

The man started to laugh. "You are certainly not what I expected, if I might say so."

The woman linked her arm through Isabelle's. "Come along then, Princess Isabelle. Your chariot awaits."

"How wonderful," Isabelle said as she settled comfortably in the backseat of the limousine. "I can hardly wait to see where you are taking me."

Chapter Eighteen

Maxine called Daniel at the office a little after four o'clock. "Something's wrong," she said, her voice tight. "Isabelle is gone."

It struck Daniel that there was nothing unusual about a grown woman being out on a beautiful day in late spring, but Maxine sounded so distraught that he packed up his briefcase, told Phyllis to forward his calls, then headed for home.

By the time he reached the apartment, Maxine had worked herself up into a state bordering on panic.

"Calm down, Maxine." Daniel put his arm around her shoulders and led her into the living room. "I'll pour you a whiskey, and we'll talk."

"The only way to calm me down is for our girl to walk through that door with her arms piled high with packages.

'Tis what I've been fearing," she said, her voice shaking. "Something terrible has happened, Daniel, something terrible."

He knew all about the Irish and their love of signs and portents. He'd grown up with talk of banshees and leprechauns and things that went bump in the night. He sat down on the sofa next to her. "Now, back up and tell me what's going on."

"If I knew, would I be carryin' on like this?"

Daniel forced a laugh. "I'm not going to answer a loaded question like that, Maxine."

Her eyes filled with tears, and she twisted Ivan's engagement ring around her finger. "Isabelle's an impulsive girl, but she's learned to be thoughtful. Where on earth can she be?"

While Daniel was on his way home from the office, Maxine had called Dr. McCaffree, the obstetrician, and two local hospitals and had come up empty each time. Daniel's gut knotted tighter as his anxiety level rose.

"Would you be thinkin' your family had the party for her today?"

"Not without asking you, Maxine."

"I wouldn't be family. In Perreault—"

"This isn't Perreault. This is America. You're family as far as we're concerned." They both knew Maxine would have been highly offended if she had been excluded from the baby shower. She'd made that fact known in no uncertain terms.

Maxine squeezed his hand. Her affectionate gesture took his anxiety level even higher. "She's too trusting by half. She doesn't know how to protect herself in the city."

Daniel couldn't dispute that fact. He'd seen the way the little princess met Manhattan with her arms open wide, oblivious to the dangers, both hidden and otherwise. He didn't want to scare the hell out of Maxine, but it was time to make a few phone calls, starting with the cops.

* * *

"You must tell me," Isabelle said as a private jet took off from Teterboro, a small airport in New Jersey. "I cannot bear the suspense."

"Patience, Princess," said the woman in Chanel. "Soon enough you'll know your destination."

As soon as the jet achieved cruising altitude, the woman excused herself to join her companion in another part of the plane. There was a surprising amount of space inside the jet, room enough for the cabin where Isabelle was seated, an office, and a sleeping compartment.

Cushy leather divans lined both sides. A video player was hidden away in a rosewood cabinet that also housed a stereo. All manner of reading material was shelved in a rosewood wall rack at the far end of the cabin, near the door that led to the bedroom.

Isabelle had grown up royal but not fabulously wealthy. She was familiar with the ways of the very rich, but still she found this whole thing quite amazing. Wouldn't you think there were any number of wonderful places in Manhattan in which to hold this baby shower? Or why not the country inn on Long Island that Cathy had mentioned? Daniel's entire family lived in New York. This simply didn't make sense.

She stopped, a smile tugging at the corners of her mouth. Florida! Connie and Matty were vacationing down there. Certainly they would never hold a family party without the matriarch of the family present. Apparently they considered it preferable to bring the entire party down there to Connie instead of bringing Connie up to the party.

"Americans," Isabelle murmured as she leaned back in her seat and tried to get comfortable. What an amazing lot they were.

Daniel called his sister Cathy to make sure the baby shower wasn't under way.

"I don't want to scare you, Danny, but the party's next week."

"I didn't think you'd forget Maxine."

Cathy sounded affronted. "Of course we wouldn't. Maxine is family."

"That's what I told her."

"Besides, Mom and Pop are still in Florida. How could we have a shower without Mom?"

"I don't have any answers, Cath."

"Have you called the police?"

"Yeah, but they won't do anything until she's been gone twenty-four hours."

Cathy was quiet for a moment. "I don't know how to ask this, Danny, except to just ask it: Could she have walked out on you?"

"What the hell kind of question is that?"

"One that has to be asked."

"No, she wouldn't walk out on me."

"She's an unmarried, pregnant princess who's thousands of miles away from everything and everyone she knows."

"Save the analysis for the paying customers, Cath." He slammed the phone down.

Maxine entered the room. "What did she say?"

"You don't want to know."

With that, Maxine burst into tears. "Something terrible has happened, Daniel. I can feel it in my bones."

He tried to comfort the woman, but his own nerves were stretched so taut he felt like he was ready to snap. "Wait a minute," he said. "Did you call the Poconos?"

"Ivan's house?" Maxine shook her head. "I wouldn't be thinking she'd go all that way."

"Who knows?" countered Daniel. "Anything's possible." She could have called for a radio car and taken a spin up to the mountains. She was crazy about the place, all those mountains and lakes. She'd said it reminded her of Perreault.

Maxine punched the number in, then handed the telephone to Daniel. He listened to it ring five times. Ten. Twenty. He handed the phone back to Maxine. "She's not there."

"Or she's not answering," said Maxine, hands trembling as she replaced the receiver in the cradle.

Another cold blast of fear iced his blood. "Or she can't answer." He grabbed her car keys from the sideboard. "You stay here in case Isabelle calls."

"Where are you going?"

He met her eyes. "Ivan's place."

Maxine crossed herself. "Dear God, I pray she's there."

He didn't know which prospect scared him more: finding the house empty or finding her there alone and in trouble.

"Call as soon as you get there," Maxine said, giving him a swift hug.

"She'll be there," he said. She had to be.

Connie Bronson had never mastered the art of traveling light. An overnight trip for Matty's wife required a pullman suitcase, carry-on luggage, and a tote bag that doubled as a pocketbook. In the early years of their marriage, Matty had railed against her inability to leave home without everything she owned, but with time had come patience. Now, after almost fifty years as husband and wife, Matty was able to shrug his shoulders and chalk it up to one of the differences that made life interesting.

"Do you have the carry-on?" Connie asked as they deplaned Delta 104, Orlando to JFK.

"I've got the carry-on."

"The Mickey Mouse T-shirts?"

"I've got the T-shirts."

She stopped midpoint in the jetway, to the consternation of the two hundred thirty-five people behind her. "We forgot the Cinderella watch for Katie."

He patted his breast pocket. "Got it, Connie. Now can we get the lead out?"

Frank was waiting for them at the luggage carousel. "Good to see you back, folks," he said, pumping his boss's hand. "Things aren't the same without you around."

"Frank!" Connie exclaimed, giving the man a hug. "What are you doing here? Your tonsils."

"Piece of cake," said Frank with a grin. "They decided not to do it. I'm on enough antibiotics to kill an elephant's tonsilitis."

"I'm so relieved," said Connie. "Danny had his tonsils out when he was twenty-one. Dreadful for an adult."

They kept up a running discussion on the pros and cons of modern medicine while they waited for the luggage to appear. Matty tapped his foot impatiently.

"Could be halfway home by now if it wasn't for all your junk," he said to Connie who rolled her eyes and ignored him.

Twenty minutes later, each lugging a considerable load, they made their way out to the street where the Lincoln awaited them.

"Hey, Mr. B.!"

Matty spun around. A big, burly skycap beamed at him. "Joe!" He offered his hand. "Great to see you, pal. Where you been keepin' yourself?"

"I been everywhere, Mr. B. International, the shuttle. Even managed Teterboro for a while, real close to home, but the money's better over here. Got my son hooked up over there, though."

"Say hi to Ronnie, would you? Last time I saw him he was in Little League."

"Will do."

Matty turned to leave, but Joe had more to say. "He saw Danny's princess out at Teterboro a little while ago. Said she was even cuter in person than on TV."

"She's a doll, all right. We're all looking forward to that baby."

"Coming soon?"

"First week in July."

"Ronnie said she looked like it was any time. He kinda wondered what she was doing flying off someplace."

Matty frowned. "Flying off?" He turned to Connie. "Were Danny and Isabelle going anyplace?"

Connie shook her head. "Isabelle said they'd be staying close to home until the baby comes."

"That's what I thought."

"Look," said Joe, "maybe I got it wrong."

"Don't worry about it," said Matty, clapping him on the back. "We'll figure it all out when we get home."

Isabelle stared out the window at the endless blackness of the Atlantic Ocean. They had been airborne for almost four hours. She'd accepted the explanation that they were flying over the water in order to avoid heavy traffic from commercial airliners, but it seemed to her that it was more than time to see the lights of the Florida coastline twinkling below.

She unbuckled her seat belt and put the latest issue of *Vogue* down on the table in front of her. Rising slowly to her feet, she massaged the small of her back. Her muscles were cramping from sitting for so long. Even her legs hurt, whether from the inactivity or the cabin pressure she didn't know, but she felt perfectly dreadful. A pleasant cabin steward had checked with her periodically, offering her beverages and more reading material, but he had only smiled politely when she asked questions and had neatly sidestepped answering any of them.

Carefully Isabelle made her way toward the bifold door that separated the cabin from the rest of the plane. Gripping the handle, she made to pull it open but was met with resistance. Locked? She tugged at it, harder this time, and was rewarded with a "Just a moment" from inside.

She stepped back, her heart pounding faster. Listening carefully, she heard the faintest click of a lock, then the door folded open. The woman in the blue Chanel suit smiled at her, the same kind of pleasant smile as the cabin steward's.

"So sorry," said the woman. "We often have difficulty with the hinges."

"It was locked," said Isabelle, hands clasped over her belly.

"You're mistaken," said the woman, still pleasantly smiling. "Why on earth would we lock the door?"

"That is the second question I wish to ask." She met the woman's eyes. "I must demand to know where we are going."

The woman's smile didn't falter. "Now, you wouldn't want to spoil the surprise, would you?"

"At this point, yes, I would." She gestured toward the window. "I know we're on the way to Florida for the baby shower. Shouldn't we be seeing land by now?"

"Oh dear," said the woman. "How on earth did you guess?"

"Well, it wasn't terribly difficult." Her royal hauteur reasserted itself. "Although I must say by the time we reach the baby shower, I shall be ready to go to bed."

The woman patted Isabelle on the hand in an overly familiar fashion. "I'm so sorry, dear. We didn't want to worry you, but there is some heavy weather up ahead, and we've been diverted temporarily."

Isabelle frowned. "Do we have enough fuel?"

"Absolutely."

"I'd like to make a telephone call."

"I wish we could accommodate you, but we don't have the equipment to do so."

"Would you ask the pilot to relay a message? Perhaps someone on the ground would place a call for me."

"Of course," said the impeccably groomed older woman. She disappeared for a moment then returned with a piece of watermarked white paper and a pen. "Please write your message down, and I'll make certain the pilot relays it."

Somewhat relieved, Isabelle jotted a note to Daniel that she was fine, even though he certainly must know she was en route to the baby shower. "Thank you," she said, handing the note to the woman.

"Our pleasure. I only regret we've given you the slightest

apprehension." The pleasant smile reappeared. "Now if you would, please return to your seat and buckle your lap belt. As I said, there are storms in the area, and we like to take all precautions."

Isabelle did as the woman requested. There was nothing wrong with taking precautions. Given her condition, it was a prudent thing to do. "Everything is all right," she said out loud as the plane cut its way through the darkness. There was absolutely nothing she could do about the storms. She should be relieved the pilot was exercising a high degree of care. Better to arrive tired and grouchy than to have something dreadful happen.

"Positive thoughts," she admonished herself. She stifled a yawn and glanced at her watch. The glitter of gold from her bracelet made her smile despite her fatigue. Almost seven in the evening. She was hungry and tired and not at all in a party mood.

She closed her eyes and willed herself to sleep. Perhaps she'd feel more cheerful after a nap.

Daniel turned the wheel sharply and made a left into the driveway. The truck screeched to a stop, kicking up dirt and gravel. Immediately he noticed Ivan's cottage was dark. Leaving the engine running, he sprang from the truck, raced up the path to the front door, and jammed the key into the lock.

"Isabelle!" He swung open the door and switched on the lights. "Princess, are you here?"

No answer. He glanced around the living room. It looked exactly as they'd left it a few weeks ago. The fear that had been building inside him exploded. She wouldn't do something like this. She wasn't the kind who got her kicks out of making the people she cared for worry themselves sick.

He searched the rooms, the closets, looked under the beds. Nothing. He was about to check the garage when the telephone blared. He was on it before the second ring.

"Did you find her, Maxine?"

"It's not Maxine, Danny. It's your old man."

For the first time in his life he understood how it felt to be scared to death. Death would be easier than the crushing sense of terror closing in on him. "Whatever the hell it is, Pop, just say it."

"We've got trouble, Danny. She's been kidnapped."

Daniel broke all the speed limits between Ivan's house and the airport where Matty said a private jet would be waiting for him within the hour.

Kidnapped. He clutched the wheel as beads of sweat broke out along his temples and the back of his neck. What kind of son of a bitch would kidnap a woman in the ninth month of pregnancy? If Matty hadn't bumped into Joe at the airport earlier, they'd still be beating their heads against a brick wall, trying to figure out where Isabelle had disappeared. Matty had immediately called in a few favors and reached the traffic controller at Teterboro. The plane belonged to Malraux International, and it was a safe bet it was en route to Perreault.

He reached the airport in record time. Matty was waiting for him on the tarmac next to their chartered jet. The plane was small and sharp-nosed. The pilot could propel it across the Atlantic fueled only by Daniel's rage.

"We've got a problem," Matty said as soon as Daniel joined him. "Interpol's involved. They want us to stay out of it. We might endanger Isabelle and blow their operation."

"Fuck Interpol. I don't give a goddamn about their operation."

"They can get nasty."

"Let 'em try. They'll have to kill me first."

"Don't tempt them, Danny. When you get to this level of shit, even the good guys play rough."

Daniel started up the steps to the plane with Matty on his heels. "What the hell are you doing? You're not going alone."

"Do me a favor, Pop. Stay home."

"I love that woman, too," Matty said, "and that's my grandbaby she's carrying."

"I don't have time to waste fighting with you," Daniel said, entering the cabin. "Let's get the hell out of here."

Once they were airborne, Matty filled Daniel in on the details of Juliana's death.

"She died two weeks ago?" Daniel stared out the window at the vanishing earth below. "Why didn't it hit the news?"

"They're keeping it under wraps, going to claim it was a suicide. Postpartum depression."

"But it wasn't?"

Matty shook his head. "Afraid not."

As far as Interpol could tell, Juliana had been injected with an overdose of barbiturates. A suicide note had been found next to her body. Whether it had been forged or written under duress nobody knew.

"Damn it. This doesn't make any sense," Daniel said, dragging his hand through his hair. "Juliana was exactly what Malraux needed. She's played ball with him from the beginning, right down to marrying his son. What the hell did they have to gain by killing her?"

Groggy and unrefreshed, Isabelle gave up the quest for sleep. She'd dozed fitfully, her dreams tangled and surreal, leaving her perception of time out of kilter. Early morning sunlight filtered through the cabin windows. Impossible. Opening her eyes, she glanced at her watch. Not quite midnight. She reached over to lift the shade.

"Oh, my God." Instead of the Florida coastline she saw the jagged peaks of snow-capped mountains. She knew those mountains. It was all as familiar to her as her reflection in the mirror.

Perreault. She'd never thought to see it again, never wanted to see it again. Dawn's light cast a pinkish glow across the mountains. As a little girl she'd believed it was the touch of a magic wand, transforming the tiny country into a wonderland. How little she knew what constituted magic.

The woman entered the cabin. "Good," she said, "you're awake. We're about to make our descent into the airport."

"Orlando?"

The woman looked mildly embarrassed. "It will all be made clear, your highness."

Your highness? There was something about the way the woman said it that alarmed Isabelle even more than the fact that she'd been abducted back to her homeland. *Stay calm,* she told herself, moving her hands in small circles on her belly. Getting upset wouldn't be good for her or for the baby.

The woman seemed to sense her thoughts. "You are in no danger whatsoever, your highness. I am a licensed obstetrician. Your well-being is our top priority."

Isabelle nodded curtly. "I am relieved to hear that." She thanked God for the glass wall of reserve that most members of royalty employed upon occasion. Coolly she turned to look out the window. "We're landing at the little airstrip near the castle? The runways there are scarcely more than paths in the dirt."

"There have been some improvements since you left, your highness. I think you will be well pleased."

What possible difference did it make if Isabelle were pleased or not? Whatever was going on had nothing to do with her pleasure and they both knew it. "I suppose this is my sister's idea of a fitting punishment," she said as the plane knifed through the clouds. "What Juliana giveth, Juliana taketh away." This was probably an elaborate ploy to strip her once again of her money so they could fund more improvements to the airfield.

"This isn't a police state." She shifted position in an attempt to ease the cramping muscles in her lower back. "Juliana has achieved her goal. I request the jet be refueled so I can return home immediately."

"Perreault is your home."

"Perreault is where I was born, Doctor, but it is not my home." Home was in New York, with Daniel and Maxi and Ivan and all of the Bronsons. They were the only true family she'd ever known.

"You will understand everything soon, your highness, I promise."

The plane touched down, bumping its way across the runway. The seat belt cut into her lower abdomen as the pilot braked to a stop. Daniel must be wild with worry. He'd probably called the police or the FBI or whoever it was Americans called in situations like this. She wouldn't put it past Juliana to try to hold her for ransom. Why settle for her trust fund when Juliana could tap into the Bronson fortune? If it didn't mean being stranded in Perreault, she wished Daniel would tell her sister to go straight to hell. And Maxi—she couldn't bear to think how Maxi would feel, knowing the two girls she'd raised were once again battling.

The doctor stood up. "We can deplane now."

"I'd rather not."

"I strongly urge that you comply."

Isabelle arched a brow. "Is that a threat?"

The doctor looked genuinely horrified. "Of course not. It is only that there are people waiting who must not be disappointed."

Awkwardly Isabelle rose to her feet. "I should hate to disappoint my sister."

An odd look passed across the woman's face, but she said nothing.

"This way, ladies." The cabin steward motioned them toward the door.

Isabelle followed the doctor down the metal steps to the tarmac where, to her surprise, Eric awaited them.

His expression was duly serious—the perfect expression for a man about to meet his kidnapped sister-in-law—but she did note with satisfaction that his eyes were drawn repeatedly to her enormous belly. She wondered how it was she had ever believed herself in love with him.

"Darling girl." He made to kiss her cheeks, but she stepped away. "I wish the circumstances could be different."

"As do I. It is sad to see a grown man performing his wife's less pleasant chores."

He looked at the doctor who shook her head. "There are things you do not know."

"And there are things about which I do not care any longer. Juliana has accomplished her goal. My trust fund reverts back to her, and my life has been disrupted. She has proved herself superior in every way. Now I would like to return home."

"Darling girl, this is your home."

She was growing wearing of that sentiment. "You do not believe that any more than I do, Eric."

"Darling girl, you must listen to me. Something has happened—something dreadful."

She'd never heard that tone in his voice before or seen that particular look in his eyes. She waited, her hands moving reassuringly across the expanse of her belly, refusing to help him in any way.

"It's Juliana," he said, blue eyes welling with tears. "She has taken her own life."

Chapter
Nineteen

Eric talked about Juliana's depression after Allegra's birth, about how much her sister had desired a son, but Isabelle's mind was numb. His words simply had no meaning. As they drove up the mountainside to the castle, she saw her sister as a little girl, her blond pigtails like spun gold in the Alpine sunlight. The young Juliana always rose with the first light to pick flowers from the garden or to walk the path to the stables. She'd lived a charmed life, one of ease and privilege, safe within the walls of the castle with their father happy to wipe away her tears.

Isabelle had envied her with all her heart. How strange, how heartbreakingly sad, that Juliana lay dead by her own hand while Isabelle knew a joy unlike any she'd imagined possible in this lifetime.

". . . the funeral will be late this afternoon," Eric said,

patting her hand. "Once that is past, the news will be made public."

"Where is—I mean, I would like to . . ."

He shook his head. "It is best that you remember her as she was."

Isabelle wished she felt something more than a bitter-sweet regret that things had not been different between herself and Juliana. "I'd very much like to see the children." The only true innocents in the entire tragic situation.

"They are with my mother in Paris. When Allegra was born, it quickly became obvious that Juliana was not—" He stopped and regrouped his thoughts. "I am sure you'll have an opportunity to see them before long." He made to pat her hand again, but she moved away. His wry smile told her the gesture did not go unnoticed. "I see that you will be adding to the family very soon."

"That fact should have been considered before dragging me onto the plane."

"We did provide a doctor for you, darling girl. The last thing we wanted was to endanger your health in any way. You must believe that. We simply found it imperative to bring you here as quickly as possible."

"Did you think me so heartless that I would not attend my sister's funeral if at all possible?"

"I apologize for any discomfort or apprehension we might have caused you, darling girl. We erred on the side of caution."

"Kidnapping someone is hardly erring on the side of caution."

Eric seemed genuinely surprised. "Kidnapping?" His features hardened into something approximating a frown. "A damn mishandling of the situation. You were to have been informed that it was a family situation right from the start." He reached for her hand and kissed it before she could react. "We wanted only to have you with us in our sorrow. Never would I do anything to cause you a moment's unease."

That from the man who had slept with her while he was busy impregnating her sister. It was all Isabelle could do to keep from laughing out loud.

They reached the castle at last. Eric parked the Daimler under the porte cochere, then turned off the ignition. She reached for the door handle, but he raced around to the passenger's side before she got the door open. The castle was draped in the black bunting of mourning, as it had been for her father little more than a year ago. It seemed as if a lifetime had passed since then.

"Where is Yves?" she asked as Eric led the way into the drawing room. Yves always greeted visitors at the door. "It's terribly quiet in here."

"This may be Yves's morning off. We are running on a skeleton staff this week, darling girl. There has been a certain reluctance to serve since Juliana's unfortunate demise."

A chill ran up Isabelle's spine despite the warming sun. "The curse of Perreault."

"It has acquired a certain validity in the past year."

For the first time, she understood what Maxine meant when she talked of feeling the brush of evil. The castle felt different, as if there had been a fundamental yet invisible change that rendered it alien to her.

As the hours passed, Daniel found it progressively harder to pretend he wasn't thirty thousand feet over the Atlantic Ocean with nowhere to go but down.

"You okay?" Matty asked.

"Yeah."

"Rough trip."

Daniel met his father's eyes. "I hadn't noticed."

"The plane's been bucking like a damn bronco."

"Thanks for the update, Pop."

Matty leaned forward in his chair, elbows resting on his knees. "Your mother and I were talking on the plane up from

Florida. Damned if we can figure out where you got this flying phobia. The rest of us took to it like ducks to water."

"It's fear of heights, Pop. The flying part is secondary."

"Where'd it come from is what I want to know."

"Why don't we get Interpol to run a background check for you?" He knew his old man was trying to keep his mind off what lay ahead. He appreciated it but couldn't get into lightweight banter the way he usually could. His emotions were too raw, too close to the surface. He cleared his throat. "I owe you one, Pop. If you hadn't—" He couldn't finish the sentence.

"Dumb luck," said Matty, puffing nervously on his cigar. "If Joe wasn't such a blabbermouth, we might not've found her. Let's just hope they're going to Perreault."

"They're going to Perreault. Malraux will try to use Isabelle the way he used her sister."

"I still say let Interpol handle it. They know what they're doing."

"Yeah," said Daniel, "but they're not in love with her."

Matty looked at him. "So you finally realized it. I was wondering how long it was going to take you."

"Too goddamn long." He'd sell everything he owned and start again at the beginning just for the chance to tell her.

She had expected to be put in her old suite, but Eric led her to the opposite wing of the castle where he showed her to a room on the first floor. It was small, decently appointed, but isolated from any hope of companionship.

"I would prefer my old apartment," she said, running her finger across the slightly dusty top of the nightstand.

"So sorry, darling girl, but there's a spot of trouble in that wing. The old plumbing has had its day."

"I suppose it doesn't matter," she said, trying to ignore the prickle of apprehension moving up her spine. "I'll be leaving right after the funeral." She looked at him. "When will it be?"

"Four P.M."

She rubbed the small of her back. "I do not know what I'll do for clothing. This is not the proper attire."

"Do not worry, darling girl. All will be taken care of." He kissed her on both cheeks. "Sleep. We can discuss everything when you wake up."

He closed the door after him, leaving Isabelle alone. A basket of fruit rested on a tabletop. She helped herself to an apple, but found it was mealy after spending the winter in the cellar. The castle was quiet, much too quiet for this hour of the morning. She stood by the window, looking down at the gardens below. The hedges were untended, new growth leaping upward in random patterns that were nothing like the crisp, geometric designs Isabelle remembered. The stone pathways her father had walked on his rambles with the dogs were barely visible through the encroaching weeds. And the rose bushes Isabelle had loved as a child were gone, ripped out and planted over with azaleas.

She felt as if she'd been dropped into some alternate universe where the normal landmarks had been changed just enough to lend an air of unreality.

From the vicinity of the kennels came the yipping of her father's beloved Corgis. Bertrand had been adamantly opposed to kenneling dogs. "They're social creatures," he had said with great indignation. "Not meant to be locked away in a cubicle." It had always struck Isabelle as odd that he had done exactly that with his younger daughter on the day he sent her off to her first boarding school.

It was obvious Juliana had had no difficulty banishing the Corgis to the canine dungeons. *Poor things,* thought Isabelle. They probably had no idea why they had been cast aside, any more than she had understood why she was no longer good enough to live in the castle with her family.

Memories were everywhere. Her beautiful mother. Her thoughtless father. Juliana and the two little girls she'd left behind. *Why did you do it, Juli? How could you leave them alone?* It wasn't that long ago that she had been left without a mother, and her heart went out to the nieces she had never met. She yearned to hold them close, to give them—even for a moment—a mother's love. Perhaps it was a good thing they were in Paris with Celine. Isabelle was unsure if she could resist the temptation to spirit them away to America where they could grow up surrounded by love.

She moved her hands across her belly. "I'll never leave you," she whispered. "No matter what happens, I'll always be there for you."

And so would Daniel. She'd never met anyone like him. Sharp. Opinionated. Strong and loyal and more wonderful than any man had a right to be. He'd grown up surrounded by all the love and security a child could want, and Isabelle knew that together they would provide the same for their baby.

What a shame it was that their child would never know the country of its mother's birth. Perreault was part of her, no matter how she tried to deny it. Being here again brought it all back to her. The hopes and dreams she'd nurtured. The plans she'd made for her own future. How she wished she could banish the curse of Perreault and turn the principality into the wonderful country it could be.

But it wasn't her place. The throne would go to year-old Victoria, and Isabelle had no doubt that Honore and Eric would be making the decisions on her behalf. If only there were a way to stop time, to somehow ensure that Victoria and Allegra would know more happiness than she and Juliana had.

Suddenly the room seemed too small, too stiflingly hot to stay there another second. Turning away from the window, she glanced about for a telephone, but there was none to be found. She needed to hear Daniel's voice, to let him know she would be on her way home again before the day was over.

She opened the door slowly, then peered up and down the corridor. Not a soul in sight. Not a sound. "Goose," she said out loud. What difference did it make if the hallway was clogged with servants? She wasn't a prisoner here.

A back muscle spasmed, and she paused a moment in the doorway and waited for it to pass. The corridor was long and narrow and dimly lit. She was unfamiliar with this wing of the castle. In the past it had been used for servants and less important guests. It occurred to her that a person could disappear in this deserted wing and never be heard from again—certainly not the kind of thought a woman in her last month of pregnancy relished.

"At last," she murmured, seeing the spill of light up ahead.

She was just about to step into the huge rotunda when she heard footsteps behind her. Spinning around, she found herself face to face with Yves. Dear God, what had happened to him since the last time she was there? Although it hardly seemed possible, his gaunt frame was even more so, and his dour expression had become downright tragic. Juliana's death must have hit him terribly hard, she thought, glad in a way that someone found it in his heart to care.

"Mademoiselle," he said, executing a swift bow. "You must leave this place."

She stared at him. The man had always been proper to the point of being obsequious. His dislike of her had been veiled in the painfully correct behavior of one born to serve.

He grabbed her by the wrist and pulled her into an empty room, closing the door behind them. Her heart beat so wildly that she feared for her child. "There is danger everywhere, mademoiselle. I have heard them talking. Leave now!" His breath smelled strongly of alcohol.

"Good Lord, Yves, have you been drinking?" Poor man. He was so griefstricken that he'd sought solace in the bottle.

He tightened his grip on her wrist, and frantically she wondered how she would manage to kick him when she had not seen her feet in months. "The Princess Juliana—God rest her soul—was murdered."

Certainly his words were those of a madman. "You are mistaken. She took her own life, Yves."

He shook his head, his eyes wild with fury. "She was

murdered, mademoiselle. She had discovered too much. She knew that your son——"

Isabelle raised her hand. She didn't need the ramblings of a drunken servant, especially not one who had never liked her. "That is quite enough, Yves. As you can no doubt see, my child has not yet been born."

"You carry a son."

"I carry a child," she corrected him, feeling once again the icy wings of fear against her face. "Whether it is a son or a daughter I do not know." The man was mad. There could be no other explanation.

"They know," said Yves as she struggled to break free. "Why else would they have brought you here?"

She stomped down hard on his instep. He cried out, releasing her from his grasp. Moving as quickly as she could, she darted from the airless room and hurried into the center hallway.

"Dear girl!" A familiar voice called out. "I have been looking for you."

She stopped, then turned to see Honore Malraux swiftly making his way toward her.

"Isabelle!" He was at her side in an instant. He gripped her by the shoulders and kissed her warmly on both cheeks. *"Mon dieu,* my darling child, what has happened?"

"What on earth has been going on here? I believe that Yves has lost his mind."

Honore's face registered no surprise at her statement. "I am so sorry you had to see him that way. He has been having a difficult time of late."

"I never knew Yves was a drinker."

"Ah, the things men will turn to in an hour of need. They are myriad, my dear, and deadly." He stepped back to look at her. "More beautiful than ever. You are your mother come back to life."

She took a deep breath as a wave of dizziness came over her.

"Darling child!" Honore propped her up with his arm. "You are unwell?"

"It is so stuffy in here," she said. "I don't remember the castle being so dreadfully stuffy. I cannot bear this place another second."

"One moment," said Honore, leading her to a gilt chair. "I shall be right back."

He returned minutes later with a cold glass of spring water which she gratefully drank. He placed the crystal goblet down on the floor, then helped her to her feet.

"Come," said Honore, taking her by the arm. "This is all too much for you. You need time to assimilate the changes."

"I should like to use the telephone first. Maxine must be frantic with worry."

"No," he said smoothly, "first you must regain your composure. You sound distraught, my dear. You would not want to cause Maxine undue concern, would you?"

"Disappearing off the streets of Manhattan might have caused her a bit of worry, wouldn't you agree?"

"I am appalled at how dreadfully this situation has been handled. Maxine has no call for alarm. She and I had a long chat while you were en route. All is well. I am concerned that my staff did not tell you that."

The stepped outside into the sparkling sunshine of a Perreault morning. The smell of pine—the rush of the wind—so many memories. *I'm never coming back—not as long as I live.*

"How did Maxine take the news of Juliana's death?"

"As one would expect," Honore said, guiding her carefully across a footbridge. "With enormous sorrow."

"Will she be here for the funeral?"

Honore shook his head. "I did not think it advisable."

"Did Maxine understand?"

"She is a wise woman."

She refrained from asking questions about Daniel. Both men had campaigned for the right to build in Perreault. Hard feelings between them would not be surprising.

She heard the sound of footsteps running close by and the heavy thunk of a car door being slammed shut. Loud voices, arguing in French, echoed in the stillness and were punctuated by the growl of an engine.

Honore seemed oblivious to it all. "Eric told me you were concerned about your lack of wardrobe for the services this afternoon."

Isabelle blinked at the abrupt change of subject "Yes, I am," she said, gesturing toward her bright teal jacket and white pants. "This outfit is highly inappropriate."

Honore chuckled. "My dear girl, you could not be inappropriate if you tried, but if it will ease your mind, we shall search out proper garb."

"I would suggest a search through my old wardrobe, but I fear nothing would fit in my current condition."

Honore was too much the gentleman to look down at her belly. "A new shop has opened in town. Celine is quite taken with it. Perhaps they can provide something suitable."

"I would greatly appreciate it."

"You are not too tired?"

"I can't bear the thought of going back into the castle, Honore. Yves was—" She shuddered. Between Yves and the bittersweet memories around every corner, she would just as soon never see the castle again. "A ride would be a welcome diversion."

The jet landed at the small airport on the French side of the border. Daniel barely noticed the way it bounced across the tarmac like a runaway bumper car.

An Interpol agent, a tall man with a bad attitude, was waiting for them. "You're not going any farther," the agent said without preamble. "The operation is under way."

"I'm going."

"I have the jurisdiction to stop you by force, if necessary."

"You'll have to kill me," Daniel said.

"I will, if it comes to that."

Matty stepped forward. "We have a car waiting. You can't stop us from getting in it and driving away."

"No, but I can stop you from crossing that border," said the agent.

Daniel looked at his father.

His father looked at the Interpol agent. "You drive a hard bargain, pal."

The agent's expression remained impassive.

Daniel gauged the distance between himself and the agent's car.

Matty stepped back, smiled pleasantly at the agent, then delivered a right hook that sent the guy to the tarmac.

Daniel jumped into the car, and he didn't look back. He took the curves at full speed, not noticing any of the Disney World scenery. The only important thing was Isabelle.

It seemed to take forever, but at last he reached the castle. The drive was clogged with cars. Interpol agents and local detectives swarmed the grounds. A cluster of suspects lay on the grass face down and handcuffed while a score of frightened employees stood at the edge of the path and watched in silence.

Daniel screeched to a halt behind a van, then ran straight toward the action. He collared a man who had the look of Interpol all over him. "What's happening? Did they find the princess?"

The guy shook his head, obviously preoccupied.

"Shit." He scanned the area. Eric was cuffed and standing next to one of those nondescript-looking European cars that made Daniel think of Nazis and sirens in the night. He grabbed the bastard by the collar. "Where the hell is she?"

The elegant young Malraux spat in his face.

Daniel considered beating the living shit out of him, but the bastard wasn't worth the effort. Only Isabelle mattered. Only their child.

He headed for the castle.

"Don't waste your time," someone yelled. "We've got the place cleared. There's no one in there."

He ignored the guy. He couldn't explain it, but something was calling him inside. The last time he'd seen the place it had been filled with music and candlelight and the laughter of wedding guests. Now it seemed like a royal ghost town. His footsteps echoed in the hallway. He knew the layout of the land around the castle from his spec sheets from the ski resort plans, but he knew only the basics about the castle.

If he was looking for a hiding place, where would he go? The servants' quarters? Isabelle's suite of rooms? The dungeon, wherever the hell that might be?

He laughed out loud. Those Interpol guys would never think of the dungeon. It was too obvious, too much a part of the old world for them to even notice. How did you get into a dungeon? There had to be a door or a staircase somewhere. Off the kitchens maybe? He ran full out through the ballroom, through the dining room, toward the back of the castle.

A pot of water boiled on the stove. Dozens of cans and jars were piled high on the counter. Broken glass and red preserves littered the floor. He swung open a door, but it was only an empty pantry. He looked more closely. Could it be? He pulled out the shelves and pushed against the back wall. Nothing. He pressed along the outer edges, and the door swung inward. A series of stone steps led down into the bowels of the castle. The only light was what managed to filter down from the kitchen.

"Isabelle!" His voice rang out. "Princess, if you're here, say something!" Anything. If this was a dungeon, he understood why people chose to fight to the death. Being trapped here would be a living hell.

"Isabelle!"

Nothing. No sound. No movement.

He moved deeper into the room. His right foot hit something soft, human. Terror grabbed him by the balls.

"M'sieur . . ." The voice was low, indistinct. Definitely not Malraux's.

Daniel crouched down. "Who are you?"

The man's breathing was labored. Waiting for him to form his words was agony. The fact that he spoke them in French added to the difficulty. The sickly sweet smell of blood was everywhere.

"Yves . . ." The man coughed hoarsely. "The chalet . . . she didn't believe—"

"Who didn't believe?"

"The princess . . . and Honore—"

That's all he needed to hear. "I'll get help for you," he said, stripping off his suit jacket and pillowing it under the wounded man's head. "Don't worry, Yves. I'll make sure a doctor sees you."

Another hoarse cough. "*Je suis votre servi—*" His voice faded as Daniel charged up the steps.

"This isn't the way into town," Isabelle said as Honore guided the Bentley up a narrow, curving path. "Where are we going?"

"Trust me, dear girl." He smiled as he negotiated a sharp right-hand turn. "We'll tend to your wardrobe."

"I would rather go into town," she said, trying to ignore the insistent pain in her back.

"We wouldn't wish to attract attention now, would we?"

"I have no need to hide."

"I think only of you," Honore said smoothly. "There has been a great deal of—talk since you left."

She laughed out loud. "There was a great deal of talk when I was here. I have always been good for idle gossip."

"There are some strange stories circulating about your condition. I should hate to see you made uncomfortable."

"I am unmarried," she said, "but I am also unashamed."

He patted her hand. "As well you should be. Bearing a child is an act of God made visible."

The words were uttered with great conviction and obvious sincerity. She wondered why her skin crawled as he said them.

"We're heading toward Papa's chalet," she said as they continued to climb the side of the mountain. "What are you thinking, Honore?"

"There is a closet off the master bedroom that is filled with women's clothing. I know you will find something suitable."

"What on earth would my father have done with a closetful of women's clothing?" Bertrand had had an active social life, it was true, but his women had always provided their own attire.

"Your mother's clothing, dear girl. Bertrand was a sentimental man."

"Turn around now, Honore," she ordered. "I do not find any of this amusing."

"You know so little of your mother," he said, ignoring her statement, "and there are so many things you need to hear."

There was something uncomfortably familiar about the conversation. If only she could put her finger on what it was. "There is nothing more I need to know about my family. I have a new family now, and they are all that I need." Bronson and the baby, Maxi and Ivan, Matty and Connie's wonderfully enormous brood.

"Blood is all, darling child. You must understand that— especially now."

Her back muscles cramped, or was it her belly? "It isn't always enough, Honore. Juliana and I were fine examples of that."

"But love triumphed," he said as the Bentley climbed a steep incline. "In the end that is all that matters."

A cold sweat broke out at the back of her neck. "Juliana was a suicide. I hardly see how that constitutes a triumph for love."

"A tragedy," Honore said, sounding chillingly unconvincing. "But from the sorrow comes something wonderful."

"I—I do not understand."

"You and my son, darling Isabelle, and the child you are carrying." He swung left onto the road that led to Bertrand's chalet. "My grandson."

Chapter
Twenty

Honore's words seemed to hover in the air between them. Had the whole country gone mad? "I must be mistaken. You did not say 'grandson,' did you?"

"Of course I did, darling child. You did not believe you could keep the wonderful secret forever, did you?"

"I do not know what on earth you're talking about."

Honore sighed. "Please. We are alone. We are friends— family, or soon to be so. Now is the time for truth." He met her eyes. "Eric told me the child is his, as Juliana had feared it to be."

Her belly cramped violently as if in protest. "I do not understand what this is all about, but I can tell you with certainty that Eric is not the father of my child."

"Your circumspection was understandable while your sister was alive, but she is gone now, darling child. You are free to shout your happiness to the world. A son is the culmination of a man's dream. A grandson is the beginning of new dreams." He patted her hand. "You have made me a happy man, Isabelle, and I reward those who make me happy."

"I do not wish to be rewarded. I want you to understand me when I say this child is not Eric's." She rubbed her belly as much to soothe herself as the child. "And there is no way on earth that you could know the sex of my baby."

Honore told Isabelle of Juliana's investigation. He hinted that the chance meeting with Eric in New York might not have been an act of chance at all. Eric had neatly tied it in with Juliana's own suspicions, and this was the horrifying result.

"This grows tiresome, Isabelle. We have a copy of your sonogram. The fetus is a male." He glanced at her as the car climbed higher up the side of Mont Vollard. "And he is a Malraux."

The side of a mountain—the damn chalet was built in the side of a mountain.

Rivers of sweat ran down Daniel's back as he pushed the car faster along the sharply curving incline. How high up was he now? Four thousand feet? Maybe five? He half expected a plane to go by and tip a wing in salute.

The air was getting thinner. No doubt about it. He struggled to get more oxygen into his burning lungs. There were no guard rails on these roads. A few inches too far to the right and he'd plunge down into that picture-perfect valley, smashing into a mass of twisted steel and bone.

"Hang on," he told himself. "It can't be much longer now." *Or much higher.* He'd find the cabin and he'd find Isabelle inside, safe and sound. There was no other way it could be.

Her belly cramped with anxiety as she considered her options. Honore was driving more slowly than usual, and she debated the wisdom of throwing herself from the car as a means of escape, but she feared the baby might not survive. That was the only thing that was important to her. The truth she'd been trying to avoid for the past two hours hit her square in the chest. She was in labor.

The sporadic back pains had become more regular, joined by a deep, powerful cramping in her belly, the rhythmic contractions of her womb as the baby prepared to be born. *Please, God,* she prayed, *not like this.* Daniel should be by her side, sharing the miracle of birth as he had shared the miracle of creation. She took a deep breath and counted down slowly from ten. The pain eased, and she exhaled a long shuddering sigh.

"Darling child, is something wrong?"

"I am fine," she lied. "It is just a terrible shame that the situation is such that it is."

Honore relaxed. "The situation is even more complicated than you realize. I am a man of many complex businesses, Isabelle, and some of them are not understood by the common throng." She listened, struggling to mask her mounting horror, as he told her that the gendarmes had been on their way to arrest him when he and Isabelle climbed into the Bentley not forty minutes ago. "This is not something with which I care to burden you—these misunderstandings are commonplace—but we must remain at the chalet until I receive word that we can return in peace." He patted her hand. "I will protect you and your infant with my life, darling child. I have waited a long time for a second chance."

"A second chance? Do you mean now that Juliana is gone?"

He nodded. "Juliana had become difficult. We did what was necessary to facilitate the proceedings. In the end I am sure it was a blessing for all concerned." His smile returned. "Still, we must thank her for discovering you were pregnant. Eric was elated, as was I. We understood full well that your

sister had made it impossible for you to share the truth with
us at the time.''

*I'm not really hearing any of this. I've known these
people all of my life. Things like this simply do not happen.*

Bertrand's chalet was situated halfway up Mont Vollard.
Clever architects had carved out a parcel of land that
extended out over the valley, providing a panoramic view
from almost every window. Honore swung into the gravel
drive, then leaped from the car to help Isabelle.

"Lean on me." He put his arm about her shoulders. "The
path is steep."

His touch caused bile to rise into her throat, but she
forced herself to accept it with grace. Everything depended
upon how well she was able to carry out the charade. The
gendarmes would find them—they had to. Perreault was a
small country. Sooner or later, they would be discovered.
She prayed that would happen before her baby was born.

Daniel saw the chalet a thousand feet above him, jutting
out into space. He didn't know what architectural magic had
made it possible to build a house in midair, but the illusion
was amazing. He was parked off the road, hidden by the
cover of the woods. He thought he heard the echo of
Honore's car door slamming shut.

He was only going to get one chance and he had to get it
right the first time. The only thing he had going for him was
the element of surprise.

His gut twisted as he looked up at the steep, densely
wooded slope. "You gotta do it, Danny," he said out loud.
"If you love her, this is the way it's gotta be."

The first hundred feet weren't so bad. He went from
foothold to foothold with relative ease. He was feeling more
secure, less convinced he was going to drop off the side of
the mountain, when his right foot lost its purchase and he
grabbed for an outcropping of rock, his fingers trying to
penetrate the stone. Damn it to hell. Leather soles weren't
made for rock climbing.

Reeboks, he thought as he regrouped and tried again. Nikes. Baseball cleats. He ran through the list of alternative footwear in an attempt to distract himself. He made it another two hundred feet then lost his grip and fell ten feet onto a large and prickly bush. His left cheek hit the sharp edge of a rock, and he tasted blood inside his mouth. The knees of his pants were blown out, the shoulder seams on his jacket were ripped, and the sleeves hung by a thread.

He got to his feet and attacked the side of the mountain yet again.

The inside of the chalet was sparsely furnished. The warmly cluttered room she remembered had been replaced by a sleek, functional decor that felt coldly impersonal. She ran a hand across the lacquered surface of a tabletop. Of course there was no dust.

"Even your gestures are like Sonia's," Honore said. "The resemblance is uncanny."

He approached her, and she took an involuntary step backward. Juliana's wedding, she thought suddenly. That long and intimate conversation in the library. At the time she'd thought his memories of her mother were remarkable in their detail, but she'd never questioned why.

"My mother's clothes," she said, hiding her trembling hands behind her back and praying another contraction wouldn't choose that moment to strike. "Are they really here?"

"Carefully stored," he said. "After you deliver, you might enjoy modeling some of them. French *Vogue,* I am certain, would welcome you once again." He smiled. "Perhaps with your new husband."

Dear God, don't let me be sick. She took a seat near the window as a contraction started. "I never knew my father to be so sentimental."

"It was not Bertrand," said Honore. "I stored them against the day her beautiful daughter would wear them for me."

She dug her fingernails into the arms of the chair as the pain subsided. "That is not funny, Honore."

"It was not meant to be." He knelt down before her and placed his hand on her belly. She struggled not to recoil from his touch. "Sonia destroyed my child, but now, through you and Eric, that child has come back to me."

She tried to stand, but the force of the contraction made that impossible. "This child is mine," she said. "Mine and—" She stopped, horrified by what she had come so close to saying.

Honore rose and moved toward her slowly, steadily, with the same deliberate movements a trainer used to gentle a skittish pony. "There is much you do not know, Isabelle, about how your mother and I were lovers that last year— about the way she aborted my child as if it were nothing more to her than an old sweater to be discarded. Family is everything to me," he said, his words a twisted parody of a beautiful sentiment. "She had to pay for that crime, for taking my child away from me."

That rainswept night—a hairpin curve—a Maserati with faulty brakes that spun out over the edge of a cliff and into oblivion, taking the Princess Sonia with it—

"My God!" He'd killed her mother for betraying him. He killed her sister for getting in the way of his goal. And he would kill her as soon as she delivered her child.

His hands caressed her belly. "You have given back to me one hundredfold, darling child. The son you're soon to bear will carry my bloodline and yours into the future and retain the throne of Perreault for its rightful owners."

"No!" She struggled to modulate her tone. "I mean, my child will not inherit the throne, Honore. That belongs to Victoria. She was Juliana's firstborn."

"How little they teach you about your own homeland. The first male child inherits, Isabelle, whether he was delivered of you or Juliana. She failed to live up to her responsibilities. You, darling child, would never disappoint."

He explained that if two generations had passed without male issue, the entire principality would have reverted to French/Swiss rule under a treaty signed three hundred years ago by the first ruler of Perreault.

His hands moved up over her belly and cupped the heavy fullness of her breasts. "Sonia's breasts were large," he said in a lazy voice. "Her nipples were perfect dusky circles." He pulled her shirt out of the waistband of her white trousers then slipped his hands inside. His touch scalded her skin, made her feel violated and dirty.

"Don't," she whispered, her eyes filling with tears. "Please don't."

His fingers forced their way under the band of her maternity bra. "Already heavy with milk," he said approvingly. "My wife did not have enough milk to nurse Eric. You will not disappoint in that regard."

Something inside her snapped, and she struggled to her feet in an attempt to get to the door, but he grabbed her and threw her down on the sofa. She fell clumsily, half on her side, half on her stomach, as another contraction overwhelmed her.

"This is for your own safety," he said, binding her wrists behind her back with the telephone cord. Then he bound her ankles with his silk tie. "I cannot have you stumbling over the rocks outside, not when you are so close to delivering my grandson."

A wild scream tore from her throat. He slapped her hard, shocking her into silence, then shoved his silk pocket square deep into her mouth. She gagged on the smell of his cologne.

"I will not hurt you, darling child," he said, his hands so close to her breasts. "You are much too important for that."

Pressing his body flat, Daniel eased himself up and onto the deck. He tried not to dwell on the fact that he was suspended a mile over the valley below. On his stomach, he inched his way toward the window, careful to stay below the

line of vision of the occupants. The only thing he had going
for him was the element of surprise, he thought again. If he
lost that, he lost everything.

He heard voices from within, but he couldn't make out
the words. He moved closer, stopping for a long moment
when a board squeaked in protest. From far below came the
sound of car engines, and he prayed Malraux didn't hear
them. He'd hoped Interpol wouldn't be far behind, but he
also knew that Honore wouldn't hesitate to use Isabelle as a
pawn.

*You're going to make it, princess, hang on a little longer.
We're going to come out of this, and then I'm going to say
all the things I should have said a long, long time ago.*

Her scream broke the Alpine stillness. It bounced off the
mountains and back at him. It filled his gut and set fire to his
soul. Looking into the window, he saw Malraux with his
hands on Isabelle's breasts and a few thousand years of
evolution went up in smoke as he realized he was about to
kill a man.

Honore's hands were greedy, proprietary. He cupped her
breasts as if he had the right to touch her, as if he owned her
and the baby she carried. She tried to scream, but the gag
made it impossible. Her throat felt as if it were being torn
apart with the force of her fear and rage.

Oh, Bronson . . . she thought, trying to project herself
back to the warmth and safety of his arms. *I should have
told you I loved you.*

Honore was saying something, but his words held no
meaning for her. She wasn't there—not really. This wasn't
happening to her—not his hands against her—not the
contractions—not Daniel's face in the window—

She was going insane, that's what it was. She'd conjured
him up from her dreams, from the deepest part of her soul.

With a roar, Bronson exploded through the window in a
shower of broken glass. Honore turned at the sound, but
Bronson was too fast for him. He sprang at Honore like a

guided missile. Honore staggered. Daniel landed a blow to his jaw that sent the older man to the floor.

Honore lay there, apparently knocked cold.

Daniel turned toward Isabelle. It was all there in his eyes, everything she'd ever wanted to see, everything she'd ever wanted to hear.

He pulled the gag from her mouth. Behind him Honore, not unconscious at all, struggled to his feet.

A bullet whizzed past Daniel's cheek and splintered the wall behind Isabelle's head. She screamed, then Daniel saw her body go rigid with fear. He had to get Malraux out of the chalet and into the open. When Interpol finally showed up, he didn't want Isabelle anywhere near the showdown. If anyone got hurt, he wanted it to be him.

The thing to do was draw Malraux's fire. "You're finished, bastard," he said, moving toward the man. "It's over."

Malraux fired again. The bullet grazed Daniel's scalp. "Lousy shot, Malraux. What's the matter? You didn't have any trouble killing Juliana." Daniel backed his way toward the door. "You're going to have to kill me to stop me, and even if you do, you're not going to get rid of me, because I'm going to keep coming at you all the way to hell."

Malraux took the bait. "Arrogant bastard." He fired another shot. Blood soaked Daniel's right shoulder. "I've been toying with you, but I am tiring of the game."

Hang on, he told himself. *Get outside.* Reaching behind with his left hand, he unlatched the door. He had to get Malraux away from the princess and out in the open so Interpol would have a clear shot at the son of a bitch.

Malraux followed him out onto the deck, stepping around the trail of blood Daniel was leaving behind. "You're nothing," he said. "Not worth the bullet."

Daniel laughed in his face. "What's the matter, Malraux? Don't have the guts to pull the trigger?"

Malraux raised the gun and aimed it at his heart.

*   *   *

Isabelle struggled wildly against her bonds, but the contractions were sapping her strength. She had to get to Daniel—she had to help him. Honore was an expert shot. His prowess with a gun was well known throughout the continent. He'd been toying with Bronson, postponing the inevitable. He'd killed before. She had no doubt he would be more than happy to kill again.

And Daniel had played right into his hands. She knew what Bronson was trying to do. He'd lured Honore out onto the deck in order to protect her and the baby. *Damn you, Bronson!* She worked desperately, trying to free her hands from the knotted telephone cord. *I don't want a dead hero!* She wanted him exactly the way he was—happy, angry, scared, and everything in between.

She heard the sound of a scuffle from out on the deck followed by the loud crack of a gunshot. Everything fell silent. *You're fine, Bronson,* she thought fiercely. *You wouldn't dare let something happen to you when we need you so much.* She would keep him safe with the power of her will, surround him with so much love, so many hopes for the future that no harm could befall him.

Minutes passed. Finally the silence was broken by the whine of an engine as a car made its way up the hill.

Two men in dark suits burst through the front door.

"Interpol," said one, thrusting an ID at her. "Where—?"

"The deck," she said, praying they were who they said they were. "Honore has a gun."

The men drew their own guns, then headed for the deck. She waited. Fear was a living, breathing mass tearing at her chest. She closed her eyes, putting all of her energy, all of her power, into keeping him safe.

"I love you, Bronson," she whispered. "More than you'll ever know."

"What was that, princess?"

Please, God, please . . . She opened her eyes. His face

was bruised and bleeding. His shoulder was soaked with blood, and the front of his white shirt was shredded to ribbons.

"You're hurt," she said, starting to cry as one of the Interpol agents quickly untied her hands and feet, then went to call for help.

"Yeah," said Bronson with a loopy grin, "but you should've seen the other guy." He swayed on his feet and sank heavily onto the sofa next to her.

She met his eyes, afraid to form the question.

"He's dead," said Bronson, gesturing toward the deck.

"He killed my mother, Bronson." Her voice caught. "And Juli." She hesitated. "After the baby was born, he would have—"

"He's gone, princess. You're safe. You'll always be safe."

She began to cry in earnest. "I want to hug you, but I'm afraid I'll hurt you." She waved her hand in the air. "Oh, Bronson, what has he done to you?"

"Nothing that can't be repaired." His beautiful green eyes met hers. "This isn't the way I had it planned, princess, but I've waited too long as it is to say it."

Her heart beat so fast inside her chest she thought she would faint.

"I love you, Isabelle, and I'm not about to let you go again."

"Is that a proposal?"

"Fair warning: I don't intend to take no for an answer."

"You know that I—" She stopped midsentence as another contraction began.

"Princess?" He watched, eyes wide, then yelled for the agents. "Something's wrong, damn it! She's in pain. Call a doctor."

"Help is on the way, Mr. Bronson," said the taller of the two. "Just relax. You'll be fine."

"I don't give a damn about myself," he roared. "She's in pain—"

"I—I'm not exactly in p-pain," Isabelle managed after a moment.

"The hell you're not. I saw the way—"

She touched his wrist. "Bronson," she said, "I'm in labor."

Chapter
Twenty-one

Edouard Christopher Matthew Bronson was born four hours later at the hospital of the Sacred Heart. Three weeks early, he weighed seven pounds, one ounce, and the doctors pronounced the heir to the throne to be every bit as healthy as he looked.

His mother and father were exhausted but elated. Isabelle dropped off into a deep, satisfied sleep while the doctors finally convinced Daniel to let them care for his wounds.

Honore Malraux's body had been recovered from the base of Mont Vollard. His son, more devious than anyone had realized, would stand trial on charges ranging from drug smuggling to murder. Celine Malraux had been arrested at her apartment in Paris. Theirs had been a true family affair—Celine had overseen a major money-laundering operation from her elegant pied à terre. As for Juliana's babies, they were not with Celine at all. Instead, they had been hidden away in Isabelle's old suite of rooms, where they were cared for by a harsh-voiced nanny with all the warmth of an Alpine winter.

Baby Edouard was now the nominal ruler of Perreault, but the real power rested with Isabelle. All around them things were changing with the speed of light, but Daniel was determined that nothing would destroy what they'd fought so hard to hang onto.

"I've never seen you like this before," said Matty as Daniel glared at his bruised face in the hospital mirror. "You're acting like a bridegroom."

"That's what I'm shooting for, Pop."

Matty's smile was wide. "You've got a terrific woman waiting for you, Danny. Don't screw it up."

"I'd call you out on that one, but I can't move my arm." He was pieced together with bandages, gauze, stitches, and hope. "You'll take care of that other matter?"

Matty nodded. "You've got my word."

Daniel grinned at his reflection. "Do I really look this bad?"

"Yeah," said Matty, "but she'll never notice. She's in love."

"Maybe," said Daniel, "but she's also in charge. Things are different now, Pop. She may not want the things she wanted before all of this happened."

"Go to her," said Matty. "Tell her. I guarantee you won't be disappointed."

Daniel walked down the corridor toward Isabelle's room. The door was slightly ajar, and he pushed it open.

She looked up at the sound. Her dark hair was pulled back into a ponytail. She wore a hospital gown, her gold bracelet with the tiara charm, and the most beautiful smile he'd ever seen. Their child was cradled against her breast.

"He's asleep," she whispered as Daniel sat down on the edge of the bed.

"I thought he was nursing."

"He was." It didn't seem possible, but her smile grew even more beautiful. "Our son has an amazing appetite, Bronson."

Our son. Emotions he'd never imagined grabbed his heart and wouldn't let go. "You did a great job, princess."

The baby nuzzled closer, and she stroked the tiny pink cheek with the tip of her index finger. "I couldn't have done it without you."

"Can you do the rest without me?" Damn it. What had happened to the words of love, the sweet promises he'd planned to make?

"Not terribly romantic, Bronson."

"I'm not handling this very well, am I?"

"Whatever it is, just say it, Bronson." The world was in her eyes, and he took heart.

"Marry me." A statement, not a question. Plain, simple, powerful. He met her eyes. "I love you, princess, and I can't imagine growing old with anyone but you."

Her beautiful dark eyes welled with tears. "Everything is different now, Bronson. You might be getting much more than you imagined."

"I know exactly what I'm getting."

She gestured toward the world beyond the window. "Perreault is on the verge of collapse. We have no money, no industry. We don't even have a reputation any longer. Certainly not a good one. I want better than that for our son."

"Marry me," he said for the second time. "We'll go back to New York, and you'll never have to see this place again. You said you loved New York, and it sure as hell loves you."

"But I love Perreault, as well." She sighed deeply. "I didn't realize how much until I saw Eddy's face and thought of all the wonderful things I could never share with him if we turned away."

"So what are you telling me?" he asked over the painful

lump in his throat. "That it can't work? That you're going to stay here and—"

The baby fussed, and she stroked his cheek agan.

"You're not listening to me, Bronson. I can't live without you, and neither can our son. A long time ago you saw a way for this country to make a mark for itself. A way for us to grow."

"You're talking about the ski resort?"

"Anything—whatever you think will work. Papa was wrong, Bronson. We have to embrace the future, otherwise there won't be a future for Perreault at all."

"It's not too late," he said, considering the idea. "It'll take a lot of effort, a hell of a lot of PR, but I think it can be done."

"Is it a deal, then?" Her dark eyes glittered with excitement.

"Remember, I have a company to run, princess. New York is still my home base."

"I know," she answered, that royal hauteur reappearing. "And I have a country to run."

"Equal partners," he said. "Otherwise there's no deal."

"Equal partners," she agreed. "But I get the final say on what happens with Perreault." She overflowed with ideas, some of them crazy, many of them brilliant. "Every woman in this country can embroider as well as I. I can help them increase their annual income and give Ivan's Princess line a boost at the same time. Think of it, Bronson! The possibilities are limitless."

"That's all terrific, princess, but I'm not going to spend the rest of my life locked away in that castle."

"I am glad to hear that." She shuddered. "It will take a while before I'm ready to live in the castle again. Right now I would like nothing better than to return to New York with you and plan our wedding. I'll come back here whenever I'm needed."

"We're going to be spending a hell of a lot of time in airplanes."

"I know you hate flying, Bronson."

He hooked his finger inside the collar of his shirt and lifted the chain with his Saint Christopher medal dangling from it. "It doesn't bother me now that I have protection."

She leaned forward. "What on earth happened to that medal?" The heavy silver was dented, and a piece from the bottom was missing.

"A bullet," he said.

"That's not possible."

"Dumb luck," said Daniel. "The doctor said he saw it twice during the war."

"A miracle."

"No," he said, looking down at his son. "The real miracle is in your arms."

"Can I come in?" Matty's voice boomed from the hallway.

"Keep it down, Pop," Daniel said. "Eddy's sleeping."

"Close your eyes, Isabelle," Matty called out, more quietly this time. "I have a surprise for you."

"Roses," said Isabelle, doing as he asked. "I love roses."

"Sorry, princess," said Daniel. "It's not roses."

She opened her eyes and saw Matty standing next to the bed, holding Victoria against his right shoulder and Allegra in the crook of his left arm. She saw herself in their eyes, and she saw Juliana. All of the pain, all of the loneliness—she would make sure it never happened again, that these two little girls would never know how it felt to be second best. Most important of all, she knew that Bronson understood.

"You knew I wouldn't be able to leave them, didn't you?" she said to Bronson.

"Somehow I always figured you'd be a package deal, princess. We're already an instant family. What's two more?"

Matty sat year-old Victoria down on his son's lap, then rested tiny Allegra next to Isabelle in the hospital bed. A brand-new family was forming right there before his eyes, those magical bonds of love and hope drawing the five of them closer together until the differences between them no longer mattered.

Matty stood in the doorway, trying to commit the sight and sound of love to memory. There would be tough times ahead. Life didn't come with guarantees. His boy and the princess both had hard heads and hot tempers, but that would only make it more interesting. The love was there and the commitment. Those three beautiful babies were proof of that.

"I love you, Bronson," Matty heard her say. "So much more than you'll ever know."

Daniel turned, and Matty thought he caught the glitter of tears in his son's eyes.

I knew it, Danny. Sooner or later it was going to get you, too. You could fight it all you wanted, but when the right man met the right woman, there was only one way the story could end. Daniel was a Bronson, and Bronsons were family men. He couldn't change that if he tried.

Smiling, Matty walked down the corridor to the telephone and placed a long-distance call to his wife.

Turn the page for a special preview of
Barbara Bretton's

Shore Lights

Available May 2003 from Berkley Books!

Once upon a time in the Emerald City there lived a woman named Maddy Bainbridge who believed she could move back home with her mother and not lose her mind.

Maddy was old enough to know that the things that drove you crazy when you were seventeen would probably drive you even crazier when you reached thirty-two, but her mother's offer came at a moment when her defenses were down and her options were extremely limited.

"I need help, and God knows you need a job," Rose said during the fateful phone call that changed their lives. "The inn is doing turn-away business, and I'd rather share the profits with my daughter than a perfect stranger."

"I appreciate the thought, Mother, but I'm just going through a dry spell here." An eight-month dry spell but Maddy wasn't about to put too fine a point on it. "I'm sure the voice-over work will pick up any day now."

"You're an accountant, Madelyn. You have a degree. You can do much better than voice-over work for a used car dealership."

"I was an accountant," she reminded her mother. "Not much call for bean-counters when there aren't any beans left to count." The great dot-com collapse of a few years ago had littered the landscape with the fallen careers of fellow accountants from Washington down to Baja.

"Be that as it may, you have a child to support and no husband to help you out. You need a chance to get back on your feet, and I need someone I can trust to help me with the business. Give me one good reason why this isn't the perfect solution for both of us, and I'll never broach the topic again."

Are you listening, God? Just one good reason . . .

On any other day, Maddy could've given her twenty, but that evening she couldn't come up with a single one.

"Hannah has a brand-new dog," she said finally, knowing her mother's negative stance on anything furry or four-legged. She had spent part of her childhood wishing she could turn Rose into an Irish setter. "Her name is Priscilla, and she has a few issues."

"What kind of dog?"

Oh, how she longed for something large and prone to drooling. Bulldog! St. Bernard! Irish wolfhound with an overbite!

"A poodle," she mumbled, praying it sounded like bull-mastiff on Rose's end of the line.

"Did you say *poodle*?"

"Yes," said Maddy. "A poodle."

"How big a poodle?" Rose sounded amused.

Maddy glanced down at the tiny bundle of curly fur asleep in her lap. Sometimes the truth was a royal pain. "Too soon to tell," she said, "but her paws are gigantic." For a stuffed toy. There was always the chance Priscilla might make it to a whopping five pounds if she pigged out on Purina.

"No problem," Rose said calmly. "Just so long as she doesn't piddle in the common areas."

Was this her my-way-or-the-highway mother talking, the woman revered in three counties as the undisputed Queen of Clean? Rose had been known to change her sheets after a fifteen-minute nap. "Okay," Maddy said, "now I get it. My real mother is trapped in a pod in the basement behind the washer and dryer."

Rose's answer was a surprisingly long span of silence. No snappy comeback. No withering maternal observation. Just enough silence to unnerve her only child.

Maddy would have liked to match her mother silence for silence, but Rose had thirty years on her and she had no doubt her mother could stretch that silence until Christmas if she felt like it. "I was making a joke, Mother. You were supposed to laugh, not take me seriously."

Rose cleared her throat. "Quite frankly, I don't see what's holding you there in Seattle now that Tom has . . . moved away."

"He didn't just move away. You can say it. I promise I won't fall apart. Tom married somebody else. I've made my peace with it." Which, of course, was a big enough lie to grow her nose to a size worthy of the men of Mount Rushmore.

"Maybe you have," Rose said, "but Hannah certainly hasn't. She's the one you should be thinking about."

Instant guilt, supersized with fries. This was no pod person; this was her mother.

"Hannah is the main reason I'm staying in Seattle. This is the only home she knows." She paused, waiting for a response from her mother. Rose, however, remained silent. Rose had never been one to play silence to such advantage. "Besides, Hannah will be starting preschool in a few weeks."

"We have schools here in New Jersey."

"All of her friends are here."

"She's four years old, Madelyn. She'll make new ones."

"Seattle's our home."

"Home is where your family is. What Hannah needs right now is to be surrounded by people who love her." People who won't leave her. Oh, Rose didn't say those words but then she didn't have to. She had already wheeled out the heavy artillery and aimed it straight at Maddy's heart.

Oh God, Mother, you're right ... of course, you're right ... I can't argue the point with you ... was this how you felt when Daddy went back to Oregon ... did you lie awake every night and stare up at the ceiling and worry about me the way I worry about Hannah ... it's been so long since I heard her laugh ... I can't even remember how long it's been ... I don't go to church anymore, but maybe I should because I'm beginning to think it will take a miracle to make Hannah happy again.

But she didn't say any of it. The words were trapped behind all the years they'd spent away from each other, all of their differences both large and small. The ghost of the lonely little girl she once was rose up between them and she wouldn't go away. Only this time, the little girl looked like Hannah.

How Hannah adored her father! Her world had revolved around their Sunday brunches, their excursions to the Space Needle and Mariners games, strolls along the waterfront where he taught her how to eat crab. The loss of those weekly visits had turned her happy child into a sad-eyed little girl Maddy barely recognized. How did you tell the child you loved more than life that not every man was cut out to be a 24-7 father?

"This wasn't part of the plan," Tom Lawlor had said the day Maddy told him she was pregnant. It hadn't been part of her plan either but sometimes life handed a woman a miracle and trusted her to do the rest. Tom's children had children of their own and he had been eagerly anticipating retirement from the company he owned and a life that didn't include potty training and the tooth fairy.

Not that Maddy had been ready to punch her ticket on

the Baby Express herself. Children had been out there somewhere in the shadowy future, a concept to be dealt with at a later date. She had never doubted that somehow, some day, Tom would warm to the idea of another child, a child of their own, but until then she was quite content with the life they shared. She took her birth control pills religiously, popping one each morning with her orange juice, trusting her future to God and country and modern pharmaceuticals.

A fierce bout with the flu—and one tossed pill—had shown her the folly of her ways.

The easy carefree relationship she and Tom had enjoyed before her pregnancy was soon nothing more than a memory. He still cared for her and she knew he loved Hannah, but sometimes it seemed to Maddy that he loved their daughter the way you would love a golden retriever you had to send to college. A part of his heart remained distant and not even the sheer wonder of their little girl had been able to change that fact.

Why didn't they tell you the truth when they handed you that squalling, slippery, precious newborn? They congratulated you and wished you well. They gave you coupons for disposable diapers and baby wipes, but they didn't so much as whisper about the things that really mattered. Why didn't they tell you that the feeding and diapering were the easy part; a baby cried when she was hungry and she fussed when she was wet. Even the newest of new mothers could figure that out without too much trouble. If only someone, somewhere, could tell you what to do for a little girl with a broken heart.

"Promise me you'll think about the idea," Rose urged as they said good-bye.

"I'll think about it," Maddy told her mother and then she did her level best to put the entire idea from her mind.

But a strange thing happened. The more Maddy tried not to think about Rose, the more often her thoughts turned to her mother. Twice in the next few days she found herself reaching for the phone, only to catch herself middial. What on earth would she say? It wasn't like she and Rose were friends. They didn't share the same tastes in books or movies. Their child-rearing methods were poles apart. Rose was a realist who believed only in what she could see and hear and touch. Maddy believed in those things, too, but she knew there was more to this world than met the eye.

The first time Maddy brought home an invisible friend, Rose put the entire family into group therapy so she could figure out where they had gone wrong.

When Hannah showed up with her first invisible friend, Maddy set an extra place for supper.

Still this odd yearning for her mother lingered. Rose was the last thing she thought about at night and her first thought in the morning. So much time had passed since they had last lived together under the same roof. So many things had changed. Maybe the idea of moving back home again wasn't quite as crazy as it sounded.

"Leave Seattle for Jersey?" Her cousin Denise e-mailed her when she first got wind of Rose's offer. "Are you nuts?" What woman in her right mind would trade life in the Emerald City for a one-way ticket back to the Garden State? Crazy didn't begin to cover it.

"DON'T DO IT!" Her cousin Gina's warning practically leaped off the computer screen. "You're the only one of us to make it west of the Delaware River. Don't blow it now!"

The senior members of the clan also weighed in with their opinions.

"You'll make your mother so happy." Aunt Lucy IM'd her, then surrendered the keyboard to Aunt Connie, who added, "I don't know why you moved out there in the first place. We have coffee in New Jersey, too, Madelyn."

Every morning Maddy woke up to an inbox stuffed with E-mails with subject headers like "Come Home, Maddy" and "Don't Do It!!!" until she began to feel like she was being spammed by her own family.

The weeks passed and she was still no closer to making

a decision than she had been the day Rose made the offer.

The day before Hannah started preschool, Maddy was rummaging through a huge trunk of old clothes that she'd stashed in the condo's storage area when she came across the beautiful fisherman's sweater Rose had knitted for her when she started grade school. The thick cream-colored wool was still supple and lustrous and smelled only faintly of Woolite and mothballs. Large bone buttons marched smartly down the front, fitting neatly into the beautifully finished buttonholes. Rose was a perfectionist and her needlework showed it. Every stitch, every seam was meticulously crafted and designed to last. Only the pockets showed serious signs of wear, faint ghostly outlines of small fists jammed deep inside, of crayons and candy bars and half-eaten PBJs.

That sweater was probably the last gift Rose ever gave Maddy that didn't come with strings attached. Even the presents for the baby had come with warnings about the perfidy of men, about the impermanence of love, about how if Maddy had half a brain she would stop wishing on lucky stars and start pumping up her 401(k). All the things her nine-months'-pregnant daughter hadn't wanted to hear.

All the things that had turned out to be painfully true.

September waned and she continued to duck Rose's demand for an answer, but the yearning for something more than they had shared before lingered and grew stronger. In early October she packed Hannah and Priscilla into the Mustang and drove down to Oregon for her father's seventieth birthday party. He knew all about Rose's offer and Maddy's reluctance, and his take on things surprised her.

"It's time you went home," Bill Bainbridge said as they watched Hannah pretend to have fun with his neighbor's children. "You need your mother. You both do."

Maddy pondered his statement. Was that possible? She was a grown woman, the single mother of a small child. She was long past needing anyone. She was the one who wiped away Hannah's tears, the one who lingered at the bedroom door, listening to the holy sound of a sleeping child. Rose hadn't done any of those things for Maddy when she was growing up. At least not that Maddy could remember. Rose had been too busy selling pricey real estate to people with more money than brains, sure that the example she was setting for her daughter would put Maddy on course for success.

Nothing had prepared Rose for the rebellious under-achiever who sprang from her womb with a mind of her own.

"It's not that I don't love Mother," she told her father as they wiped away the remnants of cake and ice cream from every surface in his kitchen. "I just think we do much better with a continent between us."

"She's reaching out to you," Bill said as he tossed a used paper towel into the trash. "Rose never reached out to anyone in her life. I say it's time you gave her a chance."

"Easy for you to say," Maddy grumbled as her father pulled her into a clumsy hug. "You were only married to her. I'm her daughter: I'm doing life."

They both laughed but Maddy sensed Bill's heart wasn't in it. She wanted to kick herself for making such a thoughtless remark. It was no secret that her father had never quite managed to get over his first wife. He had gone on to make a successful second marriage that had ended with the death of his beloved Irma, but there was little doubt that the love of his life was the fiercely independent redhead from New Jersey who didn't believe happily-ever-after existed anywhere but in the movies.

"We don't get a lot of second chances in this life," Bill said when he kissed her good-bye. "Go home for Hannah's sake, if not your own. You won't regret it."

"We could move in with you," she said, only half kidding. "I'm a pretty good cook and Hannah's great company."

He smiled and shook his head. "You know your old man's hitting the road next week. I promised Irma I'd make that trip we'd been planning and it's a promise I intend to keep." Oregon to Florida and back again, with scores of stops along the way. Irma had been working on the last of the itinerary when she lost her long battle with breast cancer.

Maddy's eyes filled with tears at the memory of her stepmother. "Has it gotten any easier?"

"Nope." He glanced away toward the curb where her Mustang idled loudly. "Didn't expect it to."

"You'll stop by and see us in Seattle during your travels, won't you?"

He grinned and tugged on a lock of her hair. "Not if you're in New Jersey."

"Fat chance."

"Six months," he said as she hugged him good-bye. "Give your mother six months. What can you lose?"

"My sanity," Maddy said. They laughed, but the truth was out there and she couldn't take it back. Sometimes even the most independent woman was only a daughter at heart.

—∞—

PARADISE POINT, NEW JERSEY—
THREE WEEKS BEFORE CHRISTMAS

Rosemary DiFalco swore off men in August of 1992, and, as far as she could tell, that was when Lady Luck finally sat up and took notice. All her life Rose had been waiting for her ship to come in and when it finally sailed into view she swam right out to meet it.

You didn't get anything in this world by being shy, and you sure as hell didn't get anything by waiting for some man to hand it to you on a silver platter.

For longer than she could remember her mother, Fay, had rented out rooms in her ramshackle old Victorian house, sharing their living space with retired schoolteachers, penniless artists, and an assortment of hard-luck cases whose only common ground was the bathroom on the second floor. When Fay died, she left the house to her four daughters, three of whom wanted absolutely nothing to do with it. Rose, however, saw possibilities lurking behind the cracked plaster and faded carpets, and she bought out her sisters' shares and settled down to the hard work of building a new life for herself.

She took early retirement then traded in her fancy condo on Eden Lake. She cashed in her 401(k) and plowed the proceeds into the house where she had grown up, a wreck of a Victorian that just happened to boast ocean views from almost every bedroom.

The Candlelight Inn was born and Rose never looked back. To her delight, she found that she enjoyed the constant parade of guests. She loved the challenge of staying one step ahead of the needs of a nineteenth-century house with a mind of its own. Most of all, she loved the fact that the Candlelight's success had made it possible for her to offer her daughter a way out of the mess her life was in.

Any way you looked at it, this should have been a slam dunk. Rose needed help running the place; Maddy needed a job. The perfect example of need meeting opportunity.

So why did Rose wake up every morning with the sense that she was preparing for war? She had created an oasis of peace and tranquillity for her paying guests, a place people came to when they wanted to leave the stresses of the real world behind. You would think at least a tiny bit of that tranquillity might spill over onto the innkeeper's family. Take this morning, for instance. Maddy had been holed up in the office working on the Inn's website for hours now. Rose hadn't seen hide nor hair of her since they'd laid out the breakfast buffet in silence. They had exchanged words late last night over something so trivial that Rose couldn't even remember what it was, yet the aftermath had left her wondering for the first time if she had made a terrible mistake inviting Maddy and Hannah to come back home.

It was painfully clear they weren't happy. Her daughter was prickly and argumentative, more reminiscent of the seventeen-year-old girl she had once been than the grown woman pictured on her driver's license. And Hannah—oh, Hannah was enough to break your heart. The delightful little girl who had entertained Rose with her songs and stories last Christmas in Seattle was now a withdrawn and painfully sad child whose smiles never quite reached her stormy blue eyes.

Rose knew that Tom and Maddy's breakup had nothing to do with her, but decades of guilt were hard to ignore. She hadn't prepared Maddy for the real world of men and women. She had taught her how to balance a checkbook, shop for the best auto loan, and make minor plumbing repairs, but she hadn't taught her the fine art of living with a man.

The truth was, she hadn't a clue herself. Rose had grown up in a world of women, with an absentee father, three sisters, and more aunts and nieces than you could shake a bra strap at, and between them all they had about as much luck at keeping a man as they had at the slot machines in Atlantic City.

Some women were lucky in love. Some were lucky in business. One look at the bare ring fingers and flourishing IRAs of the four DiFalco sisters and you knew which way the wind blew. Lucy, the youngest, said a DiFalco woman couldn't hold on to a man if she had him Krazy Glued to her side. Over the years Rose had come to realize the truth of that statement.

In the best of times love was a puzzle Rose had never been able to unravel. She had married a wonderful man, the salt of the earth, and still hadn't been able to find a way to hold on to love for the long haul. He offered her the world and she had found herself longing for the stars. She had a beautiful daughter who was bright and talented and loving yet somehow that wasn't quite enough for Rose, either. She wanted Maddy to have everything she never

had, to be everything she could never be, and when Maddy
had turned out to be lacking the ambition gene, Rose's disappointment knew no bounds.

Maddy was a dreamer, same as her father. She followed
her heart wherever it led, and she never thought to leave a
trail of breadcrumbs so she could find her way safely home.
Maddy's unplanned pregnancy had filled Rose with a combination of elation and dread. She hadn't known Tom Lawlor well, but she did know that he had already earned his
parenting stripes and wasn't in the market to add a few
more to his sleeve. He was her age, after all, and she understood him even if she didn't approve.

But not Maddy. Not her daydreaming, foolish optimist
of a daughter. She hadn't seen it coming, not even when
he spelled it out for her in neon letters a foot high. She had
still believed they would find a happy ending, believed it
right up until the moment Tom and Lisa flew off to Vegas
for one of those quickie weddings in a chapel on the strip.

She longed to gather Maddy and Hannah up in her arms
and kiss away their tears, mend their broken hearts until
they were better than new.

All of the things she didn't have time to do when Maddy
was a little girl.

Instead there she was, a successful sixty-two-year-old
businesswoman with the hottest B&B between Rehoboth
Beach and Martha's Vineyard, trying to summon up the
guts to knock on the door to her own office and see how
her daughter was getting on with the website. Rose had
bearded wild bankers in their lairs, charmed free advertising
out of jaded local radio stations, spun pure gold from straw.
Spending five stress-free minutes with her only child should
be a piece of cake.

So what if she and Maddy had exchanged words last
night? It wasn't the first time and God knew it wouldn't be
the last. They were mother and daughter, hardwired to get
on each other's nerves. Nothing was going to change that
fact, but she could make it better. She knew she could.

If she could just bring herself to knock on that door.

Barbara Bretton is the award-winning, *USA Today* bestselling author of more than forty books. She currently has more than ten million copies in print around the world. Her works have been translated into twelve languages in at least twenty countries. She lives in New Jersey.